Journey Through the Video Game World

ALSO BY ASHAD MUKADAM

Kicking From Beyond The 40 (Only available in paperback format)

Journey Through the Video Game World

By:

Ashad Mukadam

Published 2014 by Ashad Mukadam in Calgary, Alberta, Canada
Printed by Lulu.com

Journey Through the Video Game World
Paperback 1st Edition

Ashad Mukadam
Calgary, Alberta, Canada
http://ashadmukadam.wordpress.com

ISBN: 978-0-9938038-0-2

Printed by Lulu.com

Cover Image © [Kirsty Pargeter]/Fotolia
Cover Design by Ashad Mukadam via Lulu.com Online Cover Designer
Editing by Ayuz Mukadam and Ashad Mukadam

To my parents, Nizar and Nasim, and my brother, Ayuz

CHAPTER ONE

Ronald Charlton was playing video games in his family room on his two-month-old Invisio 4 late in the morning of August 3, 2013. He still lived at home with his parents, Harold and Monica, and his brother, Mitch. They had lived in the same 2000 square foot home located near Nose Hill Park in Northwest Calgary for many years. His family was deeply worried about him because he hadn't done much besides working out and playing video games since being laid off from his job in February. His 27th birthday was fast approaching, being on the 21st of the month, and his family was looking at planning a nice birthday party for him. However, Ronald didn't really care much, as he felt it was just another reminder of his layoff.

"You're playing that thing *again*?!" asked his girlfriend, Dawna Langston, whom he had been dating since university, as she came down the stairs. "That's *all* you ever do these days! You *never* go anywhere anymore, not even for *nature walks* with *me*!"

Ronald, who was 6'4", 209 pounds, and had black hair, green eyes, just ignored her, and continued playing his basketball game. "Are you even *listening to me*?! Did you even hear what I just told you?!" she asked again, now getting really angry at Ronald.

"Leave me alone, Dawna," Ronald said, annoyed at the interruption. "You know that this is all that I've got now since I was laid off. That, and working out. At least with video games, no one treats you poorly, no one threatens you with layoffs, and no one lays you off just so they can hire their friends and make a mockery of what you worked so hard to accomplish."

"But you can't just sit here all the time playing those stupid things! I'm even surprised you made it for my birthday party!" she responded.

Dawna, who had turned 26 on May 29, was referring to the big birthday party her family had thrown for her on that date. She was 5'10", had shoulder-length brown hair, and brown eyes. A natural athlete, she played

1

lots of sports growing up, and in university, she played volleyball, which was sort of how she and Ronald had met. She still kept herself in shape, including being an avid weightlifter. In fact, she was able to lift well over 300 pounds, which explained her muscular build. Not only that, but she also had tattoo sleeves on both arms, as well as tattoos on her back, down her sides, and a large tattoo on her upper chest. Dawna was also considering getting additional tattoos on her stomach and her legs. She also had a number of piercings, including three in her nose (one in each nostril, plus one through her septum), one in her tongue, a labret piercing, two through her left eyebrow, and one in her belly button. On this day, she was also wearing her nose chains (one for each nostril, and two for the septum), and her belly chain.

"Hey, I go for workouts, don't I?!" Ronald responded, now getting irritated because he felt Dawna was excessively nagging him to do something else. He not only got flak from his girlfriend, but also from his family. "Do I let myself get fat? No! So leave me alone!"

"But we're all worried about you!" she said. "I mean, you can't play video games and work out for the rest of your life! You have to get out of the house do other things once in a while!"

"Oh, you mean so that people can look *down on me* and say, 'Oh, look at that man! He's not working anymore! He's useless to society now because he doesn't work!' No, thank you!"

"Come on! There are lots of people being laid off, not just you! Everyone knows that the *real* economy in this province isn't as rosy as the media and government say it is!"

"But people constantly put you down when you're unemployed! I mean, a couple of my friends got laid off last year, and they've had trouble finding work since then. Anytime they go for interviews, all employers do is put them down and insult them. And other people they talk to put them down and insult them, too," he said. Pointing to the TV screen, he added, "At least *these people* don't say anything like that! They respect me, and like me for who I am. They don't care about whether or not I'm working! And I know that they won't fire me, because no one fires you in a video game!"

However, Ronald didn't always behave like this. And, his demeanour used to be better, too.

Ronald was actually a very sociable and friendly person. While he was never popular in high school, he got along with everyone, and no one had any complaints about him. He has also played on his high school basketball team, though he was not one of the starters. He also liked hockey, baseball, and football, and even played floor hockey and little league baseball growing up, though his baseball team never made it to the Canadian championships. However, he despised golf, a sentiment that still remained, because he found it to be elitist, environmentally destructive, and boring to watch. In fact, once he had tried to watch a round on TV, and fell asleep to the point where Mitch had trouble waking him up to let him know that he had to have a shower. He finished high school in June of 2004, but decided to take a year off to figure out what he wanted to study after high school. During this time, he volunteered a lot, and found out that he really liked marketing and research. Around January of 2005, he decided to apply to the Calgary University School of Business to major in Marketing, with the intention of starting in September of 2005. He was a great student, though he could never get onto the Dean's List because of how hard the business courses were. Ronald didn't work during the school year because he already had quite the workload to deal with, having taken five courses per semester, and adding a job would have been too much to handle, especially after hearing of the demands many employers had of their student workers. Instead, he worked the summers in various student positions because he found them to enrich his knowledge base, and also to help him pay for school so that he didn't have to take out huge student loans. In May of both 2006 and 2007, he was also able to travel to Greece and Spain, respectively, because he was fortunate enough to find jobs with employers who were willing to be patient and wait a month before he started his summer employment. Ronald also inquired with some of his classmates about the Co-op Program, and those who were in it had advised him that he might not find the program to be as beneficial, depending on what positions he may be placed in. They especially highlighted the fact that he would be able to find some of the positions offered through the Co-op Program on his own as regular summer jobs, but with the advantage of not being forced to stay until the end of the placement term if things were just not working out.

Ronald made a lot of friends during university, especially with students from other faculties. While he had made some friends in the business school, he found that he couldn't relate to most of them because their primary focus was money, which was not his primary motivation for wanting to get into marketing. He also found that many business students really loved golf, and talked about how they would do business on the golf course, with further made it difficult to find something in common with these people. Instead, he was better able to relate to the non-business students because they shared his views and outlook on life. They would talk about things such as their philosophies on life, what they hoped to accomplish, how they could help the world, and what their dreams for the future were. Ronald also enjoyed debating and discussing the subject matter of his non-business courses with these other students because he found he would learn more things from them, which was not the case with the business students. After graduation, Ronald was still able to keep in touch with some of them, though some did leave Calgary due to better work opportunities being available elsewhere. Ronald felt fortunate that some of these friends did end up working at the company he used to work for, and even though they were working in different departments, they used to get together for lunch, or after work to hang out.

It was also during university that Ronald met Dawna. Dawna had lived in the northeast of Calgary near Sunridge Mall for her entire life, and still lived there with her parents. She was the youngest of three, and had a brother and a sister, both of whom were already married, having married young, and both of them were already parents. Her sister already had a son and was currently expecting another baby, and her brother had two daughters, and his wife was expecting their third child. Dawna enjoyed being around her nieces and nephew, and made a point to visit them as much as possible. Growing up, Dawna enjoyed playing and watching most sports, though she absolutely hated golf for the exact same reasons as Ronald. In high school, she played multiple sports, including basketball, volleyball, and badminton. She finished high school in 2005, and, like Ronald, took a year off before going on to post-secondary to figure what she wanted to do. During her year off, she played in a volleyball rec league because she wanted to make the Canadian National Women's Volleyball Team. She was heavily scouted by the team during high school, and when she told them she was taking a year off before starting university, they highly recommended to her that she play in a rec league during this time in order to stay on the team's radar, especially since they attended those games to continue following other players they were interested in that also weren't attending university immediately after high school. It was during this time that she decided to major in Kinesiology, partly because she enjoyed the idea of being a Physiotherapist, and partly because she wanted to understand what her team trainers were doing when treating injured players. In September of 2006, she started her post-secondary education at the Calgary University's Faculty of Kinesiology, majoring in Athletic Therapy. She also tried out for and made the university's women's volleyball team. After her first year, Dawna was able to get volleyball scholarships, along with a few academic ones due to her good grades.

Ronald and Dawna formally met during one of her practices. However, Ronald fell for Dawna much earlier than their first meeting. During the Fall 2007 term, they happened to be in an option class together. One day Ronald was sitting in the back with his friends and was talking with them when, while looking around the room, he noticed a beautiful, muscular girl who had various piercings and tattoos sitting in the front with her friends talking and laughing. He instantly became infatuated with her. After that, he kept plotting to try and sit next to her so that he could talk to her and ask her out, despite his friends' objects that she would never say "Yes" to him because someone like her would never be interested in a guy like him. At first, Ronald was foiled in his attempts to sit next to her because Dawna always arrived to class right on time, and her friends and teammates would save her a seat, as they were in a class of 300 people. Not only that, Dawna's friends and teammates would sit in a different place from class to class. At one point, Ronald had decided to give up, and went back to sitting with his friends in the back. Then one day in late November, the 20th, he found out that she was a volleyball player when she answered a question and used her volleyball games to illustrate an example. After this particular class, he talked it over with his friends, and they agreed that the only way he would ever meet her was if he went to one of her practices. One of them told him that they were aware of a practice later that day at 3:30 in the Gerry Morgan Memorial Gym, and, as luck would have it, Ronald finished classes at 3:00 in the Kinesiology building. At the end of that day, Ronald told his friends that he was going to attend the women's volleyball team's practice so that he could ask Dawna out. "Good luck," one of them said. "Tell us how it goes."

"I don't know why you're bothering with doing this," said another. "A hot chick like that doesn't go out with guys like us. Don't come crying to us tomorrow if she rejected you because you're not her 'type.'"

"Hey, at least give him a *chance!*" said a third. "Maybe he'll prove us wrong, and show us that guys like us *can* go out with girls like her."

After finishing classes, Ronald went to the practice, and it was intense. The coach was very demanding, and made the players conduct the various drills at a very high pace. Ronald easily spotted Dawna, though she wasn't wearing her nose and belly chains. He watched her the whole time, and saw that she was really good, and that saw that she was a natural athlete. After practice was over, and just as the players were heading to the locker rooms, Ronald yelled from the stands, "Hey you! With the piercings and tattoos! Wait a minute!"

Dawna stopped and turned around, wondering who was yelling at her. Ronald came running down the stairs, and Dawna was totally shocked that someone had actually watched the volleyball practice inside the gym, as most people would watch it from the windows in the hallway that led to the Calgary Speed Skating Centre. She asked, "Yes? Can I help you?"

"What's your name?" Ronald asked.

"Dawna. Dawna Langston."

"Oh, that's such a beautiful name."

"Thank you," she responded. She was still confused that a guy was talking to her, as most guys considered her a freak, especially because she had so many tattoos and piercings. "And what's your name?"

"Ronald Charlton."

"Oh, okay. So, why did you want to talk to me?"

"Well, we're in the same Sociology 101 class, and I usually sit in the back, and I just can't keep my eyes off of you."

"Uh, okay, that's a little scary to hear," Dawna said, who was starting to get a little freaked out.

"No, no, it's not anything bad like that. I mean, I think you're really beautiful. I just haven't been able to talk to you because you're always with your friends, and you always come to class just on time and sit with your friends."

"Thank you," she said, now getting a little flattered that someone had actually said that she was beautiful, and not a freak. "So, what do you need to ask me? My coach is starting to get impatient over there."

"Would you like to go out with me sometime? And, could I have your number?"

"Oh, really?!" Dawna said, somewhat confused, and yet somewhat excited. Then, confused, she asked, "You want to *date* me?"

"Yes I do."

"Um, well, can you wait maybe 15 minutes?" she said. Then, pointing to the windows, she said, "Would you be able to meet me up there? I have a team meeting that I have to go to, and we're kind of holding it up."

"Sure, I can do that. I don't want to keep the rest of your team waiting any longer than I already have."

"Great! See you then!"

Ronald waited in the hallway that led to the Speed Skating Centre for about 20 minutes, when he saw Dawna approaching him from the doorway leading to the locker rooms. She said, "Sorry for being late. The coach was mad at me for holding up the meeting, and then she took *forever* discussing strategy."

"That's okay," Ronald said. "You didn't keep me waiting for long."

She reached into her bag, pulled out a pen and a piece of paper, wrote down her number, and gave it to Ronald. She then said, "I can't go out this week because I'm crazy busy, especially with road games this weekend in Brandon. But, how about next Tuesday? I don't have a practice that day, and besides next weekend is a home series."

"That will work. It actually works for me as well, because I too am pretty busy. On the bright side, I'm fully done all my assignments and midterms this week."

"Lucky! In a couple of weeks, I still have a few more things due! Anyway, what is your major?"

"Marketing," Ronald said, rather embarrassed because some business students didn't have a great reputation with the rest of the student population.

"So, you're one of *those* people, eh?"

"Don't worry, I'm not like them. There's more to me than just business."

"Oh! I think you're the first business student I've met that has said that."

"What's your major?"

"Kinesiology. I'm majoring in Athletic Therapy."

"Oh, so you want to be a personal trainer?"

"No, physiotherapist."

"Oh, that's nice. I know there is a lot more demand for that in Calgary compared to some of the other majors."

"Well, I just like helping others overcome their injuries. And, it helps me to understand what the trainers are doing when someone goes down with an injury. I want to be of more help to them than just standing around wondering what to do."

"Okay," Ronald said. Then, he looked at his watch, and said, "I've got to get going now. I'll see you next Tuesday!"

"Okay, see you then!"

Ronald left, and while he was walking, he entered Dawna's number into his cell phone's contact list just in case he misplaced the piece of paper with her number on it. The next day, he told his friends that Dawna agreed to go out with him, which left them in disbelief that he actually was able to get a date with her. On their first date, Ronald and Dawna had gone to an Italian restaurant, and then a movie, splitting the evening's bill. Ronald was shocked, as on all of his other dates, the girl *always* expected him to pay, even if she had money, and this attracted Ronald to Dawna even more. Dawna also enjoyed the date, as she found Ronald was quite easy to talk to. They continued dating from that point forward, and quickly became exclusive. Their friends couldn't believe it, as they all thought that those two would be single for a long time. But, they quickly accepted the relationship, and they all became friends with the two of them.

Ronald started watching volleyball more, and even attended some of Dawna's games. During university, the Canadian National Women's Volleyball Team scouts and coaches continued scouting Dawna, and were so impressed with her that they named her to the team for the 2008 and 2012 Summer International Athletic Competitions, as well as the World Championships during that time span. However, Ronald wasn't allowed to join her because the National Team's head coach was very strict, and did not allow the players' boyfriends to accompany the team in order to avoid any distractions, though he did allow the players' spouses and children to join them so that they had family there. He didn't have the money to attend the 2008 International Athletic Competition on his own anyway, and, in 2012, he had to deal with more responsibility at work, and also couldn't attend the World Championships anyway. As a result, Ronald watched both International Athletic Competitions, as well as all of the World Championships, on TV.

When Ronald introduced Dawna to his family in June 2008, his mom, Monica, was shocked at what she saw. As it was a hot day out, Dawna had decided to wear a short top that revealed her tattoo-covered arms and belly-button piercing. She had also worn her nose and belly chains, despite Ronald begging her not to. He was already nervous about how his mother would react to Dawna's appearance with her many tattoos and piercings, and felt that her wearing the chains was over the top. Ronald also knew he would get plenty of questions from Monica, as she had always thought her sons would end up with "clean girls," or those without any body modifications. However, Dawna firmly told Ronald that his mother would have to accept her for who she was and what she looked like, and therefore wore all of the adornments. When they arrived at his house, Ronald took a deep breath, and then he and Dawna got out of the car, and went inside his house. When Ronald and Dawna entered the house, Monica just froze in shock, and said, pointing at Dawna, "*You're* Ronald's girlfriend?"

"Yes I am, Mrs. Charlton," Dawna said. "It's really nice to finally meet you. Ronald's said a lot about all of you."

Monica became even more shocked when she saw Dawna's tongue piercing as she talked. "You've got something in your *tongue!*" she said.

"Yes, it's a tongue piercing," Dawna said.

"But, *why*?!"

"Because I wanted it, and I like it," Dawna said, confused as to why she was being asked the question.

"Well, I can certainly say that Ronald hasn't told us *everything* about you, Dawna."

As they went for lunch, Ronald whispered to her, "See?! I told you that my mom would have an issue with the chains!"

"Well, she'll have to deal with it because this is me, and this is what I look like," Dawna whispered back. "Besides, when she gets to know me, she'll forget about all of these things on my body and on my face."

During the rest of the time Dawna was there, all Monica could do was stare at the tattoos, piercings, and chains that were all over her body. She still couldn't believe that Ronald brought someone home like Dawna. However, Harold and Mitch didn't mind, as Harold was already working with people whose appearance resembled Dawna's, and Mitch also saw people like that at school. When Ronald left to drop Dawna home, Monica immediately told Harold, "I can't believe he brought *her* home. He-He-He...I didn't think he would end up with someone like *her*! She's not '*clean*!' I always imagined he would end up with a 'clean girl!'"

"Look, Monica," Harold said. "She was such a nice and sweet girl. Remember how Ronald described some of the other girls he had dated? They were 'clean girls' at that, and turned out to be horrible people."

"Well, he could have kept looking," Monica responded.

"Mom, not all people with tattoos and piercings are bad," Mitch said. "I actually liked her. Hey, she was willing to play some video games with us, which a lot of girls don't."

"I guess," Monica said.

"Besides, some of the people I work with look sort of like her," Harold said. "And they are real professionals. They don't let those things get in the way of their work. Furthermore, they are actually nice people. Just give Dawna a chance."

"Okay, I will," Monica said grudgingly.

And she did, as eventually grew very fond of Dawna because of how nice and down-to-earth she was. She was even more impressed with how kind and gentle Dawna was, and how she always put others ahead of herself. However, Monica still referred to the tattoos, piercings, and body chains as "imperfections."

When Dawna was not busy with volleyball, sometimes she and Ronald would head off to the mountains for weekend trips to do nature walks, which was an activity that they both enjoyed. They mostly visited Banff, Kootenay, and Jasper National Parks, though sometimes they would head off to Kananaskis and Canmore. They also would head off to Nose Hill and Fish Creek Parks for some day hiking, especially in the springtime, to see nature come alive.

Ronald was ecstatic in the Spring of 2009 when he completed the final courses for his degree, as it marked the completion of the hardest part of his life to that point. With the economy in Calgary still being really bad after finishing his schooling, and the fact that he was really exhausted after completing up his studies, Ronald decided to take the rest of 2009 off, and resolved to start his job search in January of 2010. This allowed him to not only go on vacation to BC and Banff National Park at the end of July, but it also allowed him to attend his graduation in November 2009, which Dawna was also able to attend. At the ceremony, Ronald looked up at the Gerry Morgan Gym's stands, and saw her sitting next to his family, and it made him very happy that they were all there for his big day. He even got the chance to see some of Dawna's volleyball games that fall, and felt quite happy because he knew he didn't have to scramble home after the games to finish up his school work.

When he started looking for work at the beginning of 2010, Ronald saw that there were not many jobs available in Marketing, and guessed that there would be a ton of applicants for them. But, he applied anyway, and hoped for the best. On Monday, January 14, he received a pre-screening interview from someone in the Human Resources Department at Pacific IT and Consulting for a Marketing Assistant job that he had applied to a week earlier. After a couple of days, he found out that he had passed the initial phase, and was being called in for a second interview on the 17th of January (that Thursday) at the company's offices located on 6th Avenue S.W. in Downtown Calgary. Here, he not only met the HR person that had talked to him on the phone, but also the Marketing Director, Thom Gerty, as well as one of the members of the Marketing Department. During the interview, he found out that everyone in the department reported directly to Thom, who didn't believe in having middle managers below him because he felt that middle managers had a habit of treating their employees poorly, and only promoted people they liked, including friends. Thom was firmly of the belief that an employee should be promoted based on their merit, and not on who their friends were, nor who could play the political game the best. Thom had formed these attitudes from his own personal experiences as he was rising through the marketing ranks in various other organizations, where mangers purposely never let him move up the ranks. Due to these experiences, Thom promised himself that if he ever reached the executive ranks, he would always base recruitment on a person's merit, and preferred a system where his staff would report directly to him. If any team was in need of a leader to help them stay organized on track with their projects, he would name a team lead rather than a manager. The team lead was required to send in a truthful report stating exactly what everyone, including the lead themselves, had contributed to the project.

Thom had been with Pacific IT for 12 years as the Marketing Director, and was given autonomy over his department as soon as he took over because the CEO, COO, and CFO strongly adhered to a "hands off" policy when it came to how the various departments were run. They were of the belief that the executives that they had hired to run the departments had more experience and knowledge for those areas, and therefore deserved as much discretion as possible. Moreover, the executives would only intervene if necessary. Upon starting his position, Thom immediately dealt with his inherited staff, keeping all of the non-management employees while letting go of all of the middle managers in order to implement his direct reporting policy. After that, he then implemented his merit-based policies for promotions, only giving higher-level positions to those who were deserving them. Because of these policies, and also because of how approachable he was, everyone thoroughly enjoyed working for Thom. This translated into higher productivity and strong morale in the Marketing Department. If anyone within the Marketing Department ever left the organization, it was either because they wanted a new challenge, or someone wanted to start their own business.

During the interview, Ronald had been grilled about the various aspects of marketing, and what he would do in various situations. This was to see if Ronald had the right attitude and competencies to be able to succeed in the department. Despite his best efforts, Ronald was really nervous during the interview, and sometimes struggled during the interview. After it was over, and as he left Pacific IT's offices, all Ronald could do was look down in shame, thinking that he had blown the interview. As he had another interview with another company coming up the following Monday, he knew he couldn't worry too much, and prepared as best as could for it. While that interview went a lot better, Ronald was in for a shock after he got home. As he entered the house, Monica and Harold told Ronald that there was a message for him from Thom, who had asked Ronald to call him back. Mitch wasn't there because he was in Regina, where he had been attending the University of Regina since September 2007, majoring in English. Ronald then turned his cell phone on to check his voicemail for any messages, as on his résumé he had listed both his home and cell numbers. The phone vibrated after a few seconds, indicating that he had a new voicemail message waiting for him. It was Thom, who had left the exact same message on his voicemail that he had left on the home answering machine. Ronald immediately called him back, and Thom answered, "Hello?"

"Uh, yes, hello, Thom? It's Ronald. Ronald Charlton," Ronald said.

"Oh, yes, Ronald! How are you today?"

"I'm doing okay. I'm just returning the message you left."

"Yes. I just wanted to let you know that you're being offered the Marketing Assistant position that you interviewed for last Thursday."

Ronald went silent for a few moments, shocked that, despite the fact that he thought he blew the interview, he was being offered the job. "Hello? Ronald? Are you still there?" Thom asked.

"Yes, I am," Ronald replied. "I'm just surprised because I thought I blew the interview."

"No, no!" Thom said, laughing. "You were just nervous. We're not the type of company that holds that against a candidate. We've all been there before. Remember, I was in your position once. And, we don't get to hold the Number 1 spot in the Top 100 Employers listing by using things like that as an excuse to reject a candidate."

"Oh, that's a relief," Ronald said, breathing a sigh of relief.

"So, are you taking the position?"

"Yes, I will," Ronald replied with excitement.

"Great! I remember you had said something about being able to start next Monday. Does that still work for you?"

"Yes, it does."

"Great! Okay, you enjoy the rest of your week, and if you have any questions, feel free to contact me We'll have all the paperwork that you need to fill out ready when you come in next Monday. When you enter the reception area, just be sure to ask for me at the front desk. I will come and escort you to the floor then."

"Okay. But, I do have one question. Why did you hire me? A lot of my friends that have applied for similar positions are getting the 'no experience' response from a lot of employers. They are starting to look out of town, out of province, and even at other countries because employers here don't want to give them a chance."

"That's actually a good question, and I'm glad you asked that. I'm *very* aware of that 'no experience' attitude amongst other employers. And it's not just here in Calgary, but its also the case across the country. In fact, when I was your age, the exact same thing happened to me, and this was in the '70s, when employers were more willing to train and give people a chance. It took me a couple of years before someone was willing to give me a chance, and I vowed that I would *never* do that to anyone that I was hiring because I know how it feels, and how frustrating it can get. No one starts with experience, and no one starts with knowledge of all of these software programs. Did you know that was actually the main reason why there was a 'brain drain' in the 1990s? I remember when I started here at Pacific IT, a lot of people in the industry were complaining about how a lot of Canadian graduates were going to the States or Europe. And yet, these exact same companies would not hire those graduates because they had no experience! What did they expect would happen? That these graduates wouldn't take offers from places that were actually interested in hiring them, and that they would just sit around waiting for some Canadian employer to have an epiphany that they needed to hire new Canadian graduates if they ever wanted to continue to be successful? Experience can only be gained by working, and that means giving people a chance. Software can be taught, especially software like the ones used here at Pacific IT, where we seem to be the only company in the industry that uses them. So, who's going to know these programs without working here? That's actually one thing that I like about this company. We're not a company that believes in hiring the most experienced candidate, or the most proficient in all of the software programs, but the one who has the right attitude, the willingness to learn, and who can get along with others."

"Okay, that's great, but you didn't answer the question *why me*."

"Oh? I didn't? Sorry, I tend to ramble a bit. The reason we hired you specifically was because we could tell from your answers that you would have the right attitude, and would work well with others. And, that you were genuinely interested in making a career at this company. Many of the other candidates had an arrogance about them, especially the experienced ones, who acted like they were the greatest and therefore we would be fools not to hire them. And some of the other candidates seemed to be more interested in the experience and the money, and would leave quickly once they received their experience and training."

"Okay, thanks. I'll see you next Monday, then."

"Wonderful! And if you have any other questions, don't hesitate to give me a call."

During that week, Thom emailed Ronald a copy of his employment contract. Among other things, it said that he would be given about a three months of training to give him an overview of the company, learn all of the different software programs used by the company, and meet with members of all of the various teams so that, in case someone from marketing was needed, he could talk to them. This was to be followed by a three month probationary period so that both parties could evaluate if there was a fit. Ironically, Ronald also received a call that Thursday from the other company that he had interviewed with, and was told that they couldn't hire him because he didn't have experience. Ronald just took it in stride, and thanked them for letting him know, and said that it wouldn't have worked out anyway because he already had accepted another job offer.

On Monday, January 28th, Ronald arrived for his first day of work at 8:00 am, and was excited, while at the same time nervous. After filling out the paperwork, Ronald started his training, as per the email Thom had sent a week earlier. During this time, he learned everything he could about his job, including the software, the different roles in the Marketing Department, how his position interacted with them, and all the other various aspects of the company.

Pacific IT's primary business was to create desktop and mobile applications for all types of organizations. They also did consulting work for clients on the other systems that Pacific IT was knowledgeable in. Their office was located in a skyscraper on 6th Avenue S.W. in Downtown Calgary, and took up 10 floors of this building. While every floor had pretty good views of the city, the best views were on the top floor, where most of the executive offices were located. The Marketing Department was a floor below that, and Thom's office was the only one there, as he didn't believe in being separate from all of his staff, and wanted to be as close to the action as possible. He also wanted his staff to have easy access to him, and always kept his office door open in case someone wanted to talk to him. This was also the only floor with an open office concept, as Thom felt that cubicles were not conducive with a collaborative, team-oriented work environment. The other floors had a lot of cubicles, and the manager offices were located as close to their teams as possible. There were also lots of meeting rooms around Pacific IT's offices so that a last-minute meeting could be called, and the company kept private "breakout rooms" for employees to be able to make personal calls to ensure that they could have their privacy if they had to make such a call. Each floor had its own lunch room, which contained a full fridge, a stove, garbage cans, a water cooler, vending machines for snacks, pop, and food, juice and coffee machines, and a prep area. There was also a cafeteria on the main floor of the Pacific IT office space.

Pacific IT's Marketing Department was essentially the first point of contact for clients, where proposals and presentations were made to clients when there were RFP (Request for Proposal) posts. The department also responded to client inquiries about other services that Pacific offered, as well as non-IT related questions from current clients. Members of the Marketing Department also handled internal and external communications, including advertising, newsletters, social media, any media requests, and the company's website, as well as attending trade shows.

During Ronald's probationary period, Dawna was finishing up her Kinesiology degree, and completed her course work in April. As she would be graduating in June, she asked if Ronald would be able to attend her graduation, and Ronald told her that he would have to ask Thom if he could attend. When he did, Thom was very happy to oblige, as he also felt that no one should miss the important events such as this. At the graduation, Dawna looked around to see if Ronald was there, and when she saw him and his family, she couldn't contain her excitement, as she stood up from her seat and waved to them. They waved back, and she sat back down, just as the ceremonies were about to begin.

After Ronald had finished his probation, Thom immediately promoted him to Junior Marketing Analyst, as he was very impressed with Ronald's work ethic, quality of work, abilities, and attitude. While Ronald had done more administrative work during his probationary period, he was doing more research and analysis of market trends in this new role. He was also more involved with the development of some of the proposals to potential clients, and was even asked to help out with other marketing duties such as advertising, cold calls, presentations, and emailing clients. Mitch finished his schooling in April 2011, and graduated in June of that year, and Ronald felt fortunate that Thom gave him permission to attend Mitch's graduation. By mid-2011, Ronald had been promoted to Intermediate Marketing Analyst, which allowed him to be more involved with the Department's projects.

When Thom retired in June 2012, he left Ronald in charge of the entire Marketing Department while the search for a new Marketing Director was going on because he felt that Ronald was the most capable of leading. No one objected. The respect that Thom's workers had for him was reflected by the fact that all of Pacific IT's staff attended his retirement party. Everyone from Marketing thanked him for giving them a chance when no one else would, for being the best boss they ever had, and for treating them with dignity and respect. Ronald also thanked Thom for giving him a chance, mentioning that another company that interviewed him had rejected him, using the justification of him not having enough experience. He also thanked Thom for saving him from having to go through the long period of unemployment that some of his friends had to go through, and for showing so much faith and trust in him. Thom was very humble in receiving the well-deserved accolades, and said that he did what he felt was right, just, and fair. He also imparted a final teaching, which was that no one should ever forget what they had to go through when they were starting out.

During the time that Ronald was essentially the interim Marketing Director, he found it difficult to balance his duties as an Intermediate Marketing Analyst while also leading the entire department. He asked for a lot of help, and because his co-workers loved working with and for him, they were happy to oblige. Ronald always treated them with respect, and made sure that everyone's contributions were rewarded. He also received a monthly bonus during this time, mainly because Thom demanded it from the executives, who were hesitant to do so because they were receiving pressure from their peers in the industry to not give bonuses to those below the managerial ranks. If someone happened to be jealous of Ronald or anyone else in the department, he dealt with it respectfully, and made sure that the person understood that he didn't actively lobby for more responsibility or promotions, and instead Thom made the decision on his own. Ronald made sure that the person was aware that he didn't have any authority over hiring and promotion decisions in the department, as his official role was still Intermediate Marketing Analyst. This time period from June 25, 2012 to the end of 2012 would mark the high-water mark of Ronald and the rest of the Marketing staff's tenure at Pacific IT and Consulting.

That was because in the beginning of December, the executives found their new Marketing Director, Betty Morgan, who was going to start on January 2, 2013. As the Marketing Department would soon find out, Betty was a nasty person, and only liked working with her friends, who came only from high school and university, as she didn't bother trying to make any new friends once she finished her schooling. While she was a popular person with her friends, she treated others very poorly. All that was known about her educational background was that she went to high school in Calgary, and then attended the University of London (Ontario) Management School, majoring in Marketing. There, she completed a Bachelor of Commerce degree, but never went on for an MBA, which was typical for many within the executive ranks of all organizations. It left many people in Pacific IT's Marketing Department, including Ronald, who had no intention of getting an MBA, wondering, "If she didn't have an MBA, how on earth did she become the Marketing Director?"

It was actually quite simple for Betty. The reason that she was able to get such a position without completing an MBA was because she was very good at presenting herself as the most competent candidate, and that the company would benefit from her leadership. In all of her previous jobs, those that worked with and for her found out that her work ethic was horrible, as she spent more of her time at work promoting herself rather than actually doing any work. When she was rising through the ranks, she had a habit of coming in later than all of her co-workers, but leaving much earlier than the rest. She lacked any competence at doing her job, and showed indifference during any training sessions that she attended. She even bullied her co-workers by insulting them and putting them down. However, she didn't get fired, and instead received promotions, because she would take credit for the work done by her co-workers, even though she didn't contribute much during the entire duration of her teams' projects. Once becoming a manager, things got worse, as she became known for bullying most of her staff in any way she could, as she would put them down, and made their lives miserable. She was never available for her staff's questions, instead deriding them for bothering her, and telling them that she didn't have time to talk about their "petty issues." Betty continued arriving later and leaving earlier than everyone else, and yet forced her staff to stay late into the evening, even hiring a spy to make sure everyone was complying with her order. She intentionally gave those not in her inner circle poor performance reviews, even if they did a good job. These employees would have to appeal their performance reviews to HR as per the appeals policies in place, and in all cases the reviews would be changed as HR agreed that Betty was completely out of line giving such reviews. Not only that, Betty would consistently threaten those outside of her inner circle with termination. Sometimes, Betty would fire them without cause, and only because she didn't like them. Due to this, some former employees sued the company for wrongful dismissal, and many of them won their cases. Despite all of these issues, Betty still wasn't fired because her bosses still believed she was doing a good job. However, she was the nicest person in the world if a co-worker or employee happened to be one of her friends. As a manager, she gave them great performance reviews regardless of whether they actually deserved them or not, never firing them, and always defending them in any dispute. While she didn't have final hiring authority as a manager, she sat on the hiring committees for her teams, and did her best to promote her friends that had applied. However, she was overruled many times when it came down to making a hiring decision, as many of her friends showed poor attitudes and incompetence in the interviews.

During Betty's career, she never lasted longer than three years at a company, as her immediate boss would either leave for another company, or would retire. And when a new boss came in, the other staff immediately booked a meeting with them, minus Betty, to discuss their grievances about her. Once an investigation had been completed, their first major decision would be to remove Betty from her position because of her poor work ethic when she wasn't a manager, and because of her poor treatment of her employees when she was a manager. However, because Betty had been fortunate that she was able to use her friends and previous bosses as references, and her new employers would not contact her old employers, she was always able to get another job quickly.

She had lost her previous job in October 2012 because her attitude got her into trouble with her boss. After another one of her employees had left the company, there was an opening that she thought would be perfect for one of her friends from Ontario, who was looking for jobs in Alberta because of a lack of job prospects in Ontario. The friend was brought in for an interview, with the company paying the travel expenses. During the interview, the HR Manager and her boss noticed that Betty's friend didn't have the right qualifications nor the right attitude for the position. After all of the interviews had been completed, and when they were deliberating over the list of candidates on who to hire, Betty insisted that her friend should be hired over more qualified candidates. However, her boss and the HR Manager overruled her, telling her that her friend was not the right fit for either the position or the company. Betty became livid, and questioned the authority and competence of both her boss and the HR Manager. Suddenly, Betty heard her boss say, in a very firm tone, "Betty, as of this moment, you're no longer an employee of this company!"

"What?" Betty asked, surprised. "What does that mean?"

"It means that you're fired, Betty!" the HR Manager said as she phoned security.

Grudgingly, Betty accepted the decision, though she voiced her displeasure over it. However, the dismissal did not mark the end for Betty, as she immediately started looking for work. She received an interview with Pacific IT and Consulting at the end of November, and it was two rounds of interviews. In both cases, when explaining why she lost her previous job, she simply stated that it was a difference of opinion on how the company was being run. She was an expert at playing politics, and as such she was able to impress both the CEO and HR Manager, who decided that she was the most suitable candidate. She further solidified the position by saying that she would question authority if she felt that a decision was wrong. After she received and accepted the job offer, she was asked when she could start in her new role. She told them that she wanted to spend the holiday season with her family, and could start January 2, 2013, and that was it: Betty Morgan was the new Marketing Director. When she heard that she would have full autonomy over the decisions of her department, including who she wanted to hire and promote, a wide grin came across her face because she had finally been given the full autonomy she had sought when she began her new job search.

As soon as she started at Pacific IT, Betty immediately treated her staff just as poorly as she did in her previous jobs. She belittled her staff, questioned their competence, and made them work longer hours, threatening to fire them if they did not. And just like at her previous companies, she arrived late and left really early, and hired a spy to keep an eye on her staff to make sure that everyone stayed late. And even though everyone's work was up to the quality that Thom liked, it was not good enough for Betty, and she made them start all over because she would find some imaginary mistake in it. On one occasion, when Ronald mentioned that Thom would have approved of his report on market conditions, Betty snapped back, "Well I'm not Thom, *am I*?! I have different standards than Thom! Now, do that over before I fire you for insubordination!"

Ronald and the other staff did their best to work with Betty, even asking her for a meeting to find out what her expectations were, or express their concerns. However, she turned them away every time, telling them, "Hey! Get back to work! I'm *way* too busy to talk! Now, stop interrupting me before I fire you!"

The staff all tried to talk to the CEO about Betty's behaviour, but their complaints fell on deaf ears, as he kept saying to them, "Look, we need people like Betty because she might see something that isn't right, and then we can fix it right away. So, that's probably what she is doing. That's why we hired her: she's an independent thinker. Now, please, return to your desks."

As it turned out, Betty already had plans in place for the Marketing Department. Unknown to everyone, when she first started, she researched the company's policy book about handing out layoff notices, and found out that she had to give two-weeks-notice. Once she got this information, she started working the phones to determine which of her friends wanted to come and work for her at the company. After talking to all of those people, she determined that the earliest that everyone could all start together on February 25, 2013. Therefore, layoff notices to the current staff would have to be handed out on February 8, 2013, at the latest. And without the executives willing to question what she was doing, she encountered no resistance from them when she sent the notices for approval. In fact, the executives agreed with her on the need for a culture change within her department.

When February 8 came around, Betty got to the office at 7:00 am, much earlier than usual, and before everyone else. That was because she wanted to personally place the layoff notices on her employees' desks. When Ronald and the rest of the staff came in at about 8:30 am, they were stunned to see the layoff notices. They immediately went to the CEO and asked him what these were all about, as they weren't given any warning about layoffs. The CEO simply said, "Well, ask your boss. It's her decision as to who she wants on her staff."

Ronald was very angry, and barged down to Betty's office. He asked her angrily, holding the layoff notice, "What's the meaning of this?"

"Well, Ronald, we're trying to create a different culture in this company," Betty said slyly and without remorse. "And, you don't fit into this new culture."

"But *all* of us?" Ronald asked, demanding an answer.

"Yes," Betty said arrogantly. "You see, I was evaluating everyone, and no one fits the new culture that we're trying to create."

"Who said that?! There was definitely nothing wrong with the culture in this department! Thom worked hard to create an inclusive culture here!"

"Well, that may have been this *Thom's* culture, but it's not *mine*. I need people that I can work with, and all of you don't *fit in* with what I'm trying to build here. And, I have the backing of the executives about the need for a change in culture, otherwise they wouldn't have approved these layoffs."

"You mentioned culture change across the company. Is this happening right now in other departments, or just this one? Because I haven't heard anything about a culture change from my friends that work in the *other* departments!"

"I can't speak for the other departments, but I feel that *this* department needs a change in culture. Think of this as your first life lesson: Life is never fair!"

Ronald snorted, and then stormed out of the office. During their final two weeks at Pacific IT, the staff showed their displeasure over their layoffs. They worked much slower, and didn't stay past 3:30 pm because, since they couldn't be fired once they either gave a notice of resignation or were given a layoff notice, there was nothing anyone could do to change the behaviour. The clients and potential clients noticed the drop in morale, and they, too, were upset because such a good set of people were being let go for no reason other than a boss didn't that like them. As it turns out, one of Betty's former employees ended up working at one of Pacific's clients, and had said that the most likely reason for the layoffs was because Betty only liked working with her friends. This just made Ronald and the rest of the staff even angrier, as it became obvious that Betty had never intended to give them a fair chance. On their final day, February 22, everyone arrived at 7:00 am, cleaned out their desks, and left, as they didn't really see any reason to stay the whole day and deal with Betty. Company policy allowed workers to stay as little as they wanted to on their last day, so it wasn't as if anyone could do anything about it. When Betty arrived at 9:00 am, she could only smile, as she was impressed with herself at her handling of the situation. For the rest of the day, she just let the phones ring, ignoring the calls coming in from both clients and potential clients. She also fired her spy because the person was no longer needed.

Problems began almost immediately after Betty's friends started the following Monday. The new employees did not have the best work ethic, nor were they the most competent. After filling out their paperwork, they immediately started in their new positions in the Marketing department because of their previous "experience" in other companies. However, they still had to go through the mandatory three-month probation period, and were also required to attend the necessary meetings during those three months to learn about the company and its business. However, the new employees showed very little interest in these meetings, as they knew Betty's personal policy was to never fire her friends, nor to ever give her friends bad reviews. Betty's new staff also showed a lack of punctuality, as they consistently arrived late, and left early, meaning that no project was ever completed on time.

This further translated into a substandard product, as the quality of the work that was being produced was far below the standards seen under Thom's leadership. Many of the proposals that were sent to the company's clients and potential clients were so bad that they were rejected outright, and those companies soon started looking elsewhere for their IT needs. Furthermore, the Department's staff were very rude to the clients, which accelerated the loss of business away from Pacific IT. Moreover, the new employees gave little credence to the corporate communications, which led to poor quality on the company advertising, flyers, brochures, and newsletters. This was also extended to the company's website and social media accounts, as they were barely updated, if at all, which further angered Pacific IT's current clients. On top of that, Betty and the rest of the Marketing Department rarely interacted with the other departments, which led to a great deal of disconnect between Marketing and the rest of the company.

Ronald took the layoff really hard. After he got home with his things on February 22, he immediately went to sleep. After sleeping for about four hours, it was lunchtime, and he went downstairs, upset at the course of events that had taken place. "Don't worry, Ronald, everything will be okay," Monica said. "That *woman* will get what's coming to her! Don't you worry, God will give you justice for her actions."

"But, the economy sucks right now," Ronald said. "There just aren't many marketing positions right now, and the ones that *are* out there get *tons* of applicants! I don't stand a chance!"

Mitch, who had been working since September of 2012 as a fundraiser for Common Goals United of Calgary, was off that week because of the Family Day long weekend. He didn't have a girlfriend because he felt that right now, they were too expensive and too time consuming, as he felt that they required constant attention and got mad if their boyfriend did anything without them. Not only that, but he also felt that girls would distract him from his goals in life, so he intentionally made sure he didn't have a girlfriend, at least for now. His parents and Ronald weren't worried, because he said that he would eventually look at settling down, but it just didn't make sense at the moment. He consoled Ronald by saying, "Hey, how about this? I know some people that might be able to help you out in the non-profit sector. Do you want me to contact them?"

"You know, I just don't want to look for work right now," Ronald replied. "I've heard stories that, with the job market still being pretty bad, and people still getting laid off, there are many managers out there just like Betty Morgan. And you know what? I don't want to deal with anyone like that. Not after *this*."

Dawna, who had been working at a physiotherapy job since November 2012, also tried to cheer up Ronald, but to no avail. As time went on, it was quite obvious that he had gone into a deep depression, as he didn't want to go on nature walks with Dawna anymore, nor really do anything for that matter. Ronald had started playing in floor hockey and basketball recreation leagues after he finished school because he wanted to ensure that he had a life outside of work. Thom had encouraged playing sports, and didn't get mad if Ronald left work a little early on the odd occasion so that he could make it to the games on time. However, Betty did have a problem with that, and never let Ronald leave early, saying that it only showed that he didn't care about his job. But, after losing his job, he began feeling ashamed about being unemployed, and stopped going to the games. The friends that he had made in those leagues started calling him to find out what happened. After finding out that he had stopped coming to the games because he was ashamed about his layoff, they tried to come to his house in early March to convince him to come back, as they missed him and needed him. But replied back with, "Why? So that everyone there can make fun of me for now being unemployed? I know how everyone talks about the unemployed, as if it is *their* fault No! I will not go to the games anymore!"

"But, there's other players there that have been laid off as well!" one of the players said. "Come on, no one will say anything bad, because they themselves are going through the same thing, or know someone who is."

"No! This is humiliating for me!"

It was around early March that Ronald became addicted to video games. One day, he came down to the family room, and noticed the Invisio 3 that he hadn't played since the Christmas holidays, and decided to hook it up and start playing it. As he played, he started noticing that the games were giving him compliments, and all he could think was "At least *these* people appreciate me!"

At first, his family and Dawna weren't worried, as they figured that he was just blowing off some steam. However, March turned into April, April turned into May, and May turned into June, and Ronald still continued playing his video games non-stop. The only other thing that he did was work out. And they started getting very angry with him. One day in May, Monica said, "Ronald, dear, I think you need to stop playing these video games! You've been playing these things non-stop since early March! You *need* to start looking for a job, or start doing something more *productive!*"

Ronald just brushed her off, saying, "Hey, Mom, at least I'm not doing drugs, or alcohol, or gambling! If I was doing one of those things, *then* you would have something to worry about!"

"But Ronald, *this* is no better because you're just doing *nothing!*"

"Mom, *these* people respect me! They compliment me! And they value me! No one mistreats you in a video game! And no one fires you from a video game!"

"Ronald, you can't spend the rest of your life playing video games! You have to go to other places besides the gym!"

"Well, maybe in the future, but this is the right thing to do right now!"

"Whatever happened to your plans to eventually travel to Germany, France, and Italy?"

"Well, I got laid off, and those plans are on hold indefinitely. Besides, things are even *worse* there! Why would I want to be reminded of what I am going through?"

"Ronald, I don't know what I'm going to do with you!" Monica said, before storming off.

Dawna was even more angry, as she did not like being constantly ignored. She understood that sometimes people needed to be left alone and be given their space to recover, but this addiction was becoming ridiculous to her. And Mitch was upset because Ronald no longer wanted to play basketball with him when he had some time off, instead wanting to stay indoors and play the video games, or head off to the gym to work out. His family cancelled the family vacation they had booked to BC because they were afraid that Ronald was never going to get off of the sofa in the family room. Monica and Harold's rule for family vacations was that if one of their kids couldn't or didn't want to go, then no one went on vacation. And his friends kept calling him, but they, too, were unsuccessful in getting through to him. It got even worse, as in June Ronald waited in line to buy the new Invisio 4, and the sports, adventure, and racing games that were released in conjunction with the system. He later bought more games for the system as they were released. His family, friends, and Dawna were irritated at him that he was willing to go out of the house to buy video games, but not for anything else but working out at the gym. However, Ronald felt a deep sense of shame for being unemployed. He started believing that the only ones that cared for him were the characters in the video games, as they were the only people who appreciated him, respected him, praised him, congratulated him, and comforted him. As a result, they were the only ones that he was willing to interact with on a regular basis.

CHAPTER TWO

Back at Ronald's house on August 3, 2013, Dawna did her best to get Ronald to stop playing video games so much. She insisted that he had to start getting off the couch to do something else. He finally snapped, and curtly said, "Look, Dawna! I don't want to do anything else today! Now leave me alone! I have to concentrate on this basketball game! The opposing team is really tough!"

Dawna stormed upstairs in frustration, and looked around for Monica and Harold. After finding them sitting in the living room, she went up to them and said, "Mr. and Mrs. Charlton, Ronald's playing those stupid video games *again*! He just won't stop!"

"We know, Dawna," Monica replied. "I don't really know what to do. We keep trying to talk to him, but he just won't listen."

"And," Harold added, "the only way for him to fix the problem is to first admit that he has a problem."

"But this is getting to be too much!" Dawna said. "He needs to stop! He won't spend time with me anymore! He only focuses on those stupid video games!"

Just then, Mitch arrived home after helping out at a fundraising event for work. This weekend, the Common Goals United of Calgary had held a golf tournament. As he opened the door, he said, "Hi Mom. Hi Dad. Oh, Dawna! You're here too."

"Hi dear," Monica said.

"Hey Mitch," added Dawna.

"Hi Mitch! How was the tournament?" Harold said.

"Well, it was golf," Mitch said. "It's not one of my favourites, but we did raise a good amount of money that will help a lot of people."

"I hear you," Dawna agreed. "But like you said, the funds raised will help a lot of people."

"Always look at the positive," Harold said. "In fundraising, golf tournaments are popular because many people enjoy the sport. And those in need will be helped."

"I know," Mitch said. "So anyway, where's Ronald?"

"He's downstairs playing those stupid video games," Dawna said.

"*Again*?!" Mitch said angrily. "He's been doing that for, what now, 5 months?!"

"I know! And, I tried to get him off, but he just won't!" Dawna said, visibly irritated.

"It's not like we haven't been trying, either," Monica added. "And, we've been trying to tell him for months that he's not the only person that's ever been laid off."

"Yeah, that's right," Mitch responded. "I mean, at the tournament, there were a good number of people there that said that they had been laid off, and some for reasons similar to Ronald. They showed a lot of sympathy and empathy towards him because they were experiencing it themselves. And, some of the managers from our sponsors that were there were saying that they've noticed an uptick in applications for their job postings. They also showed empathy because they realized that not everything was as good as what the government and corporate media have been reporting."

"But, Ronald keeps saying that many interviewers are really rude based on what his friends have had to go through," Dawna said. "So, how do we get him to see that no one is against him?"

"I don't know," Harold replied. "I mean, even at our company, we're getting people with years of experience and lots of education applying for lower-level positions because of how bad things are. From what I've observed and listened to, some people, including those in HR, are out of touch because they don't have to worry about *their* jobs going anywhere anytime soon."

Harold would know. He started recalling about how he himself had trouble getting settled down in 1976 after he had finished his Bachelor of Arts degree in Historical Studies at Calgary University. After finishing school, Harold, who was from Drumheller, decided to stay in Calgary because there was more work available here, and also because he wanted to be more independent. He bounced around various white-collar positions because the managers didn't trust him with responsibility to the point where he became frustrated, or the companies that he worked for just did not appeal to him as a place to work long-term. Finally, in the early 1990s, he completed a Contracts Analysis certification on the advice of a manager that saw that he had potential to really succeed in that field. When he finished the certification, Harold immediately was moved into a Contracts Analyst position in that company, and he just loved the work. He could now say that this was the type of work that he was looking for all of this time, and wished that his previous managers had taken more interest in him as this one did.

He stayed at that company until 2003, when he was laid off after the company's new owners downsized the company and outsourced many jobs overseas in order to cut costs, despite the fact that the business was already very profitable. That company did not last for very long after that, as most of its clients moved to service providers that were still located in Calgary because they actually needed to meet with the consultants and other staff in person, and not just over the Internet. Harold had been with his current employer, a junior oil and gas company, for ten years as a Senior Contracts Analyst, and enjoyed working there because of the positive corporate culture, including the organization placing emphasis on training younger people, which allowed him to be a mentor to them.

Harold also smiled when he thought of how he had met Monica during a lunch break on a warm day in June 1979. He had been walking around Downtown Calgary, and happened to look into the window of one of the cafés there. Through the window he saw Monica reading a mystery novel, alone, and not aware of what was going on around her. After staring for a few minutes, he went inside to introduce himself to her. When he did, a surprised look came to Monica's face. Nevertheless, they ended up eating lunch together, talking about their lives and their interests. At the end of the date, they exchanged numbers. They continued dating for two years, and got married in December 1981.

As he was daydreaming, Ronald came upstairs because he was getting hungry, and also because he finished his basketball game. Monica asked, "So, are you finished playing those things for the day?"

"No," Ronald retorted. "I'm hungry, so before I start another game, I will eat lunch."

"All you ever do these days is play those games!" Mitch yelled at him. "You have to do other things!"

"How many times do I have to tell all of you?!" Ronald said angrily. "I don't want anyone to put me down over getting laid off! It's not like the economy is great! And all these people that put me down believe everything that is said in the news!"

"Well, you can't play video games forever!" Dawna said.

"It might not be forever," Ronald responded. "But, those people respect me."

"Well, you have to start doing more productive things," Harold said. "Playing video games isn't going to solve anything."

Ronald ignored that last statement, and he went to the kitchen to make his lunch. He asked Dawna, "Dawna, do you want me to make something for you?"

"No!" she said. "I'm leaving!"

"What? Why?"

"Because there's no point staying here if all you're going to do is play those stupid games!"

"Hey, I never said you couldn't play with me!"

"I want to do something different! I played those games with you when you weren't addicted! But I won't play with you when you won't do anything else!"

"Fine! Be that way!"

Dawna got her things, and, still upset, slammed the door before driving home. Harold, Monica, and Mitch came into the kitchen and were not happy. "How could you do that to her?!" Monica asked.

"What do you mean?" Ronald asked.

"Ronald," Harold said, "Dawna is such a good girl. She cares about others instead of just herself. Remember how much you complained when you dated some of those other girls? Like how they would expect you to buy them expensive gifts, but would only buy you some cheap stuff that you didn't want? Or how they expected you to *always* take them out to expensive restaurants, and expected you to pay the entire bill? Dawna doesn't do that, does she?"

"No, but she just doesn't understand," Ronald said.

"Oh, I think she does," Monica said. "She has been really patient with you, but I can tell you that it is wearing thin. Despite all of her 'imperfections,' which for the life of me I cannot understand *why* she doesn't just get rid of them, she is kind, and has done her best to support you through this time. But, if you're not careful, you could lose her."

Ronald just snorted, and then ate his lunch. After he finished, he went back down, and started up another game. After playing for about an hour, Ronald finished his game, and went up to his room to get his workout clothes. He came down, and just as he was leaving his house, he lifted up his gym bag and yelled, "See? At least I don't let myself get fat!"

He left the house, and went to the nearby gym. After working out for a couple of hours, he came back home. He went up to get himself cleaned up, and then came down for dinner, where everyone was waiting for him. Monica then asked, "So, Ronald, when exactly are you going to look for a new job? It's been almost six months since you got laid off."

"Yes," Harold added, "and you have had more than enough time to rest."

"I don't know." Ronald muttered. "The economy is bad, and a lot of other companies are laying off their employees, so I don't know if I'll apply or not. Besides, if employers don't show any loyalty, why should I? Look where loyalty gets you! Straight to the unemployment line, with no way of getting out."

"But I met a lot of people at that golf tournament today," Mitch said. "Some of them are going through exactly what you are. And the managers of sponsors were empathetic. They even said that I could pass along your résumé to them, and they genuinely seemed interested in you after I told them about the responsibilities you had at Pacific IT and Consulting."

"Why?! So that they can put me down and insult me in person?!" Ronald retorted. "No, thank you!"

"Okay, fine," Harold replied calmly. "You don't have to look for a job if you don't think you'll be respected. However, you could start your own business. You could volunteer. You could do consulting work. You could even travel to just get away from Calgary for a while."

"No way! Starting a business requires money, and none of the banks are lending to people like me," Ronald said. "And, as for doing some of those other things, people will just remind me of my situation, and then will put me down."

"Ronald! I did *not* give up my career for you and Mitch just so that you could waste away the rest of your life playing video games!" Monica said, who was quite angry at the responses that Ronald was giving.

She began recalling of the days gone by. Monica, who was born and raised in Calgary, used to work as a Consultant for a major international consulting firm that had an office in Calgary. She too had attended Calgary University, and had studied in the Faculty of Management from September 1972 to April 1976. She did this in spite of the objections of her friends, who had tried to convince her to be a model. However, she firmly told them she wanted to get an education. She graduated in June 1976 with a major in General Business, as she didn't want to be pigeon-holed into any particular field by prospective employers, as had happened to some of her business friends that had chosen a specific major and had applied to jobs outside of that major.

After she had finished school, it took her about six months to find a job because some of the firms she had applied to were a little intimidated by a smart woman entering their company, especially since many still had the attitude that women would quit their jobs once their children were born. However, she finally found an enlightened consulting firm, and started out as an Assistant. After a year, she earned her first promotion, followed by another promotion a couple of months after she met Harold in 1979. A year after she and Harold were married, Monica earned another well-deserved promotion, and was working in a Senior Consultant role. When she found out she was pregnant with Ronald, she was due for another promotion to a Managing Consultant role. However her employer gave it to someone else because they were worried that she wouldn't be able to spend as much time at the office with a child on the way. Monica had become quite upset, but decided to wait until after her baby was born before she made any rash decisions. After Ronald was born, she started doing some research about whether or not she could have a career and raise a small child at the same time. After some soul searching during her maternity leave, she decided to become a stay-at-home mom in order to be there for her kids. She and Harold were in agreement with the decision, and felt it was the right thing for them.

In the midst of her flashback, she heard Ronald yelling, "Look, I've told you multiple times how I feel, and nothing's going to change that. Besides, it's not like I've gotten into drugs, or alcohol, or gambling, or shopping. You have nothing to worry about!"

Then, he remained silent for the rest dinner. After he finished eating, he went downstairs, and started playing more video games until he went to bed.

The next day, Ronald was in the basement playing his 16-bit video game system when his family came down, thinking about trying to hold an intervention for him. "Ronald, pause this game this instant!" Monica demanded.

"Why?" Ronald asked.

"Because, we need to talk to you!" Harold said.

"No, I can listen while playing," Ronald said, not taking his eyes off of the screen.

Mitch then stood in front of the TV, blocking Ronald's view. Ronald tried to look around him, but because Mitch was so big, it was hard. "Can you move, please?" Ronald asked.

"No!" Mitch said. "This needs to be done *now*!"

"Fine!" Ronald said.

He then paused the game, and asked, "What is it?! I was about to hit a high score!"

"Ronald, you need an intervention," Monica said. "Ever since you got laid off, you've been depressed and irritable. For the past five months, all you do is play these games, and you don't go anywhere except for the gym. And, it's time to deal with it."

"What, did Dawna tell you to say that?" Ronald asked, annoyed because he wanted to return to his game.

"No, she did not!" Harold said. "And you show your mother some respect!"

"We tried calling her, but I guess she's out or something," Mitch said. "Her mom said that she was going to go to the mountains on her own, and that she wasn't going to wait around forever for you."

"What?! How can she say that! I've been good to her!" Ronald angrily replied.

"Not for the past five months, you haven't!" Monica said.

"How many times do I have to tell you...!" Ronald started to say.

"Look, you have to start doing more with your life than just this!" Harold said. "We are getting pretty sick and tired of you coming down every day to do nothing but play these games!"

"I work out, don't I?!" Ronald said.

"But, do you talk to anyone while at the gym? No, you don't!" Mitch said.

"How would you know what I do there, and who I talk to there?" Ronald asked.

"Because Dawna has friends who go there, and she told us," Monica said.

"Why would she throw me under the bus like that?" Ronald asked. "What girlfriend does that to her boyfriend?"

"She's just worried about you!" Harold said. "You are just so blinded by these games that you don't see that she cares about you! Do you really want to lose her?!"

"But, it's not like I ignore her!" Ronald replied.

"Yes, you do!" Monica yelled. "When was the last time you called her?! When was the last time you did *anything* with her outside of playing and talking about these video games?!"

"I called her last week, on my own free will," Ronald said.

"That's not enough!" Mitch said. "*I* even know that girls require constant attention."

"Uh, Mitch, we'll talk about your girl situation later," Harold said rolling his eyes. "Right now, let's deal with Ronald's problem."

"Great," Mitch said sarcastically.

They then continued arguing with Ronald about his video game addiction, and how they wanted him to start doing something more meaningful with his life. They made it quite clear that starting after the long weekend, he would give both Harold and Mitch copies of his résumé so that they could distribute it to their friends and acquaintances. Ronald told them he didn't want to, and then added, "Besides, none of you know what it feels like to have to be treated so viciously by someone that never met you, like how Betty Morgan did after she took over the Marketing Department at Pacific," Ronald said. "You don't know what it feels like to give everything to a company, only for them to betray you like this!"

"Excuse me?!" Harold asked in an annoyed tone. "Is that how you *really* feel?! How do you think I felt when I had to deal with indifferent, and in some cases verbally abusive, managers that did not give me a real chance and made me feel worthless when I was bouncing from job to job after finishing school? They never took the time to get to know me! How do you think I felt when I had to find a new job ten years ago because the company that I worked for about 12 years was sold to new, and greedy, owners who wanted to make even more money, even though it was already a profitable business?! When they took over, and without warning, these new owners, who by the way had never met me or any of my co-workers, just told us one day that we were out of a job because they wanted to cut costs and were moving much of the work offshore! I, too, was hurt. But did I just sit around this house moping, playing video games or being unproductive?! No, I did not! Instead, I looked for another job and gave my best effort to my new company, because that's what you do, especially when you have bills to pay, and a family to feed!"

"And," Monica added, "how do you think *I* felt when I was denied a promotion just because I got pregnant with you?! I was very upset with what they did! When I heard their excuses about how I might not be reliable and trustworthy when I returned from maternity leave, I was even more furious! I even considered going to court! But, in the end, I decided that I would make my choice after my maternity leave was over so that I didn't do anything in anger! Just before my leave was over, I handed in my resignation to my manager because I decided that family is forever, and that was more important than career. I have no regrets putting *you and your brother* ahead of my former career. Life is about prioritizing what's important to you, and accepting the consequences from the choices you make. I talk about you kids with pride because I am happy about how you turned out. I shudder to think what would have happened if I had gone back to work and told them I was ready to focus on my career again. So before making such assumptions, think about everything we're discussing right now! Life moves on, and you have to face the challenges!"

"Well, right now, it's like that everywhere," Ronald said. "And yet, despite putting in all of that hard work, the good workers get laid off while the idiots stay behind. They make a mockery of the excellent work that was done by the people who were there before. At least, that's what some people who are still at Pacific have told me. They have said that clients are leaving Pacific in droves because of how rude and incompetent the Marketing Department has become since Betty Morgan and her friends came in. And they're telling me that the executives think it is the Consulting and IT departments that are causing the problems, and not Marketing! So the executives have been monitoring those other two departments, while leaving Betty and her staff alone! So, why would I want to go back into *that* world?!"

"But-," Mitch started.

"No!" Ronald interrupted. "At least with these games, my accomplishments are rewarded. And appreciated. No one makes a mockery of my work."

"You know, Ronald, you are *so* addicted to these games that one day, you will get trapped in them!" Monica said.

"Ha!" Ronald responded. "As if *that* is ever going to happen! This is reality, not science fiction or fantasy!"

"Well, you never know," Mitch said. "Strange things can happen."

Ronald's family then left, visibly frustrated that they still couldn't get through to Ronald. Meanwhile, Ronald resumed playing his game, and reached a new high score in the process.

CHAPTER THREE

The next Sunday, August 11, 2013, Ronald was, once again, playing video games, this time on his Invisio 4. At breakfast, he was asked by his family if he was interested in joining them on a trip to buy a new stereo system, as the old one had broken down a few days earlier, to which he promptly replied no. It was also raining outside, and the forecast called for thunderstorms later in the day, which put Ronald in less of a mood to go outside. He decided to play an adventure game that would keep track of his score, and he wanted to try to beat the high score that he had set a month earlier. However, he was having trouble beating it because his character was always dying before he could get halfway through the game. He constantly wondered what he was doing wrong today that his character kept dying, and what he had done previously to get that high score. After about three hours, he took a break and paused the game to eat lunch, during which his family returned with the new stereo system. Upon finishing his meal, he returned to the game to continue his quest to beat his previous high score. After another hour, he was finally doing pretty well, when he suddenly heard thunder, which caused him to jump up in fright. He looked outside, and saw some lightning, and said to himself, "Hopefully, that lightning doesn't get anywhere near here!"

"Ronald, I heard you scream," Mitch said as he ran downstairs to check on his older brother. "Are you okay?"

"Yeah, just a little startled," Ronald said. "Feel this, my heart is pounding in fear!"

Mitch then put his hand to Ronald's chest, and said, "Yeah, I feel that. Just try to relax."

"I will. Hopefully, this game here calms me down."

All Mitch could do was roll his eyes and shake his head. He then went back upstairs. Ronald continued on with his game, quite happy at the progress he was making. The lightning and loud thunder and continued, and Ronald was doing his best to ignore it. After about an hour, he had completed three-quarters of the game, and saw that he was coming close to beating his high score. He said, "Finally! I'm almost at the high score! Just a bit more!"

As he pressed on, the lightning became more frequent, and seemed to come closer to the house. Ronald paused the game a few times, and looked outside to see what was going on. Suddenly, just as he was about to beat his old record, lightning struck the console, and an electric pulse immediately flowed down the wire to Ronald's controller. While the pulse didn't electrocute him, it seemed to surround him, as if it was trying to create a portal for him to travel through. In an instant, the pulse made him disappear from the sofa, and sent Ronald straight into the Invisio 4 console, pausing his game in the process. Before he knew it, he was being transported through some sort of a long, 3D tunnel, and, as he looked back, he noticed his family room going farther into the distance. As he was falling through the tunnel, Ronald yelled, "AAAAAAAAAHHHHHHHHH! What's going on here?!"

After falling for what seemed like ten minutes, Ronald suddenly was dropped into a 3D-pixellated city, and fell hard onto the ground. "Ooph!" Ronald said made as he landed hard on the ground.

Although Ronald was fully conscious, it took him a few moments to regain his composure. As he got up to a sitting position, he rubbed the back of his head, and checked to make sure he wasn't hurt, before saying to himself, "Ow! That was a long fall! I'm surprised that I didn't get hurt!"

"Yeah, that looked like a really nasty fall you took there!" he heard a female voice say.

That was Pixie, a resident of this strange new city that Ronald now found himself in. She was known around these parts as *The Traveller* because she travelled through the video games of this world, mostly as an observer, although there were times when she was an active participant. She had come to this city from a game called The Simulation of Real Life - People Version, a people-creation game that allows people in the real world to control the actions of the virtual people that they created. Pixie, who looked like a fitness model, but who could also fit in nicely in any magazine specifically targeted towards men, was 5'9" with blue eyes, long, curly blonde hair that went up to her waist, and always wore a cowboy hat, a short, belly-revealing tank top, short blue jeans, and cowboy boots. The reason why she looked like this was because the real-life person that had created her, a man in his mid-20s, had always fantasized about dating a model, and wanted a girlfriend who looked just like Pixie. He was also careful to make her an adult upon creating her, but didn't provide her with a "family" or any roommates. However, Pixie, who looked to be around either 24 or 25, left The Simulation of Real Life - People Version game after finishing university, which she had attended when the player was not playing the game, because she wanted to travel the "world," meaning the video game world, and did not want to be stuck inside one video game for the rest of her life. When she had decided to leave the game, she simply looked towards the player, and told him that she was done with the game, and was leaving forever to travel the "world," and would never come back. The player was shocked and dumbfounded, wondering what had just happened because in The Simulation of Real Life - People Version, the adult characters usually left only when they had either died or lost a fight with another character. Also, the person playing the game never thought that video game characters actually had a mind of their own. When Pixie had first come to this pixellated city, she had asked the government of the video game world, officially called *The Video Game Government* but commonly referred to as *The VGG*, if she could stay forever without becoming a civil servant, which left them shocked because no character that had left a video game had made such a request before. After deliberating, they asked her why she wanted to stay permanently, to which she explained that she just wanted to travel the "world," and did not want to be left at the mercy of a person in the real world, and didn't want to be stuck working in an office. The VGG deliberated some more, and then agreed to Pixie's request, on the condition that all she was to do was travel through the games, and not get involved in them unless she was asked to either by The VGG or the in-game characters. However, she was not allowed to change her clothes unless she travelled to a game that required her to do so, as she was not born in this city, was not intending on working at VGG Hall. She was also granted immortality because since she was no longer going to be a permanent character in any one game, and rather was going to be a traveller, requiring her to have mortality would not make sense since her "life" would not be on the line.

Ronald, who was still on the ground, looked up, and saw Pixie just standing there. "Are you okay?" she asked.

As he got up, Ronald said, "Yeah, I am. Where did you come from?"

"Well, you fell here right in front of me. A few more inches and you would have landed right on top of me, and then *I* would have been checking to see if *I* was hurt."

He then looked around, and noticed that he was definitely not in Calgary anymore. He then looked at himself, and noticed that he was a 3D-pixellated person. He then looked at Pixie, and saw that she was a 3D-pixellated woman. After staring at her for a few moments because he had never seen anyone like her before, she asked, "Are you sure you're okay? Because, I've never seen anyone look at me like *that* before."

"I'm sure," Ronald replied. "Sorry. I'm struck by your beauty because I've never seen the perfect woman before. Did you know that-."

"I look like a fitness model?" Pixie interrupted. "And that I could easily be on the cover of any men's magazine? Yeah, yeah, I know. I've been to the game with all of those models before, and I was constantly asked to stay in it because I fit in so well. I know how I look. I have a mirror, you know."

"Oh, I've heard of that game! Wait a minute! How the heck could you have *been* to that game before? Don't you mean that you *played* that game before?"

"No, I mean I actually visited it."

"How is that possible?"

"Because I travel between video games," Pixie responded, confused as to why Ronald was asking such an absurd question. "What game are you from?"

Ronald just stared at her blankly, wondering what she meant by what game he was from. He then said, "Game? I'm not from any game."

"Oh?" she responded. "Then were you born and raised here? If not, do you work at VGG Hall?"

Ronald looked around, and noticed some other 3D-pixellated people walking around, and stared at Pixie again. "I-I-I guess not. This definitely doesn't look like Calgary," he told her. "And I'm *certainly* not working at this moment."

"Oh, okay. Wait a minute! Calgary?! What's a *Calgary*?!"

"It's a city in the province of Alberta, in the country of Canada."

"Alberta? Canada? Province? What are you talking about?" Pixie asked, with a blank look on her face.

"I'm not in my home anymore, am I?" Ronald asked, in a confused and scared tone.

"I don't think so, because the stuff that you're talking about is not computing with me."

Ronald then looked around once more, and looked back at Pixie. "If I'm not in Calgary anymore, then where exactly *am* I?" he asked her, still quite scared that he wasn't in Calgary anymore.

"Video Game City," Pixie said.

"Video Game City?!"

"Yeah. It's an important part of the video game world."

Suddenly, Ronald's eyes widened while his mouth dropped in a look of shock. "You mean to tell me that I'm in the video game world?!" he yelled.

"Wait, are you telling me that you're *not* from this world?" Pixie replied.

"Yes, that's *exactly* what I'm telling you," Ronald said as he nodded his head.

Pixie then looked around to make sure that no one was listening to their conversation. When she saw that the coast was clear, she said to Ronald, "Come with me. We'd better not stand here too much longer or something bad may happen to you. People here have never seen someone who is not from our world before, and I don't know what they'll do if they see one."

"Come with you? Where?"

"To my apartment. It's not far from here. When you fell from the sky, that's where I was headed. Now let's go! You don't want to draw attention to yourself, do you?"

Still confused about his new surroundings, he merely nodded and followed Pixie as they walked a few blocks to her apartment building. On their way there, he asked her, "So, what's your name?"

"Pixie. What's yours?" she responded.

"Ronald. Ronald Charlton."

"Nice to meet you, Ronald."

"Nice to meet you, too. What's your last name?"

"Well, I don't have one."

"What?! How is *that* possible? Are you like some of those celebrities who only use their first name?"

"Celebrity? What's a celebrity?"

"A famous person."

"Oh. In that case, no, I'm not like those 'celebrities' you speak of. I'll explain when we get inside my apartment."

Soon, they then arrived at the building, and Pixie opened the door. After they entered the building, they went up a couple of floors to her apartment. She looked around for her key, and then opened the door, after which they entered her apartment.

After once again making sure that Ronald was not injured, Pixie told Ronald to sit down at the table near her kitchen. Pixie's apartment was a standard one-bedroom apartment. The kitchen had a fridge, stove, microwave, sink, dishwasher, and cabinets and drawers for dishes, pots and pans, silverware, and small appliances. The bedroom had a twin bed, a closet, a dresser, a mirror, and a bookshelf. The bathroom had a shower, a tub, and a toilet, and the living room had a TV, a computer, and a sofabed. "You know, I've lived here for about five years, and you're the first ever guest that I've *ever* had!" Pixie told Ronald.

"Five years?! But, you don't look older than 24 or 25!"

"Well, I am immortal, so it's not a big deal for me."

"Immortality? How is that possible?"

Pixie then went on to explain how things worked in the video game world, including how pretty much everyone that was a video game character had immortality so that they didn't cause problems in their respective video games. The only game that didn't have immortality was The Simulation of Real Life - People Version, and she went on to explain how she was once a part of that game, and had decided to leave because of her desire to travel the "world," and was given immortality as a result. She then talked about how things worked in Video Game City. In this city, it was the place to stay for those who no longer wanted to be a part of one video game, and either wanted to work at VGG Hall, or wanted time to figure out what game they did want to be a part of. If the reason was to move to another game, they were given a time limit to make a decision, otherwise they would lose their immortality and would be placed in a video game chosen by The VGG. Pixie then went on to explain as to why she had lived here for so long, and why she was going to continue to live in this city, which amazed Ronald. Pixie also said that sometimes, some characters of video games came to Video Game City for "vacation," that is, when they needed a break from their video games, and not because they wanted to leave them. These "vacations," which were allowed by The VGG, required the characters to register with The VGG how much time they were going to be on "vacation," a period which could not exceed a two month time period. Only after The VGG approved the "vacation" could the characters arrive. Pixie made sure to mention that Video Game City existed outside of all video games, and acted as a hub and capital city for the video game world that people could go to when they needed to get away from their games, or when they needed to discuss a matter with The VGG, whether privately or in a "town hall" setting. Ronald was still grasping the fact that there was a living world inside of the video games, one with living, thinking intelligent beings. However, he decided that he might as well find out as much as he could about this place. Ronald then inquired about what happened to people that were born and raised here, to which Pixie replied that sometimes, the characters from other video games that had come to the city, whether for a "vacation" or to leave their games completely, had kids here. And because the parents had to take care of the kids, they were allowed to stay here permanently to raise their children. After the kids became adults, the parents were then given a choice as to whether or not they wanted to continue living permanently in Video Game City. When the kids became adults, they too were given a choice as to whether or not they want to be a permanent character in a video game, or if they wanted to stay here. Pixie also mentioned that most of the people that had left their video games didn't age, with the exceptions being those who had come from The Simulation of Real Life - People Version, and those who had kids in this city and didn't leave for another game. The children of those people also didn't have immortality, and neither did any of their other descendants if they were born in Video Game City. The reason for the parents of children born here, as well as their kids and their other descendants born in Video Game City, not having immortality was that The VGG felt that it was only fair to those who were only interested in working at VGG Hall, or were only going to be staying in Video Game City temporarily and were not interested in having children here. For those who came from The Simulation of Real Life - People Version, mortality was kept to maintain the continuity of the aging dynamics of that game. As a result, the permanent residents of Video Game

City started up their own businesses, or worked at VGG Hall, where The VGG's headquarters were located. Pixie didn't forget to mention that schools were set up for the kids of Video Game City, and they were taught not just the nuances of the video game world, but just enough about the real world so that they would have the same basic knowledge that everyone else in the video game world had.

"Now, how does this tie in with you not having a last name?" Ronald asked Pixie after she had finished explaining the workings of this new place he found himself in.

"Well, when we leave a video game, we have the option of whether we want to keep the full name that we were given prior to us leaving, or whether we want to keep parts of our name, or if we want to adopt a new name altogether."

"Okay."

"Have you played The Simulation of Real Life - People Version before?"

"Yes, I have. In fact, I have all the iterations of the main series for the PC."

"Okay, then. So, you know how in that game, the characters can only be given first and last names?"

"Yes, I do."

"Well, I chose to keep only my first name because I liked it. I absolutely despised the last name that the person who created me gave me. But, *most people* around the video game world know about me, mainly because I'm the only Pixie in this world and I'm the only traveller of this world."

"Well, what was your last name before you dropped it?"

"It's embarrassing."

"Don't worry, I won't tell anyone. Consider it our little secret."

Blushing, Pixie then said, "Well, it was Armageddon."

Ronald looked at her blankly, and then said to her, nodding his head in agreement, "You were right to drop that last name. Pixie Armageddon just does not sound like a good name."

"That's exactly why I dropped the last name," she replied, happy that Ronald agreed with her. "I didn't want to be associated with anything of a negative nature."

"Has anyone else who hasn't had kids asked to live independently of the video games since your request?"

"Only those wanting to work at VGG Hall. And they have been told that if they ever quit their jobs, then a new two-month residency limit will be in effect from their last day of work."

"Does that also apply to you?"

"I wouldn't be surprised. Not that I would quit being a traveller. I love doing this."

"Okay. Now, you mentioned a VGG? What is this VGG? Is it some sort of government?"

"Yes, it is," Pixie said. "It's actually called The Video Game Government, but we all usually simply refer it to as The VGG."

She then explained how The VGG represented all the video games in the "world," even the old arcade ones, and were based at VGG Hall. It was a council consisting of five people, who were elected by all of the video game characters once every ten years through a secret ballot vote. The ballots were ranked, and the top five candidates won the seats. The ten year term allowed the council to maintain independence and helped prevent short-term policy-making. To ensure that there was no usurpation of power, no leader was elected, all councillors were equal, and each one had an equal vote and say on decisions. If ever there came a situation where a councillor became power-hungry, and tried to establish an office of President of The VGG in order to become the sole ruler of the video game world, including trying to circumvent the rules, they were immediately dismissed and by-elections would immediately be called. That member was also barred from ever running for office again. If the member refused to leave, the police and security were immediately called in to remove the member, who would then be escorted straight to a maximum-security prison for life with no chance for parole, and their immortality was immediately revoked.

"Wow! Now *that's* holding someone accountable!" Ronald said, impressed with the level of accountability in place over the video game politicians compared to the ones in real life. "I wish there was more accountability in *my world*! We have some leaders that throw their colleagues under the bus for questioning them. Such accountability may do them some good! They are really no better than some of the people that they *do* put in prison! And to arrest them on the spot, even if the cameras are rolling? *That* would keep the politicians where I come from humble!"

"Really? What type of place do you come from?" Pixie responded.

"Well, how do I explain this? You see, I'm from what you probably refer to as *out there*," he responded, pointing.

"What do you mean by 'out there?'"

"Well, you see, I'm from the real world. I'm one of the many people out there that play, well, as *you people*."

"You mean to tell me that you are a real life human being that has to deal with corruption and mortality?"

"Well, yeah, though not *all* of us are corrupt."

"And the city you come from is, what was the name of it again?"

"Calgary."

"And the region of the real world?"

"Alberta, Canada."

"Huh. This is strange. We've never *had* anyone from the real world come *here* before. I mean I've heard that it *could* be possible, but this is the first time that it's actually *happened*. How did you get here, anyway?"

"I was just playing video games in my house during a thunderstorm, and lightning struck my Invisio 4 console. It created some sort of electrical pulse that travelled up my controller and surrounded me. The next thing I know, I'm falling down this 3D tunnel, and then I fell down in front of you."

"That is *very* unusual."

Ronald then suddenly remembered that his family might start worrying about where he had gone off to. He asked Pixie, "Will my family notice that I'm not home anymore?"

"What do you mean?"

"Well, I live at home with my parents and my brother. And when the lightning struck the console, I was playing video games, and they *knew* that I was playing them. If they saw the lightning enter the house, they may check up on me. If they see that I'm not there, they'll get *really* worried!"

"Oh! Well, *that* you don't have to worry about! You see, time in the video game world travels independently from the real world. I remember learning something about this in university. You see, time in our world is constantly moving, even if a game is paused. So, what may be a few months in your world, it's like a few years here. I don't exactly remember what the equivalent is. So, when you get back to your world, only a few minutes would have elapsed, at *most*."

"Oh, that's a relief! So, how *do you* keep track of time here?"

"Well, it's a very complicated calendar, and certainly not like the 365 1/4 day, 12 month one used in the real world."

"You know about that?"

"Yes. I just told you that we learned about it in university, didn't I?! And don't forget that most games these days have save support, so we know the exact date the player saved the game on. Also, if a game has microphone support, and the player turns their microphone on, we can listen into the conversations."

"But you said on our way here that you didn't know about the exact location of where I am from, or what a celebrity was."

"Well, I don't know *everything* about your world! I've only been travelling for five years, and there are *tons* of games out there already, with so many *new* ones being created everyday! So, it certainly would be tough to visit every single game in such a short period of time! And most of the games I've been to so far either don't have microphone support. And in those that *do*, the players don't either have a microphone, or they keep them turned off. So, it's not like I would have heard about this new information before I met you."

"Yeah, that would make sense."

Then, Ronald suddenly thought about the whole aging dynamic in this world that Pixie explained earlier, and asked her, "I've got another question: Will I age while I'm in this world?"

Pixie then started laughing, and said, "No, no, you won't. We also learned in school that if a real world person *did* ever come here, they're immortal. They only lose their immortality once they return home."

"That's a good thing! I don't want to return home being a few years older!"

They then realized they had been talking for quite some time, and they both agreed they were getting quite hungry. Pixie then proceeded to make dinner. During the meal, they talked about each other's pasts, including their friends and Ronald's family. Ronald mentioned his job, how he was laid off, and the depression he was going through. Listening to this, Pixie was just happy that she didn't have to deal with such a situation in this world. Ronald then mentioned Dawna, and Pixie was shocked at the fact that it wasn't just people in certain video games that looked the way Dawna did. However, she was quite impressed that Ronald saw beyond Dawna's tattoos, piercings, and chains. She could also see that Ronald deeply cared for Dawna, and that he showed regret for how he had been treating her since losing his job. She then said that when she was in The Simulation of Real Life - People Version, the guy that created her made her fall in love with some guy that she had no interest in, and how she independently ended the relationship without the player noticing. Pixie also said that she didn't have a "family" or roommates because the player didn't want to give her either as he was creating her. Ronald then asked, "So, what's with this outfit you're wearing? How come you don't change clothes?"

Pixie immediately gave him an annoyed look. She then told him, "Well, the guy that created me and played as me, and just so you are aware I was created as an adult, probably saw me as some sort of a fantasy girlfriend. I mean the name he gave me, and the fact that he made me look like this, and the fact that he refused to change my clothes while I was in the game, I can't come to any other conclusion. Ever since I arrived in to Video Game City, don't you think that *I wish* I could change clothes? Unfortunately, I'm not allowed to."

"Why not?"

"Because, people who come from The Simulation of Real Life - People Version aren't allowed to change clothes once they leave that game. They can only change clothes once they become a permanent character in another game. And since I'm not going to do that, I'm stuck in these clothes forever. If I had known that, I would have changed clothes before I left."

"Oh. How old was this guy who created you?"

"I don't know! Maybe he was as old as me, since he didn't look older than 25 or so. The Simulation of Real Life - People Version doesn't have microphone support, so I couldn't listen into his conversations to be able to give you a definitive answer."

"Oh. So, how exactly *did* you leave? Did you get into a fight with someone? Because I have played that game before, and as far as I'm aware, you can only leave either by fighting someone or by dying. And, well, obviously you didn't die, so you must have gotten into a fight and lost."

"No. I just turned to face the player and told him that I was done, and that I was leaving and would never come back, as my life ambition was to travel the 'world,' and I didn't mean the world of The Simulation of Real Life - People Version. I also told him off for giving me the name that he did, for making me dress this way, and for never letting me change into more modest clothing."

"Whoa! I bet he was livid! I know I'd be, and then I'd call CreatorWorld to tell them about a defect in the game!"

"Well, I don't know if he was mad. But he certainly was confused. I bet he thought we video game people didn't have minds of our own! But, what is this 'CreatorWorld?'"

"The developers of The Simulation of Real Life - People Version. They've created a number of games under that name, including the main The Simulation of Real Life - People Version line."

"Oh. I would not know, because I've lived in this world all my life. And in school, we were never told about *who* created the games."

Ronald then remembered that adults created in The Simulation of Real Life - People Version, at least from the user's point of view, couldn't go to school, let alone university. Confused, he then asked, "How could you have gone to school if you were created as an adult?"

Pixie replied, "I can only speak for myself, but I went to school, and this also includes university, when the guy wasn't playing the game."

"Wow! I thought video game characters didn't have a mind of their own. I thought they were just programmed by the developers of the games, and that the actions and thoughts were controlled by the players of the game."

"Ha! You thought *wrong*! We *do* have minds of our own! You just don't *see* it because we live our lives when the games are turned off!"

"So, when the people of the video game world leave a game, or go into a new one, do the real-world players notice it? Because I'm *sure* that would cause a lot of problems."

"Except for The Simulation of Real Life - People Version, they don't really notice. Most of the time, the people in charge of each game just assign someone else to that role, and give them the same name as the person that left, and that's it. When players are playing those other games, to them, all the characters are the same because they look the same, and talk the same. Only we in the video game world would notice that someone else has taken the place of the previous character."

"Oh. So, the next question is, how exactly *am I* going to get home? I don't want to live here for the rest of my life because I've got a life in Calgary."

"I don't really know. I mean, I just travel between video games. You know, maybe The VGG can help! They are really nice people, and don't ever turn down a request unless it is one that harms other people."

"Well, if they're the ones to go to, then let's do it. Let's go!" Ronald said, getting up.

"We can't go right now!" Pixie responded, getting Ronald to sit back down. "VGG Hall is closed! We'll go tomorrow morning."

Ronald could only nod his head in disappointment, and then he got up to clean the dishes. After he was done, they went to the living room, talked some more, and relaxed for the rest of the evening before getting some sleep.

The next day, after breakfast, Ronald and Pixie made their way to VGG Hall, which looked more like a small high-rise building. The building contained a main office with cubicles and offices for the civil servants and bureaucrats. The assembly hall, where all of the debates and decisions occurred, was located in the centre of the building. The main hall had 50,000 seats to accommodate everyone in the video game world that wanted to attend the town halls. There were also some smaller rooms located on either side of the main hall for smaller discussions. At the end of the hall was a long, rounded table with five sets, one for each member of The VGG. This was were they sat all day, as they themselves had no offices to ensure that they were easily accessible to everyone in the video game world.

Before they entered the building, Pixie told Ronald, "Now, you stay quiet until The VGG asks you to come forward and discuss what your business is. We don't need any trouble here."

Ronald nodded his head, and then they entered. They went up to the reception area, and Pixie asked the person sitting there, "Hi Teresa. Is The VGG busy right now?"

"Hello Pixie," Teresa said. "No, they've got nothing going on right now. You may enter the assembly hall."

"Thanks. And this…guy is with me…."

"That's fine. I'll just let them know that you're here."

As Pixie and Ronald entered the assembly hall, Ronald noticed five men sitting at the front of the hall. "What? No women?" Ronald whispered to Pixie as they approached the front.

"No, the women who had run for office were not very good candidates," Pixie whispered back. "Part of their platforms were things that would have screwed up the harmony in this world."

"Is that how you people feel about women? Because, in the real world, we have women that are political representatives, and we *never* hold the attitude that they'll screw things up. We say that about *individuals*, but not the entire gender."

"Well, we also hold those same views. We all felt like the women that were running were going to screw things up. We've had women represent us before!"

"Oh."

After reaching the front of the hall, VGG Member Duncan said, "Oh, hello Pixie. What can we do for you today? I don't think we have a game for you to travel to at the moment, so you'll have to come back in a few days if that's your reason for coming today."

"No, actually it's not about that, Member Duncan. It's about an issue that has just come up," Pixie replied.

"Oh? And what is this issue?" VGG Member Mooris asked.

Pixie then explained about how Ronald had landed in Video Game City the day before. She talked about how he had a life in the real world, and how that was where he belonged. After Pixie had finished, Ronald asked, "So, is there a way for you to send me home?"

"Well, we do have a way to send people that come from the real world back to their realm if by chance they ever ended up in our world. Even though it was taught that as a theory in school, a past Video Game Government didn't take any chances. But it is not as simple as opening up a portal or a tunnel that will lead them back directly to their houses," VGG Member Wakawaka said. "We also don't have a plane or any special mode of transportation that will take you home."

"You see, you're not in *your* world anymore, you're in the video game world," added VGG Member Yealos. "The rules here are different, although I'm sure there are different rules governing the various regions of your world. In our world, if someone from the real world were to ever find their way here, the only way for them to go back home is to play a certain number of video games. After all, that is what this world is about, and that is the only fair way to deal with this issue."

"And, they must be played in the order that *we* decide. And they must be completed from the beginning to the end," said VGG Member Pathos. "When you complete the game, or as you people in the real world say, 'beat it,' a portal will open that will lead you to the next game, except for the final game, as that portal will send you home."

"So, how many games do I have to play?" Ronald asked.

"Well, it's going to be a lot. We have to make sure that you're *serious* about wanting to leave this world and return home," replied VGG Member Wakawaka.

"But don't worry, you'll have a guide with you," said VGG Member Duncan. "We want to make sure that you don't get lost or stuck while playing these games. It's important that you at least have *someone* around to help you out in case you are having trouble with something."

The VGG then told Pixie and Ronald that the Council would need some time to deliberate on who would be Ronald's guide. After discussing the matter for several minutes, VGG Member Mooris then said to Pixie, "Pixie, since you are The Traveller, and know so much about our world due to your travels, would you be willing to be Ronald's guide?"

"Sure! I'd love to!" Pixie said. "It might be fun having a travel companion for a change. It's certainly going to be a unique experience!"

"Good," said VGG Member Pathos. "So, Ronald, we hereby declare that Pixie will be your guide. In some cases, she may even be allowed to fight alongside you. When you enter each game, we'll send her the details you need in order to start the game. Also, when you finish the final game, we'll inform her that the final portal, the one that sends you home, has opened up. However, we must emphasize, *you will not know* when you have reached the final game. That is to ensure you don't try to take shortcuts, as we frown upon that. We want to keep the integrity of the games intact."

The VGG then pressed several buttons that were located underneath the desk, after which the first portal opened up. Pixie and Ronald looked to each other for a few seconds, and then Pixie asked, "Are you ready? This is going to be a very difficult journey."

"Well, I'm as ready as I will ever be," Ronald replied. "It's going to be different actually being *in* the games where I will have to perform the various tasks *in-person*, instead of looking at a screen with a controller or a mouse in my hands."

"Okay, then, let's go."

Just as Ronald and Pixie were about to enter, VGG Member Duncan stopped them. "Oh, Ronald, we need to warn you of something!" he said.

"What is it?" Ronald asked.

"We have to let you know that if you *do* take *any* shortcuts, you'll have to start the games all over," VGG Member Pathos said. "That means if you're in the last game, and you try to take a shortcut, you'll be sent all the way back to the first game. So, don't cheat or take any shortcuts."

"And, there is one more thing," VGG Member Wakawaka said. "If you do not complete the game you are in, meaning that if you do not complete all of the tasks required, you will have to start that particular game again. So that means that unless you finish every task required, you will be trapped in that game, and in our world, forever."

"Okay, that's good to know," Ronald said. "I'll make sure not to use any cheat codes or shortcuts."

"Good!" all the VGG members replied in unison.

Pixie and Ronald then took a collective deep breath, and then entered the portal, beginning their journey so Ronald could go back home.

CHAPTER FOUR

After exiting the first portal, Ronald and Pixie found themselves in a 3D version of a New York university. "Hey, I think I've read about this place on Wikipedia!" Ronald said as he looked around.

"Huh? What's a Wikipedia?" Pixie asked.

"It's a free encyclopaedia on the Internet. It has stuff on *everything*."

"Oh. We don't get access to those types of things here."

"Really? You don't have access to the Internet?"

"We do have an Internet, but we don't have anything like a free encyclopaedia. It's mostly email and other communication methods so that we don't lose touch with our friends from Video Game City and the games themselves. There are also websites used by The VGG and some of the businesses in Video Game City to relay information to everyone around the 'world.'"

"Oh, that's too bad. You're missing out on *a lot* of information."

Suddenly, Ronald noticed his clothes change to safari clothing, while Pixie's didn't change at all. "What the...? What is this?" he asked as he examined his new clothes.

"Well, you see, in the video game world, if the game you are required to participate in requires a clothing change, then the clothes change automatically," Pixie responded. "So that means that this game does require a clothing change for all participants, which is why you're now wearing something different. And since my clothes didn't change, I can only be an observer. Although, I have heard from some people that there are games out there where the attire of non-participants also changes, mainly because it's necessary for the conditions present in those games. Anyway, if you need my help for this game, just yell 'pause,' and I will come by and answer whatever questions you have."

Pixie's phone then rang, and she saw that The VGG had sent her a message. "It looks like this game is called Hunt for the Lost Treasure of Morocco," she said. "It's set in 2000, and you're the main character. Your task is to find a lost treasure located in the Atlas Mountains of Morocco."

She then received another message, and said, "Oh, The VGG forgot to tell you a couple more things. First of all, you don't have to go back to Video Game City anymore, which we already had guessed when they said that after each game before the final one is finished, the portal will send us to the next game. And...oh! It also looks like you'll have unlimited health throughout your journey, so you don't have to worry about, say, dying in a fight. You will be able to recover in-game."

"Okay, that's great," Ronald said. "So, what exactly am I supposed to do here on campus?"

Pixie then looked at her phone, and said, "Okay, on campus, you're supposed to find a map, a compass, a whip, a backpack, a machete, and a historical document that contains information about the treasure. Now, go! And remember, if you need me, just yell 'pause.'"

Ronald then went on his way. He decided to find the map first, as he figured that would be easier. He went around the campus and asked many students and professors, and they all told him that they didn't know what he was talking about. When he asked if they knew someone that might, they said they couldn't answer the question. He decided to ask Pixie for help, and yelled, "Pause!"

"Yes, Ronald? How can I help you?" Pixie asked.

"Who the heck am I supposed to ask about this map? Every person that I have asked doesn't have a clue, and when I ask them who might know, they say they aren't aware of anyone that might know."

"Well, maybe go to the geography department. Or the archaeology department. Or even the history department. They may have an idea as to where the map is."

"Thanks."

"You're welcome. Time for me to go."

The game then continued, and Ronald asked around as to where the geography, archaeology, and history departments were located. It didn't take him long to find someone who showed him where he had to go. After receiving the directions, he first headed to the building where the geography department was located. None of the students and professors knew where the map was, though they were aware of its existence. They said they knew of some history students and professors that would be able to help them, and gave Ronald their names and where he would find them. Ronald then headed to the history building, and located the first professor on his list. "Oh, hello there!" the professor said when Ronald entered the office.

"Hi, professor," Ronald said. "I'm here to inquire about this map."

"Which map?"

46

"It's a map of Morocco's Atlas Mountains. I think it's from the 1800s, when rumour first started that there was a treasure located somewhere in those mountains."

"Ah, yes! You've come to the right place!"

The professor then told Ronald about the history of the map, and how, because the scientific knowledge of the time wasn't as advanced as today, many explorers had trouble finding it. He also mentioned that the document, which was only recently discovered, contained important information about the treasure. Without this information, the treasure would be tough to locate. "That's great, but I need to know where this map is located," Ronald said after the lecture was given.

The professor directed Ronald to the basement of the administration building. Ronald asked why it was located there, and the professor said that it was there to ensure that no one had exclusive access to it. The professor mentioned that it was a problem at this university that a department stored an artifact within their offices, and as a result, not many people had access to such documents. Ronald thanked him, and then headed straight to the administration building, which was located near the place where he started. He then headed to the basement and asked to see the map. After he received it, he looked at his checklist and saw a checkmark magically appear. Ronald was amazed, as he thought that, since he was *physically playing* the game, he would have to do everything manually, such as mark off the list. He then decided to find the compass, and asked some of the students and professors where he could find it. All of them said that he would have to buy one, and that there was an adventure store located near the campus. Ronald realized that he didn't have any money, and was wondering how he would be able to afford it. He then yelled, "Pause!"

"Yes, Ronald? How can I help you?" Pixie said.

"Okay, that's the second time that you have said that exact set of words when I yelled 'pause.' Can't you say anything else when I yell 'pause?'"

"No, I can't. Don't you think I checked that when you started playing? I know how annoying it is to hear that every time you yell 'pause.' I too get annoyed that I have say the exact same thing over and over again. However, it is part of the rules."

"Oh. That sucks."

"Yeah, but what can you do? Anyway, what do you need help with?"

"I'm looking for this compass, and I found out I have to buy it. But, I don't have any money on me! What do I do?! I can't cheat, otherwise I'm going to have to start over!"

"Check your wallet. You've got a debit card linked to a bank account that has funds in it. Later on in the game, you will receive more funds, but right now, you will only have enough funds to buy the things that you need at this point in the game."

"I don't have a wallet with me. When I got sucked into this world, I was wearing a T-shirt and shorts, and I definitely didn't have my wallet with me since I was home."

"But, your clothes changed when you entered this game, didn't they? And in this game, you *do* have a wallet. Check your pockets."

Ronald immediately checked his pockets, and in one of his pants pockets he found a wallet. He opened it, and saw a debit card in there, just as Pixie had said. "Cool! One more thing. Where's the adventure store?"

Pixie gave him the directions, and then said, "Okay, time for me to go."

Ronald then headed to the adventure store, and found the compass. He also found a machete, whip, and a backpack, but wasn't too sure if he was allowed to buy them together. He yelled, "Pause," and Pixie came.

"Yes, Ronald? How can I help you? And, before you say anything, I know that's annoying to hear every time you yell 'pause!'" she said.

Ronald laughed, then asked, "I found the machete, backpack, and whip here, as well as the compass. Am I allowed to buy them together, or do I have to make separate trips?"

"Actually, you're supposed to buy them altogether. For some reason, every player in the real world that plays this game makes separate trips."

"Thanks."

"You're welcome. Time for me to go. And before you say anything, I know that is also annoying to hear all the time!"

All Ronald could do was laugh, and then he proceeded to buy the whip, compass, machete, and backpack together. Finally, he went to find the document. He returned to the campus, and asked around where he could find it. A couple of students and a professor gave him the names of two professors that had studied the document, one who was an archaeology professor, and the other one who was an ancient history professor. They gave him the directions to their respective offices. After receiving this information, Ronald yelled, "Pause!"

Pixie came, and, holding back a laugh, she said, "Yes, Ronald? How can I help you?"

They then started laughing, and after composing himself, Ronald said, "Okay, so I have to go and see an ancient history professor and an archaeology professor. Which one should I go and see first?"

"Well, let's think about this for a minute. Who would be the first to study the document?"

"The archaeology professor?"

"Are you sure? Because wouldn't an archaeology professor need to have some information about a treasure before he or she heads off to start up a dig? And how would he receive that information?"

"So, what you're saying is that he could try to locate the site of the treasure, but it would be in vain without any foundational knowledge. And, the document was written in some ancient language that only an ancient history professor would understand."

"Yes. So, who do you think you should go to first?"

"The ancient history professor."

"That's right. Okay, time for me to go."

Ronald then proceeded to talk to the ancient history professor. After arriving at the office, he asked the professor about the document, and the professor quickly retrieved it for him. He then told Ronald about the history of the treasure, and the history of the document. He then told Ronald that he still had to talk to the archaeology professor, as they were both working on this mystery together, and handed Ronald the document. Ronald thanked him for his time, and then headed straight to the archaeology professor's office. When he found the archaeology professor, he introduced himself and asked him about what he knew about the document. The archaeology professor then explained the importance of the document, including the history of the previous unsuccessful archaeology expeditions that had been undertaken in an effort to find the treasure. He then marked on the map where, based on the document and other research, the treasure was believed to be located. Before sending Ronald on his way, the professor told Ronald that before he could head off on his journey, he would have to go to the bank to sign some papers. "Why?" Ronald asked.

"Because, since you're the leader of the expedition, you have to sign the papers in order to release the funds that we need to finance the expedition."

"Didn't the university already do that?"

"Yes, the university did give its approval to fund the expedition. But, they hadn't yet assigned a leader at the time. Remember, when you started this game, the university assigned you as the leader. Therefore, you will have to sign the papers."

"Okay."

Just as Ronald was about to leave, the professor said, "Wait! There's one more thing!"

"And that is...?" Ronald asked.

"The rest of your team is waiting for you in Lima, Peru, so you will have to travel there to get them before you head off to Morocco."

"Okay, thanks for letting me know. I forgot to ask you, where is the bank located?"

The professor then gave Ronald the directions to the bank. Ronald thanked the professor, and then headed for the bank. While making his way there, Ronald looked around, and was amazed at the level of detail in this game, even though it was created and released during 2004. "Man, I remember when this game came out, we thought that this was as good as it would get. It has some amazing details in it, but it's surreal to think at how much *more* realistic these games are now with these new systems!" he said to himself.

When he arrived at the bank a few minutes later, Ronald headed straight to the customer service desk and told the representative that he was there to sign some papers. The representative paged someone, and a few minutes later, a banker came out, and introduced himself. However, since he had never played this game before, Ronald didn't know that this particular banker was actually the bad guy. Therefore, Ronald didn't keep his guard up, and talked a lot about his adventure with the banker. However, all the banker talked about during the entire meeting was how valuable the treasure would be to a collector, if it existed, and if it were to be found.

"You know, a collector could sell this treasure for millions of dollars if they had it in their possession," the banker said. "They'd be set for life! Especially someone who is just getting by like me."

"I guess," Ronald said. "But, I think it would be better to put it on display in a museum."

"Such a shame. Stuff like that should *never* be locked under some glass collecting dust! I mean, these days, museums merely display things for a few months, and then put it under storage for *years* before it ever sees the light of day again! However, a collector can display it in their houses all the time, just *waiting* for someone to pay them a *king's ransom* for it!"

"What's wrong with it being in a museum? It is, after all, a way to educate and enlighten the public about civilizations that were once considered lost in the context of history. Especially in the countries where those civilizations existed, those residents would get to know who lived in their areas before, and what conditions their ancestors endured."

"I think it's just a complete waste to let people see things either for free or a very small fee. I mean, the money that could be made from those items...."

"Well, if we don't understand the past, we can't learn the lessons for the future. If a treasure just sits in a collector's home, it's just better off if those items were *never* found. Such valuables would be under such secrecy that it would be just like the items *were* in storage in a museum."

"But, you could extort a lot of money from those countries that want it back."

"No, that's not my thing. I consider this a public service, as we need to learn about our history. I mean, in a private home, the only ones that get to enjoy the items are the residents of the home and invited guests. It's as if the collector is hoarding the items, rather than sharing them."

"Who cares about sharing? I only care about money."

All Ronald could do was roll his eyes. After the papers were signed, the banker entered the information into his computer. When everything was finished, he said to Ronald, "Okay, the money is now released. The funds are in the bank account, and you can access them via the debit card that you have. Good luck."

"Thanks," Ronald said.

Ronald then left the bank and started for the airport. After Ronald had left the office, a wide, evil grin had come across the banker's face, while he also steepled his fingers together. "Finally! Now I can put my plan into action!" he said to himself in a very evil tone.

Just as Ronald was leaving the bank, he was suddenly ambushed by some thugs in business suits who were trying to steal his debit card, as well as his other supplies, from him. Little did he know that these thugs had been sent by the banker to attack him. To ensure that no one suspected him, the banker stayed in his own office, and had instructed these minions that they had to dress up as ordinary business people and make the attack look random. Ronald was able to fight off the toughs using his athletic abilities, as well as some karate skills he had learned from watching TV. After they had run off, Ronald said to himself, "I wonder who they were. Those guys just came out of nowhere!"

He checked to make sure that he was okay, and noticed that, just as The VGG had promised, he didn't have any injuries or bruises. He then made sure that he still had all of his supplies. Once he was sure that everything was there, he called a cab, and made his way to the airport. "You know, maybe video games aren't as safe as I thought," he said to himself during the ride to the airport. "I mean, they may not fire me, but they definitely will try to injure me! And, it seems like they don't respect me as much as I thought."

Ronald arrived at JFK International Airport approximately an hour later. After paying the cab driver, he headed straight to the ticket counter. Little did Ronald know that some more of the bankers thugs had followed him, and were standing just a few feet behind him. After Ronald bought his ticket, and had his bags checked in, the hired bandits attacked him, forcing Ronald to fight them off. Some of the patrons came to Ronald's aid and helped him defeat the thugs, after which some other bystanders rushed to Ronald to ask if he was okay. He said he was fine, and just a little shaken up. They then asked him who those people in the suits were, to which Ronald could only reply that he had no idea. But in his mind, he was starting to suspect that they had been sent by someone who wanted the treasure for themselves. After all, he had access to the information on the treasure, and had already been ambushed twice within a short period of time. However, this was no time to be scared.

Ronald checked that everything else was intact, and then boarded the plane for Lima, Peru. By the time the plane took off, it was already late in the afternoon. Shortly after takeoff, Ronald was served dinner. Not long after finishing, he fell into a deep sleep. When he woke up six hours later, Ronald wondered why he was so tired. While he accepted the fact that the fights with the thugs had taken a lot out of him, didn't The VGG say that he would have unlimited health? But as he looked at his hands, he realized again that there were no scrapes on him. He smiled and realized that they hadn't said anything about not getting tired. After another 1 hour and 46 minutes on the flight, followed by another 30 minutes dealing with customs, Ronald finally met the other ten archaeologists that were part of his team. The archaeologists were: Mr. Ortiz, Mr. Donovan, Mr. Youlade, Mr. Kaynes, Mrs. Tedlow, Dr. Buttress, Dr. Havana, Mr. and Mrs. Fred, and Ms. Gould. However, the spokesmen for this group were Ortiz, Donovan, and Youlade, as the others were very quiet, not to mention very shy. Just as Ronald was introducing himself to them, some thugs hired by the New York banker after the hired guns from New York were unsuccessful, attacked them. Ronald, along with the other members of his team, and aided by some bystanders at the airport, fought them off. Shortly after they were defeated and restrained by security, the Lima police arrived and escorted the thugs to prison. "Who were they?" asked Mr. Ortiz.

"I don't know," Ronald said. "But, this is the *third time* I've been attacked by thugs in business suits since yesterday!"

"Really?" asked Mr. Donovan. "Why would they attack you?"

"I don't know why they're targeting me," Ronald said. "But, I'm starting to think that *someone else* is after the treasure, and they really want to get their hands on the map and the debit card."

"When did they start attacking you?" asked Mr. Youlade.

"Right after I left the bank," Ronald replied. "You don't think there's a connection, do you?"

"Well, it's possible that someone from that bank is after the treasure," Mr. Ortiz said. "Then again, it could be some corrupt businessman that has also heard about the treasure. They could have been trying to extort the university for funds for this trip, and were refused. And now that you have the funds, and most of the necessary items, they no longer need the university."

"How would you know about who the possible suspects could be?" Ronald asked Mr. Ortiz.

"Well, one of my friends that used to be in this game is now in some new adventure game where there is a lot of corruption," Mr. Ortiz replied. "My friend said that he likes that game because he gets to be the one to tackle all of the corruption going on."

"But how do you keep in touch with him? Aren't games sort of independent of one another?" Ronald asked, confused as to how the characters in video game world communicated with one another.

"You see, we have an Internet here as well," Mr. Donovan said. "Just like the one in your world, we have similar infrastructure. However, we can only stay in contact with those people that we meet in Video Game City, and with those that were in our own game, but left. Except for Pixie. Because she's The Traveller, she can maintain contact with *everyone* she meets in our world."

"How do you know that I'm from the real world?" Ronald asked, amazed that these characters were aware that he came from the real world. "And how much do you know about it?"

"To answer your first question, the VGG informed us when you arrived in the game, and that Pixie was your guide," Mr. Ortiz said.

"And to answer your second question, we don't know *everything* about the real world," Mr. Youlade added. "While we do have screens that allow us to see all of the people playing the game, with our current player's screen enlarged, we do not know where they are physically located. And this game doesn't have microphone support, so we can't learn anything about the lives of the players by listening to their conversations."

"We did, however, learn about your world's Internet in school," Mr. Donovan said. "That, and a few other things, such as the nuances of our particular games, and any information about the real world that is relevant to us so that we can understand what is going on. However, we are never taught exactly *who* the developers of our games are, nor are we taught where they are located."

"Are you ever able to approach the screens? Or even go *through* them in order to enter the real world?" Ronald asked, worried about what he was hearing.

"No, we're not," Mr. Ortiz said. "While we can see the screens, they are always far away. So if we try to move towards them, we can never get close to them. And even if we could, we wouldn't have the ability to go through them. It's something that The VGG put in place to prevent anyone from our world from causing havoc in your world."

"You didn't think we were aware of the real world?" Mr. Youlade asked.

"No," Ronald said, shaking his head with a scared look on his face. "Just like I told Pixie, I thought you people didn't have minds of your own. And I thought you were just told what to do by the developers."

"Oh, we very much do have minds of our own," Mr. Ortiz said. "We just get to use them when the games are either paused, or when they are turned off."

"And, I didn't think that video games had an education system," Ronald said. "I just thought they were given the required knowledge by the programmers."

"Oh, no," Mr. Donovan said. "We have to *learn* how to do these things. Did you know that anyone that is new to the games, including those who came from a different game, have to go to school to learn the nuances of their new roles?"

"No, I did not," Ronald said.

Then he looked around and noticed that there were no screens or cameras appearing anywhere. He then turned to the rest of the party and said, "Wait! What gives?! I don't see any screens in this game!"

"You see," Mr. Ortiz said, "this game is existing outside of the other people that are playing this game at this moment."

Ronald then asked, "Why is that?"

"The VGG has purposely done this to ensure that you aren't distracted by anyone you may know in the real world currently playing this game," Mr. Ortiz said. "They forgot that the theories taught in school also said that if a person from the real world *did* find their way into our world, they could actually get close to the screens, and even go *through* them. They realized after you entered the portal to this game that if you saw the screens, and you recognized someone, you may try to plot an escape before you're done with whatever games you're supposed to play."

"Oh," Ronald said.

"Well, we'd better not waste anymore time here," Mr. Youlade said. "It's already really late, and we need to get plenty of rest before we head off to Morocco."

The party then got their things and checked into the airport hotel for a couple of nights using Ronald's debit card. Since the university only gave Ronald access to the funds, he was required to pay for any necessary expenses.

The next day, the party went over their itinerary, including a list of supplies that they would require after they landed in Casablanca. Afterwards, they rested for the rest of the day, and slept early, as their flight would leave the next day at 9:00 am, sharp. The following day, they boarded the plane, and were off to Morocco. On the flight, they enjoyed well prepared meals, and also got as much rest as they could. During the flight, Ronald asked, "You know those funds that the bank released for this trip? What are they for, beyond paying for the supplies, tickets, and hotel room?"

"We get paid from these funds also," Mr. Ortiz said. "If you hadn't signed those papers, we wouldn't be on this trip because we told the university that we said would not be participating unless we received a stipend."

"The funds are also used to pay the interpreter," added Mr. Donovan. "He, too, made it clear he wouldn't join us unless he was paid."

"We also needed to give the money to the village we'll be staying in," Mr. Youlade said. "They only accept outsiders for a mission like this if they are compensated."

Ronald was satisfied with the answer and dropped the topic. When they arrived in Casablanca about 12 hours later, they were immediately ambushed by more of the banker's thugs. The party was able to fight them off, although the thugs were able to scatter off before the police could arrive. Ronald said, "You know, I'm starting to think that someone doesn't want us to find the treasure."

"Either that, or they want it for *themselves*," Mr. Ortiz said.

After brushing themselves off, they gathered their things, and met their interpreter, who would be helping them communicate with the villagers inside the village that they were travelling to, which was located in the Atlas Mountains. They then went to a local supply shop to buy the rest of their required supplies. After purchasing the remaining needed supplies, they rented a vehicle and headed for the Atlas Mountains, with the interpreter driving. A few kilometres outside of Casablanca, Ronald noticed a black van with tinted windows following them, and said, "I think we're being followed."

The archaeologists turned around, and also saw the van. "No, maybe they're also just travelling, and have to use this highway to get to their destination," Mr. Youlade said.

As Ronald kept looking, he saw that the van had no intention of changing lanes to pass them, and instead seemed like it was headed straight for the party's car. "Then why is that van coming at us at high speed, as if it is trying to ram us from behind?" Ronald replied, worried about what was unfolding.

Suddenly, they saw several men in suits come into view outside the windows with guns in tow. They too had been hired by the banker to steal the party's supplies and information in order to secure the treasure for himself. They started shooting at the party, causing some dents in the van. The interpreter asked for a phone, and first phoned the police to report that they were being shot at. He then phoned the car rental agency to inform them that the car may have some damage because the party had been shot at. The agent reassured him that they would still get a full refund of their security deposit, given the circumstances. After hanging up, the interpreter then asked for a gun, and told the rest of the party to pull out their guns and start shooting at the thugs. While the interpreter put the car into autopilot, the entire party did as they were told, and started shooting at the van. After a lengthy shootout, Ronald's party was able to shoot the tires of the van. The van crashed, killing the hired guns. When everything seemed safe, Ronald said, "Now I *know* that someone is trying to get our stuff so that *they* can get the treasure."

"Well, that means we'd better get to it first!" Mr. Donovan said.

After driving for a few more hours, they arrived at the mountain village. They were immediately welcomed by the village's mayor and its citizens. After the initial welcome, they participated in a local celebration. Over the next few days, the party then learned several mountain survival skills, including mountain climbing skills. Ronald took it all in, and learned a lot more than he thought he would, as his nature walks with Dawna seemed quite easy compared to some of the things that he was learning here. They also learned about some of the local animals, and how best to deal with them if they ever encountered them.

A few days later, when Ronald and his party were getting ready to leave, the village was suddenly attacked by more goons hired by the banker. They had a tough time locating these people, as GPS was only in its early stages. However, the banker had been tipped off by a local informant that the party was staying in the village. He then sent out an all-out attack on the village, with the intention of killing everyone. Most of the bandits came via helicopter, while some of the goons ambushed the village from the ground. The goons that attacked from the ground were dealt with by the villagers, who used their knowledge of the area to fight off the thugs. Meanwhile, the thugs in the helicopter, who began shooting at the ground, were dealt with by Ronald and the archaeologists, who fired back at their attackers with their guns. After a lengthy battle, the hired killers on the ground were killed, and the helicopter crashed into an undisclosed location.

Once the battle was over, the party thanked the villagers for their hospitality, as well as helping them fight off the thugs. The village's mayor responded by thanking them for saving the village, and gave them a reward. After the completion of the ceremonies, they headed off into the mountains for the final part of their journey. The party made sure to put on their winter gear, as the villagers had warned them that the Atlas Mountains were known for being cold and snowy, and thus it was essential that they wear warm clothing.

The trek into the mountains was difficult, just as the villagers had said. It was cold and snowy, and at times quite windy, which forced the party to stop several times. They followed various trails, and camped more than they had intended to. However, with the map and compass in hand, they were slowly able to navigate their way to where it was believed the treasure was located, all without getting lost. They reached their destination a few days later, and decided to make camp here. The location at the entrance of the cave was ideal, as it was not too cold, snowy, or windy, and they all needed a break after a tiring journey. During camp, Ronald debated in his head whether or not he wanted to take the treasure back to New York. He remembered watching documentaries and other TV shows that stressed at just how upset the local populations had become whenever a treasure that had been found was taken away by foreign archaeologists, with the artifacts then being displayed in foreign museums around the world. He yelled "pause," and Pixie appeared. She then said, "Yes, Ronald? How can I help you?"

"Pixie, is there an alternate ending to this game?" Ronald asked.

"What do you mean?"

"I know that in this game that we have to take the treasure back to New York once it is found, but I don't feel right about taking it from the Moroccan people."

"Oh."

"Yeah, so is there some sort of alternate ending that would allow me to let some Moroccan museum take the treasure, which would allow the local Moroccans to be able to see the treasure without having to travel to a museum just to view them?"

"Well-," Pixie started.

"You know, the problem in the real world is that foreign archaeologists find lost artifacts, and then steal it from the countries that they found it in," Ronald interrupted. "And they then display it in a 'prestigious' museum located in some 'world class' city, justifying the decision by saying that local populations do not deserve to have these artifacts returned to them because they will not know what to do with them. I know for a fact that some countries are trying to recover such items, but the countries where they're being displayed in are refusing to give them back."

"Before you interrupted me, I was going to say that there is an alternate ending to this game. And it does involve giving the treasure to a museum located in the Moroccan capital. However, I can't tell you what to do. It's up to you as to how you want to end the game."

"So, The VGG will not be mad if I decide to go with an alternate ending?"

"No, they won't. It's something that is entirely *your* decision, as you won't be cheating or taking any shortcuts."

"Thanks."

"You're welcome. Now, it's time for me to go."

After Pixie left, Ronald took some time to think. At dinner, he still looked distracted, and Ms. Gould asked him, "What's wrong, Ronald? You seem distracted."

"Were you ever aware that there is an alternate ending to this game?" he asked them.

"Yes, we are," Mr. Youlade responded. "But, whenever we play this game, the players *always* go with the regular ending."

"Are you happy with that?" Ronald asked them.

"Well, we do it because we have to," replied Mr. Donovan. "If it were up to us, we would happily go with the alternate ending, just to see what would happen."

"You know, it actually would be *fun* to go with the alternate ending, just once," Mr. Ortiz added. "It's something that I, too, have been curious about."

The other archaeologists then started talking about how they wished that the players of this game would try the alternate ending, even if it was just once. Ronald then discussed about how things worked in the real world, and how he always got upset because he wished that when someone found an artifact, they would, for once, keep it in the country where it was found. He elaborated about how he disliked the thought that much of the local population would probably never get to see them when the artifacts were taken away. He also mentioned how he had watched shows that stressed how local populations were not happy at this, and in fact were quite upset that the countries that currently possessed such artifacts refused to give them back. "You know what?" Mr. Ortiz said. "Ronald's right. It's just not right to take these things back to the US."

"I agree," Mr. Donovan agreed. "I feel that we should finish the game with the alternate ending, and give the treasure to the people of Morocco."

The other archaeologists nodded in agreement, to which Ronald said, "So, it's settled then. When we find this treasure, we will give it to a museum in Rabat."

"Yes!" the rest said in jubilation.

They then slept for the rest of the night, as in the morning, the final part of their expedition was going to start.

The next day, the party packed up their camp, and held a quick briefing before entering the cave. "So, does everyone know what to do?" Ronald asked.

"Yes, we do," Mr. Donovan said. "We stick together, and check out every tunnel. We don't have a map of this cave, so we can't afford to split up."

"And, we have to make sure that there are no booby traps in there," Mr. Ortiz added.

"Plus, we have to keep an eye out for more thugs," said Mr. Youlade.

"Great!" Ronald said, before adding, "Now, let's go through all the supplies that we need for this cave."

They pulled out flashlights, the whip, the machete, gloves, and trail markers so they could trace their steps back out of the cave. After putting on the gloves, they entered the cave. It was a long and dark cave, and the flashlights came in handy here. However, the party did not know that they were being followed this whole time by not only the banker's goons, but also by the banker himself. As they were walking, they dropped trail markers on the cave floor, knowing that they would light up when someone shone the flashlight on the ground. When the party reached a semi-lit portion of the cave, they found some statues, and promptly Ronald warned them, "Okay, we have to make sure that there are no booby traps here."

Mrs. Fred pulled out a frisbee, and threw it across the hall. Nothing happened. Then, a ball was taken out of the backpack, and rolled along the floor of the hall. Again, nothing happened. However, as the party moved across the hall, members of the party suddenly began disappearing. In all, Mr. and Mrs. Fred and Ms. Gould were kidnapped, while Ortiz, Donovan, and Youlade were ambushed and killed by the thugs. When Ronald reached the end of the hallway, he turned around and noticed that six members of his team were missing, and that there were only six left. The banker and his thugs had been quite efficient in their operation, being careful not to be seen by anyone. Therefore, Ronald did not grasp the danger that he was facing.

While worried about what had happened to the others, he continued on with whoever remained. However, the remaining members of his team were kidnapped, with Drs. Buttress and Havana getting killed by the goons. As Ronald approached what seemed like the entrance to the room where the treasure was hidden, he said, "I think this is it! It looks like that the treasure, if it exists, is behind this boarded up tunnel!"

All he heard was silence. Confused, Ronald said, "Hello? Is anyone else here?"

He turned around, and saw that he was all alone. "Where is everyone? What's going on here?"

After calling out to the rest of his party a few more times, he decided to continue alone, and used his machete to break the boards. He entered the tunnel, and, using his flashlight, he navigated his way to a larger room, which was lit with torches. On a pedestal, he saw a gold treasure sitting on it. "It *does* exist!" Ronald said in excitement as he approached the pedestal. "What a relief! I don't have to start this game over!"

As he took the treasure off of the pedestal, he heard a male voice say, in an evil tone, "Aha! You found it! Now, hand it over, nice and easy!"

Ronald turned around, and saw that it was the banker from New York, and that he was pointing a gun directly at Ronald. "Hey! You're that banker that I had to deal with earlier in the game!" he said. "What are *you* doing here?"

"Yes, that's right!" the banker said with an evil scowl on his face. "You have made things much too difficult for me! You may have outlasted my goons, but you won't overpower *me*! I want this treasure for myself. It will be a nice addition to my collection!"

"What?! *You* were the one who sent all of those thugs to attack me and my party?"

"That's right! I thought I could kill you, much earlier. But no problem, as you have led me straight to the treasure anyway! Now, hand it over, otherwise I'm going to shoot and kill you, right here, right now!"

"No! This thing belongs to the people of Morocco!"

"Well, that's just too bad for the Moroccan people, isn't it?! I collect lost treasures! Anytime a university or country is looking for a lost treasure, *I'm* the one who finances it! And, don't think I won't kill anyone who stands in my way! Don't be alarmed, I do give the treasures back. Of course, provided the countries of origin pay nicely for it. If they pay, I'm happy to give them back! If not, well, I benefit too, since other collectors are willing to pay my price!"

"So *that* explains all that talk about collectors and king's ransoms when we first met!"

"Yes! But you have foiled me at every turn! *You* were a lot tougher and resilient than I thought! Now, hand it over before I kill you!"

"No!"

"You're making a *big* mistake! What are these pathetic and poor people in Morocco going to do with it? *I* can do more with this than some poor idiot located here!"

"They can learn about their history from this artifact from a museum that is accessible to them!"

"Not for long!"

Just as the banker was about to shoot, he was hit in the head by a backpack by Ms. Gould, who had fought off her kidnappers, thus knocking the gun out of the banker's hand. "Are you okay, Ronald?" Ms. Gould, who was out of breath, asked.

"Yeah, I am now that you're here," Ronald said. "What happened to you, Ms. Gould?"

"I was kidnapped by this idiot's goons!" Ms. Gould responded, pointing to the banker. "I was lucky I could fight them off. Those kickboxing lessons really paid off! But, some of the others have been killed!"

Ronald then kicked the gun away. The banker, who by then had regained his composure and got up off the ground, came charging at Ronald. In self-defence, Ronald killed him with the machete when the banker got close. Then, Ms. Gould noticed the treasure and said, "Oh! You've found it!"

Ronald took the treasure, and then said, "Yeah, I found it. Now, let's go!"

They ran from the room, and then looked for any remaining members of their party that were alive. They found the interpreter, Tedlow, Kaynes, and the Freds, and fought off the remaining minions of the banker in the process. Once they left the cave, they immediately called for a helicopter, which took them straight to Rabat. The banker's surviving hired killers, meanwhile, were arrested and taken into custody. In Rabat, the party went to the information building, and asked where the museum was located. After receiving the directions, Ronald called the museum to let them know that the party was coming to donate the treasure to them. Once they arrived at the museum, Ronald asked for the director, who came down, and was quite grateful with the generosity shown by the party. "You know, so many people have played this game, but you are the *very first* to actually do this for us!" the director said.

"Well, with the way things go in the real world, this seemed like the right thing to do," Ronald said.

"We really appreciate it! Thank you so much!"

"Hey, no problem. I mean, I know how important this is to you and to the people of Morocco."

The entire party was given a reward for their generous and selfless donation. The story about the donation even made Moroccan papers. After being recognized by local officials, they headed straight for the airport to buy their tickets to New York, and headed for the US.

A week later, the party was recognized for their discovery at a news conference. As it turned out, the banker was well known to the authorities. But because of his stealth, no one could pin the previous heists and murders of expeditionaries squarely on him. Because the banker was killed, his entire family was arrested by US authorities, as they were considered accessories to the crimes for not doing anything about his behaviour. They were also charged for extortion and hoarding of cultural artifacts that were neither registered nor were legally owned by them.

After several speeches, including ones delivered by the university's chancellor, the party was asked about their adventure, including how they were able to survive the dangers faced given that so many other expeditions failed. They explained that they had more training to deal with such situations than the previous groups. Suddenly, a reporter noticed that the treasure was not there, and asked, "So, where's the treasure?"

"It's in Rabat, Morocco, in a museum," Ronald said. "The people of Morocco now have the chance to learn more about their ancient history."

A murmur erupted in the audience, as no one in this group of people even knew about the alternate ending to the game. "What does he mean?!" whispered one reporter.

"Forget what he means. What is he *doing*?!" another reporter responded in a whisper.

"I don't know! *This* isn't how the game is supposed to *end*!" replied another.

"I know!" the first reporter responded. Then, pointing to the heads of the well-known museums, she said, "Isn't he supposed to bring that treasure back here, and give it to one of *our* museums?!"

"Well, this game isn't crashing," the second reporter said. "You don't suppose that there's an alternate ending to this, do you?"

"I don't know," the third reporter said. "Let's ask him."

Then, a question was asked, "Why did you give the treasure to the Rabat museum?"

Ronald then explained the way things worked in the real world, and how he felt that it was not right to keep such a treasure. He also mentioned about how he had promised himself that if he ever had a chance to be in the same position, he would do the right thing and make sure that local treasures stayed in the country that they came from. When asked if this was some sort of alternate ending, Ronald said, "Yes, this is the alternate ending. The problem is that most players of this game in the real world never take that route."

Another murmur erupted. After a few minutes, the news conference continued, and the other archaeologists were asked questions about what it was like to work with Ronald, and what they had learned during their adventure. They replied that it was quite refreshing to work with Ronald. He was clearly an independent thinker, and thought outside of the box.

Ronald was then asked about his team, and he said he was happy to work with tough and dedicated people who were never ready to give up, in spite of all the challenges they faced. The news conference then ended at that point, and a portal opened up at the side of the stage. Ronald's clothes changed back to normal, and Pixie appeared, saying, "Hey Ronald. It looks like you've finished the game successfully. I just received word from The VGG that that portal goes to the next game. So, we'd better leave."

Ronald looked over, and saw the portal. He then looked at Pixie and said, "Oh, okay, Pixie. Let me just say goodbye to these people."

He then went over to Gould, Kaynes, Tedlow, and the Freds and said, "Well, it looks like I have to go now and continue on my journey so I can get home."

"Okay," Ms. Gould said. "It was a pleasure working with you, Ronald."

"Yes," Mrs. Fred said. "Without you, I don't know if we could have *finished* this game."

"And, we learned some things about ourselves during the adventure," Mr. Fred said.

"We will never forget you, Ronald," Mr. Kaynes said. "You were someone that we had fun working with."

"Thanks, guys," Ronald said, blushing. "It was also great to work will all of you."

Ronald then hugged everyone in the team. After he was done, he joined Pixie, and they entered the portal that led to the second game.

CHAPTER FIVE

After exiting the portal, Ronald and Pixie found themselves in a game that was set in a kid-friendly world, with a linear map that had doors leading to various zones. Ronald also noticed that they were in a valley surrounded by mountains. However, there was no water beneath them. Rather, they were standing on a platform that said "Start," with a path that only went up to the first door. After looking around this strange place, Ronald said, "Where are we? Are we walled-up? But instead of walls we have mountains boxing us in?"

"No, I don't think we are boxed in," Pixie replied.

Suddenly, both of their clothes changed, and they were both now wearing overalls and coloured shirts, Ronald's being blue, and Pixie's being yellow. They also were wearing some large truckers' ball caps, with Ronald's being grey and Pixie's being green. "Huh. I'm not even that good at fixing things," Pixie said as she examined her new clothes.

"Neither am I," Ronald said, as he inspected his new attire. "This clothing change must mean that we're inside of a new game."

"Yes, we are," Pixie said as she looked down at her phone. "It's something called Great Adventure Brothers 3D — Rescue the World. And, seeing as how *my* clothes also changed, I'm guessing that this is a two-player game. Though, you would *think* that The VGG would change the name of this game just for this instance, seeing as how I'm a *girl*."

Ronald just laughed, and said to her, "I'm guessing they didn't do that because there are probably other people also playing this game right now, and changing the name may confuse the real world players as to what game they're playing."

"Maybe. But the name of this game sounds so familiar. And I feel like I've worn these clothes before. I wonder why that is."

Pixie then phoned The VGG to ask them how the two-player system would work, and they replied to her that she would be required to fight alongside Ronald during the entire game. After finishing her phone call with The VGG, Pixie checked her phone to find out what the game's plot was about. They found out that an evil lord, called Ultimo Lord X, had deposed the king of the kingdom, King Relian, as well as Relian's lords in each of the worlds of the kingdom, and had replaced them with his own overlords. There were six worlds, each with its own unique theme, plus the final world that consisted of Ultimo's Castle. Ultimo had also unleashed a large number of monsters that could only be defeated by either jumping on them or using power-ups. The first six worlds contained a certain number of zones that had to be completed before the players could reach the castle of the overlord of that world, and the overlord had to be defeated in order to advance to the next world. There were also extra zones if the player wanted to play them. In order to defeat each lord, the players had to stomp on him three times, or use power-ups to knock him down. The final world didn't have any zones, and instead required Pixie and Ronald to navigate through Ultimo's castle. When they reached Ultimo Lord X, they had to stomp on him six times in order to finish the game, as he was immune to power-ups. In order to get through each zone, as well as Ultimo's castle, Pixie and Ronald had to make use of the platforms, and make sure they did not bump into their enemies when facing them, otherwise they would be returned to the previous door they finished. Ronald still would still have unlimited health, and therefore unlimited lives. And just like in the previous game, Ronald was not allowed to use any cheat codes or other shortcuts, otherwise he'd be sent back to the first game, Hunt for the Lost Treasure of Morocco.

Pixie then looked up from her phone with a worried look on her face. "Now I know why I thought I recognized the title of this game, and why I felt like I had worn these clothes before! I've *been* here before," she told Ronald. "Not only that, but I've actually been asked to *play* this game before. And it is not easy, even in a two-player situation."

"So?" Ronald said. "That means it's supposed to be a challenge. And, aren't there power-ups that we can use?"

"You don't understand, Ronald. This is a *very* dangerous game. You don't know how some of these monsters can just sneak up on you. There are power-ups, yes. But, you still need to be careful when you are battling them."

"Okay, okay. I'll be careful. And, that's why you're here with me, right? We both will watch out for each other."

"So, do you think you'll be okay?"

"Yes, I will. Look, let's just get started. It looks like this is a mountain world, and that means there will be *a lot* of climbing. So, we'd better not waste anymore time."

"Okay, let's go."

"Just one more question."

"And that is…?"

"Are there items shops along the way in this game? I've never played this version of the series before."

"No, you just have the power-ups from the zones."

"Oh, okay. Well, I'm just glad I received all of that mountain climbing training done in the first game. Not to mention actually having to *do* the mountain climbing."

They then followed the path to the first door, and entered it, thus beginning the game. Upon entering the door, they saw the scenery suddenly change from the map that they were just in. Inside it, they were in a wide valley, and the mountains were far enough away that they were inaccessible. The monsters were visible, though they were small compared to Pixie and Ronald's height. Initially it seemed that they didn't care too much that Ronald and Pixie were there. However, once Ronald and Pixie started moving forward, the monsters started attacking them. Ronald and Pixie both jumped and stomped on the monsters, and saw that they disappeared. Pixie looked to Ronald after the monsters were defeated, and said, "Now do you understand what I meant when I said that this is a dangerous game?"

"I do now," Ronald replied, nodding his head. "This is not going to be easy, or very safe."

They continued moving forward, and saw a bunch of blocks that were numbered a couple of feet above their heads. There were five in total, and were lined up side-by-side. Pixie pointed to them, and said, "If we hit these, we might get power-ups, or we might get coins, or we may not get anything."

Ronald hit one of the blocks, and saw that some coins came out. He continued hitting the block until it yielded no more coins, after which the block turned solid. "So, how do the coins help us in this game?" he asked Pixie after he finished.

"Well, they won't really *do* anything for *us*," Pixie responded. "If we didn't have unlimited lives and unlimited health, getting 100 of these coins would give you an extra life."

Pixie then hit the next block, and it just broke into a few pieces. She then hit the following block, and more coins came out, and she continued hitting it until it became solid. Ronald hit the fourth block, and it broke up. The fifth block also yielded some coins, and he continued hitting it until it solidified. They then moved forward, and suddenly saw a fire-spitting bear emerge from the bushes a few feet away from them. They avoided the fire pellets, and waited for the bear to go back into the bushes before moving on. They then saw some platforms, jumped up onto them, and walked on them for a while until they reached a gap. They jumped the gap, and went back down, and directly above them were three blocks. Ronald hit one, and saw a steak coming out of it. Thinking that this was a piece of delicious barbecue steak, Ronald grabbed it. Suddenly, a tail emerged from his lower back, and tiger ears grew on the top of his head. Ronald was wondering what was going on as he felt his scalp, finding the tiger ears, and then turning his head behind him to see the tail. "What the...? What is *this* stuff that's coming out of me?!" he asked, scared that he may have turned himself into another animal.

"That steak that you grabbed was for the Tiger Power-Up," Pixie said.

"You mean to tell me that I turned myself into a freaking tiger?!" Ronald screamed in fear.

"No, no," Pixie replied, laughing. "You have the same face and body as you always did. You just now have a tiger tail and tiger ears coming out of you. This is actually a very useful power-up."

"How is this good?! I don't want any tiger stuff coming out of me!"

"Well, for one, it allows you to fly if you get enough speed. However, I wouldn't recommend it because you're also playing with me, and the *last* thing I need is to have to chase you in order to keep up with you. And, you also can easily defeat the monsters if you spin, as your tail is so powerful that it kills the enemies."

Ronald, disgusted over having received this power-up, hit the next block, hoping for a different power-up, but instead it yielded nothing but coins. He then jumped on the block that had the Tiger Power-Up, and then hit the block above that, but it also yielded more coins. After going on a little further, they came up to another block, and Pixie hit it. Out of the block came a candle, and Pixie grabbed it. Suddenly, she saw that her clothes and hat turned red, and she was also wearing red gloves. Pixie then made fists, and big fireballs came out of both hands. She then shot the fireballs across the valley, knocking out a ton of monsters. "Cool! I got the Fire Power-Up!" she said, impressed with her new ability.

"Hey, no fair!" Ronald said. "You got the *good* power-up! I wanted that one!"

All Pixie could do was laugh. She then said, "Hey! You'll just have to wait until you get another power-up! This one's *mine*! Besides, you've got a good one, too."

Ronald just rolled his eyes in disgust, and they kept moving forward. After fighting off a few more enemies, they came to another platform, and saw a goal with a flagpole on it. "See that flagpole there?" Pixie asked Ronald, pointing to the pole.

"Yeah," Ronald said.

"In order to finish this zone, we have to raise the flag."

"Okay."

They made it to the flagpole, raised the flag, and saw a "Zone Complete" message appear in the sky. They then saw a door appear, and they went through it. Upon exiting, the door flipped over to show a "Completed!" sign going up diagonally, and the path opened up to the next zone. They followed the path, and entered the second door. This zone was more hilly, and the mountains appeared to be closer, suggesting that they were in a foothills region. "You know, a lot of the monsters are going uphill, rather than downhill," Pixie said. "So, this should be a little easier. And, we have our power-ups, so we shouldn't have any problems."

"Well, at least my mountain climbing is going to come in handy here," Ronald replied.

They quickly ran up the first of the hillsides, and when they reached the very top, they slid down the hills, knocking out all of the monsters. "How is it possible that we're able to slide so easily, on *grass* at that, without a toboggan?" Ronald asked Pixie.

"Because the video game world is different," Pixie said. "What have I told you? Things here don't work exactly the way they do in the *real world*!"

They then moved on, continuing to use this strategy to defeat all of the monsters in this zone, and then slid down the final hill to the goal. They raised the flag, and the Zone Complete message appeared, followed by the door leading out of the zone. They exited the door, which closed and had "Completed!" display once they went through, and saw the path open up in two different directions. "We should take the south path here that goes to the overlord's castle," Pixie said, pointing to the south path. "The one to the east is just a waste of time."

"Why?" Ronald asked.

"Because it's just a zone that doesn't need to be completed. And, that path just loops back to the main path. I really don't know *why* the players in your world always continue on that way. I guess they want to get more coins or something."

"Well, you know this game better than I do, so we'll just keep going the way you say to."

They then took the south path, and played in two more zones, both of which were mountainous, and therefore required them to use their mountain climbing skills. As they were going through the zones, Ronald could only think about how fortunate he was that he had received the training in the first game, not to mention having to actually do some mountain climbing in that game, as he had to help Pixie up a few times so that she wouldn't fall. In both zones, the real challenge was in climbing the steep cliffs, rather than the enemies they faced. And if any monsters did cause trouble, Pixie just unleashed fireballs, which cleared the path and allowed her and Ronald to focus on the climbing. Ronald still had not been able to change his power-up, as all the other power-up blocks had Tiger Power-Ups, which did not help him at all. He still was not comfortable with the Tiger Power-Up, but he was learning to live with it. After they had completed these two zones, they arrived at the castle. "So, what kinds of things can we expect in this castle?" Ronald asked as they approached the entrance.

"We'll have to face a few guards before getting into the overlord's room," Pixie said.

When they entered the castle door, they were greeted by a servant of the deposed lord. "Thank you, Ronald and Pixie, for coming! A major catastrophe has occurred!"

"We know what it is-," Ronald started.

"Shhh!" Pixie interrupted him. "You have to let him finish! It's part of the game!"

"Yes, well, anyway, as I was saying, a major catastrophe has occurred!" the servant said. "Our regular lord, the great Lord Mortanis, has been deposed by the evil overlord Kingly, a minion of Ultimo Lord X! We need you to defeat Kingly so that we can return Lord Mortanis to his throne!"

After this speech, they were then immediately transported into the castle. When he saw that they were now in the lobby, Ronald said, "Hey! We didn't even get to tell him that we would do it!"

"It's implied that you're going to do it," Pixie said, rolling her eyes. "Now, let's get on with the task."

As they went through the castle, they defeated the guards using their power-ups. They avoided the lava areas by using the platforms, and after a while they approached a wooden door. "That's where the overlord's room is," Pixie said, pointing to the door.

"Are you sure it's not a door that leads to a room where the ceiling rises and falls?" Ronald asked.

"Who has played this game before?!" replied Pixie, rather annoyed.

"Okay! You don't have to get mad."

They entered the door, and saw Kingly waiting there for them. "I've been expecting you two!" he said. "You may have survived the zones of this world, but you won't survive *me*!"

Ronald and Pixie stayed close to the door, and devised a plan to defeat Kingly. Pixie then whispered to Ronald, "You be the decoy and distract him, and I'll use the fire balls to defeat him from by behind."

"Why do *I* have to be the decoy?!" Ronald asked.

"Who's the one with the Fire Power-Up?"

"You are," Ronald said begrudgingly.

"And that means I can get him in one shot, right?"

"Yes, that's true."

"Okay, then, we have to get started."

Ronald approached Kingly, and said, "Yo, Kingly! Over here!"

Kingly started chasing after Ronald, who was doing his best to elude Kingly. Meanwhile, Pixie was trying to get into position to fire at Kingly. Once she had him lined up, she created large fireballs with her fists and pointed them at Kingly, and they hit Kingly directly in the back. "Noooooooooooooooooooo!" Kingly said as he became engulfed in fire.

After a few moments, Kingly blew up, and a ball with a question mark appeared. Ronald picked it up, after which he and Pixie were magically transported to the throne room of the castle. On the throne was Lord Mortanis, who said, "Thank you, Ronald and Pixie! I have been returned to my rightful place! However, you still have to conquer six more worlds. The other five lords are still in grave danger, and so is the king."

Immediately after the celebration of the return of Lord Mortanis to the throne, Ronald and Pixie were transported to the second world. Here, they noticed a jurassic setting, with volcanoes, palm trees, jungles, vines, and large, glacial lakes. "This looks like we were transported back to the age of the dinosaurs," Ronald said.

"Well, this *is* Jurassic World," Pixie said. "But don't worry, the dinosaurs here aren't that big. One stomp and they're gone. Or, we can use our power-ups to vanquish them."

"Okay, as long as we won't get *crushed* by the dinosaurs."

They followed the path to the first door, and Ronald immediately noticed that in addition to the dinosaurs, there were some monsters from the first world. He and Pixie confronted these monsters, and used their power-ups to defeat them. In this zone, Ronald uncovered many Celery Power-Ups, which he wasn't interested in despite the fact that they would have given him temporary invincibility, and more Tiger Power-Ups. They continued on by using the platforms, and quickly reached the goal. After raising up the flag, they exited the door, and then continued on the path. After a couple more zones, they entered the fourth and final zone of this world they would have to face before reaching the overlord's castle. Ronald hit the first block directly in front of him, and saw an army suit emerge out of it. Curious as to what this was, he grabbed it and saw the tiger tail and ears disappear. His clothing also changed, and he was now wearing a camouflage coloured bounty hunter costume and now had a bazooka. Once Ronald saw this, a big smile came across his face. "Now *this* is more like it!" he said in an excited tone.

"This is the Bazooka Power-Up," Pixie said. "Be careful with that thing, especially where you point it! It can be *very* dangerous if you're not careful with it!"

Ronald nodded, and they proceeded along. During the rest of the zone, Ronald didn't even give Pixie a chance to use her Fire Power-Up, as he used the bazooka at every enemy that he could find. "Ronald! Let me at least defeat *some* of these enemies!" Pixie yelled at him. "This isn't a *one-player* game! We're supposed to be a *team*!"

"What?" Ronald responded, shrugging his shoulders. "I have a powerful weapon, and I'm going to use it. Besides, you got to use your fire power in the first world more than I got to use my tiger abilities."

"But, at least I let you *defeat* some of those monsters!"

"Fine, when we get to that overlord's castle, you can defeat some of the guards."

"Thank you!"

They finished the zone, and then headed to the overlord's castle. The servant at the door said, "Oh, Ronald and Pixie! It is so good you have arrived! A major catastrophe has occurred! Our regular lord, the great Lord Yeinius, has been deposed by the evil overlord Tyrannous, a minion of Ultimo Lord X! We need you to defeat Tyrannous so that we can return Lord Yeinius to his throne!"

After they were transported to the castle's lobby, Ronald said, "That sounds just like what the servant at the door of the last castle said."

"Well, that's how they talk. You're going to hear the same thing before entering almost every castle," Pixie replied. "I think it's different in the last two, but I don't remember."

"Oh," Ronald said. "That's even more annoying to hear than the stuff you had to say every time I yelled 'pause' in the first game!"

"Well, you'll just have to deal with it."

"I guess the programmers were just being lazy when they made this game, at least with the first five castles."

"Just get on with the mission!"

They then made their way through the castle, and encountered many guards along the way. Here, Ronald kept his promise and allowed Pixie to defeat all of the guards with her fire ability. When they got to Tyrannous' room, they saw a t-rex standing in front of them. "I see that *you two* were able to make it this far! But this is as far as you will get on your journey!" Tyrannous said in a thunderous tone.

"We'll see about that!" Ronald said, holding up his bazooka.

Before Pixie could say anything about a strategy, Ronald fired a shot directly at Tyrannous before he could get into a fighting stance. The shot hit Tyrannous straight in the chest. The dinosaur, clearly caught off-guard, yelled, "What the...? This can't be happening! You didn't even give me a chance to attack you!"

Then, just before he blew up, Tyrannous yelled, "NOOOOOOOOOOOOOOOOOOOOO!"

"I didn't cheat, did I?" Ronald asked after the hit, realizing that he may have been a little too impatient.

"No, Ronald, you didn't," Pixie said, quite upset that Ronald had not worked with her in defeating the dinosaur.

"Okay, good. What about a shortcut? That wasn't a shortcut, was it?"

"No, it wasn't. You just didn't wait for me to come up with a strategy!"

"Oh! Well, in that case, no harm done!"

All Pixie could do was roll her eyes and shake her head in disgust. A ball with a question mark then appeared, and Ronald picked it up. The two of them were then transported to the throne room, and a celebration was held for the return of Lord Yeinius to his throne. "Thank you, Ronald and Pixie! I have been returned to my rightful place! However, there are still five more worlds to conquer. The other four lords are still in danger, and so is the king!"

Immediately after the celebration, Ronald and Pixie were whisked away to the third world. Here, there was nothing but a desert. The only things visible were cacti, sand, and dunes. "You know, hearing that last bit by the last lord was annoying, as he said *exactly* the same thing as the lord in the first world, except for the number of worlds and lords left," Ronald said. "You would think that the programmers of this game would give a bit of variety."

"Like what? Everything seems okay to me," Pixie responded.

"Well, they could mix things up. I don't know, maybe say, 'Thank you, but your journey is still dangerous with so many worlds left to conquer!' I mean, it just gets repetitive to hear."

"Just deal with it, okay?" Pixie said as she sighed.

They then entered the first door, and Pixie told Ronald, "Okay, there are a variety of power-ups in this world. So, you don't have to keep that bazooka."

Ronald then fired a shot and cleared out the landscape. "Why? I'm not giving this thing up unless I *have to*!" he responded.

As they travelled throughout all of the zones of this world, if Ronald hit a block with a power-up, he would just let that power-up pass him by, as he clearly was not interested in relinquishing his bazooka. While he used his weapon to clear out the landscape, he also allowed Pixie to use her fire power to defeat some enemies to ensure that she didn't complain that he was not letting her participate. This world also required them to go through a pyramid. After entering it, they had to follow a path, along which they encountered many monsters on their way to the goal. Here, Pixie and Ronald really worked as a team in defeating the monsters in what were tight quarters. After that, they reached the castle that used to belong to Lord Harinion, but was now occupied by Ultimo's minion Pindener. Pixie and Ronald met the servant of this castle at the front entrance, and listened to a message that was similar to that given by the previous two servants. After the formality, they went inside, where they used each of their power-ups to defeat the various guards, utilizing the platforms where necessary in order to avoid any dangerous areas. After entering Pindener's room, they heard Pindener say, "Well, I'm surprised that you two were able to get *this far*! But, this is where your journey ends! You will *not* defeat *me*!"

Ronald then asked Pixie, "So, what's the plan?"

"We'll both shoot at him!" Pixie replied.

Ronald then aimed his bazooka at Pindener, while Pixie aimed her fists at the overlord. They then fired at the same time, with both the fireballs and missile hitting Pindener right in the chest. "Noooooooooooooooooooooo!" he said, as he was about to blow up.

"Boy, they *really* don't know how to say anything else, do they?" Ronald said as Pindener blew up.

"I'm not getting into any arguments with you," Pixie replied. "Just play this game, and don't worry about what the characters are saying."

Pixie then picked up the question mark ball, and they were then immediately sent to the throne room. After the celebration, including hearing Harinion deliver the same speech as given by the previous two lords, they were then transported to the fourth world.

When they landed on the "Start" platform, Ronald immediately noticed that it was a water world. "Will we have to do a lot of swimming?" he asked.

"Yes, we will," Pixie said. "And, you will have to give up that bazooka in this world."

"Why? I *love* using this thing! It makes the battles *so* much easier!"

"Because it's not going to be effective in the Water World! The missiles fizzle out when they touch water!"

"We'll see. Let's go into the first door and find out!"

"Okay, but don't tell me that I didn't warn you!"

They then headed for the first door of this world, and promptly entered it. At the start, they were standing on a platform, and looked into the water below. They saw that it was very deep, and there was a path within the water that eventually led to the exit. Ronald immediately pulled out his bazooka, and fired a shot into the water. He saw that it didn't do anything, and tried to fire another shot. "What the...? Why isn't it working?" he asked, after a third shot fizzled out.

"I *told* you that it wouldn't work here, didn't I!"

"Well, you did...."

"And you didn't believe me, did you?!"

"No, I guess not," Ronald said, looking down embarrassed.

"Okay, so let's go find a different power-up, okay?"

They then entered the water and swam to look for blocks that contained power-ups. As they were swimming, Pixie used her fire power to get rid of the approaching monsters. After a while, they finally came across a group of blocks, and Ronald hit one, and saw that a candle came out. He grabbed it, and his clothing immediately changed, and he was now wearing red overalls, a red shirt, a red cap and red gloves. "Okay, well, at least I have *something* that'll work," he said.

The two of them continued along the path, and worked as a team, combining their power-ups to defeat their enemies. This strategy allowed them to efficiently and effectively reach the end point of the first zone quickly. For the remaining three zones in the world, they used the same strategy of combining their power-ups to defeat their enemies. More importantly, Ronald was learning to work together with Pixie, not to mention trust her. However, these three zones were really difficult, as both Ronald and Pixie had to avoid man-eating fish, fireball-throwing seaweed, and spiked fish that would require them to have to start the zone over if it touched them. Not only that, but this world required a great deal of swimming in order to reach the final platform. This tested their endurance, and both Ronald and Pixie found that their legs and arms were getting tired. After the gruelling voyage, they finally reached the overlord's castle, where they were met by a servant at the front door, and were given the same speech as delivered by the previous servants. The only new piece of information they received was that the water world used to be ruled by Lord Tanker, who had been overthrown by the evil minion of Ultimo Lord X, Lord Washreed. Once inside the castle, they worked as a team in defeating the guards that attacked them, and then reached Washreed's room. Once inside, they heard Washreed say, "So, you were able to make it this far! But your journey ends now! *I* will succeed where the others *failed*!"

Ronald and Pixie then went over their strategy, and surrounded Washreed. They then collectively used their fire powers to hit him in both the back and the chest, and thus defeating him in the process. Washreed yelled out in pain, "Nooooooooooooooooo!"

After he blew up, Ronald picked up the question mark ball, and were whisked away to Tanker's throne room, where they celebrated his return. After the formalities were finished, including participating in the celebration, Ronald and Pixie moved on to the next world.

As they arrived at the "Start" platform of the Forest World, Ronald immediately noticed how spooky this place was, even though he was just looking at the map. There were old trees without leaves on them, spooky-looking trees with leaves on them, and a lot of strange flowers. "This looks scary," he said to Pixie. "Are we going to be safe here?"

"This is the *second most* dangerous level in the entire game," Pixie said.

"What? You mean that what we just went through was easier than this?"

"Yes, that's right. You see, in those other levels, we didn't have to deal with ghosts, weird-looking flowers, and other creatures of the night."

"Like what?" Ronald asked, his tone cracking in fear.

"In this level, there are bats, spiders, and things that can suck the energy out of you if they touch you," Pixie replied.

"And there's no way we can skip this level?"

"No, not unless you want to go all the way back to the beginning of the first game."

"No, that's okay. Let's just get through this level quickly."

They then travelled along the path to the first door, and then entered it. Once inside, the setting was even darker and spookier than the one outside. Ronald hid behind Pixie, and asked her, "Will our Fire Power-Ups work here?"

"No, we will have to get Sword Power-Ups," she said. "For some reason, the ghosts and other monsters of this world are immune to fire, but not the sword. Until then, we have to just stomp on them."

As they moved forward, they encountered many monsters along the way. They had to stomp on any monsters that attacked them in order to defeat them. It took them a while before they finally came up to a series of blocks. As they approached these blocks, Pixie pointed to them and said, "The Sword Power-Ups are under these blocks. Just keep hitting them until it comes out."

Ronald hit the first of the blocks, and saw a shield coming out. "That's the Sword Power-Up! Grab it before it disappears," Pixie told him.

He did as he was told. When he picked up the power-up, his clothing changed, and he was now wearing knight's gear, including a knight's armour, helmet, a sword and a shield. "So, what does this mean?" he asked her.

"It means that you will be immune to a lot of different attacks," Pixie replied. "Now, let me get mine."

Pixie hit the next block, and it just produced a lot of coins. She then hit the adjacent block, and another shield came out. She picked it up, and her clothing changed as well, and was now wearing knight's gear, too. "Wait a minute," Ronald said. "How come you have the exact same costume as me? Shouldn't you be wearing women's armour?"

"The programmers of this game made the main characters men," she replied, rolling her eyes. "So that means I have no choice but to wear men's armour. That was also the case when I played it before. It's not like I have much of a choice."

"Oh. Well, let's keep moving. We've still got a lot of work to do."

They continued travelling through the forest, using their swords to defeat any ghosts and other forest creatures that tried to attack them. As they neared the end of the zone, they had to deal with the energy-sucking monsters that came out of nowhere to try and kill them. However, the monster had trouble attaching to their bodies, as both Pixie and Ronald were wearing metal suits. They then defeated the monster with their swords, and made it to the finish line, where they raised the flag to end the zone. They then entered the door that appeared.

The next three zones that they had to encounter were just as dangerous. However they didn't let go of their Sword Power-Ups, as it provided them with the best protection against the monsters. They were able to make it through all of the zones by looking after each other. They finally then approached the lord's castle. Here, they went through the same servant introduction as in the previous worlds, and found out that the rightful lord of this world was Lord Franko who had been deposed by Ultimo's minion Ghastly. They went through the castle, defeating the various guards that attacked along the way. Eventually, they reached Ghastly's room. They heard him saying, as they opened the door, "Oooohhhhh! You made it heeerrrreeee! But nooooo morrrre! You are finnnnissshhhed!"

"So, what's the strategy?" Ronald whispered to Pixie as they approached Ghastly.

"Same as the last lord, only this time we attack him with our swords," she replied.

They surrounded Ghastly, and then started stabbing him with their swords. After stabbing him three times in unison, he started staggering. As he was about to blow, he yelled out, "Nnnnnooooooo! I've beeeen deeeeffffeeeattttted!"

Ghastly then blew up, and Pixie picked up the question mark ball, which transported them to Lord Franko's throne room. They witnessed the same celebration seen in the previous worlds, and issued the same warning as given by the previous lords. After the formalities had finished, they were sent to the next world.

Almost instantaneously, they were standing on the "Start" platform of a tropical-looking world. However, the map showed that they were going to constantly be travelling on a beach, and would not have to navigate through any jungles. And while there was also a volcano in the middle of the territory, they were not required to travel through that zone. "All right! I can take these clothes off and get some sun!" Ronald said excitedly.

"Ronald, wait!" Pixie said. "This isn't a fun level! And, you won't even have a *chance* to lie down on the beach here! If you get distracted for even a *second*, you'll get ambushed!"

"By what?"

"Well, there are poison-shooting plants here. And, there are nasty crabs."

"Good thing you're here, otherwise I would have been screwed," Ronald replied gratefully.

They then followed the path to the first door, and entered it. Inside, they immediately encountered a beach that was anything but friendly. It was teeming with monsters, and didn't have any sunbathers or other visitors. And, it was really hot outside, which made Pixie and Ronald were very uncomfortable as they were still wearing their knights suits. As a result, they immediately headed to the set of blocks right in front of them to find Fire Power-Ups, which not only changed their clothing and hats to the red coloured attire that they had on earlier in the game, but also made things more bearable in dealing with the heat. They then proceeded to use their fire power to eliminate all of the enemies that they faced, and were able to finish this zone relatively quickly. For the next three zones, they continued to use their fire power to eliminate all of the monsters that attacked them, and then headed straight for the lord's castle after completing these zones.

At the entrance, they encountered another servant, but he said something different what from the previous servants had said. "Oh good!" he said.

"You have made it this far! The terrible thing, the deposition of the great Lord Relaxo, has happened. In his place is the minion of Ultimo Lord X, the evil lord Darkness! You must get rid of him this instance!"

When Pixie and Ronald were sent to the lobby, Ronald said, "Well, it was nice to hear something *different* for a change at the entrance to this castle."

"Don't worry about *that*," Pixie said. "We've still got to finish this game."

Once inside the castle, they encountered many guards, and worked together to defeat them. They then navigated the rest of the castle, and eventually reached the room of the lord Darkness. "So, you made it here!" he said to them. "Well, I will *not* let you move on! Your journey ends *now*! You will *not* get to Ultimo Lord X!"

The lord Darkness immediately attacked them before Ronald and Pixie could devise a strategy for the fight. They quickly jumped out of the way, and had to dodge him as he attacked them separately, and yet very quickly. Finally, Ronald decided to just aim his fists in the direction of Pixie, and told her, "Get out of the way, Pixie!"

Pixie rolled out of the way just as the fireballs were coming towards her, and they hit Darkness, who was just about to attack her. He cried out, "Noooooooooooooooooooooo! I've been hit! This wasn't the way it was supposed to be! I have failed you Ultimo Lord X! Now, you will have to fight on your own!"

Darkness blew up, and then Pixie picked up the question mark ball that appeared in his place. After being transported to Lord Relaxo's throne room, they participated in yet another celebration. However, this celebration was quite different compared to the ones Ronald and Pixie had encountered in previous worlds. This was due to the fact that the next world was Ultimo Lord X's castle, which used to be inhabited by King Relian before Ultimo had overthrown him. Also, the lords from the other worlds were in Lord Relaxo's castle to celebrate the defeat of Ultimo's minions. Lord Relaxo told Ronald and Pixie after the celebration, "Ronald and Pixie, thank you for returning me to my throne. All of the lords of this kingdom are now back in their rightful places. However the job is not yet done. King Relian is still in grave danger, as Ultimo Lord X still runs the king's castle. There are dangers in that castle, and you must be careful. On behalf of all the lords, I wish you good luck, and we know you two can do it!"

A cheer rang through the room, after which Ronald and Pixie were whisked away to the final world, where Ultimo Lord X currently reigned.

Upon arriving, they noticed that there were no zones here, or even a "Start" platform. Instead, it was just the castle which they had to travel through. The outside of the castle was spooky, and it definitely looked like it had been redesigned to look more evil and uninviting by Ultimo Lord X. When King Relian was in power, the outside was white in colour with blue spires on the towers. However, Ultimo Lord X had changed it to a dark black colour, and it now resembled the castles that evil beings lived in. The gate, which used to be white and draped in flowers, was now black, and creaked when opened, with the flowers replaced by thorns and weeds. The walls surrounding the castle also used to draped with flowers, but those, too, had been replaced with weeds and thorns. The courtyard, which used to be vibrant with flowers, gardens, statues of the king, and flowing fountains, was now littered with dead trees, weeds, broken statues, and gargoyle statues. "Well, I guess this is it," Ronald said. "The final level of this game."

"Yes, it is," Pixie said. "And this is the most dangerous part of the game at that! You really have to be careful here."

"So, exactly how *do* we get through this level? I don't see any 'Start' platforms, or any paths."

"We will have to navigate through the castle until we reach Ultimo Lord X's room."

"Oh, okay. Well, let's get going, then."

They went through the gate, and were welcomed by a servant of King Relian. "Oh, we are so happy that you made it here!" the servant said. "Ultimo Lord X has made a mess of this castle! It was once vibrant, but now it is filled with monsters! Please, be careful! And, please, defeat Ultimo Lord X!"

Pixie and Ronald then entered the castle, and were immediately attacked by the guards, which they defeated by using their fireballs. As they made their way through the lobby, they saw that the room was dark and spooky, and not in the vibrant Renaissance look that Relian had maintained. The walls were painted in black, and were covered with photos of Ultimo Lord X and his minion overlords that had been defeated in the previous worlds. Pixie and Ronald had to keep their guard high, as they had to battle with many monsters that tried to ambush them. They were able to defeat them by using their fireballs. They continued through the castle, defeating more monsters along the way, when they finally they reached the throne room. Ultimo Lord X was in the room, sitting on the throne, and was waiting for Ronald and Pixie. "So, you finally made it here!" he told them. "I didn't think you had the wherewithal to make it this far! I *surely* thought that the lords would beat you, if my monsters couldn't!"

"Where is the king?" Ronald asked him.

"He's in a cell in the dungeon, where he belongs! I guess *now* it's up to *me* to defeat you, since my minions couldn't do it. I still want to rule this kingdom!"

"You will *not* defeat *us*!" Pixie replied.

"We'll see about that! And good luck trying to use your Power Ups! They are useless against me!"

The battle then started, and Ronald and Pixie devised a plan where they would alternate who would distract Ultimo Lord X, and who would stomp him. It was decided that Ronald would first be the decoy, and Pixie would stomp first. Ronald then put the plan into action, and distracted Ultimo, saying, "Come on, Ultimo! Try and get me!"

"Fool! You are going to perish!" Ultimo Lord X replied.

He did his best to attack Ronald, but Ronald kept eluding him. With Ultimo Lord X's back turned, Pixie stomped on him. "Ow! Who was that! Oh, I see it was this guy!" he said as he turned around.

"I'm a *girl*!" Pixie replied, annoyed that there was nothing that she could do to change the script.

"Whatever! You will *die* for doing that to me!"

Ultimo Lord X then went after Pixie, and she made sure that he kept his eyes on her. With Ultimo Lord X distracted, Ronald stomped on him, and Ultimo now went after Ronald. With this strategy, they were able to get in the necessary six stomps, after which Ultimo was defeated. "Noooooooooooooooo! My plan has been foiled! I can't believe I've been defeated by these two!" yelled out Ultimo.

He then blew up, and the castle magically returned to its previous look. King Relian was released from the dungeon, and the kingdom was returned to normal. A celebration was held in the courtyard for the return of peace and normality to the kingdom, including the return of King Relian to his rightful throne. At the celebration, King Relian bestowed awards onto Pixie and Ronald. "Ronald, Pixie, I and the rest of the kingdom thank you for returning peace to our land, and for returning it to the state that it was in before Ultimo Lord X and his minions came in," King Relian told them. "Please accept these medals and wreaths as a reward for your bravery, and as a gift of gratitude from us."

"Thank you," Ronald said as he received his medal and wreath. "I wasn't expecting anything."

"This is *always* how the game ends," Pixie whispered to him, smiling as she accepted her gifts.

"You are very welcome," King Relian said, smiling back. "Now, I wish the two of you good luck on the rest of your journey."

As soon as the presentation was finished, he portal to the third game opened up, and Ronald and Pixie's clothing returned to their normal state. Ronald and Pixie then said their goodbyes to King Relian and the rest of the citizenry that had gathered in the courtyard. They then entered the portal, and journeyed on to the third game.

CHAPTER SIX

When they exited the portal, Ronald and Pixie found themselves in the lobby of a dance hall. It resembled the Downtown Calgary Concert Hall's lobby, though this hall had different features. The stage was located straight ahead, which would be where Ronald would have to go and dance in order to complete the necessary tasks of this game. There was also a nightclub located to the right of them, where some of the dancers and spectators went to either to enjoy the night or in some cases, try and find a date. The nightclub also contained pool tables, dartboards, pinball machines, a dance floor for those that just wanted to dance, and a lounge for those that just wanted to go there for a meal. To the left of them was a practice facility, which contained its own set of platforms that allowed in-game players to practice their dancing prior to starting the game on the stage. The dance hall was located in the downtown area of a city, though the exact city was unknown, and was situated near hotels and restaurants so that in-game tourists who wanted to see the sights of the city, including the dance battles of the stage, could do so. Sometimes, the dancers and the spectators at the dance hall would also eat at those restaurants if they didn't want to go to a bar for food.

Ronald looked around the lobby of this place, and said, "This looks like we're in the Downtown Calgary Concert Hall."

"What's that?" Pixie asked, confused as to what real-world place he was referring to.

"It's a performing-arts theatre in Downtown Calgary. There are a lot of shows that are held there."

"Oh. In Video Game City, we don't really have a real arts scene because of the transient population. I mean, I don't think there are enough permanent residents there to *have* a thriving arts scene."

"That's too bad. While the arts scene in Calgary still isn't the greatest, there are still many wonderful performances that take place. And, the booming population over the past ten years has led to its increased development."

"Well, the issue never really has come up for us because of the reasons that I just stated."

Ronald nodded his head, and then looked around again, and asked Pixie, "So, am I home now? Because if we are, I can just hop on the LRT and take some buses home. You know, it's quite awesome because there's a bus stop right near my house."

"No, you aren't home yet!" Pixie responded as she looked at her phone. "Does this Downtown Calgary Concert Hall have a nightclub located to its right, and a practice facility with dancing platforms situated to its left? And is it located near hotels and restaurants?"

"Well, I know there are a couple of restaurants located nearby. And there is an upscale hotel that is fairly close to it. But, it *certainly* isn't located *anywhere* near the Calgary nightclubs, and it *definitely* doesn't have a practice facility with dancing platforms."

"That means that you're nowhere *near* your real-world home, then. In fact, I don't even know what city we're actually in. I'm looking up the information of this game, and I'm not getting any details about the specific physical location of this game. It just says we're in a dance hall that has a stage straight ahead, a nightclub to the right, a practice facility to the left, and that it is located close to some hotels and nightclubs."

She then continued scanning the phone, and added, "Huh. That's funny. This is also a tourist destination for people from Video Game City and the *other* games. I didn't know that you could travel *here* without repercussions."

Pixie then continued looking and said, "Not only that, but it's one of the 'tourist games,' whereby people from all over the video game world can go to if they don't want to take their vacation in Video Game City. And, these 'tourist games' are where people from Video Game City go for vacation. I didn't know there were such things as 'tourist games!'"

"Well, looks like you learned something new."

Ronald then looked at his and Pixie's clothing, and saw that nothing was changing. He said to her, "Well, if our clothes didn't change, and I'm not home yet, then what game are we in?"

"It's something called Dance Party 10," Pixie responded.

"Oh no! Not *that* game!" Ronald said with a look of fear on his face.

"Why? What's wrong with it?"

"I hate the music in this game!"

"You hate dance and pop music? I think you're the first person that hates both of those."

"Well, I can tolerate good dance music, but *not* the 'stupid dance' that's in this game! And I absolutely *hate* pop music, *especially* teen and bubblegum pop! And I know that this game contains *that type* of pop music!"

"Ronald," Pixie said, rolling her eyes, "you have to play this game whether you like it or not. Remember, you have to beat all of the games in order to get home. And if you refuse to play this game, you'll be stuck in it *forever*. Do you want to go home, or do you want be stuck in this game just because it contains music that you dislike?"

"I want to go home," Ronald said begrudgingly.

"Then that means that you'll have to suck it up and deal with everything that this game contains, including the music!"

"So, do I still have to use dancing platforms in this game? Because in the real world, we have to play it using those special platforms. And, since I'm actually *in* the game, I'm not sure if there's anything different or not."

"I *think* you still have to use platforms. I've never been to this game before, so we'll have to find out. Now let's head to the stage area."

They then walked straight ahead to where the stage area was. It had two dance platforms that were set up in the exact same format as seen in the real world. It also contained a DJ booth, where the DJ would play the songs that the players would have to dance to during the competitions. Surrounding the stage in a circle was the seating area, which was six levels high, and allowed the spectators to sit and watch each of the duels. "Looks like you *do* have to use the platforms," Pixie said, pointing to the centre of the stage.

"So, what exactly *do* I have to do in this game?" Ronald asked.

Pixie then checked her phone, and said, "Well, it looks like you have to win 10 duels."

"Duels? What do you mean by duels?"

"Well, those platforms there are where you have to play the game, right? Well, you have to battle against another person in a dance competition, and that is called a duel. You have to win 10 of those in order to open up the portal to the next game."

"So, do I have to beat *you* 10 times?"

Scanning her phone, Pixie said, "No, I'm not even allowed to participate in this game."

She then looked up, and added, "I'm only allowed to sit in the stands. But, if you want to take a break from dancing, you just simply get off of the platforms. In that case, I'm allowed to answer any questions you may have."

"Now, how do these duels work? Because there's only me, and yet there are two platforms," Ronald asked.

Pixie looked at her phone again, and then looked up and said, "Well, you'll be competing mostly against real-life players, and they'll appear as holograms on the platform that you're *not* on. However, they won't recognize who you really are. On their screens, you'll appear as one of the in-game characters."

"Oh. So that means if one of my friends is playing, they won't even know that I'm trapped in this world?"

"No, they won't. It says here that this game has a one-player mode whereby the real-world players can compete against the in-game players."

"Another question: How exactly do I start these duels? I don't see *anyone* here, and this place looks dead, save for that DJ there."

"I think you have to just stand on one of the platforms. But ask around just to be safe."

"I'll go ask the DJ."

"Okay, I'll go find a seat in the stands before they fill up."

Pixie went up into the stands to find a place to sit and watch the duels, while Ronald went up to the DJ. As he approached, the DJ asked him, "Yes? Can I help you?"

"How do I get this game to start?" Ronald asked him.

"Just stand on one of the platforms, and that will inform me that you want to start a duel. I will then check my screen here to see what song the real-world player has chosen, and I'll load it up."

"And, how exactly do I play the game here? Because if I'm standing on the platform, I won't see the arrows."

"You *will* see the arrows. They'll be appearing in front of you, on a virtual screen."

"Oh, okay. Just one more question: Why is this place so dead? You're the only other person I see here."

"Well, there are various places where this game is being held. The VGG sent you here because they wanted to ensure that you weren't waiting for hours, or even days, for the other in-game characters to finish their turns before you could get started on your task."

"Oh, okay. Thanks."

"You're welcome."

Meanwhile, Pixie took a seat in the front row, so that she would get a good view of the action. Ronald then went up to the left platform, and stepped onto it. Suddenly, the lights changed to strobing lights like the ones seen inside of a nightclub. Then, everyone heard, "WELCOME TO DANCE PARTY 10! PLEASE WAIT WHILE THE GAME LOADS!"

Scared and confused, he turned around to the DJ and asked him, "What's happening?!"

The DJ yelled back, "You see, when you stand on one of the platforms, the game starts up, and begins to load. Don't worry, it always does that at the start of the game. That's the only time you'll hear it, unless you decide to leave for a while. Also, you will notice that the stands are now starting to fill up."

Ronald then turned back around, and looked towards the stands. He saw Pixie sitting there right in front of him, and waved to her. She waved back, and smiled. He then looked around the hall, and did see that people were coming in to watch the duel, after which he took a deep breath. He then heard from the PA system, "SONG CHOSEN! GET READY TO DANCE!"

After a few moments, a hologram of a 13-year-old girl appeared to his right, and this girl was from Frankfurt, Germany in the real world. As it turned out, she was a dancer, and had dreams of one day becoming a professional dancer. Ronald also noticed that she had a look of confidence on her face. The PA system then blurted out, "Ready? Set! DANCE!"

The duel began, and arrows appeared in front of both Ronald and the hologram of the girl. It was a really fast-paced song, and Ronald had a lot of trouble keeping up with the arrows. It was so bad that Ronald didn't even pay attention to the song, he just wanted to get in some hits. However, the girl had no issues keeping up, and looked like she was having fun playing the game as well. About halfway through the duel, he was already hearing boos from the audience, and Pixie had a concerned look on her face. She felt bad for Ronald, and wished she could do something, but knew that she couldn't. Ronald easily lost this duel, and the crowd continued to boo him for his lacklustre performance, while cheering the 13-year-old girl for her victory. She jumped up and down in excitement, and even said, "Wow! That was easy! And I chose *hard*. They must have chosen an *idiot* for this game!"

Ronald was clearly upset at this, as he started yelling at the girl. "She can't hear you!" the DJ yelled. "On her screen, it displays something else, and that means that she can say whatever she wants to you, and she won't have to face any consequences."

"Great!" Ronald mumbled to himself.

After about five minutes, the PA system blurted out, "SONG CHOSEN! GET READY TO DANCE!"

A hologram of a 27-year-old man from Edmonton then appeared on the right platform, who looked worried about whether or not he could win the duel. They then heard, "Ready? Set! DANCE!"

This song was a little easier for Ronald. However it was a teen pop song, which did not make him happy. Making things worse was that it was one of his least favourite songs of all time. In spite of this, Ronald kept tried to maintain focus on the arrows, and made sure that he didn't miss anything. Meanwhile, his opponent was having a lot of trouble, and just wanted this song to be over so that he could get away from this. As it turned out, the guy was at a friend's party, and he had been forced to play despite protesting. Inside the dance hall, the audience was noticing Ronald's effort, and cheered him on while booing the other guy. Ronald won the duel, and raised his hands in celebration, although there was a shocked look on his face that he had actually won. The crowd cheered and celebrated with him. However, Ronald's jubilation ended when the DJ suddenly interrupted the cheer by saying, "The winner by disqualification, Marty Linden!"

"WHAT?! WHAT ON EARTH IS THAT?!" Ronald yelled in anger as he turned around towards the DJ, and now had a look of fury on his face.

With the audience booing the decision, Pixie became worried about what Ronald would do next. The DJ told Ronald, "You didn't show any of the right emotions."

Ronald then came off of the platform and stormed towards the DJ booth. "WHAT DO YOU MEAN THE 'RIGHT EMOTIONS!' WHAT THE HECK?! I WON THAT DUEL FAIR AND SQUARE!" he yelled as he walked towards the DJ.

"You didn't look like you were having fun, and therefore you've been disqualified."

"WHAT?! THERE'S NOTHING IN THE RULES OF THIS GAME THAT SAYS YOU HAVE TO LOOK LIKE ANYTHING!" Ronald screamed and pointed, getting into the DJ's face. "I KNOW, BECAUSE I PLAYED THIS GAME IN THE REAL WORLD AT A FRIEND'S HOUSE!"

"Hey!" the DJ replied. "You're no longer *in* the real world anymore! You're in the video game world! This is *my* dance hall, and *I* make the rules! Either you follow them, or else I will send you back to the first game so fast that you won't know what hit you! You will wish that you *never* got into my face like this! And don't think I don't have the power to do that, because The VGG has given me that power!"

Pixie then jumped out of her seat and ran onto the stage, and raced towards Ronald. She got in between him and the DJ, and pushed Ronald back, trying to restrain him. "Ronald, just cool down, okay?!" she said as she pulled him back. "We don't want the people from the first two games to get annoyed with you because they have to deal with you again!"

"But that's not fair!" Ronald replied. "How can he just do that to me?!"

"Look, you have to *remember* that you're no longer in *your* world! You're in *our* world, and you have to *follow a different set of rules*!"

She then yanked him outside the dance hall and said, "Look, you need to cool down, okay?! Let's just go for a walk."

"Fine," Ronald said with a look of disgust.

They then walked for a while, with Ronald still seething about how he had been disqualified. He soon started to realize that, unlike everything that he had been telling his family and Dawna, it seemed like that the people in the video game world may not in fact treat others right, and may not even actually respect him. He started rationalizing that the only reason as to why he was receiving those positive and respectful messages from the games that he had been playing was because the programmers designed it that way so that people would actually buy the games. There was never any thought given to the possibility that the video game people may not have been thinking the same positive things, but said them because they were forced to say them. Suddenly, as they were talking, Ronald let it slip out to Pixie that he had been playing video games because of his depression from being laid off, and she said, "*That* explains *everything* that just happened in there."

"What do you mean?" Ronald asked.

"You see, we've seen people play video games because of depression before. Remember those screens that those archaeologists were talking about in the first game?"

"Yeah."

"Well, I remember travelling to some games and continuously seeing through the screens the same depressed-looking people through them, as if they were hiding something and using the games as an escape from their problems."

"It wasn't me, was it?" Ronald asked, worried that Pixie might suddenly remember him from when he was playing his video game systems over the past five months.

"No, it wasn't you," Pixie replied. "There have been a lot of other people. For example, one of them was a girl. I think she was in a really bad relationship, but couldn't end it because her parents wouldn't let her. You see, this guy she was dating was someone that the parents had set her up with because he had a *ton* of money!"

"How do you know that?"

"Well, she kept talking about it, as she was playing a lot of games that had microphone support, and she had left her microphone on."

"Did you get to know where she was from?"

"No, that was a piece of information that she kept to herself."

"Oh. And, how does this relate to me?"

"Well, she felt that the only escape she had was through the video games, thinking the exact same things that *you* have been thinking. That we respect the real-world people, that we don't put them down, and that we are *always* their friends. But, as you've seen, that's not *always* the case."

"Yeah, I've noticed that."

"And, you see that sometimes, we actually talk *badly* about them when the games are off."

"Yeah, I've noticed that, too."

"So, from what I have seen prior to that outburst, you're actually a pretty good guy, and you actually *do* care about others. But, it seems like that layoff has really gotten to you, because otherwise you wouldn't have had that outburst that you did."

"Well, it's not *just* the layoff."

"Oh? What else could there be?"

"You see, at my job, I used to have a great boss. Someone who treated everyone with respect, and always cared about others. If you had any concerns, his door was always open. And, he would come out of his office to talk to the other staff just to see how they were doing. He even took the time to get to know us personally. And a few times, if we were short-staffed because of vacations or people calling in sick, he would fill in wherever we needed help. Then, he retired, and I was left in charge temporarily, and I kept running things in the same fashion as he did, because *if it ain't broke, don't fix it*. Then, at they end of last year, meaning 2012 in the real world, the executives hired someone else to replace my former boss, and she was a horrible person. She treated everyone poorly, she bullied them, and she *never* had a nice thing to say to *anyone*. Not only that, she was *never* willing to listen to *anyone's* concerns. She never even *tried* to get to know *anyone*. Her door was *always* closed, and even locked at times, so that no one would bother her with *any* questions or concerns. She always threatened to fire everyone, even if she didn't have a good reason to do so, and made us stay late just because she had the power to do so, even hiring a spy to ensure that we complied with that order. As it turned out, she wanted us out so that she could only work with her friends. She made sure to set everything up right so that she could do exactly that. And, I also found out that she has never tried to make any new friends since finishing university, meaning that all of her friends came from her high school and university days. Also, from what I've been told, she has *always* treated her employees and co-workers like that, at least the ones that were not her friends, at all of the other companies that she worked at. And she's *always* shown a preference to only working with her friends, and has *always* treated her friends better than everyone else."

"Oh? How did you find out all of this information?"

"As it turns out, one of her former employees worked for one of my former clients. And that person quit because they just couldn't deal with my old boss' abuse anymore. That person told us all of this."

"And, I guess this old boss of yours had final say over who would work for her, and laid you and the other staff off so that she could hire her friends."

"Exactly. And now, those people are making a complete mockery of all of the hard work that we did there."

"How so?"

"Because, they're rude to clients, and they won't help them out when they have any questions. Moreover, they don't make very good proposals to the clients, and the proposals are *far* below the quality that our previous boss would have ever approved of. In fact, they're written so poorly that the clients reject them outright, and now are looking for other IT providers. And, these new people that my old boss hired, and even my old boss, are spending more time planning parties than working. From what I've heard, they're also always on their personal social media accounts, or on the

Internet doing non-work-related things. Some even waste time talking and texting on their cell phones all day."

"How do you know all of this if you don't work there anymore, and if all you've been doing is playing video games?"

"One of my friends that works in another department is still working there, and I've talked to him a few times when I take a break. And he is not happy. He said that he has noticed his workload going down like crazy. He's even more frustrated because he feels like that the executives seem oblivious as to the real reason for the sudden loss of business. And now his department, Consulting, as well as the IT Department are being blamed and scrutinized. I mean, a lot of the employees have gone to talk to the executives to say that Marketing is causing all of the problems. But the executives just brush them off, saying that the problem is either that the clients now need something different from what currently Pacific provides, or that Consulting and IT are the ones driving away business because of how they're treating the clients."

"Oh, and I bet that when you got disqualified, those memories came back, and you took it out on the DJ."

"Yeah. I mean, if he just knew what I had to go through...."

"Okay, okay. You know what? When you feel you're ready to get back onto that stage, let him know about all of this, okay? But, not right now. You clearly need to practice, as it's quite obvious that you have to get used to the faster songs before you start duelling again. *Especially* if you don't want another teenage girl making fun of you!"

"But the songs, I just don't like that style of music."

"You know what? Maybe you can come to an agreement with the DJ. As I was restraining you, I noticed that he had some songs on his monitor that you might like."

"Is that even allowed. The *last* thing I want to do is to have to start all over from the adventure game."

"That's why you have to talk to the DJ. If The VGG gave him control, that means that he's allowed to do whatever he wants in this game."

"Okay, then. I'll ask him."

"In the meantime, let's just get some sleep. It's better if you're fully rested and calm. We don't want you to start duelling so soon after that argument. The DJ will especially need *more* time than you."

"Okay. So, where do we go?"

Pixie then led them to a hotel near the dance hall. She paid for the room, and they then went up and got some sleep.

The next day, Ronald and Pixie went back to the dance hall, but they did not go to the stage area. Instead, they turned left and went to the practice facility, where the dancing platforms were set up in the style of an arcade. In the facility, there were also some of the in-game characters that were just playing for fun. When Ronald and Pixie entered, everyone stopped what they were doing and just stared at them in silence. Then, one of the female dancers asked, "So, are you here to mouth off at *us* as well?"

"No, just here to practice," Ronald replied.

"Sure, that's it," she replied sarcastically. "You big baby! You should realize that right now, you're in *our* world, and not whatever world you *came from*! You *cannot* mouth off at us like you did yesterday!"

"It wasn't *you* that I got mad at," Ronald told her. "I got mad at the DJ."

"But, the DJ is one of our *friends*!" a male dancer responded. "And when you mouth off at one of our friends, you mouth off at all of *us*!"

"Look, if you understood my past, you would understand why I reacted the way I did, okay?" Ronald replied, getting angry. "And besides, none of this concerns you. The only people that this concerns are me and the DJ."

"Whatever," the female dancer said. "You have to realize that in this game, it's also about having fun, and not *just* whether or not you hit all of the arrows on time."

Ronald just snorted, and then he and Pixie proceeded to one of the platforms. Ronald loaded up the game, and made sure that he chose a one-player practice game. He made sure that he picked a dance song that he actually liked, and then started the game. While he did his best to keep up, he struggled with it, and ended up losing the game halfway through it. As Ronald became frustrated, Pixie did her best to calm him down, and told him to just try it again. Ronald did what she said, but continued to have problems with the game. "Dang it! This thing is *impossible* to beat!" he said, growing even more frustrated with his lack of success.

"Look, Ronald, you have to calm down," Pixie said. "You just need to keep trying until you get it. Otherwise, you'll be stuck here *forever*!"

"I don't want that! I want to get home!"

"Well, then, use *that* as motivation."

"I'm *trying*! But, I just can't do it!"

"Well, run that song again, and then maybe we'll be able to see what you're doing wrong."

Ronald loaded up the song again, and he struggled yet again. "Dang it! What am I doing *wrong*?!" he said, now very angry.

"You know, it seems like you're hitting the steps when they're in the hit zone," said another female dancer. "You have to hit them *just before* they get there."

Ronald turned around, surprised that one of the dancers was actually giving him advice. "What? You're actually *willing* to help me?" he asked her.

"Yeah," she said. "I've had issues with this DJ as well, so I know *exactly* how you feel. I mean, some of the other DJs in the game understand that you're just trying to focus on making the hits. They know that you're probably having fun on the inside, but just not showing it on the outside.

But this guy, he's *really* strict. He expects you to *show* that you're having fun. With this guy, sometimes, you just have to fake it to win the duels."

"Well, there you go," Pixie said. "I didn't even know that because this is the first time *ever* that I've been to this game. So, I wouldn't have been able to help you out at *all*."

"Do you mind if *I* coach him?" the dancer asked Pixie. "He *needs* someone that has experience with this DJ, and knows the songs inside-out."

"Sure, go ahead," Pixie told her.

Ronald looked to Pixie and whispered to her, "Is this allowed? Wouldn't this be considered cheating or taking a shortcut?"

"No," Pixie whispered back, shaking her head. "First of all, this is practice. And second, *she* came to *you*. You didn't ask for help from anyone but *me*. She offered, and therefore it's not against the rules."

Pixie then moved aside, thus allowing the dancer to stand beside Ronald. She then said to him, "Now, load up that song again. Oh, and by the way, my name is Marissa."

"I'm Ronald," he told her. "I really appreciate this."

"You're very welcome," Marissa replied. "I don't mind helping others out."

Ronald smiled, and then loaded up the song again, and attempted to dance to it again. However, he was still having trouble keeping up. At the end of the song, Marissa pointed out to Ronald everything that he was doing wrong, explained to him what he needed to do to correct these errors. Ronald took her advice to heart, which showed as he was more successful in the next attempt. After a few more tries, he mastered the song, and went on to the next song. Using Marissa's coaching and advice, he was able to master all of the songs in the game, after which a look of relief came across his face. *"Finally!* I can go in there and at least *try* to get out of this game!" he said, with a sense of calm.

"That's great! It took awhile, but you're ready now," Marissa said. "To make sure that you're okay, I'll be sitting in the stands next to...."

Marissa then turned to Pixie and asked her, "What's your name?"

"Pixie," she replied.

"Yeah, I'll sit next to Pixie," Marissa said. "*Every* competitor should have their coach near them for guidance."

"Is that allowed?" Ronald asked. "Wouldn't *that* be considered cheating or taking a shortcut?"

"No," Marissa said, shaking her head. "I've seen *plenty* of coaches sit in the stage area with this DJ. He doesn't mind that."

"Well, in that case, thanks," Ronald said. "I would actually prefer that, as I don't know exactly *what* is going to happen in there."

He then got off of the platform, and the three of them headed to the stage area so that Ronald could make another attempt at the duels. After they entered, Ronald went to talk to the DJ, while Marissa and Pixie went to the seating area to find a place to sit in the front row, right in front of the platforms. When he got to the DJ booth, Ronald told him, "Hey, dude, I'm sorry about what happened yesterday."

"Well, I accept your apology," the DJ replied. "But, you should know that I don't tolerate that type of behaviour!"

Ronald then went on to explain why he had reacted the way he did, including his layoff, and how he was treated by Betty just before his layoff. He also told the DJ about his depression, and how he had become even more upset when he learned that his old company was going down due to the way Betty and her new team were running the Marketing Department. After Ronald had finished, the DJ said, "Whoa! That explains a lot! I should apologize too for the way I handled things! I should have told you *before* you went onto the platform about my rules, so that I did not strike a nerve with you! If I had known, I *certainly* would have done things differently to ensure that you didn't get so upset."

"I accept your apology as well," Ronald said. "I think that maybe we should have talked a bit more before the duels started yesterday."

"Yeah, that's for sure. I mean, I think we just got off on the wrong foot."

"Yeah. So, is there a way that maybe we can talk about the songs that you play?"

"Sorry, I can't do that. This game is strictly designed to play the song that the user wants, not what the in-game characters want."

"Oh, okay," Ronald said, disappointed. "Well, then I'll just go to the platforms."

Ronald then headed to the platforms, and then stepped onto the right platform. He waved to Marissa and Pixie, who waved back, and then waited patiently for the game to start. Soon after, the introductory message blared through the PA system: "WELCOME TO DANCE PARTY 10! PLEASE WAIT WHILE THE GAME LOADS!"

By now, the seats had begun to fill up, and the lighting changed to the nightclub-style strobe lights. Then, he heard, "SONG CHOSEN! GET READY TO DANCE!"

On the other platform, a hologram of a 23-year-old woman came, and she was from Calgary. Ronald looked, and he thought he recognized her from one of his trips on the LRT, but he wasn't too sure. After a few moments, they all suddenly heard, "Ready?" and he at once returned his focus to the screen.

Then, "Set! DANCE!" blared through the PA system, and the duel began.

It was a rock 'n' roll song, and a wide grin came across Ronald's face, as he finally heard a song that he liked. As it turned out, the woman next to him was part of an aspiring rock 'n' roll band, and she wanted to dance to the music as practice for her gigs. Ronald used the training that he had received from Marissa to perfection here, as he was able to make all of the hits, while the woman really struggled dancing to the song. Even the crowd noticed, and cheered loudly for Ronald. Pixie and Marissa were also very impressed, not to mention being happy for him because he was doing so well. Ronald easily won the duel, as the woman was kicked out halfway through because her score was so low that it didn't even register. "And the winner is, Ronald Charlton!" the DJ said from his booth.

Ronald raised his arms in the air in celebration, and the audience cheered. However, Ronald stayed on the platform, and got ready for the next duel. Everyone could see that while Ronald was relaxed, he was also completely focused in his mission to win this game. And Ronald was determined to defeat the rest of his opponents. And the determination showed, as he easily won the next duel, and the remaining eight to finish his task. It also helped that the songs that the real-world players chose were ones that Ronald liked, especially the rock and country ones, as well as a dance song that he actually liked.

At the end of the final duel, Ronald raised his hands in celebration, and then got off of the platform, and bowed to the crowd. Just a few moments later, the portal to the fourth game opened up, and Pixie and Marissa got up from their seats and went onto the stage. Ronald first went to talk to the DJ and say his goodbyes to him. Then, as Pixie stood in front of the portal, Ronald went to talk to Marissa one more time before they left for the next game. He told Marissa, "I want to thank you for helping me with this game. I couldn't have done it without your help."

"You're very welcome," Marissa replied. "And, if you play this game in the real world, I hope you never forget me."

"I won't. I mean, I could have been stuck here *forever* if it weren't for you."

"I'm just glad I was able to help you on your journey."

"So, I guess you can't come with us, can you?"

"No, I can't. You see, unlike Pixie, I'm not a traveller. Otherwise, I'd have to leave this game and head to Video Game City to get permission to become a traveller as well. And, unlike Pixie, I have no intention of becoming one."

"Why not?"

"Because I like it in this game. It's fun, and there's *always* something to do. My friends are also here. And, I don't have to worry about only being an observer in this game. I can participate whenever I want, wherever I want. Furthermore, I can interact with the tourists that come here, even those that have come from the other games! If you're a traveller, you can only interact with characters from other video games in certain circumstances. I also don't have to leave home for long periods of time. If I'm tired, I can just go home to relax for as long as I need to."

Pixie then approached Ronald and grabbed him by the arm, saying to him, "Ronald, we have to get going. We still have got a lot of games to get through."

"Okay," Ronald said to her.

Pixie then went back to the front of the portal. Ronald then turned to Marissa and said, "Well, I've got to get going."

"Okay, bye. Good luck the rest of the way," Marissa said.

"Thanks."

Ronald then walked towards Pixie, and said to her, "Well, let's continue on."

"Okay, let's go," Pixie said.

They then went through the portal, and continued on their journey.

CHAPTER SEVEN

When they got out of the portal, Ronald and Pixie found themselves in a hockey arena. "Where *are* we?" Ronald asked. "I mean, I know we're inside a hockey arena, but what city are we in?"

"I don't think that we're in any particular city," Pixie replied as she looked at her phone for information on the game they were now in. "It just seems to be a general hockey arena."

"So, then, what kind of game is this?"

"From what I see here, it's a game called Hockey Powerhouse 2013."

"Hey! I have that game! I've played it a *lot*!"

Pixie looked up and said, "Great, I guess. At least you know the general rules of this game. However, you don't know what the task is in order to open up the next portal."

Pixie then looked back at her phone to search for what tasks Ronald had to complete in this game in order to open up the portal to the fifth game. She found the necessary information and said, "Aha! I found it! It looks like you have to win the League and International Cups in either the Season or the Franchise Mode of this game."

"Well, I've done it before," Ronald said.

"But, have you done it at International Star level? Because that's what you have to do here."

"Yes, I have."

"Without cheats or shortcuts?"

"Without cheats or shortcuts."

"Okay, well, you should be okay, then. So, what do you want to do? The reason I ask is because it looks like I have to enter in the information here."

"I'd like to do it in Season mode because that'll be easier. It will allow me to concentrate on just playing the game, and not having to worry about any of the front-office stuff."

Pixie entered in the information, then asked, "What types of rules do you want?"

"Keep the regular league rules, but don't allow trades," Ronald said. "I don't want my team to get screwed up by the CPU to the point that I have to start this game over again."

"How could that happen?"

"Sometimes, the CPU makes stupid trades that causes a team's roster to get messed up. Like trading superstars for lousy players, which turns a contending team into one that misses the playoffs."

"Oh, okay. Well, I don't play sports, and I don't like sports. Therefore, this is the first time I've ever *been* to a sports game. So, I wouldn't know anything about how these things work."

"Really? There are lots of people in the real world that don't play sports, and even hate them, and *still* go to the games to watch."

Pixie just laughed at that. She then entered in the details for the rules, and then asked Ronald, "What team do you want to play as?"

"My hometown team, of course!" Ronald replied.

"That Calgary thing you keep talking about?"

"Yes."

"Let me see where it is."

Pixie found the Calgary team, and entered it in. Suddenly, the arena changed to the look-and-feel of the Calgary Arena, including the ceiling and the jumbotron. Ronald looked around with a confused look on his face, and asked Pixie, "Huh? What just happened here? This place suddenly looks like the inside of the Calgary Arena!"

"Calgary Arena?" Pixie asked, looking up. "What's that?"

"It's the hockey arena for the professional hockey team located in Calgary."

"Oh."

Pixie then also looked around the arena, and said, "I don't know what happened. This is really odd. *None* of this happened in the first three games."

She went back to the phone, and saw that she had to create Ronald and put him on the Calgary team before he could play the game. She then asked him for all of his personal details and physical attributes, as asked by the game. Finally, she asked him for what ratings he would like, and Ronald, of course, asked to be a top-notch player on the team. She entered in the information, selected his team as the Calgary team, after which a message appeared on the screen that said, "Player created and placed on the Calgary team!"

Pixie then got out of the Create Player screen and returned to the Season Mode's main menu. Out of nowhere, gym bags with equipment appeared in Ronald's hands, and he just looked at them. "What are *these*?" he asked as he lifted them up.

"I think that's your equipment," Pixie said. "It seems that after I created you and placed you on the Calgary team, it gave you your equipment. And that seems to be what you have to wear in order to participate in this game."

"Oh, okay. Are *you* allowed to play in this game?"

"Probably, *if* I created myself. Are girls allowed to play in this game?"

"Well, this hockey game doesn't have any in-game female players, nor is there a way to create them."

"Oh, okay. Well, I guess that means that I'm not allowed to participate, then. And since I don't play sports, I wouldn't have wanted to participate anyway."

"Oh, okay. Although, it would have been fun to play side-by-side."

"I think I would have been a spectator for most of the games, since I *know* I would be terrible at this game," Pixie replied, laughing. "So, it would have been a moot point anyway."

"You could have made yourself into a superstar," Ronald replied. "That's what *I* did."

"But, when you're in *this* world, you still have to know how to *play* the sports!"

"Oh, well then, that would be a problem for you. In Calgary, I used to play in a recreational hockey league until I was laid off. I stopped playing because I felt embarrassed that I was unemployed."

"You see? You have played hockey before, and I haven't. So even though I can make myself a great player, that still doesn't hide the fact that I'm terrible at the game."

"Yeah. So, if you're not playing with me, what happens if I need your help?"

"You can yell 'pause,' and I can help you out with a few things, such as menu items. But if you need help with other things like strategy, I would not be of much help. I think this game has coaches, and they are the only ones that can make the in-game decisions. Be mindful that this game is different compared to when you're sitting and playing at home, where you have control over everything related to the team."

Ronald nodded and said he understood. He then asked, "Where will you be watching this game, then?"

"I'll sit in one of the seats here."

"Oh, so you'll be somewhere in the stands?"

"Yes, that's where I'll be."

"Okay, well, I guess I'll see you after the whole season is over."

"Okay, bye. Good luck with this."

Ronald then proceeded down the hallway towards the locker rooms, while Pixie made her way to the stands to take a seat. Ronald walked around for a while searching for the locker room. After getting lost, he finally asked the arena staff where the locker room was, and they pointed him in the right direction. After finally finding the locker room, he entered and saw that it had the logo of the Calgary team on the floor, walls, and in the stalls. In addition to the players' stalls, it also had a coach's office, stalls for each of the players, as well as a hallway leading to the team's showers. Each stall except for one contained the player's jersey, as well as their equipment. Ronald guessed that the empty stall was his, and went to it to put his equipment away. As he did that, he continued looking around the locker room, and saw some of the players filing in. He also saw the coach coming out of his office, and Ronald figured that this would be a good time to introduce himself to all of his new teammates, as well as the coach. He then walked towards them, and held out his hand, and said, to them, "Hi, I'm Ronald Charlton. I'm your new teammate, and I hope we get along really well this season."

Some of the players shook his hand, as did the coach. Then, one of the players, Hank Poloy recognized him, and said, "Wait a minute! Ronald Charlton?! Don't you live in Calgary?"

"Yeah, I do," Ronald said. "How do you know where I live?"

"Because, we see you through the screens all the time when you're playing this game!" another player, Greg Watson, said. "In fact, don't you usually choose *Franchise Mode* so that you can deal with all of the front-office issues? I even remember you had traded *me* once for some draft picks!"

"So *that's* where I know you from!" a third player, Pete Peterson, said. "I *thought* you looked familiar! And, to further answer your question, sports games have a location description underneath the screens of each respective player, similar to what you see on the sports stations on TV."

"But, what are you doing *here*?" Poloy asked. "Why aren't you on your couch playing?"

Ronald then went on to explain how he had lost his job, the ensuing depression, and how he had been transported to the video game world via a lightning strike on his video game console. He explained that The VGG had ruled that he had to play a number of video games in a certain order, only known to them, before he could get home, and that the only way to advance was to beat the current game, after which the portal to the next game would open up. Only when he had successfully completed the final unknown game would the portal home open up, and so he was stuck in the video game world until he had completed all of the required games. At the end of this, the coach said, "So, that explains why the trades were turned off. You want to be sure that 'management' doesn't mess around with your quest to get back home."

"Exactly," Ronald replied. "Otherwise, I'll be stuck here forever."

"Well, since it's just going to be us this season," said another player, Carlos Rotiz, as he was motioning to everyone in the locker room, "let's win everything for Ronald! We've got to get him home!"

"Yeah!" the rest of the players said in unison.

The players, now all fully energized, then headed to the ice for their practice, where they went through a lot of drills in preparation for the upcoming season. One day, during the preseason, Ronald asked the team, while they were in the locker room, "So what's up with the changing of the scene? I mean, when I started this game, one minute I'm standing in a generic arena, and the next, I was standing near ice level at the Calgary Arena. I don't understand what happened."

"Well, it's a very unique thing to the video game world," Watson said. "You see, in the sports games, there are no 'cities' in the way that there are in the real world. While, yes, we represent a real-world city, we don't actually *live in* or *travel to* those actual cities."

The other players on team went on to explain that in the games that were played in indoor arenas, such as basketball and hockey, all the games are played in the same arena. It was only the interior that changed based on the design of the real-life arena of the home team for that game. This meant that the centre ice logo, the advertisements, and the seating arrangements changed to reflect how they would look in the real-world arena. Therefore, any pictures that the real-world players saw when the games were loading up were just that: pictures of the real-world city where the arenas were located. They also mentioned that the seating capacity for most of the arenas were between 18 000-20 000, although there were a few that were much lower. For the games played in stadiums, such as soccer, baseball, and football, they, too, were located in the same 'city' in the video game world. And just like the indoor arenas, the interior merely changed to reflect the home team's stadium in the real world, with visible scenery present outside of the actual stadium being added for outdoor venues. All of the arenas and stadiums had press boxes, locker rooms, weight rooms, practice facilities, and management "offices," even though the players on the team never got to see the managers that ran the teams. However, that was as far as it went.

"Wow! So, you never get to see the real sights of New York, or even Calgary? You never get to go to Italy, or France, or Spain, or Germany, and see the differences in culture there compared to North America?"

"No, we don't," the coach said. "And we never will. You know, when you first arrived here, you mentioned something about an addiction to us. Well, I hope that this as a wake-up call for you. Staying indoors all the time to play video games actually deprives you of everything that life in the real world has to offer. While we can leave this game if we want, we'd then have to go to another game, and can only take in the sights, sounds, and smells of just *that new* game. Or, we're only allowed to take a maximum of two months vacation to either Video Game City or the 'tourist games,' and only have that amount of time to take in what those places to offer. Unless we choose to work at VGG Hall, whereby then we have unlimited time to see what Video Game City has to offer. But still, we don't get to see the things that the real world has to offer. You, on the other hand, can literally go *wherever* you want without restriction-."

"Well, not without restriction," Ronald interrupted him. "I mean, some countries have no-travel areas due to their local laws. Plus, some travel groups can sometimes prevent you from seeing some of the things that you want to visit. And, you *still* need a passport if you're travelling to another country!"

"Okay, fine," the coach said. "But, you can still travel the world, the *real* world. You're not stuck in one place for your entire life. You can appreciate everything that the real world has to offer."

"So, if that's how these sports games work in your world," Ronald said, "where do you guys live?"

"For us," another player had said, "we sleep in apartments located outside of this arena."

"Just the team?" Ronald asked.

"No," the coach responded. "*All* of us."

"So, everyone on the team," Ronald replied.

"What he means is, all of the players, coaches, and management of all of the teams in this game live in a huge apartment complex located just outside of the arena," said Peterson.

"Really?!" Ronald said, surprised at what he was hearing. "So, when do you people come out of the apartments?"

"When it's *our* 'game day, or a practice,'" Poloy said. "Otherwise, we aren't allowed to leave the apartments."

"You mean to say that you don't have houses, or families to go home to?"

"No," Rotiz said, shaking his head. "Maybe our real-world counterparts do, but we certainly do not own houses or have families that we must support. We are only virtual representations of real-life players. And the drafted players? Just made up players that may or may not exist in the real world."

Ronald looked confused because he was wondering about whether or not these players actually went to school, just like all of the other people in the video game world, if they were only virtual representations of the real-world players. "So, does that mean you guys didn't have to go to school?" he asked.

"No, no, no," laughed Poloy. "We *still* had to go to school! The rules of the video game world clearly state that you have to go to school in order to understand your game, regardless of whether or not you are a representation of someone from the real world!"

Ronald then started thinking about how locker rooms in this particular hockey game were handled. "So, how did we end up in the locker room? We seem to have the *same* locker room as all of the *other* teams," he asked.

Rotiz shook his head. "You see, with this arena, it is designed in such a way we only see our *own* facilities. So, at this moment, there are other teams meeting in their locker rooms. However, we don't see that because it is sort of like they are in a parallel universe. We can see them in the apartments. However once we arrive at the arena, the entrances change based on the arena that we are going to. The only other time that we see the players from the other teams is when we are playing against them."

"How does that work?" Ronald asked.

The players looked at each other trying to determine who would answer him. Then, Peterson said, "Well, you know that marker that is on the front of your sports bag?"

Ronald looked down at his bag to look for it, and saw a bar code with the Calgary team's logo above. "Oh, you mean this thing?" Ronald asked as he pointed at it.

"Yeah, that's the one," Peterson said. "Well, there's a sensor at the entrance to the arena. And it looks for that marker. When it catches it, it causes everything to magically change so that you're in the arena you're supposed to be in, depending on if there's a practice or a game that day."

"And what about the fans that come to the games?" Ronald asked. "Where do they live? And how do they know that they're going to the games of the right team?"

"I know they live all over the city," Rotiz said. "There's enough fans in the city to ensure that all of the games for all of the teams in all of the sports can be sellouts. Though, as you've noticed when you play this game at home, that's not always the case."

"And, they also have that special barcode on their tickets," Watson added. "If I'm not mistaken, they are asked when they enter this game what their favourite team is in each sport, and are only allowed to enter one per sport. And I believe that they are only allowed to buy the tickets for their favourite teams."

Upon hearing this, Ronald really started to miss home. He missed the fact that he could see other places, and especially missed the fact that he could see other people in real time, instead of only being able to see them when things like parallel universes didn't apply. Ronald especially did not like hearing that sports fans here could only like one team per sport, and were only allowed to buy game tickets to only those teams they entered as their favourites. He was realizing once again what Dawna, Mitch, and his parents were saying, and he was hoping that he could complete the final set of games, including this one, so that he could start enjoying his life once again, the way he did before Betty became his boss at Pacific IT and Consulting.

This Calgary team was not rated very high in this game, as many of the other teams had more superstars and skilled players than the this team. The overall rating also would not change as a result of the trade function being turned off by Ronald and Pixie at the start of the game. However, this season was different. In this season, Calgary was extremely motivated because they wanted to help Ronald get home as soon as possible. This reflected in their performance, as they worked that much harder. That effort also reflected in the standings, as they won a lot of games. In fact, they even broke the old record for the longest winning streak to start a season in this game, which used to be 20 games, by winning 30 in a row before they lost one. The entire league saw that this Calgary team had a lot of focus and a purpose. And the team never took their eyes off the end goal. They played a team game, and made sure that they took advantage of their offensive chances, while emphasizing team defence and goaltending. Even the virtual Calgary Arena sold-out every game, as the virtual Calgary fans didn't want to miss a minute of their team that was playing so well. They were excited that the team may actually have a shot at winning it all.

During one of the "days off" in between games, Ronald was asked by his teammates about the people that he had in his life when he wasn't playing video games. He explained that he was surrounded by a wonderful family, and a terrific girlfriend in Dawna. Ronald especially described Dawna in detail, including her wonderful personality, and her appearance. They listened intently, and were quite happy that he had a terrific support system. Some of his teammates expressed their shock that he was dating someone that had so many tattoos and piercings, as Ronald did not come across as the type of person who would date someone like that. They mentioned that they had thought that he would be dating someone more conservative, like some of the girls that they saw in the stands. However, they also mentioned to him that he should appreciate his girlfriend more, especially since she had been so patient throughout his entire depression. They also told him that he needed to change his attitude with his family, as they were clearly being patient and compassionate with him, despite everything that was happening. They emphasized that they knew of parents who did not treat their kids well, unlike Ronald's, and that he needed to start being more grateful. Ronald could only nod in agreement, because he was realizing how strongly he was being supported.

As the season wore on, the Calgary players worked hard to ensure that none of the other teams caught on to Ronald's predicament by keeping his plight a secret from the players on the other teams, whether they were in the apartments or in the games. They knew that if the players, or even the "management," of the other teams knew about Ronald's journey, it would be used as motivation to *defeat* the Calgary team to ensure that they *didn't* make the playoffs. And that would mean that Ronald would be stuck in this game forever. Already, many of the league's managers, coaches, and players kept wondering about this Calgary team, "How is it that they are so *good*? What is their secret? How is it that an average team without any real superstars can beat us, and *handily* at that? It's quite obvious that they aren't *cheating* or *using shortcuts*, otherwise The VGG would have said something. So, what is going *on* in that locker room?"

However, all they could do was wonder, because the players ensured that no one could beat this Calgary team. After dominating the regular season, the Calgary team continued to dominate in the playoffs, only losing once. During the League Cup Finals against the Pittsburgh team, they were able to take advantage of many selfish plays by the superstars on that team to score many goals in each game. In fact, the Calgary team won every game by at least, and outscored their opponents by a combined score of 34-5. They swept the series in four games, earning them the League Cup and an entry in the International Cup as the North American entry. The team celebrated their League Cup victory at centre ice, clearly ecstatic at their accomplishment. But they knew that they still had one more task ahead of them before Ronald could continue on his journey.

The teams in the International Cup tournament were no match for this determined Calgary team. All that they could do was wonder who this team was. Calgary easily defeated every team that they faced in the round-robin portion. This dominance continued in the playoff rounds as well, with Calgary winning the semi-finals and finals with ease. In fact, in the International Cup Final, Calgary played with such dominance, they won 8-0! Their opposing team was left in awe, wondering what had just hit them. After their victory, Calgary celebrated, and this one was extra special. They knew Ronald could now move on to the next game, and they gave him big hugs, happy that he could move on. Pixie too was beaming because she was so happy that Ronald was successful in winning this game. She came down to the bench, but didn't go onto the ice because she didn't have ice skates on. Ronald started to skate over to her, and saw that his clothes were changing back to normal. He rushed to the bench, and made it just before his skates disappeared. The team went over to the bench, and asked him who the beautiful girl was, to which she replied, "I'm Pixie."

"Oh!" one of the players, Yannick Parent, said. "So *you're* the traveller we've heard so much about!"

"Yes, I am," she replied, blushing.

"How come you haven't been here before?" Watson asked.

"I'm not much of a sports person," Pixie replied, still blushing with embarrassment.

"Well, we're glad you came," the coach said. "We really appreciate The Traveller being able to see what our game is all about."

"Well, the reason that I came was because I'm Ronald's guide in this journey," she said. "So, it's not like I had a *choice*!"

"Either way, we still appreciate it," the coach replied. "We always like seeing The Traveller observing our game."

"You're welcome," Pixie said.

Just then, the portal opened. Pixie looked down at her phone and said, "The VGG says that is the opening to the fifth game. So, we'd better get going."

"Okay," Ronald said. "I'll be there in a minute."

He then turned to his now-former teammates and said, "Well, it looks like I've got to get going. But, it was a pleasure to play with all of you. I learned a lot, and I hope you guys did to."

The coach said, "It was a pleasure to work with you as well."

"Yeah," Parent said. "You were an *awesome* teammate! It was great getting to know you!"

"Good luck on the rest of your journey," Peterson said. "We're all rooting for you to get home as soon as possible."

"Thanks, guys," Ronald said. "I really appreciate that."

He then hugged everyone on the team, who were all sad to see him leave. After finishing his goodbyes, Ronald walked over to Pixie, and told her, "Okay, I'm ready. Let's go."

Pixie nodded her head, and they both entered the portal, travelling to the fifth game.

CHAPTER EIGHT

As soon as they exited the portal, Ronald and Pixie's clothes automatically changed, and they were now garbed in Medieval-era attire. Ronald now found himself wearing knight's clothing, but without the helmet, while Pixie was now dressed in an early Medieval-era woman's dress, but without the head covering that was common for women during that period. They also had pouches for coins, and bags to carry other items. "What kind of game is *this*?" Ronald asked as he examined his new attire. "I mean, the only other time I wore this type of clothing was in the second game, and that was only because of the power-up."

"I don't really know," Pixie said. "I mean, I've *never* been to a game where I was covered from the neck-down."

Pixie then examined her dress, and said, "Although, if I was allowed to change clothes in Video Game City, *this* is something that I would consider for everyday wear. Unless it is boiling hot outside, then I'd have to look for something more comfortable."

After admiring her new clothing for a few minutes, she looked at her phone to find out the details of the new game they were in. As it turned out, they were now playing The Quest to Defeat the Sorcerer, whereby an evil sorcerer had kidnapped the princess of this kingdom. The sorcerer's castle lied within a mountainous area, and Pixie and Ronald would have to travel through various landscapes to get there. During the quest, they also would have to defeat various monsters that had been unleashed by the sorcerer to terrify the people of the kingdom, and discourage anyone from trying to rescue the princess. "So, essentially, we're going to have to handle things like we did in the second game," Ronald said.

"No," Pixie replied. "If we did, we both wouldn't have swords and shields. That means we can't jump on any enemies, otherwise we'll hurt ourselves."

"Then, what kind of game are we *in*?"

"I don't know."

"Well, are you at least *allowed* to participate in this game with me?"

"Let me check."

Pixie looked at her phone, then said, "Yes, I'm allowed to participate. This game actually allows for up to four real-world players to play at once. But since it's just us two, we're only allowed to go through a two-player game."

"So, what should we do now?" Ronald asked.

"I guess we should just walk west until we get to the next village. The information coming on this phone says that we'll get further details from one of the villagers when we get there."

They then started walking west, examining the landscape in the process. Ronald then realized that it reminded him of some childhood stories he had read. He said to Pixie, "You know, this reminds me of a number of books that I read when I was a kid. Some of them have since been made into films."

"Oh? How does it remind you of that?" Pixie asked.

"Well, the books and the films were mostly set in a Medieval setting," Ronald replied. "They also had a fantasy element mixed in there. But a lot of the animals and characters in them were based on Medieval legends."

"Okay. And what, may I ask, is Medieval?"

"Um, how do I explain. Well, you see, it was a time of kings and knights, and lineage of the monarchy was only through the *eldest son*. Though, if there were brothers, sometimes jealousy would cause at least one younger brother to fight with his siblings over the crown. Also, women couldn't be queens unless they were already married to a king."

"Okay. So, how is that different from now?"

"Well, I am aware that sometime in history those rules were changed. If the monarch had no male children, but did have female children, then the eldest daughter could become queen without having to marry. However, that didn't stop some kings from killing their wives for not producing a son. And sometimes, the king so badly wanted a son that they would kill their daughters."

"Wow. It is amazing to think that people in a past era of real-world history would go to such lengths for a son. What's even more amazing is that it even *took so long* to change the rules to allow a woman to rule by herself. But, have those rules changed since then?"

"Yeah. In more modern times, the countries that still have a monarchy have changed the rules to say that the eldest *child* will be heir to the throne, regardless of whether they are a boy or a girl."

"Wow! It makes the video game world seem so much more advanced. But that *still* doesn't answer the question about this whole Medieval thing you were talking about."

"Oh, right. Well, in the early part of that era, there were knights, which explains why I'm wearing this, although I don't understand why I didn't get a helmet. Early Medieval women's fashion was just like yours, although they also wore a head covering that went down to the shoulders. That covering would completely cover their hair, and some women even wore a veil. But for some reason, your clothing doesn't include those last two items. Instead, you're dressed the way women were later on in the Medieval era."

"Maybe whoever programmed the game decided to combine periods of that era."

"Yeah, that's possible. And, in the Medieval era, all monarchs, nobility, and feudal lords lived in castles that were either located on huge hills, or were surrounded by moats, with their courts living there as well. How do I explain how they looked? Have you ever played chess?"

"Yeah."

"Well, you know the rook piece?"

"Yes, I know that piece."

"Well, they were sort of like that, but wider. The rook piece resembles what the outside corners of the castles looked like. They were used as lookouts by guards to keep an eye out for approaching enemies. The rest of the castle was also built with security in mind, and only used stone and other impenetrable materials. Most castles were built in either a rectangular or square shape, though some were built in other shapes."

"Oh, so they didn't build castles like you see in fairy tales?"

"I *think* some castles looked like that, but that was later on."

"And how did people get into these castles?"

"Usually, there was a drawbridge that would lead into the main courtyard of the castle, which was typically located in the middle of the structure. However, some castles did have their courtyards on the outside of the castle, and some contained both external and internal ones."

"And what went on in these courtyards?"

"It really depended on the castle. For some, they were used only for various celebration and events, with some space allocated for storage of supplies and animals. For others, they had huge gardens in these areas. Other castle courtyards had haystacks, stables, fruit trees, vegetables, and wells. A few castles allowed the courtyards to be used for their local markets. And in those castles where there were multiple courtyards, all of these activities were incorporated."

"Okay, that's interesting. And how did the ordinary people live?"

"Many people lived in villages, and each village had a feudal lord that owned their own castle, located close to town, though they did not necessarily live in them. The common people had a tough life, as they had to work hard on the land from dawn till dusk, and had to live to live a subsistence lifestyle. Not only that, most didn't even own their own land.

Instead, the feudal lords owned most of the lands, and therefore most of the villagers were tenants. Moreover, some villagers were serfs, or near-slaves of the lords."

"Ouch! I'm glad that we both don't have to go through that type of hardship! Were there any cities or towns?"

"Yes, they did also exist, though there were fewer of them because, after the previous civilization had fallen, a great deal of the population had also decreased in number. Those that survived ran off to the countryside because they felt it was safer there. Anyway, the cities and towns too had castles that were located nearby, and it was either members of the nobility or monarchy that lived in them, depending on who the king allowed to live there. And the king primarily lived in his main castle in the kingdom's capital city, and would use his other castles as his residence for official visits to those cities and towns. The towns or cities also contained some markets, and villagers would travel to them to sell their items, as well to buy things that they couldn't find in their villages. However, villagers usually travelled to a town rather than a city because the distance was shorter, especially given the insecurities of that time."

"And did *everyone* in this period live in the villages, towns, or cities?"

"No, not everyone. There were travelling merchants, troubadours, who were the Medieval era's travelling musicians and singers, and journeymen, who were travelling craftsmen and tradesmen."

"Well, that's great to know. Were there any shops and inns in the villages, or were those just in cities or towns?"

"I wouldn't be surprised if the villages had shops. I mean, if they had permanent residents, there probably *were* things that they could make at home that they could then sell to their neighbours without having to travel to the towns. As for inns, it's possible, since the travellers would *require* a place to stay at if they wanted to stay the night before continuing on their journey, especially since night travel was dangerous. If I'm not mistaken, I did read somewhere that a lot of villages and towns had pubs and alehouses, and those were where the inns were located."

"Oh, okay. You also mentioned some sort of legends and fantasies. So, what were they?"

"Aside from sorcerers, which we already know are in this game, there were also fairies, wizards, griffins, fauns, centaurs, elves, and other types of creatures. Although, many of these creatures originated in the legends of the Ancient era, and I guess the Medieval people appropriated them for their own purposes. Anyway, some of those other creatures might also be in this game."

Ronald's history lesson made time go by quickly, as they didn't realize how long and far they had travelled when they arrived at the village they were supposed to go to. After entering the village's gates, Ronald and Pixie looked beyond the settlement and noticed a forest, and guessed that they would have to travel through that in order to continue their quest. Once inside the village, they visited the various shops to see what types of items were being sold. They saw that these shops were selling a lot of upgrades for their gear, as well as potions, matches, candles, pots, and fruits and vegetables. Because they were still only at the beginning of the game, they couldn't buy anything, as they didn't have any money with them. They then asked around the village about the sorcerer's castle, and how to get there. Initially, they received no response from a lot of the villagers. After a while, a woman sitting in front of the village square said, "What?! Why would you want to go to that horrid place? And why would you want to travel outside of the safety of this village."

"Well, we have to rescue the princess," Ronald said.

"Why would you want to do that? It's too dangerous to travel," the woman said sternly.

Pixie then tried to explain to her that they had to defeat the sorcerer so that Ronald could continue his journey to get back home, but it seemed like the woman didn't understand. In the meantime, another villager came up to them and said, "I probably will be of more help to you. I think I might have the information you need."

"Okay," Ronald said. "So, what do we need to do?"

"I don't want to explain here," the man told them. "The last thing I want to do is scare the village. They're already petrified because of the dangers that exist."

"Oh," Pixie said, rather confused.

"Yes. Come with me," the man said, motioning to them.

He then led Pixie and Ronald to his house, and asked them to sit down at the table located at the front of it. He explained to them that the kingdom had been relatively peaceful, save for the odd war. People living in the villages could travel freely. Some of them would head to the other villages in the kingdom if they had the necessary funds for the trip, and some would even travel to the king's castle, which was located to the north of this village. However, one day, an evil sorcerer came to the kingdom with bad intentions, and threatened the king that he would kidnap the princess if his demands were not met. Specifically, the sorcerer wanted a large section of land within the kingdom, his own magic guild, and unlimited access to the citizenry for apprentices. However, the king refused. Then, one night, the sorcerer kidnapped the princess and took her back to his castle in the mountains. He told the king that unless his demands were met, the princess would remain his prisoner. The king accepted the demands, but the sorcerer continued to keep the princess prisoner, and made more demands, including asking for his own personal army and a large stake of the kingdom's treasury to be sent to him each year. The king refused these additional demands, and instead pleaded to his citizens for a hero, or a set of heroes, to come forward and rescue his daughter. The king stipulated that whoever came forward and was successful in rescuing the princess would be rewarded handsomely. Many heroes stepped forward in an attempt to rescue the princess. However, the sorcerer had unleashed powerful monsters throughout the land, and all of the heroes that had stepped up perished in their attempts to rescue the princess. When word spread of all of these failed attempts, no one else was willing to step up, scared that they, too, would share the same fate as those heroes. Now, the sorcerer kept everyone in the kingdom terrified, and all of the citizens stayed inside their villages. Outside travel had become too dangerous, with all of the monsters roaming the land. Still, the sorcerer remained apprehensive that someone new would attempt to reach his castle to try and free the princess.

"So, you do see how dangerous it is for you continue on with the quest, right?" the man asked after finishing his story.

"Yes, we do," Ronald said. "But just one question: how come we didn't get this information when we first arrived in the game?"

"Because the storyline of the game requires you to come to the village and talk to me," the man replied.

"Oh, okay. Well, we'll have to deal with these dangers if I want to get home," Ronald replied.

"Yeah. So, do you have any tips?" Pixie added.

"Those upgrades in the shops will be *very* important," the man said. "That means that when you get some coins, you'd *better* get the upgrades as soon as you can. And it's also a good idea to buy food, candles, and pottery. Plus, you might want to buy some potions, as they will be very useful. Any other items are nice to haves, but are not absolutely necessary."

"And how will we get to the sorcerer's castle?" Ronald asked.

"In this game, there is a linear path that leads west to the mountains, which is where the castle is," the man replied. "You will need to follow that path and survive all of the landscapes, especially all of the monsters lurking in these areas. In between the landscapes are other villages, where you will be able to rest at the inns and buy items at the shops. I'm sure you noticed the forest to the west of this village, right?"

"We did," Pixie said.

"Well, that's the first landscape you must travel through," the man said. "Good luck on your journey. I wish you well."

"Okay, thanks," Ronald said. "Pixie, we'd better get a move on."

They then exited the man's house, and went on their way. As they didn't have any coins with them, they headed straight into the forest. The forest was densely covered with all sorts of trees, with only the path they were on being completely clear. "Well, let's get this done," Ronald said as he looked around. "There's no time to waste."

"Yeah," Pixie replied. "I mean, this place looks scary, but we have no choice. We *have* to beat this game so you can eventually get home."

They moved along the path carefully, looking out for any beasts that may have been hiding in the shadows and behind the trees. After travelling for about 500 metres, they suddenly heard a ruffle in the trees. They looked, and saw that the bushes were moving. "What is that?" Ronald asked in a scared tone.

"I-I don't know," Pixie responded, also quite petrified.

Suddenly, an elf appeared, and started to examine Pixie and Ronald. "What-What are you?" Pixie asked him.

"I'm an elf," the elf responded. "Say, what are *you two* doing here? Don't you know that the forest is dangerous?! The sorcerer has unleashed many dangerous monsters throughout the kingdom!"

"We're going to rescue the princess," Ronald replied in as brave a tone as he could muster.

"Really?!" the elf replied, eyebrows raised. "You must be *very* brave people, then."

Pixie then explained to the elf about Ronald's journey to get home. After hearing all of this, the elf said, "Well, that *is* a good reason to want to continue on. But, you do realize that your journey is going to be very difficult, don't you?"

"We've been warned," Pixie replied, rolling her eyes. "And we're still going to do it."

"In that case, you'll need some help, because it will take more than the two of you to fight the sorcerer. He is very powerful, and it will require a lot to defeat him and return normalcy to the kingdom," the elf replied.

"So, do you want to join us?" Ronald asked him.

"Sure, I'd be happy to!" the elf replied. "I have some abilities that you might aid you during your quest."

"Like what?" Ronald asked.

"I can hide myself very easily," the elf replied. "And, as I'm smaller, I have the ability to sneak up on people. I can *easily* get you more coins if you need them! I'm also a great swordsman, which will help you out *mightily!*"

"Okay, great," Pixie said. "So, what's your name?"

"Tillbury," the elf responded. "Glad to be able to help you out. I've always wanted to defeat that sorcerer, but no one's ever wanted to help me out. What are your names?"

"Pixie," Pixie said.

"Ronald," Ronald said.

"Glad to meet you!" Tillbury responded. "Now, unless you have coins in those pouches, let's get a move on!"

They then proceeded forward, and ran into their first monster very quickly. It was huge, and Ronald commented, "Well, I guess we *won't* be able to stomp on it after all!"

"What kind of game do you think this is? You think you can just stomp on these monsters and defeat them?!" a bewildered Tillbury asked him. "If you do that, he'll just swat you away, and you'll suffer a lot of damage! Why do you think you both have shields and swords?!"

"Told you so!" Pixie said to Ronald as she drew her sword and held up her shield.

"Well, I didn't know," Ronald replied. "I've never played a game like this before."

Just then, the monster let out something from its mouth, and all three held up their shields to deal with whatever substance had been unleashed. Tillbury then said, "You two surround him. I'll deal with the rest."

He then disappeared, and Ronald and Pixie looked at each other, confused as to what was happening. The monster then again released the unknown substance out of its mouth again, and they rolled out of the way. "What are you two *doing*?!" they heard Tillbury's voice say. "Surround this thing!"

They then obliged, which confused the beast. Out of nowhere, Tillbury appeared, and stabbed the monster with his sword. The monster fell down and died, and then let out some coins. "Grab those coins! They are important!" Tillbury said.

Ronald and Pixie quickly grabbed the coins, and the three of them continued along the path. After taking a few steps, they heard another ruffle in the forest, and suddenly, a fairy came out of nowhere. "Who, or should I say, *what*, are you?" Ronald asked.

"I'm Malinda The Fairy," she replied. "What are you doing in this dangerous forest? Aren't you aware of the dangers that lie in here?"

"Yes, we are," Pixie said. "And we're going to rescue the princess."

"WHAT?!" a shocked Malinda said. "Why would you want to do *that*?!"

Ronald then explained to Malinda what he had to do to get home. After hearing the story, Malinda said, "Well, that *is* a noble reason. And so is trying to get back the princess and remove that sorcerer from our land once and for all! And Tillbury! What are you doing with them?!"

"I am helping them out in their quest," Tillbury responded. "I *know* my powers can help them! In fact, they already *did*!"

"Wow!" Malinda replied, impressed with Tillbury's bravery. "Maybe I should join as well. I mean, I'm tired of the terror that evil sorcerer has unleashed in the kingdom."

"Sure," Ronald said, "if you want to. I mean, from what we're hearing, it's going to be difficult, and we need all of the help we can get."

"Great!" Malinda said. "And, I have powers that can help you out. I can use my magic to help make enemies weaker, and I can also help you avoid attacks from the enemies."

"Can you grant wishes?" Pixie asked.

"No, unfortunately I can't," Malinda replied. "You see, the sorcerer took that ability away from me to prevent me from granting wishes to remove him. And, in his current state, he is immune to my other powers. He is trying to make sure that *no one* can defeat him."

"That sucks," Ronald said.

Suddenly, another monster appeared out of nowhere, and all four of them went after it. Malinda shrunk the monster and weakened it, which prevented it from using its powers, while Tillbury disappeared and used his voice to distract the monster. Ronald and Pixie then surrounded it, and they both drew their swords. They inserted their swords into the evil creature, and Tillbury appeared to finish it off. The monster then died, and coins appeared. After Ronald and Pixie grabbed the coins, Malinda and Tillbury explained the true value of the coins. "Those coins there are valuable," Malinda said. "You can use them to buy many valuable items in the shops. Have you been to the shops before?"

"Yes," Ronald and Pixie said, nodding their heads.

"Well, you noticed the items in there, right?" Tillbury asked them.

Ronald and Pixie nodded their heads. "Well, what do those items do?" Pixie asked.

"Those items will help you out on your quest," Tillbury then said.

"I'm sure you noticed they were selling upgraded equipment, as well as food, potions, and pottery," Malinda added. "Well, the upgraded equipment being sold is better swords, shields, and more protective clothing. You can use the food to replenish your health levels, while the pottery is used to help you cook and eat the food. The potions have multiple benefits. They give you special abilities, they can heal you, or they can also do things that will aid you in defeating the monsters. Specifically, they can offer protection from monsters' attacks, especially if you aren't able to raise your shield quickly enough, or if the monster is attacking you from behind."

"Yes. And since you didn't buy anything before you entered the forest, we'd best be going back to the village that you just left to buy those items! You clearly have more than enough coins to buy the essentials!"

They all then travelled back to the village, and headed straight to the shops to buy the necessary weapons and clothing upgrades, which had immediate effects on Ronald and Pixie. They also bought a candle, an oil lamp, some pottery, matches, and some fruits and vegetables. They decided not to get any jewellery, as they decided that it was not needed for the forest. After purchasing all of the items, they returned to the forest, and immediately had to fight off a number of monsters. Using their combined abilities, they defeated all of the beasts, and continued on in the forest, but not before picking up the coins that the monsters left behind. As they made their way through the forest, they noticed that the lighting wasn't too great, and Tillbury said, "Light the candle with the matches, and put the candle inside the oil lamp! That is needed!"

Ronald did as instructed, and the lighting improved. They then ran into more beasts, and defeated this set of monsters as well by combining all of their abilities. They also made sure to pick up all of the coins that were dropped. Finally, they saw some light at the end of the path, and Pixie said, "Well, at least we made it out of that thing alive!"

"Yeah, I'm so glad we were able to," Ronald added.

Once they were out of the forest, a centaur, a creature that was half-man, half-horse, appeared, and noticed the party approaching him. "What are you doing this far away from the king's castle?" he asked.

"We're on a quest to rescue the princess," Ronald replied.

"What?!" the centaur asked, shocked. "Are you crazy?!"

"Well, we have to, if I want to eventually get back home," Ronald said.

Pixie then quickly explained the whole situation to the centaur, and after she had finished, he said, "Then all of you are very brave. I mean, you made it out of that dangerous forest alive, so you must be! And to want to go on, despite the dangers that lie beyond? That means you have no fear!"

"Yes, we are brave and fearless," Tillbury said. "What's your name?"

"Michales The Centaur," the centaur replied.

After everyone else introduced themselves, Michales said, "Pleased to meet you. You know, I, too, am tired of that sorcerer's wickedness and terror. I would like to join you on your quest."

"Do you have any special powers?" Malinda asked.

"Just my swordsmanship," Michales answered. "That, and if your feet and legs get tired, you can ride me just like a horse."

"Well, that's good enough for me," Pixie said. "We will need all the help we can get."

"Great! Let's not waste anymore time!" Michales responded in jubilation.

The now party of five continued on, and eventually came upon another village. As they approached, they noticed that beyond the village lay a deep canyon, with a ravine that had fast-moving water, and steep, rocky canyon walls. However, Tillbury and Malinda were tired from the day's journey, and wanted to rest. Before looking for the local inn, they asked around about the canyon that lay beyond the village. They were warned by some of the villagers that although it would lead them to the sorcerer's castle, it was very dangerous. They explained that there were plenty of places for monsters to hide, and they attacked all unsuspecting victims. Ronald and his party thanked them for their time, and then looked for the local inn, where they then stayed for the night.

The next day, the party first headed to the shops to buy more upgrades for each of them. Tillbury, Malinda, and Michales purchased clothing upgrades that provided them better protection from attacks, while Michales got a better sword and shield. Ronald and Pixie also upgraded their weapons and clothing. The prices were surprisingly lower than the first village, which allowed them to save some of their coins for later purchases. Once these upgrades were bought and automatically applied, they went into the other shops to buy other items, especially food, protective jewellery, and potions. After they had finished and packed their things, they made their way to the canyon.

Once inside the canyon, they saw exactly how dangerous these cliffs were. "Careful here," Michales said. "One bad step, and we will surely fall to our deaths. And that ravine there, it is not safe either. So if you want to get water, be careful that you don't fall into it."

"You know, with how difficult this canyon is, it's a good thing that I had to climb a lot of steep mountains in the first two games," Ronald said.

"Yeah, and I'm glad that I was with you in that second game," Pixie added. "Learning how to handle the footing of those cliffs like this will really pay off here."

"Oh?" Tillbury asked. "And how, may I ask, were you two able to navigate through such steep cliffs in prior games?"

"The first game was an adventure game that took me into the mountains of Morocco," Ronald replied.

"And, in the first world of the second game, we had to travel through a mountainous world," Pixie said.

"Morocco? What is that? Is that the name of another creature in this game?" Malinda asked.

"No, it's a country in northwestern Africa," Ronald said.

"Africa? What's an Africa?" Michales asked. "Is that some strange land that we don't know of?"

"Well, it's not strange to me or Pixie," Ronald replied, shaking his head. "It's a continent in the real world."

"Oh. Well, in this game, we don't have continents you speak of," Tillbury said. "In this game, we all live on one land mass. However, the lands are all divided into kingdoms, whether inland or on the coast. The oceans contain islands, and sometimes they are sailed to only for their resources."

As they walked through the canyon, monsters started appearing out of nowhere. Some of the monsters came out of the caves, while others came out from behind the rocks, just as they had been warned of in the village. Using the abilities of their party, plus some of the potions that they had bought, Ronald and Pixie were able to defeat these monsters, and collected bonus coins for defeating them so quickly. As they continued travelling through the canyon, the party encountered more monsters that were patrolling the area in plain sight. They combined to defeat all of them, and grabbed any coins that were being dropped. When they reached the canyon floor about halfway through this path, they decided to go the ravine and get some water, as a couple of members were getting thirsty. "Now, you have to make sure you don't go *into* the water," warned Michales as they approached the banks of the ravine. "If you do, you'll be asking for a sure death, as the water moves so quickly that it sucks you in."

"Okay, we'll be careful," Ronald said.

After safely reaching the ravine's banks, they kneeled down, and carefully leaned over with their water pouches. Ronald placed his hand in the water, and Michales grabbed him and pulled him back. "What are you doing?!" Michales yelled at Ronald. "You do that, and you'll get pulled in!"

"I was just checking the temperature of the water," Ronald said.

"There are evil beings in that ravine! They will pull anyone that puts their hands or feet in, and will eat them!"

"But you said that if I go *into* the ravine, that I will be sucked in due to the speed of the water. I was just putting my hand in there."

"Well, that's also dangerous! Not going in also means that you don't lay a foot or a hand in! That ravine is rife with evil water beings that have been placed in there by the sorcerer!"

"So, how do I check the temperature of the water, then?"

"In this game, the water will always be cold, okay?! That's all you need to know!"

"Okay, sorry."

Ronald then went back, and carefully filled his water pouch. Once he felt that it was full, he took a sip, and then closed the lid. The party then returned to their quest, and defeated more beasts along the way, some of which were hiding behind the cliffs of the canyons. They made sure to also grab the coins left behind, knowing how valuable they were. As they approached the end of the canyon, they noticed that the path was taking them back up the cliffs. As they climbed up, the ground beneath them became less sturdy. They were all really careful, as they knew that one wrong step would result in rocks falling off the edge. Once again, Ronald and Pixie used their mountain climbing skills to help out the rest of the party scale the cliffs, and they were able to safely get out of the canyon. Not too long after, they came across another village, although this one was located on the edge of a vast desert. As all five of them were extremely tired, they decided that they should rest inside the village, and proceeded to look for the inn. It did not take them too long to find the inn, and they checked in.

The next day, they asked around the village about what lay in the desert. One villager became hysterical because the party was actually thinking about facing the sorcerer. "Are you mad?!" the man asked. "You know that most people that go through the desert never make it out alive! In fact, how did you manage to get out that canyon alive?! I think you're the first travellers that have ever made it out of there alive since that sorcerer came and ravaged our peaceful kingdom!"

"Well, we have to, if I want to get home," Ronald said.

"Well, good luck!" the man replied. "You're going to need it! There are too many dangers in that desert there! If you stray off the path, you'll deal with dangers from quicksand to the desert creatures that lurk under the sand. You'll be lucky if you are still alive after *that* landscape!"

"You don't believe we can do it, do you?" Pixie asked.

"No! Because every hero is doomed to fail as long as the sorcerer remains!" the man said. "If you want to die, then that's your choice!"

"We *will* defeat that sorcerer!" Tillbury responded. "We have abilities that none of the other heroes ever possessed. And, we have *bravery*!"

"All of those other heroes were brave!" the man replied. "But, they didn't have brains!"

"Well, *we do*!" Ronald said. "And, therefore, we are going to finish the task!"

The man gave them all a perplexed look, and then simply said, "Well, *fools* always think they can do the impossible!"

Rather frustrated with the lack of help from this man, they then left, and headed to the shops to upgrade their equipment and clothing, and buy more items for their journey, especially food. The prices were a little higher than the previous village, but still lower than the first village.

After acquiring the necessary items, they left the village, and headed into the desert. The desert looked just like the Sahara Desert, with large sand dunes and plenty of mirages. But it also contained a few oases along the way, which would provide the party with plenty of water and shade when they needed to escape the blistering heat. Michales warned them that they had to follow the single, linear path. He reassured everyone that it would be wide enough for all five of them while travelling to an oasis. Michales also stressed, "And heed the warnings of that crazy man back in the village of straying from the path. Remember, there is quicksand, and there are creatures under the sand, so we have to be careful not to go off of it."

"Let's use this cane to see what happens," Pixie said as she took out the cane that she purchased in the previous village out of her sack. "That way, nothing happens to us."

The party stopped, and she placed the cane on the left side of the path. Suddenly, the cane looked like it was sinking, meaning that there was quicksand to the left of the path. She pulled it out with the help of the others, and then placed it in the sand on the right side of the path. All of a sudden, hands came out of the sand, and Pixie immediately pulled the cane out, and the hands disappeared. "Well, I guess those were the creatures that the crazy man was talking about," she said bewildered.

"Yes," Michales said. "So, we'd best stay off of the sand, and just use the path, since we know specifically what dangers lie underneath the sand."

As they continued walking, some monsters came running and jumping from afar and attacked them on the path. Despite the best efforts of the monsters to try and force them off of the path and into sure doom, the party managed to stay on the path, and were able to surround and kill the monsters. Specifically, Malinda used her powers to make the monsters smaller and weaker, and the other four members of the party were able to surround and defeat these monsters with a little less difficulty. Unfortunately for them, some of the coins fell outside of the path. However, they ignored these coins so as not to meet an untimely demise.

When they reached the first oasis, which was located just off of the path, Pixie used her cane to check the sand. When she confirmed that it was safe to enter, the party went into the oasis, and filled up their water pouches. They decided to camp there for the night, as they were pretty tired from the day's trek, which was intensified by the immense heat that they had to contend with. After spending a restful night, they woke up refreshed, and continued on their journey through the desert.

As they went on, they encountered more of the beasts along the way. While some of the monsters had come from afar, others popped out from behind the sand dunes, while some came out from *under* the sand. In all cases, the party used their combined abilities and weapons to fight them off, and grabbed whatever coins they could. At each oasis that came along the way, they made sure to stop and rest and also made sure they refilled their water supplies. The trek through the desert was a difficult one. But they made it through, and once they reached the end of the desert, they saw another village, with plains immediately after that. In the distance, they saw the mountains, and they now knew that they were close to reaching the sorcerer's castle. "Boy, those mountains look *huge*," Ronald said. "They look like they're bigger than the *Himalayas*!"

"What are the Himalayas?" Malinda asked.

"Are they some sort of mountain creatures?" Tillbury asked.

"No," Ronald said. "It's a mountain range in the real world."

"Oh?" Michales asked. "And where in the real world are these, as you call them, Himalayas?"

"It's in Asia," Ronald responded. "You could say they separate South Asia from East Asia."

"Oh," Malinda said. "We have never travelled outside of this game, so we wouldn't know about the landscape of the real world."

"How could that be possible?" Ronald asked.

"Remember that people in video games can only interact with each other in Video Game City and, as we found out in that dancing game we went to, other so-called 'tourist games,'" Pixie said. "While some games *are* based on the real world, and use the maps of the real world, also remember that people of the video game world cannot leave for other worlds. And, while they may know some things about the real world, they may not be aware of *everything* in the real world."

"Oh, right," Ronald said.

As they approached the village, they were suddenly met by a faun, which was a half-man, half-goat creature, who came out of the trees. "Wow!" the faun said. "You survived the desert! I have *never* seen anyone make it out of there alive since that sorcerer arrived!"

"Well, we're on our way there," Michales said, pointing the mountains far in the distance. "We're going to beat the sorcerer!"

"WHAT?!" the faun said. "Please say that you're not serious!"

Ronald then went on to explain the purpose of their journey, after which he faun said, "That's a noble reason. I mean, *everyone* should be able to get home if they've been away for a long time. But, if you want to defeat the sorcerer, you'll need help."

"What other help would we need?" Tillbury asked. "We've got all the powers that we need right here."

"But, the sorcerer will be able to attack you with his magic," the faun said. "His magic is very deep. He can find an invisible being in an instant. He can counter a fairy's magic. His magic can also attack everyone simultaneously with one wave of the hand, even if they surround him."

"So, what powers do you possess?" Pixie asked.

"I can keep him busy," the faun replied. "You see, fauns are good at distracting magical beings. Because we're so fast, not to mention the fact that we have noisy footsteps, we can distract such beings so they can't attack everyone else. You see, magical beings can only attack others when they aren't being distracted."

"He's right, you know," Malinda added. "*I'm* having trouble trying not to hit him because of how annoying the sounds of his footsteps are. And all he is doing walking and talking about his powers!"

"See what I mean?" the faun said with a wide smile. "I'm already causing issues with a magical being, and she's óne of the good guys!"

Ronald, having taken a liking to the faun, said, "Well, if that's the case, then you *should* join."

After everyone introduced themselves to him, the faun then replied, "Pleased to meet you all! I'm Rackerbild The Faun."

They all then proceeded towards the village. Once entering, they embarked on finding out enough information about the plains that lay ahead of them. And just like in the previous villages, they were warned about the monsters that hid in the plains. They were told that the plains contained many monsters, including tree monsters, grass monsters, and even some that attacked from beneath the ground. After they had finished talking to the villagers, the party decided to call it a day, and checked into the local inn and stay the night.

The next day, they went into the shops to buy more upgraded equipment and clothing, and also bought equipment and clothing for Rackerbild, They also restocked on other essential supplies, and headed out into the plains. It was a flat terrain, and had a few rolling hills, which reminded Ronald of the plains in Saskatchewan, except that there were no farms and fences. "Well, this could be a little easier," Ronald said. "I mean, it's so flat where would the monsters *hide*?"

"Don't say that!" Rackerbild said. "They can come out of nowhere!"

Just then, a monster came out from behind a small little patch of trees, and attacked the party. "See?!" Michales said. "That's why you shouldn't get arrogant!"

The party fought the monster, with Rackerbild distracting the beast, thus allowing the others to defeat the monster. After that, Pixie said, "Well, Rackerbild, if anyone had any doubts before, I think they've been put to rest. We know that you *will* be helpful!"

"Thank you," Rackerbild responded. "I really appreciate it."

As they continued travelling through the plains, they encountered many more monsters. Some came out of the ground, while some had run from afar to attack them. A few monsters also came out from amongst the bushes to try and defeat the party. Additionally, many of these monsters had some magical abilities, which were bestowed upon them by the sorcerer in order to stop anyone from continuing on any further. Up to now, the monsters had been able to thwart anyone's attempts to pass the plains and continue on to the sorcerer's castle. However, this time, the monsters were not successful. The party was able to defeat all of the beasts, using Rackerbild's ability to distract his opponents, which ensured that the monsters were not able to unleash their magic on anyone in the party. They continued on, and as they approached the final village, they saw that they were finally in the mountains, and all that lied beyond was the sorcerer's castle. Inside this mountain village, the party was triumphantly received by the villagers for their bravery and courage, as they were they only ones to be able to make it this far without being killed. Moreover, the villagers developed instantaneous hope, seeing that this party was different from the other heroes that had perished in their quest to defeat the sorcerer and rescue the princess. However, the villagers also warned them that greater dangers awaited them inside the mountains, as the sorcerer was aware that they had been able to make it this far, and he would do all that he could to stop them. They were told that the sorcerer had now unleashed more powerful monsters inside the mountains to prevent the party from reaching him. These ghouls were everywhere, including in the caves, in the valleys, and even inside the mountain rivers and lakes. However, the party remained undeterred, and they decided that they would start this trek of the journey the next day, and would spend the night inside the village. At the inn, the innkeeper let the party stay for free, unlike the other villages where the innkeepers made them pay.

The next day, they all bought their final set of upgrades, and stocked up on all necessary items, as they knew they would not have a chance to buy anything else after this. They also noticed that the prices in this village were much higher than what they were in the any of the previous villages. After being given a farewell party by the villagers, where they were all wished good luck, the party started its way through the mountains. After travelling through the mountains for a while, they looked around, and saw that the mountains towered high above the valley below. This range was definitely higher than the Himalayas, and contained wide rivers, large lakes that dotted that parts of the landscape, and thick glaciers at the top of the mountains. The natural animals of this mountain area were nowhere to be found, as they all were hiding from the monsters that lurked. "Wow," Ronald said. "And I thought the Himalayas were scary with all of the climbing deaths over there."

"Why do people in the real world climb mountains?" Pixie asked. "Are they looking for something?"

"No, they either do it for adventure, or for fun," Ronald replied.

"Climbing for *fun*?!" Tillbury said, shocked that such an option was even possible. "And for *adventure*?! Don't they have any brains to realize that you only climb if you *have to*?"

"I don't know," Ronald said, shrugging his shoulders. "I just know that's the reason why they do it now. Before, up until the 19th century, people who wanted to travel long distances, and weren't miners, would do so either on foot, on horseback, or with a horse pulling a carriage. So, if they came across mountains or hills, they would climb out of necessity. But with all the advances in technology, including being able to travel through mountain passes using trains, roads, and cars, people are driven to climb these types of mountains for other reasons."

All the others could do was shake their heads in confusion. As they continued on, they suddenly saw monsters charging out of the caves, the rivers, and the lakes with the intent of destroying the party. The party fought the monsters they faced, though it was not an easy task. These monsters were much more powerful than any of the previous ones that they had encountered. However, using their combined abilities, they were able to defeat all of the monsters they faced in this area. After slaying their opponents, they continued on towards the sorcerer's castle. When it was clearly safe to do so, they went down to the rivers and lakes to refill on water, and then continued on. Using their mountain climbing skills, Ronald and Pixie helped the others scale the more difficult cliffs, and everyone worked together to make sure that no one slipped and fell. As they approached the end of the mountainous area, they saw the sorcerer's castle in the distance. It was surrounded by high cliffs and a waterfall, but no one looked nervous. "Well, there it is," Michales said. "That is the place where the sorcerer lives, and the base from which he has caused all of this havoc on our peaceful land."

"What's the plan?" Ronald asked. "Should we just run up to it and attack it?"

"We can't do that!" Tillbury said. "If we do that, the sorcerer will just use his magic against us! I think that's *exactly* what he expects us to do!"

"So, what do we do, then?" Ronald said.

"We must approach the castle very quietly," Michales said. "We must approach it as if a tourist in your world was going to visit such a place."

Carefully, they travelled to the castle, and didn't do anything to draw attention to themselves. Unfortunately, the sorcerer had already unleashed more monsters, which gave the party a great deal of trouble, as they were much faster and stronger. "You see what I meant when you asked about just storming the place?" Tillbury told Ronald after they had slayed one of the monsters. "*This* is the magic that the sorcerer can unleash."

"Yeah, *now* I get it," Ronald replied. "What do we do, then?"

"I'll be able to help!" Rackerbild said.

Rackerbild then started running around near the rocks, trying to cause as much noise with his feet as possible. The monsters roared, annoyed at the noise that Rackerbild was making. They became angry, and started chasing after him, which was when the rest of the party struck. Malinda used her abilities to help the party avoid the attacks, as these monsters were immune to her power to weaken them. Tillbury then used his disappearing power to confuse the monsters even more, as they tried in vain to find him. And, the monsters were getting more annoyed with the noise that Rackerbild's feet were causing, which aggravated them even more. Finally, Michales, Ronald, and Pixie joined together and slayed the monsters with their swords. After collecting the coins, they continued on towards the sorcerer's castle.

At the castle gates, the party had to sneak up on the guards, and quickly and efficiently slayed the startled guards. They then went through the courtyard of the castle, which was quite similar to Ultimo Lord X's courtyard. The courtyard was littered with dead trees, weeds and uninviting flowers, as well as dark and evil statues of the sorcerer, and of his various monsters. Ronald pointed out the landscape to Pixie, who replied, "Yeah, I know. I wonder why these creepy evildoers and evil magicians always have to have the same look and feel to their castle courtyard."

"Well, some of these castles are based on fairy tales and what is shown on TV," Ronald said.

The castle itself, just like the courtyard, also looked dark, spooky, and uninviting, and was completely black in colour. Suddenly, they heard a wail from inside the castle. "Help! Oh, if there are any heroes that can hear me, please, rescue me! Free me from this prison!" they heard a female voice say.

"That must be the princess!" Rackerbild said.

"Duh! What other females could be hidden inside that castle?" Ronald said. "I mean, in every village that we visited, everyone mentioned that the sorcerer had only kidnapped one woman, and that was the princess."

"Ronald!" Pixie said. "You don't have to be rude!"

"I'm not being rude!" Ronald replied. "I'm just saying that it should obvious whose voice it was."

"Still, that was not very nice!" Pixie said in a stern tone.

"If you two are finished arguing, can we please go inside to rescue the princess?" Michales said, trying get everyone to refocus.

"Okay, fine," Pixie and Ronald said together, still quite irritated with each other.

They all then went inside the castle. The decor inside was even more spooky than the outside, as it clearly looked like an evil sorcerer lived there. The lobby led to darkened rooms, as well as a darkened staircase that led upstairs. The walls were covered with paintings, including pictures of the sorcerer, and pictures of some of the places that he had visited. "Well, we'd better check these rooms to see if the sorcerer is in any one of them," Ronald said.

They then proceeded to check each room one by one. In the first room, a monster suddenly appeared, and Tillbury said, "It would appear that the sorcerer knows that we're inside!"

The party fought the monster using the same strategies that they had used on the monsters outside of the castle, and were able to defeat it. They then continued to check the other rooms. A couple of the rooms contained beakers, flasks, and Bunsen burners, suggesting that sorcerer was working on some magic potions that were intended for evil purposes. Interestingly enough, the sorcerer hadn't deployed any monsters in these rooms, which surprised everyone. However, in the final set of rooms on this floor, they encountered more monsters, which they were able to successfully fend off. The party then headed up to the second floor, where they were attacked by more monsters in the rooms they inspected. Finally, when they went up to check the third floor of the castle, they came across the sorcerer's room. They collectively took a deep breath, and entered the room. Inside, they saw the princess tied up inside of a prison cell. The princess looked up, and said, "Oh! Oh! A group of heroes! You have come to rescue me! I finally will be free!"

Just as the party was about to go and search for the key to the cell, a magical cloud of black smoke suddenly appeared. After the smoke dissipated, a man with a long, white beard, long, white hair, and wearing a black robe with a long, pointed hood, appeared. "Aha! So you heroes have survived all of my monsters!"

"Are you the sorcerer?" Pixie asked. "Because if you are, you're toast! We'll defeat you and rescue the princess!"

"Yes, I'm the sorcerer," the sorcerer replied, rolling his eyes. "What kind of a question is that?! I didn't grow my hair and beard like this, or wear this robe and hat, in order to be called a crazy old man!"

"Well, in that case, be prepared to be defeated!" Ronald replied.

"Ha!" the sorcerer said. "You may have been able to defeat my monsters, but you will not defeat *me*! My magic is way too powerful for whatever weak skills and powers you have!"

"Want to bet?" Rackerbild said. "I know your weakness, and that is how we will defeat you!"

"You don't know of any weaknesses!" the sorcerer replied. "I only know *your* weaknesses!"

They then engaged in battle, and Rackerbild started tap dancing, which distracted the sorcerer. "Ooohhhh! That noise! That awful noise!" the sorcerer said, covering his ears. "Make it stop!"

Ronald and Pixie then went to attack the sorcerer, and hit him cleanly with their swords, but it didn't defeat him. "Ha! You'll need to hit more *more* than *that* in order to beat me!"

Tillbury then disappeared, and used his voice and improvised tap dancing to distract the sorcerer. This sidetracked the sorcerer again, who tried to attack Tillbury from the direction where his voice was coming from. As he attacked Malinda used her magic to create a magical sword, and unleashed it to magically strike the sorcerer, who was weakened after Pixie and Ronald had hit him. "Ow! What the...?! That was a magic attack from a *fairy*! Oh no! If that can happen, that means that I've been weakened! NOOOOOOOOOOOOOOOOOO!"

The battle continued on like this, with each member of the party doing whatever they could to distract the sorcerer, and another member attacking him. After five more hits, the sorcerer yelled, "NOOOOOOOOOOOOOOOOOO! I have been defeated! How-How could this be *possible*?!"

"Well, when you have a determined and focused set of opponents, *anything's* possible!" Ronald said.

The sorcerer then turned into a big puff of smoke, and after a few seconds he disappeared. After confirming that the sorcerer was defeated, Ronald grabbed the prison key and unlocked the cell, and then went to untie the princess. "Oh, thank you all so much! It's so good to be free!" the princess said as she hugged Ronald.

Suddenly, they were magically whisked away to the king's castle, and they were all now standing inside his throne room. At the same time, the sorcerer's castle self-imploded, and peace returned to the kingdom. Inside the king's throne room, a celebration was held in the honour of Ronald, Pixie, Tillbury, Malinda, Michales, and Rackerbild. "From the bottom of my heart, I thank all six of you for rescuing my dear, fair daughter, and releasing the entire kingdom from the clutches of that evil sorcerer!" the king said. "Without your bravery, focus, determination, and fighting ability, we would not be here today!"

While Ronald and Pixie quietly smiled, the rest of the party was more vocal. "Thank you, your highness," Tillbury said. "It was an honour to do this."

"Yes, and we knew it was the right thing to do," Malinda added.

"We felt that enough was enough!" Michales said.

"And, we knew that cowardice was not going to stop that sorcerer's evil terror that had been placed on the land!" Rackerbild said.

"Well, all of you succeeded where many had failed!" the king said. "Many heroes attempted to go and defeat the sorcerer. They had the fighting ability, but they didn't have the bravery, focus, and determination that all of you possess! They all perished during their journey because they became afraid of the monsters!"

The king then called for the princess, who then came forward. She then said, "For your bravery, and for your heroism in rescuing me and the kingdom, please accept this reward."

The princess then awarded each of the six of them a medal of honour, and placed it around their necks. Ronald was admiring his, and said, "Another medal? Wow. This is too much."

"Think nothing of it!" the princess said. "You deserve that reward!"

Just at that moment, the next portal opened. At the same time, two championship rings appeared on Ronald's left hand, which shocked him. "What-What is *this*?!" he said as soon as he saw the rings.

"It must be a reward for winning those championships in the previous game," Pixie replied. "They must have *just* produced them."

"Wow. And I still have that medal of honour from the second game."

"Well, sometimes you do get rewards inside the video game world. And the best part is, you get to take them home with you!"

"Cool! But what happens if I get asked about them?"

"Just say that it's stuff of yours that you thought you had lost. Or, don't say anything at all."

Pixie then looked over at the portal, and said, "Oh! There's the portal! Let's get going!"

"First, let's say goodbye to the rest of the party from this game."

"Okay. But let's make it quick"

Ronald and Pixie then went to say goodbye to Tillbury, Malinda, Michales, and Rackerbild. "Well, guys, we've got to go," Ronald said, pointing to the portal.

"It was a pleasure fighting with you!" Tillbury said in a very emotional manner. "I learned a lot about bravery fighting beside you."

"Yes, and we wish you well on the rest of your journey!" Michales added.

"I hope you eventually do get home," Malinda added. "A guy like you, who has a life in the real world, shouldn't be stuck here forever."

"And don't worry about us!" Rackerbild said. "We'll be able take care of ourselves!"

"Thanks everyone," Ronald replied. "I also enjoyed fighting with all of you. You are good beings."

"We'll never forget you!" Rackerbild said.

"We're really going to miss you," Malinda said, tears now flowing from her eyes.

"I'll miss you all as well," Ronald replied.

He then hugged Tillbury, Malinda, Michales, and Rackerbild, respectively. After Ronald was finished, Pixie hugged the others as well. After they were done, Pixie said to Ronald, "Let's go."

Ronald and Pixie then entered the portal leading them to the sixth game of their quest.

CHAPTER NINE

Upon exiting the portal, Ronald and Pixie found themselves in a crime-ridden city located in the desert. However, the city contained all of the modern infrastructure and amenities of an early-21st century city. Unfortunately, because of the crime, and especially the fear that the crime had created, many businesses had boarded up their shops. Ronald looked around, and knew that he wasn't in Calgary, and was not happy about it. "Dang it! It doesn't look like I'm home yet!" Ronald said, frustrated because he knew that he still had to go through more games. "I'm tired of these games! I just want to go home!"

"Ronald, calm down!" Pixie said. "Look, let's hide because this doesn't look like a safe place to stand and talk."

They walked over to a building that looked empty, and checked to make sure that no one was inside before walking in. "But come on! I've already played *five games* in a row, and without a break at that!" Ronald said after they entered. "I mean, I still take a break from playing video games when I'm at home!"

"Listen, we have to keep going through these games until The VGG says that you're done, okay?" Pixie said. "And remember what The VGG told you before you started all of these games?"

"That there would be a lot of games?"

"That's right. So, you'll just have to deal with it. I understand that you want to go home, and that you're frustrated that you're not. But you have to live according to the rules of The VGG, and not *yours*, or whatever the rules are in your world."

Pixie then looked at her phone to find out what game they were in, and why it was so dangerous to be standing outside on the street. The game was called Crime City: Salinas, and Ronald was required to head to the police station immediately. Beyond the fact that the game was set in a fictional city called Salinas, no other details were given. Ronald was rather puzzled at the objective of the game. He then asked, "I wonder what kind of game this is. Is it one where I have to *solve* the crimes?"

"I don't know," Pixie replied, also confused. "I'm checking my phone here, but it doesn't give me any more information. And, our clothes didn't change, so this is really strange as to what we're doing here."

"So, what should we do?"

"I guess we'd better head to the police station."

Pixie then searched for the address of the station that Ronald was to report to on her phone. After she found it, they then headed for the station, being careful not to get caught by any of the criminals that had overtaken this city. After walking for about ten minutes, they safely made it to the station, which had "Salinas Police Station No. 1" written on the exterior. Once they reached the front door, they went inside.

The station looked like a typical police station, with the reception area being in the front, and the offices, meeting rooms, classrooms, holding cells, and change rooms being located in other parts of the building. As soon as they got in, Ronald told the receptionist, "Hi. I'm Ronald Charlton. I was told that I was supposed to report to the station immediately."

The receptionist looked around her desk for any notes that indicated that Ronald was expected here, and couldn't find anything. "I don't have any messages about you needing to be here," she responded. "Is there someone who contacted you directly?"

Ronald looked to Pixie and asked, "Pixie, who did The VGG say I had to come here to see?"

Pixie looked at her phone for the message. When she found it, she said, "It looks like you have to see the captain, some guy named Bob Harringson, and The VGG told him he was in charge of this game."

Ronald then turned to the receptionist and said, "Did you catch that?"

"Yes, I did," the receptionist responded. "I'll call Captain Harringson and find out if he was expecting anyone."

The receptionist called the captain, and she could be heard saying, "Hello? Captain Harringson? I have some gentleman named Ronald Charlton waiting here. Were you expecting him? I don't have any messages on my desk here saying that he was to arrive...Uh huh...Uh huh...Oh! So he was supposed to come....Okay...I'll let him know...Okay, thanks. Mr. Charlton? Captain Harringson will be with you in a few minutes. Just take a seat there and wait for him."

"Okay, thanks," Ronald replied, and then he and Pixie took a seat.

After a few minutes, Captain Harringson, who was a large, well-built man at least 6'6" in height, came out. "Ronald?" he asked, looking around the room.

Ronald, who was reading a magazine, was a little startled when he heard his name because he was quite engaged in the article that he was reading. After hearing the captain, he jumped up, looked around, and said, "Huh?"

"Ronald? Are you here?" Captain Harringson said.

Ronald looked at the captain and said, "I'm Ronald."

"Great! Come with me," Harringson said.

Pixie also got up, and started to follow the captain and Ronald. However, she was then blocked by the receptionist, who said to her, "Where do you think *you're* going, missy?!"

"I'm going with Ronald," Pixie replied. "I came with him."

"The captain only asked for Ronald, not *you!*"

"What? I'm not allowed to play alongside Ronald?"

"No, you're *not!* You're only allowed to be an observer in this game! And, you can only help if Mr. Charlton yells 'pause.'"

Meanwhile, as Ronald was walking with the captain down the hall, his clothing changed, and he was now wearing a police uniform. After a few minutes, he realized that Pixie wasn't beside him, and stopped. He went back to the lobby just as Pixie was sent back to her seat, and he asked her, "Pixie, aren't you coming?"

"I can't," she said disappointedly.

"Why not?"

"I'm not allowed to play with you in this game."

"Why?"

"Because they won't let me. They said that I'm only allowed to be an observer, and nothing else."

"Oh."

"Ronald! We have to get this meeting started *now!*" Harringson yelled as he chased after Ronald. "Leave her alone, as she isn't allowed to play alongside you!"

"But, nothing had happened when we entered this game, and I figured that's because she was allowed to participate," Ronald replied.

"Well, she's not!"

"But why?"

"You'll get more details in the meeting! Now come with me this instant!"

"Okay. Pixie, I guess I'll see you later."

"Yeah, okay," Pixie replied, still bitter that The VGG hadn't told her earlier that she wasn't allowed to participate in this game, and instead had to find out this way.

Ronald then followed the captain to his office, which was located on the third floor of the station. Inside the office, another officer was sitting in one of the seats in front of the captain's desk. The officer got up, held out his hand to Ronald, and said, "Hi. I'm Sergeant Ivan Blesko."

"I'm Ronald Charlton," Ronald said to Ivan as they shook hands.

"This is your new partner during this game," Captain Harringson said to Ronald. "That is why Pixie's not allowed to play alongside you. You see, in this game, we want our players to work alongside one of the in-game characters, as this game is about police officers working together as a team. This game has never been a two-player game because it would hurt the morale and camaraderie of the various stations and districts. You see, our officers would not be happy about not being assigned with one of the players of the game if we allowed friends to work together all the time. What would they learn, otherwise, about teamwork, if they were always partnered up with friends? Nothing. And that would spread around the force, and suddenly we've got a lot of problems. People need to learn to work with those outside their social circle, and that is why we are strict."

"Okay," Ronald replied. "Is there a way to access Pixie in case I *do* need her help?"

"You can get access to her by yelling 'pause,'" Harringson replied. "But that's only if you need hints or tips. Nothing else! Ivan and the rest of the force will give you all the help that you need."

"It's a pleasure to be able to work with you," Ivan said, reassuring Ronald. "I'm really looking forward to it."

"So, how does this game work? I mean, when Pixie and I entered, we didn't receive much information," Ronald asked.

"We did that on purpose because in this game, the force likes to have control over the information," Harringson replied. "Otherwise, the information might get into the wrong hands, and then we are in *big* trouble. I'm sure you noticed that the streets were *very* dangerous when you arrived."

"Yes," Ronald replied, "we did."

"Well, imagine if all of the details of your missions in this game came out into the open," Harringson said.

"You might have been killed," Ivan said. "And, they would be able to foil our investigation because they would have been able to get their hands on that information. Not to mention that you would have been stuck in this game forever, since you would never be able to complete all of the required tasks. And I know that you don't want that to happen."

"Exactly," Harringson said, nodding in agreement. "Now, let me tell you about what our expectations are of you to complete this game and move on."

Harringson then briefed both Ronald and Ivan about the nature of the game. Salinas used to be a beautiful, bustling city, where everyone felt safe. The downtown was booming, people would interact with one other on the streets, they would go to the shops to buy various items, and there was a thriving arts scene. Suddenly one day, crime lords, gangs, and even a pimp moved in, and started terrorizing the population by overrunning the city with various types of crimes. As a result, people were now scared to go outside out of fear of being killed, business owners were afraid of opening their shops because they didn't want the mafia and gangs to destroy their stores and merchandise, and the arts scene died because prostitution and crime had taken over the city. Ronald and Ivan's goal was to rid the city of all of the crime, and take down the criminals. The game would be divided into a series of missions based on the crime that had to be solved. After each mission was successfully completed, Ivan and Ronald would receive their next mission. Once all of the missions were completed, the portal to the next game would open up. "Is everything clear?" Harringson asked after he was finished.

"Yes, sir!" Ronald and Ivan responded in unison.

"Okay, then, you'll now start the first mission," Captain Harringson said, as he handed them a file.

Ronald and Ivan took the file from Harringson and reviewed it. Their first mission was to stop the gang wars that were causing fear amongst the population of Salinas. These wars were preventing people from enjoying life, whether it was going downtown to shop, or enjoying arts scene, while businesses were too scared to open up their stores, fearing the consequences. There were three gangs that had set up a base in Salinas. When they first set up shop, they had reached a mutual agreement not to fight with each other, so long as they didn't trespass on each other's turf. However, as more people started joining the gangs, they each started looking to expand their territory, which resulted in encroaching on each other's turf. Such attempts for more control over the city led to the gang leaders becoming angry with one another. No compromise was reached between the gangs, and this led to an all-out war for total control over the city. When the gangs first arrived, the people of Salinas instantly became worried for their safety. However, these wars now terrified the citizens, as they feared that walking outside meant being injured, if not killed.

"So, where should we go?" Ivan asked Ronald after they finished reading the files.

"Well, from the files, there seems to be a pattern as to where they tend to fight," Ronald replied. "It seems like they always fight in front of the downtown theatres, and the fight seems to go from north to south. So I say that we head to the next theatre that hasn't been hit yet, and have a stakeout there."

"Okay, let's go."

"Hey! If you're going to head Downtown to deal with a shootout, you'd better put on your bulletproof vests!" Captain Harringson told them. "You don't want to get shot and have to restart the game, do you?"

"No, sir," Ivan and Ronald said in unison.

Ivan and Ronald put on the vests, and then headed towards the Proxy Theatre, which was where they deduced the next fight would occur. When they were within a few blocks of the theatre, they immediately saw a shootout taking place amongst the gang members, each wearing clothing unique to the gang that they belonged to. Ronald told Ivan, who was driving the squad car, to stop. "Why do you want to stop here? Why don't we just deal with that shootout over there?" Ivan asked, confused as to what Ronald was thinking.

"I already know that if they see us approaching, one of two things will happen," Ronald told him. "Either they will run away, or, more likely, they are going to start shooting at *us*, and it's going to be game over, and we'll have to start all over again."

"How do you know?" Ivan asked, perplexed that Ronald wasn't willing to just jump in and save the day. "I mean, we have the element of surprise. They don't see us."

"From what I understand, that's how it always goes in games like this. And, sometimes in the real world, based on what I've read, that can actually happen."

"So, what do you suggest, then?"

"I suggest we call for backup from *all* of the stations before we do anything. They have the numbers right now, so without backup, we're screwed."

"Okay, if you say so."

Ivan then put in a call on the APB, and said, "Calling all units, and all stations. We are in front of the Proxy Theatre in Downtown. There's a shootout amongst the members of all three of the gangs that have taken over the city. We request backup immediately! Right now it is only I, Sergeant Blesko, and Officer Charlton here, and we will not be able to handle this gang warfare on our own."

"10-4, Sergeant!" the dispatcher responded. "We will put in the call right away!"

The dispatcher said on the APB, "Calling all available officers. Gang shootout in front of the Downtown Proxy Theatre. Only two officers on the scene, requesting backup! Please head there this instance! They cannot deal with this warfare on their own!"

After a few minutes, about two dozen police cars and five SWAT units arrived on the scene, and Ronald and Ivan then got out of their squad cars and headed towards the location where the SWAT team was located. After a lengthy standoff, during which a few shots were fired, the police force was able to penetrate through and win the battle, after which they arrested the gang members. However, they couldn't locate either of the gangs' leaders, which caused confusion among the force. Inside the main police station, all of the arrested gang members were questioned as to the whereabouts of the leaders, but none of them knew where the leaders were, nor did they know exactly who their leaders even were. They simply said that they were recruited by friends that belonged to the gangs, and they were promised a large amount of loot and security for joining. That was the extent of their knowledge on the gangs. Meanwhile, Ronald and Ivan were called into the captain's office, and were given their second mission.

Ronald and Ivan looked through the files, and saw that they were now about to investigate a series of burglaries in town. They found out that one of the gang leaders was working with the mafia boss to terrorize the population further by expanding their operations into robberies, with most of the heists were home invasions and break-ins of abandoned buildings. Most of items stolen were taken to wherever the gang leader and crime lord were based, with the items then being sold on the underground market. After reviewing the files, they looked for, and were eventually able to find, a pattern in the robberies. First the gang would break into an abandoned building in a certain quadrant of town, and then invade a house in the same quadrant. They then would move to the next quadrant to the west, and do the same. They would then head to the quadrant to the south, and then to the southeast quadrant. The gang would then start the string of robberies again by going to the northeast quadrant first, and continuing on so that the police would be thrown off the trail. However, Ronald and Ivan weren't thrown off. They determined that, based on the pattern they deduced, the next target would be a house in the southeast quadrant of the city. They also found a pattern in the targeted addresses. They found that the thugs would alternate between odd- and even-numbered streets in the invasions of the abandoned buildings, with even-numbered streets being targeted first. With home invasions, they always went to streets named after prior mayors of Salinas, and it seemed to go in a northwest-to-southeast diagonal pattern. Also, the house number always started with 100, and then that number was added by 12 for each robbery. When they reached the last building number in the sequence, they would start over with 101. This helped them figure out exactly which neighbourhood the gang was going to strike next. After putting on their bulletproof vests, they headed to the location where they thought that the next robbery would take place. To ensure that the potential robbers wouldn't recognize them and run away, they wore civilian clothing, and also used an unmarked vehicle.

While driving to the neighbourhood, they bought some food for the stakeout, as they didn't know how long it would be before the gang would show up. When they arrived, they didn't see anyone, and so they waited. After about a couple of hours, they saw an unmarked van pull up in front of one of the houses, and saw some tough-looking thugs get out of the van with crowbars and other items, clearly with the intent of robbing the house. "This is it!" Ronald said. "We'd better call for backup, because if they see us, they'll run away."

Ivan put out an APB and said, "Sergeant Blesko and Officer Charlton here. We are at 101 Gaime Street, and there are gang members on scene looking to rob the house. Requesting backup."

"10-4!" the dispatcher said.

Then, on the APB, the dispatcher announced, "Robbery in progress, 101 Gaime Street. All available units and officers, please respond this instant!"

Roger and Ivan then got out of their car to confront the robbers. "Hey! You there! Stop this instant!" Ronald yelled at them.

One of the gang members turned around, and smirked. "Oh yeah?" he asked, holding out his arms as if he was looking for a confrontation. "And what are *you two* going to do about it?"

"Yeah, let's get 'em," said another robber.

Ronald and Ivan then pulled out their badges, and Ivan said, "Salinas police! You're all under arrest!"

"Oh shoot! The cops are after us!" said the third gang member. "Let's get out of here!"

"No!" said the first robber, as he pulled out a gun.

Ronald then said to Ivan, "Oh no! Ivan, let's get behind the car! Now!"

Ronald and Ivan ran behind the car, and loaded their guns. A shootout then started, and lasted for several minutes before their backup arrived. "Oh no! More cops!" said the second gang member.

"Yeah," the first gang member said. "Let's get out of here!"

The robbers then started running away, which led a foot chase, with Ronald and Ivan leading the pursuit. Because Ronald was so athletic and in such good shape, aided by to Dawna pushing him so hard in his workouts, he was easily able to catch up with the gang members. Ivan and a few of the other officers were not too far behind, and eventually caught up to the other robbers. It wasn't long before Ronald, Ivan, and the other officers were able to capture all of the robbers. As they walked back to the car with the robbers, Ronald said to Ivan, "Boy, it's a good thing that I worked out all that time since I got laid off. It really came in handy here. If I hadn't done that, and I had let myself get fat, I wouldn't have been able to catch up to these guys."

"Yeah," Ivan said. "I have to admit, you're in much better shape than me! How'd you get so fast?"

"My girlfriend taught me some things. She's a volleyball player, and has to lift a lot of weights and has to do a lot of cardio in order to stay in game shape."

"Oh yeah? How built up is she?"

"Well, she's built. Really muscular."

"Like a bodybuilder?"

"Not quite *that* built. But, she's got huge muscles, that's for sure. She can lift 300 lbs.!"

Ivan's face then showed a shocked look, as his eyes widened and jaw fully dropped. "300?! That's *insane*! I'm having trouble with *200*!"

"Geez!" said the first gang member. "Your girlfriend is built! She could bench press me!"

"Hey, you be quiet, okay?" Ronald yelled at the robber. "No one's talking to you!"

He then grinned, and said to Ivan, "Hey, I can lift that much. "So, it's not a big deal."

All Ivan could do was shake his head. They then put the robbers into the back of the car, and headed to the station. At the station, they interrogated the gang members to find out who they were working for, but no one would talk. However, they did mention which other gang members were involved in the robberies when promised a lighter sentence. Those individuals that were ratted out were then later arrested. As a result, Ronald and Ivan were now given their third mission.

The files that Ronald and Ivan received revealed that there were a series of car thefts, led by another one of the gang leaders and a crime boss. The thieves would steal a car, take it to an auto body shop, chop up the car, and then sell the parts on the underground market. The thefts were getting so bad that people were afraid of driving around the city, worried that their cars would be stolen. The pattern that Ronald and Ivan found was that the car thieves attacked malls, with the timeline of the heists showing a clear directional pattern. Using the map, Ronald and Ivan then applied the pattern to deduce where the next theft would occur. After they were confident they had the right location, they proceeded there in a squad car, but only after putting on their bulletproof vests.

When they arrived at Piccolo Mall, they noticed that the parking lot was almost abandoned. They inferred that the people of Salinas had become so scared that they didn't even want to shop at the malls. Ivan parked the car in one of the stalls, and they waited patiently in the lot. After about an hour, they saw a group of shady people approach one of the few cars in the lot, and break into it. They hot-wired it, and then drove off with it. "There they are!" Ronald said. "Let's chase them!"

Ivan then turned on the squad car, and pursued the car thieves. Meanwhile, Ronald put out an APB that they were in pursuit of a group of gang members that had just stolen a car. "10-4!" the dispatcher said.

The dispatcher then put out an APB, "All available units and officers! Car heist in progress! Unit 30185 in pursuit of the perpetrators! Please keep up to date as the chase continues, and head to the staging locations that you are assigned to cut off the thieves!"

As they chased the car around the city, Ronald and Ivan always made sure that dispatch was aware of their precise locations, and the backup cars had begun to set up blockades. However, the thieves seemed to see the backup approach just in time, and changed their direction of travel before getting trapped by the police. Suddenly, Ronald figured out a pattern that the thieves were using in order to escape capture, and voiced it over the air through an APB. Finally, after a lengthy chase, the thieves were blockaded. When they realized that they were going to be caught, the thieves stopped their car, got out, and put their hands up in the air. They were then quickly arrested, and taken to the station for questioning. At the station, the thieves were interrogated about who they worked for, and where the stolen parts were taken to. The only real information the thieves revealed was giving the location of the shop where they stripped the cars for their parts, and that was it. This allowed the police department to retrieve the evidence, namely the parts. While some of the thieves did snitch on their fellow crime partners, in exchange for a lighter sentence, no one revealed the identities of the leaders. This hampered the investigators' efforts to arrest the leaders. However, for breaking up this particular ring, Ronald and Ivan were given their next mission.

The fourth mission dealt with busting up an illegal gambling ring. The files showed that one of the gang leaders, possibly the same one that was directing the home-and-building robberies, was working with the mafia boss to try and hide the illicit money that the gang had made so that the police would be thrown off the trail of the real source of the money. Gambling was actually illegal in Salinas, therefore the casino was operating underground. This establishment was especially popular amongst the criminal element, although it also attracted the shady businesspeople of Salinas. After reviewing the files, it was decided that Ronald would go in undercover. He was to gather enough information about the gambling ring and what the money was being used for. After he had enough evidence, he was to contact the station so they could come in and bust the ring.

Ronald promptly changed into a business suit and a bow tie, and was given a large pile of money seized from one of the earlier busts. The money that he was given was unmarked, and non-sequential, so as not to draw suspicion on himself from the people that frequented the casino. As he knew that some gang members were still operating in the Downtown area, he headed there in an unmarked car. No one from the station followed him, because they all knew that if there was any hint of spying by the police, the gang would simply run away and move the casino's location. Ronald didn't wear a wire, nor did he have a voice recorder on him, as the mafia boss and gang leader had advanced technology to detect these devices. Once he reached Downtown, Ronald walked around, and noticed many shady things going on, which brought him to the realization that he still had a few more missions after this one before finishing this game. At one of the street corners, located near some business high-rises, he saw a gang member who looked like he was waiting for someone. It also looked like he would have information about any casinos in town. Ronald figured that he had to talk to this person in order to find out where the gambling ring was located. Ronald went up to him and asked, "Hi there, I've got a lot money that I don't know what to do with."

"Oh?" the gang member said. "And why are you telling *me*?! So that I can rob you, and the cops will suddenly appear?"

"No," Ronald said, shaking his head. "I'm a wealthy guy. I need to find a good way to spend my money."

"Well, what do you want to do with it?"

"I'm a great poker player, but with gambling being illegal here, there aren't any casinos around. My friends and I were once busted just for playing a friendly game of poker at my house, so I need to make sure that I can play without anyone looking to cause problems for me."

"Well, then, you've come to the right man. I can direct you to an excellent casino in town. But first, let me see how much cash you have. I don't want to be played around, you get my drift?!"

Ronald nodded, and then reached into his pocket and pulled out the stack of cash that Captain Harringson had given him, which he gave to the gang member. The thug examined it, and then gave it back to Ronald. "Looks legit," the guy said of the money. "Nothing's marked, and it's all in random order. So, I think we're good."

"Okay, then," Ronald said happily, "where's the casino?"

"Follow me."

The two of them then walked quite a distance before they arrived at an abandoned warehouse. "This way," the gang member said, motioning to Ronald as they went through the front gate.

"Why is it located in an abandoned warehouse?" Ronald asked.

"Well, the cops would *never* suspect that the casino's in an abandoned warehouse. Look at it! It doesn't look like a place for a casino. No one even drives near here anymore. If it was placed in a nicer building, or, say, in an upscale house, the neighbours would get suspicious, and rat us out to the cops, who would then start snooping around! Or, if we tidied up this place, and made it look really nice after years of no activity, without any whiff of who bought the place, people would start to wonder what was going on here."

"Oh."

They then went in through the front door. Inside, the place looked nothing like the outside. It looked really nice, like any Las Vegas casino, and had all of the games that would be found inside any casino. "I get it now," Ronald said as he admired the interior, "keep it looking rough on the outside, and have it look like Vegas on the inside to throw off suspicion."

"Well, if you mean a gambler's paradise, then, yeah, that's the idea," the gang member said. "We don't need any cops around to bust up a good thing here. They've already gotten to the robbers and the 'mechanics.'"

Ronald was then taken to the casino owner's office, where he was introduced to him. "Sir, we've got a new client," the gang member said. He then turned to Ronald and asked, "What's your name?"

"R.C. Alton," Ronald said. "Pleased to meet you!"

"Very nice to meet you!" the owner replied. "It's always nice to have a new client!"

"Well, I'm just happy to be here," Ronald said, shaking the owner's hand. He turned to the gang member and asked him, "Is your boss around?"

"No, no," the owner said, shaking his head. "Neither of our bosses are here. They *rarely* come by, so as not to draw police attention."

"Makes sense. So, what do I do here?"

"Just play whatever suits your fancy!"

The owner then handed Ronald a membership card, and told him, "You will need this from now on. You show this at the entrance, and they will let you in."

"Great," Ronald replied.

As he headed to the blackjack tables, the gang member, who continued following him, said, "Wait! I thought you said *poker* was your game!"

"Well, I just want to warm up here to get some luck before I head over there."

"Oh, okay, good luck!"

Ronald headed to a blackjack table. As he was playing, he asked some questions about where the players spent the money they had won at the casino. However, no one was answering, and after a few games Ronald decided to move on. He thanked the dealer, and went on to play some poker. At the poker tables, he asked some more questions, and unlike at the blackjack table, everyone openly answered, unaware that Ronald was working undercover. As it turned out, a lot of the businessmen and other players that frequented here would use their winnings to buy the stolen items such as those that came from the home, building, and car robberies, while others would use it on drugs, or prostitutes. In all cases, the gang members would inform their customers where they could get their "items" from. The gangs also made use of the casino as a recruitment centre, and those who were interested in joining were given the addresses of where they could sign up to become members. As he was listening, Ronald guessed that the drug and prostitution rings would be the next two missions, and that all of the crimes were somehow connected. He was of the belief that the gang leaders, the crime lord, the pimp, and the mafia boss were all working together to finance all of the crimes. He then asked, "So, do you people know just *who's* funding all of these crime waves?"

"No, we don't," said one of the poker players, a businessman. "We just win money, and spend it freely. The gang members let us know where we can get our 'stuff,' and that's all we care about."

"And, if we want to join them in the 'fun,' they let us know where we can go to sign up," said another one of the players.

Ronald just nodded his head, and after losing his fourth straight game, he said, "Well, I guess my luck isn't with me today. I'd better go before I lose *everything*. It was nice meeting you all!"

The other players said goodbye, and Ronald left. The gang member that had brought Ronald to the casino had been watching him the whole time.

As Ronald was leaving, he came up and asked, "What happened? I thought you said you were a great poker player?"

"Well, I said I was great," Ronald said. "But I never said I was the *best player in the world*! I mean, there are *always* going to be players better than me."

"Yeah, that's true," the gang member said, laughing. "Well, I hope you enjoyed yourself! Don't be a stranger!"

"Oh, I won't!"

Ronald then left the building, and walked quite a distance away from the warehouse, so as not to draw suspicion from anyone he had just met. He called the station, and passed along all the information he had found out. A few minutes later, the entire police force was briefed with of the latest revelations, and were promptly dispatched to the warehouse. Within half an hour, dozens of officers surrounded the warehouse. Once they were all in place, they all stormed the facility. Ivan and a large group of officers stormed the front entrance, and once inside, Ivan said, with the officers holding up their guns, said, "Okay, everyone! This is a bust! This illegal casino is now shut down! You're all under arrest!"

The patrons of the casino did as they were told, and put up their hands, after which they were all handcuffed and sent to the station. Once at the station, all of the criminals were questioned. However, the police were no closer to finding out just who was responsible for the crimes, as no one would reveal who the gang leaders were. But they knew they were getting closer, as they had now shut down many illegal operations, and had taken plenty of criminals off the streets. With the new knowledge received from Ronald's undercover work, he and Ivan were then given their next mission.

The file that they were given discussed the drug ring that was being run in the city. Prior to the arrival of the gangs in the city, Salinas had been a clean, drug-free town. However, once the crime leaders had established themselves, drug sales and use popped up everywhere, with the gang members distributing the drugs, and the shady businessmen and drug addicts buying them. Moreover, it seemed like the drug problem had gotten worse after the police started attacking the gangs. And since then, it seemed that someone had stepped up the effort to increase the drug trade in Salinas. While some gang members involved in the drug trade had already been caught in the earlier stings, there were still plenty more involved in the trade. And the police did not know who the leaders behind the drug trade were. This mission required Ronald and Ivan to simply take down the ring, and to try and arrest the gang leader or leaders, as well as the crime boss, that were behind the ring. It was decided that, since Ronald had busted the gambling ring in the previous mission, Ivan would work undercover in this mission.

Ivan then changed into a business suit to appear as a shady businessman looking to buy drugs, although he didn't wear a tie because he didn't like ties. He then took an unmarked car so as not to draw attention to himself, while Ronald drove in a separate unmarked car in order to back Ivan up, just in case there was any trouble during the mission. Ronald made sure that he left enough distance between himself and Ivan so that no one would suspect that they were partners. Ivan drove Downtown, and parked near the alleyway, which was behind a major high-rise building, where the files said most of the drug trade was being conducted. Ronald parked two blocks away, and waited with great anticipation. Afterwards, Ivan turned off the car, took a deep breath, and then got out. As he got out, he looked around and saw that some of the citizens were shopping on the main streets, as some businesses had reopened in recent days. This indicated to him that the police force was gaining the upper hand in the crime war, as the terror and fear of the populace was waning. However, he knew that much still needed to be done to make the streets safer. Ivan then walked into the alleyway, and saw that it was empty. He returned to the car, and pulled out a walky-talky that looked like an ordinary cell phone and asked Ronald, "Say, Ronald, this *was* the alleyway that I was supposed to go to, wasn't it?"

"Let me check," Ronald replied.

He took another look at the files, then radioed back, "Yeah, that is the place you're supposed to go. Why? What's wrong?"

"I don't see anyone," Ivan replied. "What should I do?"

"Just wait," Ronald said.

"Okay, I'll do that. But, what happens if some trouble brews?"

"Don't worry. I already asked for backup while I was driving. There are several undercover officers in the vicinity to back you up."

"Thanks. But, maybe you should ask Pixie for some help, just in case the gangs have already caught onto what we are doing."

"You're welcome. And, I guess I should see what Pixie has to say. 'Pause!'"

Pixie then suddenly appeared in the back seat of Ronald's car, and said, "Finally! It's about *time* you called on me! You know how *bored* I was waiting in that stupid lobby of the police station?!"

"Huh?!" Ronald replied as he jumped in his seat, startled that Pixie had arrived so quickly. "Oh, Pixie, it's you. Don't scare me like that!"

"Sorry about that Ronald," Pixie replied. "I didn't mean to scare you. I'm just happy that you *finally* called me so that I could get out of that lobby."

"There's not much to do there, is there?"

"No! After you left to go talk to the captain, I asked the receptionist where I had to go to observe. She told me that I was to stay put in the reception area, and I could observe all the stuff going on in the game via a monitor in there. Unfortunately, that monitor is a piece of crap!"

"So, what did you do all this time?"

"Read, talk to *anyone* that came in, just *anything* to pass the time!"

"Talk to anyone? You didn't talk to any of the criminals, did you?"

"No, but I did talk to some of the citizens that were at the station, as well as some of the officers working out of there. That receptionist? She didn't seem too keen on engaging in a conversation with me because every time I tried to talk to her, she gave me a dirty look."

"It doesn't sound like it helped you deal with your boredom."

"No! Anyway, what do you need help with? Is there something I can actually *do* on this mission? *Anything* that won't make me have to go back to that lobby?"

"Uh, no, we just were looking for hints and tips. If you get involved, the captain will get furious with me, and then I will have to start this game all over again. Or worse, be sent all the way back to the first game. And I don't want to be stuck here for that long because I want to get out of this game, especially with the progress that I'm making. I want to get home as soon as I can."

"Oh," Pixie said looking down, disappointed that she couldn't do much else. "So, what hints do you need?"

"Well, Ivan is having trouble finding the gang members," Ronald replied. "Where could they be?"

"They're around," Pixie said. "They're just making sure that the cops aren't around before heading to the alleyway."

Ronald then relayed this information to Ivan via his cell phone. "Ivan," he said, "I just talked to Pixie, and she informed me that the gang members are sweeping the area to make sure there are no cops around before they head into the alleyway. Did they arrive yet?"

Ivan, who had gotten out to search the alleyway and beyond, responded, "I think I see them. I mean, they look to be wearing the colours and gear of one of the gangs. I'd better get off before they get suspicious."

"10-4," Ronald responded.

He then turned to Pixie and said, "Thanks, Pixie. We really needed that help."

"You're welcome," Pixie responded. "So, are you *sure* you don't need me to get involved?" Pixie asked, hoping that Ronald would change his mind.

"Yeah, I'm sure. You don't want me to get into trouble, do you?" Ronald replied.

"No, I guess not. I'm just bored, and I want something to do!"

"Well, there might be *something* you could do at the station. Just ask them."

"Okay, I will."

Pixie then left, and was magically whisked away back to the station. At the same time, Ivan put the radio back into his suit jacket, but made sure to keep the radio depressed so Ronald could still hear everything that was going on. He then got out of the car and returned to the alleyway to wait for the gang members. They arrived a few minutes later, and looked around again to make sure that there were no police officers around before entering. There were four gang members, all of whom wore black hoodies, and each carrying a backpack. They saw Ivan, and one of them asked him, "Were you looking for us?"

All of the gang members kept their eyes fixated on Ivan, and looked at him inquisitively and suspiciously. "Yeah, I was," Ivan replied. "Did you see coming into the alleyway?"

"We did," another one said. "We have to make sure that no cops are around. You can't be too careful you know, especially after the casino bust!"

"I understand," Ivan said. "I mean, you certainly don't want the cops coming after you, especially now that they're regaining control of the city."

"Exactly," said the third gang member. "So, what is it that you want?"

"I understand that you might have some merchandise that I'd be interested in," Ivan said. "No one has the goods that I'm looking for, and I heard from some contacts that you're the only ones that sell it."

"Depends on what you're looking for," the fourth member said.

After Ivan described exactly what he wanted, the first gang member took off his backpack, and pulled out the item. "Well, that's *exactly* what I'm looking for!" Ivan said.

"The price is $1000," the first gang member said.

Ronald, who had been listening to the radio intently, put out an APB through the main radio for all officers to start moving in. Meanwhile, Ivan inspected the merchandise to make sure that it was indeed drugs, then said, as he reached into his pocket, "Well, in that case...."

He then pulled out his badge and said, "...you're all under arrest!"

Ivan then talked into his walky-talky and said, "Ronald, move in! We've got the evidence!"

Ronald then said on the APB, "Attention all undercover officers! Ivan has the evidence! Move in now!"

At that moment, the gang members looked around confused, and the fourth member said, "Let's get out of here!"

They started running, but two ran into undercover officers that had already gotten into place and had blocked the alleyway. The other two tried to run away, but were chased down by some of the other undercover officers, who caught up to the gang members and tackled them. They were all then arrested and sent to the station, and Ronald and Ivan were preparing to get the files on a mission to stop the prostitution ring. However, much to their surprise, this set of gang members actually cooperated with the police and revealed that they were working for a crime lord. They also gave the name of their leader, and the address of the building where they were operating out of. The whole force knew they had to move fast to catch these crooks before they escaped. After quickly changing back into their uniforms, including putting on their bulletproof vests, Ronald, Ivan, and team of officers raced to the address that was given to them by the gang members. Their hearts were racing, knowing what was at stake. Once they arrived, they surrounded the building, and Ivan yelled into the bullhorn, "This is the Salinas police! We have the building surrounded, so you have no escape! Come out with your hands up before we come in and take you down!"

There was no response for several minutes. The SWAT team, which had been called in en-route to the scene, also got into position. Suddenly, several shots were fired out of the building, forcing the officers to take cover. They returned the gunfire, which lasted for several minutes. When there was a break in gunfire, the SWAT team was asked to get into position and take the front entrance down. Some of the officers, including Ronald and Ivan, followed them. Not long after, the SWAT team, along with the officers that followed them, took down the remaining gang members one by one. After the first floor was secured, Ronald and Ivan then went up to the second-floor office of the first gang leader and the crime lord. When they arrived, they found that both the crime lord and the gang leader were pointing their guns at the street. When they heard the door open, they turned around, and the crime lord said, "So! You thwarted my chop shop! And stopped our little drug business! You will pay for hurting my profits!"

"Yeah!" added the gang leader. "And you got rid of my brothers!"

"Well, you're going down!" Ronald replied. "This is no way to live your lives!"

"Why?" the gang leader said. "The money is *way* better than what I would make in one of those office buildings!"

"And, we had a great revenue stream," added in the crime lord. "It would have bought *a lot* of planes, houses, and boats! Plus toys for my wife! And it's not like any of my clients were complaining!"

"So what?" Ivan said. "This town was in much better shape before you and your cronies arrived! I'm going to see to it that peace returns to this city!"

"Go ahead and try to do that!" the crime lord said, getting ready to fire his gun. "You'll be sorry that you messed with me!"

Just at that moment, the officers that had been climbing the exterior of the office building managed to get into the office, and were able to take down the gang leader and crime lord. Ronald and Ivan immediately handcuffed and arrested them. They were then taken to the station, where Ronald and Ivan were given their next mission.

The files revealed that there was a pimp working in conjunction with the second gang leader in a prostitution ring. The women were forced into prostitution in order to pay bills because their families had been negatively affected by the crime wave, which had forced the closure of the city's businesses. A female officer, Margot Lincoln, had already been working undercover, but was having trouble taking down the ring because whenever she caught one of the clients, they were able to escape in a getaway car driven by their partner because she did not have enough resources to help her take down the clients in the act of solicitation. As a result, Ronald and Ivan were now working undercover as regular pedestrians to help out Margot.

After reviewing the file, Ronald and Ivan then changed into street clothes, but made sure to wear bulletproof vests just in case there was trouble. They then drove an unmarked car Downtown to a high-rise building, where they then parked the car. They got out, and then walked until they reached Margot's post, where they waited for her. A few minutes later, she arrived, and Ivan was immediately attracted to her. When she came up to them, she talked to Ronald and Ivan in the way that her undercover role required her to, not realizing that it was them. Ronald then said, "Uh, Margot, we're your backup."

"Oh!" Margot replied, embarrassed. "Finally! I got the backup that I've been constantly promised!"

"Better late than never, right," Ivan said.

"Well, I guess it's good that it came eventually," Margot responded. "But, I've been having a tough time trying to take this thing down on my own!"

"Don't worry, we're here. Say, Margot, when this is all over, what do you say we go out on a date?" Ivan then asked, still infatuated with her.

"Is that a legit request? Or Is it because of how I look right now?"

"It's legit," Ivan said. "You're beautiful."

"Well, thank you, I'm flattered," Margot replied, smiling. "After everything is over, we'll see."

She then quickly briefed them about the case, and what the strategy was. This included telling them what their roles were, including where they were to be positioned. Margot stressed that neither Ronald nor Ivan were to do anything that would hurt the mission. Ronald then went to the car, and called in for undercover backup units in order to prevent any clients from taking off in a getaway car. He then returned his staging area. An hour later, a client came up to Margot, and started talking to her. She started a conversation, and took the man into the alleyway. Ronald and Ivan then took this as their cue, and went to the entrance to block it. As they got there, additional officers arrived to prevent the client and his partner, who was in the getaway car, from escaping. Margot pulled out her badge and told the client that he was under arrest. The client tried to run away, but Ronald and Ivan were there to stop him, and his partner wasn't able to help out because his car was surrounded by undercover officers. The partner was then forced out of his car and placed under arrest. After Ronald and Ivan questioned both the client and his partner about where the ring was based out of, and they were given the address. As Ronald, Ivan, and Margot escorted the client and his partner to the station, the other officers went to the address provided and stormed the building, taking everyone inside into custody. All of the prostitutes that had been taken into custody were questioned. They fully cooperated with the officers and gave them a list of their clients. This information allowed the officers to get the addresses of the clients. They then went to the houses of the clients and arrested them, which caused much embarrassment for their families because only now were they finding out about such dark secrets. At the station, the clients were offered a plea deal in exchange for information that would help them take down the pimp and the second gang leader. The clients accepted the deal, which would see them pay stiff fines but avoid other charges. They gave the police information on their "informants," which led the police force to make preparations.

Ronald and Ivan quickly changed back into their uniforms, and then quickly headed to their squad car. They then followed the rest of the officers to the house shared by both the pimp and the second gang leader. The officers assigned to this scene had already been warned that they could face anything. Therefore, they had to be prepared for the worst. Outside the gates of the house, a parade of police cars were greeted by gunfire from the guards. However, the police used their numbers to strategically surround the guards, who surrendered after a brief standoff. The officers then headed inside the house, where they dealt with more thugs along the way, sometimes having to kill them in self-defence. Meanwhile, Ronald and Ivan decided to climb up the side of the house in an effort to sneak up on the pimp and the second gang leader, who were more focused on the office door than the window. When they entered the office, Ronald said, "Freeze! You're under arrest!"

As the two crooks turned around, the other officers stormed the office. Unlike the first set of crime bosses, the pimp and gang leader didn't put up any resistance, as they saw they were surrounded and had nowhere to go. At the station, they were quite forthcoming in giving the interrogators the information requested. They revealed that both they, the third gang leader, as well as crime lord and first gang leader were all working under the mafia boss. They stressed that it was the mafia boss that had brought all of them to Salinas in the first place. When asked about how it could be possible that three different gang leaders, a pimp, and a crime lord were all working under one boss, they replied that the mafia boss had set up the three gangs, and had picked three people to be gang leaders, and they were to determine amongst themselves how they were going to divide up the territory. The mafia boss had also asked a lonely bachelor to take on the role of the pimp, and a shady businessman to take on the role of the crime lord. And when asked what the purpose was for taking such steps, they replied that this was all done in an effort to divert attention away from the mafia boss. They were then asked about how the gang wars fit into all of this, and they said that those were staged by the mafia boss to keep the population terrorized. That way, his "businesses" would continue to thrive, regardless of whether or not the police actually were successful in putting a stop to the wars. The pimp and second gang leader also made it clear that if the police wanted to eliminate crime from Salinas once and for all, they would have to take down the mafia boss, otherwise he would just find new ways to run his criminal operations. They gave the address of the mafia boss's mansion, and said that it would take a lot to bring the mafia boss down.

With this new information, the whole force started preparing strategies to take down the third gang leader and the mafia boss. Inside the large meeting room, Captain Harringson, along with Salinas' mayor and the police chief, all reminded the officers how this was the decisive battle in the war to rid Salinas from crime once and for all. They mentioned that the task was dangerous. While they would face some gang members, they would also face the employees and administration of the mafia organization that operated out of the mansion, which was located in one of the richer areas of town in the far northwest quadrant. The officers were warned that they would face opponents that would be armed, and that would work hard to defend their turf. They were told to wear protective gear, including bulletproof vests, because of the dangers of the operation. Once the meeting was over, the force took a collective deep breath, and started making their way to the mafia boss' mansion with one goal in mind: to win the final battle.

As they were driving to the mansion in their squad car, Ronald and Ivan were both nervous. "You know, if we end up losing, what happens?" Ronald asked.

"If we lose, you would just go back to the start of the mission," Ivan replied. "You see, the game autosaves when a mission is complete."

"Well, that's a relief. At least I won't have to start the game all over again."

"Wait! Let's see if Pixie can give us some help!"

"That's a good idea. 'Pause!'"

Pixie then arrived, sitting in the back seat, happy that she was able get out of the station for a while. "Thank you so much for getting me out of there! I am going *insane*!" she said excitedly.

"Well, we needed some help," Ronald replied, laughing.

"You mean you need me to help you out with taking down the last set of criminals?!" Pixie asked with enthusiasm.

"No, you still aren't allowed to get involved," Ivan said. "Rules are rules."

"Oh," Pixie replied, quite dejected. "So, what do you need help with?"

"Do you know if there are any places in the house that are unguarded that will make it easier for us to catch mafia boss or the third gang leader?" Ronald asked.

"There is a back entrance that isn't guarded. But, there is someone is patrolling the nearest hallway to that entrance," Pixie replied.

"Okay, thanks," Ivan replied.

"Are you *sure* that I can't help out in taking down the bad guys?" Pixie pleaded.

"The rules are clear," Ivan answered. "You are to only be an observer."

"Okay, then, bye," Pixie said, disgusted at the answer.

She was then magically whisked back to the police station. Soon, the police arrived at the mafia boss' mansion. "So, what should we do?" Ronald asked. "Front or back?"

"Remember Pixie's tip? Let's go to the back," Ivan said. "We'll have an easier time."

All of the officers that were on scene got out of their cars, and dealt with the guards that were at the front gate. However, they had to take cover behind their squad cars, as they were fired upon immediately by the guards. Meanwhile, Ronald and Ivan headed around to the back entrance, taking some officers with them as backup. This group had a much easier time than their colleagues at the front of the house. They kicked down the back door, and entered, watching out for the thug who was inside guarding the back door. They snuck up on him, and before he could reach for his gun, he was tackled and arrested. The officers encountered more thugs, and were forced to kill them as well because they were being shot at. Meanwhile, out front, it took a while, but the officers were managing to get the upper hand against their opponents. While the officers were lucky to avoid any casualties, they killed many guards during the shootout. After a while, the gang members and administrators of the mafia boss's organization that were still resisting were surrounded, and were forced to surrender. Inside, the mafia boss and the third gang leader appeared in the hallway, guns in hand, looking furious. "You ruined the empire that I was building!" the mafia boss replied. "You took down my confiscation business, and then you shut down my casino! Then, you had the nerve to stop the drugs and prostitutes that I was selling!"

"You took out all of my brothers!" the gang leader added. "You shut down my warehouse where I was selling all of my merchandise! And my casino! That was a great way to recruit new people and to let clients know where they could get quality goods and women!"

"That's what you get for being a criminal!" Ronald replied. "Now, surrender!"

"Never!" the mafia boss replied.

Then, the mafia boss and the gang leader started shooting at the group of officers. The officers ran for cover, and hid behind whatever would offer protection. Ronald and Ivan's heartbeats were especially racing. But they knew that it was imperative that they take down these thugs as soon as possible. They yelled to the other officers to return fire at the mafia boss and gang leader. The shootout lasted a few minutes. Ronald, sensing that now was the time to make his move, yelled out to Ivan, "Cover me!"

Ivan nodded, pulled out another gun from a holster near his foot, and fired both guns. Ronald ran to the side to get a better shot, and was able to strike both mobsters. He killed both instantly. This allowed the officers to come out from their hiding spots. They were then able to surround the remaining gang members, as well as the mafia boss's remaining underlings, and arrest them. And with that, the game was over. As soon as he found out that he had successfully completed all of the tasks, Ronald said, "Well, I'm glad *that's* over! I'm never playing this game, or any game where I would have to do the opposite of what I did here, ever again!"

They were all then whisked to City Hall for a ceremony to honour the entire police force for cleaning up the city. At the ceremony, the mayor, chief, and Captain Harringson all gave speeches commending the hard work and bravery of the officers, especially Ivan and Ronald, for making Salinas safe once again. They also announced that they would set up a new unit that would prevent crime leaders from ever setting up shop in the city again. The mayor then called up Ronald and Ivan to say something, and all Ronald could do was blush and say, "Well, it was what I had to do."

Ivan had more to say, including how grateful he was to be able to work with such a great police force, and how fortunate he was to be able to give back to such a fine community. After Ivan had finished talking, the mayor then said, "Ronald, Ivan, for your hard work and dedication in defeating those crime leaders, I am happy to present to you both these medals of honour!"

The mayor put the medals around their necks, and Ronald held it in his hand and said, "Thank you, Mr. Mayor! I wasn't expecting any rewards!"

"Well, you deserve it!" the mayor replied.

This signalled the end of the ceremony. The portal opened up to the next game, signalling that it was time to move on to the next game. Pixie, who was in the crowd, walked up to Ronald and told him that the portal was waiting for him. When he saw it, he said to the officers in front of him, "Well, it looks like I've got to get moving."

Harringson shook Ronald's hand, and he said, "Ronald, congratulations! I am so proud of you! I wish you well on the rest of your journey home!"

"Thank you, sir," Ronald said. "It was an honour to work for you."

"What about me?" Ivan asked.

"It was also great to work with you, too, Ivan," Ronald told him, with a smile on his face.

"And, I enjoyed working with you!" Ivan said. "You are a real good guy! The real world is lucky to have you!"

"Thanks," Ronald replied.

"And, we'll never forget you!" Captain Harringson added.

After shaking hands and hugging some of the officers, Pixie told Ronald, "Ronald, we've got to get going."

"Okay, let's go," he replied.

They then went to the portal and entered it, making their way to the seventh game of the journey.

CHAPTER TEN

As soon as they got out of the portal, Pixie and Ronald found themselves near the entrance of a castle at the edge of a town. They also found themselves carrying backpacks that had magically appeared. Ronald then reached behind his back to feel the backpack, and asked Pixie, "Why are we carrying *these* things?"

"I think we have to carry something around with us during this game," Pixie replied as she was also feeling her backpack. "But I don't know what it could be."

Ronald then started looking around. The town reminded him of a game that was released earlier in the century. He then said, "You know, this game looks a lot like something that I played when I was a teen."

"Well, it's not," Pixie replied. "It's something different. And I know that because I've been to that other game that you're probably thinking about, and this town seems to have a few differences from the town in that game. For one thing, in that other game, I don't think there was a castle on the edge of town."

Ronald just shrugged. They then observed that the town looked like it was in distress, as if something bad had happened and they were looking for a hero to solve whatever problems they were facing. Ronald and Pixie then walked around for a bit until they came to the west entrance, which had a sign above it that read, "Welcome to Wallapville!"

"Wallapville?!" Ronald asked, confused. "This clearly isn't the game that I was thinking about, then."

"What did I just tell you?!" Pixie answered tersely. "I *told you* that this game was different from that other game you played, didn't I?!"

"Well, you don't have to get mad."

Pixie then looked at her phone, and found out that this game was called Magnate Hunter RPG. Their first course of action was to head straight back to the town's castle, which was where they first landed after getting out of the portal. "Huh. Looks like we shouldn't have walked away from that castle. We were right where we were supposed to be!" Ronald said.

"Whatever," Pixie replied, rolling her eyes. "We had to know what this town was called, didn't we?"

"We could have asked whoever is in charge here. Or the townsfolk."

"It made more sense this way."

They then walked back to the castle. As they were walking, Ronald noticed that their clothes didn't change, and asked, "Why aren't our clothes changing? Are they going to change later, like mine did in the last game? Or is it like the dancing game?"

Pixie again looked at her phone, and then said, "Well, it looks like we're supposed to play this game dressed like this. I guess when players create their characters, they can decide what clothes they want to wear. And since we were already in our regular clothes, they didn't need to be changed."

"Oh. Does that mean it's a two-player game?" Ronald asked.

Pixie looked again at her phone, and said, "Yes, it is."

"Well, that should make you happy," Ronald said.

"Why's that?"

"Because you don't have to sit around the entire game."

"Yeah, that's true! I mean, at least I won't be *bored* this time, sitting around in some lobby doing nothing."

They arrived back at the castle a couple of minutes later, and entered the doors. Inside, they saw a group of servants crying, and also noticed a very depressed-looking king and queen sitting on the throne. They looked to their right, and saw a stand there, and guessed that it might be important. As Ronald and Pixie approached the throne, everyone in the room looked up and were excited to see them. "Oh, good, the heroes have arrived!" the king said.

"Huh? What are you talking about?" Ronald said, confused as to what the king meant.

"Well, aren't you the two people sent by the international community to help us?" the queen then asked.

"I guess we are," Pixie replied.

"Wonderful! A huge disaster has overtaken our land!" the king said emphatically.

Before Ronald and Pixie could say anything, he king proceeded to give them the background to the game. The kingdom had been a peaceful land, blessed with numerous natural resources. The kingdom had been able to also develop secondary and tertiary industries related to the exploitation of the resources, which gave its citizens further happiness and prosperity. The king and queen were the rulers of the kingdom, and had been running the land from the capital Wallapville. They also had two children, a prince and a princess. The royal family was very popular within the kingdom because they treated their subjects with respect and dignity, and personally helped out its citizens whenever they needed it. The kingdom had been divided into four provinces, with each having been run by local governors. The provinces were located to the west, east, southeast, and southwest. The provinces were given enough autonomy so that they could make the decisions required to properly deal with any issues related to their local populations. The governors were also well-liked because they were always fair, and were not corrupt. The kingdom was also bordered on the north by another country, which they had enjoyed good relations with. However, one day, an evil and greedy business magnate with magical capabilities, named Tony Demarché, came to the kingdom and demanded a large number of concessions so he could set up shop here, including the ability to buy whichever businesses he felt like. The king refused, and instead of going away, Demarché overthrew the governors and installed his own puppets to lead the provinces. He also built a mansion to the north of Wallapville, which served as his base of operations, and made it large enough to block the once unguarded border in order to prevent anyone from the other country from trying to help remove Demarché. He also installed a force field along the border for added protection. His minions were wreaking havoc on the local populations with their corruption and brutality, but the king still refused to relent. In order to put more pressure on the king, Demarché kidnapped the princess, and told the king that if he wanted to ever see his daughter again, he would have to abdicate his throne to Demarché and renounce any future claims to it, including those of his descendants. Demarché also promised his puppet governors that they would retain their positions after he had gained control over the kingdom. However, the king refused to give into his demands, and instead asked for help from the game's international powers to take down Demarché and his governors so that peace could be restored in the kingdom. After hearing of the king's plea for help, Demarché installed a force field at the north entrance to Wallapville, which completely restricted travel for the citizens. The only people that were now able travel from north from Wallapville were those personally invited by Demarché. As the king and his servants were considered his enemies, Demarché never invited them. The only way to break both force fields was to retrieve the four briefcases held by Demarché's governors, which contained special powers that allowed the force field to stay up, and the only way to completely reopen the border was to defeat Demarché and rescue the princess, which in turn would destroy his mansion. Once the king had finished his speech, he asked, "So, are you two up to the task?"

"Yes, we are," Ronald said. "We have to be."

"As ready as we will be," Pixie added.

"Wonderful!" the queen said happily. "Now, you cannot waste *any* time! We want our daughter back as soon as possible! We miss her so much!"

The queen then handed them 100 coins, and said, "This is just to start you off on your journey."

As they made their way through the lobby, Ronald pointed to the stand he saw earlier, and asked, "And what's that stand for?"

"It's for those briefcases that I mentioned," the king replied. "But it won't do you any good right now. In order for it to work, you have to get the first briefcase. Now go! There isn't anymore time to waste!"

Ronald and Pixie then left the castle, and started on their way. "You know, we don't even know how to defeat these enemies," he said.

Pixie checked her phone, and more instructions started coming in. "Oh, it's a turn-based game," she said. "So, we exchange turns in terms of attacking our enemies. We can jump on them only, so we won't get any weapons."

"Oh, so it *does* work like that other game, minus the weapons."

"Yes. And, it looks like I am the only one who is going to fight with you, as we don't get any companions that will join us in this game."

"Good to know. So, knowing all that, which way are we supposed to go?"

"It just says to ask the townsfolk, and they'll give us clues about the first puppet-governor that we're supposed to defeat."

"Okay."

They then walked around the town, and attempted to ask the people about what their task was. The initial citizens that they came into contact with would not talk. They finally came across someone who mentioned that the puppet-governor to the east, named Hylerd, was the first one that they had to beat. They found out that this person was a friend of someone who lived in the village in the eastern province. And that friend overheard a conversation about how Demarché had been informed of Pixie and Ronald's arrival, and told Hylerd to be ready for anything. "Well, I guess that's where we are headed," Ronald said.

They then thanked the person, and then started to head east, when another townsperson stopped them and said, "Wait! What are you two doing?! You're not going to travel without any supplies, are you?!"

"Why? Do we need to take any supplies with us?" Ronald asked.

"Of course! Why do you think you were given 100 coins to start with?! You know how *dangerous* it is beyond this town ever since that magnate arrived in the kingdom, don't you?" the person asked.

"What do you mean?" Pixie said. "We weren't informed of any dangers by the king and queen."

"Well, that's because they haven't travelled outside of the castle since the princess was kidnapped," the person said. "Demarché has unleashed a ton of monsters around the kingdom to prevent anyone from trying to rescue her."

"Will these items help us?" Ronald asked.

"Yes, they will!" the person responded. "They will help you to heal, and they will aid you in defeating those monsters. They are also useful against the governors, too."

"I see," Pixie said. "Well, we'd better get some items, then. Thank you for informing us."

Ronald and Pixie then headed to the nearest store. As they made their way there, Pixie looked to Ronald and said, "Well, that explains why we were given these backpacks when we first arrived in this game. We can't really carry a ton of items in our hands *and* be able to deal with all of the tasks of this game."

"Yeah, that's for sure," Ronald said. "At home, whenever I have to carry anything with me, I have trouble holding onto everything if I have more than a few items in my hands."

Pixie just smiled. When they got to the store, they stocked up on as many items as they could carry in their bags. They then left the store and headed for the eastern gate. Before they could leave, the person with whom they had spoken to before their trip to the store stopped them again. "Wait!" he said.

"Now what?!" Ronald asked impatiently. "We're kind of on a mission here! We *really* need to get going!"

"I forgot to tell you about how the turn-based nature of this game works!" the person replied.

"Oh?" Pixie replied. "Is there some sort of special system? It thought it was a game where monsters attack one-by-one, and where Ronald will attack, and then I attack after him, and then it's the monster's turn, and so on."

"Well, yes, it is basically like that," the person said. "But the tutorial is a prerequisite step for the game! Without it, you cannot move on, and you will have to start all over!"

"Okay, fine," Ronald said, rolling his eyes. "Let's get this tutorial over with."

The person then gave them directions on how the turn-based attack and defence systems worked. He also showed them how they could both get additional power when attacking their enemies during a battle. He also showed them how to attack with more strength during individual attacks in order to shorten the length of their battles. Once the tutorial was over, Ronald and Pixie were finally able to make their way to the eastern exit. They collectively took a deep breath, and started on their journey.

They noticed that the eastern area was a plains area, with rolling hills, green grass, and lots of trees. The air was really fresh, and they noticed some animals roaming around. Pixie then looked at her phone to see how to determine what their enemies were in each screen, when she heard Ronald say, "Hey, these animals look nice! I'm going to get closer to see what they're doing."

Pixie quickly looked up from her phone and yelled, "Ronald, don't!" to Ronald as he started walking towards the animals.

However, it was too late, as Ronald approached what seemed to be a friendly rabbit. Suddenly, the rabbit turned around, and its face went from friendly to evil. It then attacked Ronald, allowing it to get the first strike when the battle started. "What the...?" Ronald asked as he was attacked.

The battle then started, with Ronald and Pixie on the left, and the rabbit on the right. The rabbit then struck Ronald to finish the attack started in the field. When this happened Ronald said, "Whoa! He's not giving me any time to get prepared!"

However, Ronald was able to limit the amount of damage caused by the rabbit by using one of the defence tactics that he had been taught in the tutorial. After the rabbit returned to its position, Pixie said, "See, Ronald? That's why I *told you* not to approach those animals! They are amongst the *enemies* in this game!"

"Well, you told me only *after* I was on my way to see what they were doing," Ronald replied.

"You could have stopped!"

Pixie was quite annoyed at Ronald's attempt to deflect any blame. Ronald then said, "Well anyway, we're in the battle now, so let's just defeat this thing."

Ronald then attacked the rabbit first, using the skills that he had learned in the tutorial to increase his attacking power, all in an effort to inflict as much damage as he could on the rabbit. After just one hit, the rabbit was defeated, and Ronald was shocked. "Wow! That was easy!" he said.

"Yeah," Pixie replied. "I didn't even get a chance to attack it."

"Please don't start complaining like you did when I had that bazooka in the second game," Ronald said, sighing because he was worried that Pixie might start ranting again.

"I'm not going to complain," Pixie said with a laugh. "I know that there will be times where I won't get a chance to attack in this game. However let this be a lesson! We have to be careful in this game!"

They returned to the plains scene, and suddenly found themselves in the middle of the screen. The monsters noticed them, and collectively started charging at them. Due to the quickness of the enemies, Ronald and Pixie had to engage in battle with each of the monsters in succession. In each case, Ronald and Pixie defeated the enemies in one or two turns. After they had defeated all of their opponents, they noticed that there were a lot of coins and other items on the ground, and also saw something called "experience points" being added up on the phone. As they stared at the coins, Ronald asked, "Are we supposed to pick them up?"

"I guess so," Pixie replied. "I mean, without extra coins, we can't buy anything after we run out of the initial 100 that the queen gave us. And these items will help us out in our battles."

They picked up as many coins and items as they could before they disappeared, after which Ronald went to take a look at the experience points. "What do those things mean?" he asked.

Pixie took a look at her phone, and said, "It seems that when we get 100 of those points, our strength increases, meaning we get better attacking power and sustain less damage."

"Damage?! I thought I had unlimited health and energy!"

"Well, in this game, it seems like you can *still* sustain damage. I guess this is just a way to minimize the amount of damage that you take. But, the unlimited health allows you to restart the game from the last point you were at before your health points went down to zero."

Ronald could only shake his head. They then moved on to the next screen, where they came across more monsters. These battles took a little longer, as these opponents were much stronger, and each battle required the defeat of multiple monsters at once. Once all of the enemies had been cleared, and all of the coins and items collected, Ronald said, in frustration, "You know, this turn-based nature is getting annoying. I want to be able to defeat these enemies without having to worry about them attacking me. I mean, it's *really* annoying that I have to wait my turn to attack again. I want a quick victory so that we can move on and get this game over with. The second game was easier because you were able to get power-ups, and you could clear the whole screen using the abilities that you get from them."

"Well, you'll just have to deal with it," Pixie replied. "That is how this game works. Don't you think I miss having power-ups?! Don't you think that even *I'm* getting annoyed about having to wait for my turn to attack these things?! Especially when we have to face more than one monster at a time during each battle?"

"I'm sure you are. It's just really frustrating."

"I know. But, from what I gather, we have to play this type of game only once."

"How would *you* know?"

"Think about it. There aren't too many turn-based games out there, and The VGG only wants you to play the challenging games that you can actually pick up and play. Plus, we haven't been in *any* open-ended games, have we? That seems to be the pattern here."

"Yeah, makes sense. Anyway, we'd better keep moving."

They continued on to the next screen, and there were no enemies there. Instead, there was a river with no bridge going over to the other side. However, there was also a button a foot from the river bank. "I wonder what this does," Ronald said as they walked to the button.

"I don't know," Pixie said. "I guess you'll just have to push it to find out."

Ronald then stepped on the button, when suddenly a bridge magically appeared. "Huh, that's interesting," Ronald said. "This is similar to what I had to do when I had played that other game."

"Just because it's not *exactly* that other game doesn't mean that there won't be any similarities to the other game," Pixie replied.

They crossed the bridge, and then went on to the next screen, where they were attacked by more monsters. They were able to fend off their enemies, and after all of the battles, they noticed that their experience points were resetting, meaning that they reached 100 of these points. This meant that they were levelling up, and getting stronger and becoming less prone to damage in the process. It also resulted in the increase of their health and ability points, which were now restored to 100%. They also learned new abilities, which were far more powerful than the basic ones they had. "What do these new abilities do?" Ronald asked.

"I guess we'll find out when we get into another battle," Pixie replied.

They then travelled east one more screen before finally arriving at the village, which was called Dainty Town. Upon arriving, the townsfolk immediately rejoiced, knowing that the heroes that they had heard of were finally there. They immediately told Ronald and Pixie how much they missed their old governor, and that the puppet installed by the business magnate had made their lives extremely difficult. Hylerd was extorting tax money from the people, and spending it on himself. He was also crushing business in the village by only allowing businesses to sell products and services made and offered by Demarché's industries, although the inn in town was allowed to stay open because Demarché decreed that travellers that were going between his mansion and the governors' mansions needed a place to stay overnight due to the distance of travel. Furthermore, the puppet governor would only allow a local business owner to start up a new business after filling out mountains of paperwork, which led to numerous delays. After they finished, Ronald asked, "So, how do we get to the governor's mansion so we can get rid of this guy?"

"His mansion is located to the east," said a female villager, pointing east. "But, it's protected by a lock. To get the key that will open the locked gate of the mansion, you first have to solve a puzzle found south of the village. When you successfully solve it, you will then be given the key."

"How difficult is it?" Pixie asked.

"It's pretty difficult," replied a male villager. "None of us were able to solve it."

"Well, we'll give it a try," Ronald said.

After they had finished talking with the villagers, Pixie and Ronald headed south. They encountered more monsters along the way, which were even stronger than the ones they had faced. However, they used their new abilities to overpower these ghouls, and were able to defeat them. They collected the coins and whatever other items were left behind, and then continued south one more screen, where they found the puzzle. It was just as difficult as the villagers said it would be, as it involved trying to align blocks in a particular way in order to cause the key to be released. It took them awhile to solve it, but once they finished the puzzle, five enemies suddenly appeared, with one of them holding the key to the mansion. "What the...? Where did *they* come from?!" Ronald asked in a surprised tone, as neither he nor Pixie had been warned that this would happen upon solving the puzzle.

"I don't know," Pixie replied. "I'm just as shocked as you are."

The monsters then attacked, and a battle ensued. During the battle, Ronald and Pixie used some of their items to heal themselves, and also used some of the items to attack their enemies. They also combined their new attacking abilities with their traditional ones to thwart the monsters. However, it was a long battle, and the monsters were able to got some hits in. It took Ronald and Pixie 10 turns to defeat all of the enemies, after which the key was dropped. They also noticed that they had received about 1.5X the experience points they normally would have for facing this many enemies. They also were able to level up again, and gained a new ability. Ronald then picked up the key, and they started northward. They had to defeat more enemies that had magically reappeared, and then returned to the village. They then headed east to the next part of the village, and first went to the shops to buy some essential items before heading to the inn to rest up and heal. After they had fully healed up, they travelled east to the governor's mansion.

Immediately after exiting the village, they encountered more enemies, which they were able to defeat with relative ease, and also received a level-up in between battles. They continued east for a few more screens, and faced and defeated more monsters in the process before making it to the governor's mansion. The exterior of the mansion was just like any political leader's mansion, though there were also a few differences. It was painted in a very bright, pink colour, and was more inviting than the evil castles that they came across in the second and fifth games. Outside, they found a vibrant garden that had many flowers, as well as a large lawn that had nice statues, flowing fountains, and a bright brick pathway. As they approached the gate, they saw that it was padlocked. "I guess this key is for that lock," Ronald said.

"Only one way to find out," Pixie said. "Put the key in and see if it works."

Ronald did so, and the lock suddenly disappeared. They went through the gates, and made their way to the front door of the mansion. As they approached the front door, they came across some guards, who immediately started attacking the two of them. After a 6-turn battle, they defeated the guards. Pixie and Ronald also received double the experience points for defeating the guards when compared to what they had received for defeating the puzzle enemies, and levelled up again. They then entered the mansion, and saw that it was beautifully decorated, with nice Renaissance-era paintings. It also had portraits of the old governor, named Crossing, and his family all over the walls, meaning that Hylerd hadn't had a chance to redecorate. As they made their way through the mansion, they came across administrators, who immediately attacked Pixie and Ronald. These enemies were more difficult compared to the previous enemies that they had dealt with on their way to the mansion. In defeating this set of enemies, Ronald and Pixie received more experience points, which allowed them to level up even faster, and gave them many new abilities. Finally, after searching a large number of rooms, they finally reached the governor's office. When they entered it, Hylerd said, "Oh! You made it this far! Well, that is a surprise! Maybe Demarché's monsters and my minions were too easy for you. But not me! I am going to be *impossible* to defeat! You will meet your demise right here!"

"We'll see about that!" Ronald said defiantly.

The battle then started, with Ronald attacking first, followed by Pixie, who each used their new abilities to go after the governor. However, the governor himself had a large number of special abilities, and used these to inflict massive damage on Pixie and Ronald, who did their best to minimize the effects of his powers. After about 7 turns, and after taking some healing items, they finally were able to defeat the governor. When this happened, Hylerd said, "Oh no! I can't believe it! I was defeated by a cowgirl and a normal guy! How could this be?!"

"Believe it!" Ronald said sternly.

Then, Hylerd disappeared, and out of nowhere Governor Crossing arrived. "Thank you so much for rescuing me!" Crossing said. "I didn't know how *long* I was going to be stuck in that prison!"

"You're very welcome," Pixie replied. "It was our pleasure."

Governor Crossing then looked around his desk, and pulled out the first briefcase. Handing it to them, Crossing told Pixie and Ronald, "This is the first of the briefcases! You will need to put this on the stand you saw when you entered the castle in Wallapville! It will tell you where you need to head to next. The only way to get rid of that force field to Demarché's mansion is by defeating the other three puppet governors and retrieving those briefcases!"

Ronald took it, and said, "Thanks. So, why couldn't we just take it from the desk?"

"Because the only way to get access to the desk was by defeating that magnate's minion!" Crossing replied. "You see, *we* are the only ones with access to it. And when you defeated that minion, it magically freed me from his prison, and brought me here."

"Oh," Pixie said. "Okay, well, you're again very welcome for the rescue. Come on, Ronald. We've still got a lot of work to do!"

They then headed back west towards Wallapville, where they encountered and defeated more enemies along the way, and even getting to level up. They also passed through Dainty Town again, and stayed at the inn for awhile before starting again for Wallapville. They faced more enemies as they travelled west, and were able to defeat them. They finally made it to Wallapville, and headed to the inn, where they stayed to rest up before heading to the castle, where they would find out where they had to go to next after placing the briefcase on the stand.

As they were heading to the castle, Ronald asked Pixie, "Say, Pixie, are there any side-quests in this game?"

"Side-quests? What do you mean by that?" Pixie asked, quite confused as to what Ronald meant.

"Side-quests are quests that you can do outside of the main game. In those games that you had visited that allowed you to participate didn't they have side-quests?"

"I wouldn't know. Usually, I'm just instructed about the main story, and no one really mentions anything about these side-quests. This is the first time I've ever heard about side-quests."

"Oh. Well, can you check if there are any in this game?"

"Sure, I can do that."

Pixie then checked her phone, and was not able to find any information about side-quests. "I can't find anything here," she said. "Maybe we should ask around town."

Ronald proceeded to ask some of the townsfolk about side-quests, and a few mentioned that there were some places that they could go to if they wanted to do such things. One of the side-quests involved going around the kingdom and doing various tasks. If each task was completed successfully, then Ronald and Pixie would get a reward. "You know, Ronald, we just don't have that kind of time," Pixie said. "We need to get you home, and these side-quests, as you call them, will keep you stuck in this game for a *very* long time."

"Yeah, I don't think I am willing to waste time right now," Ronald replied. "Having to do tasks that forces me to visit and revisit places in this game over and over again is just going to get boring and very tedious."

"Okay, then. Let's head to the castle and put that briefcase on the stand to see where we need to head to next."

They then made their way to castle. Inside the lobby, they saw the king and queen standing there. When he saw them holding the briefcase, the king said, "Oh good! You have defeated Hylerd! Now, when you put that briefcase on the stand there, it will tell you where you have to travel to next."

Ronald nodded and promptly placed the briefcase on the stand. Suddenly, some magical dust and light appeared, which then formed a circle, and caused Ronald to jump back. The circle of dust and light then made its way onto the briefcase. After the light subsided, the front of the briefcase now read "W." "What does that mean?" Pixie asked the king and queen.

"It means that the next briefcase is west of here," the queen replied.

"It also means that you will have to defeat Albert Youla in order to get the next briefcase!" the king added. "Youla deposed the original governor, Francisco Martín, who is imprisoned in a dungeon somewhere in that mansion."

"You must head in that direction at once!" the queen said. "There isn't any time to waste! Our daughter needs to be rescued!"

Meanwhile, back at his mansion, Demarché was very upset at how easily Pixie and Ronald had defeated Hylerd. "He was *impossible* to defeat!" Demarché muttered. "And yet, a cowgirl and some average guy beat him! How can this be?!"

He then immediately informed Youla that Pixie and Ronald would be heading in his direction, and that Youla should be prepared for their arrival.

Pixie and Ronald first went to the shops to restock on some items that had been used in their previous battles. They then headed west, exiting through the entrance gate that they had encountered when they first arrived in the game. After going west one screen, they suddenly found themselves at a shoreline, and found that there was nowhere else to go. "So, what do we do now?" Ronald asked. "I mean, wherever we're supposed to go, we probably need a boat, since there's no other way to get past all of this water."

"Let me check," Pixie said, looking at her phone.

After a few minutes, she received some more information. She then said, "We're supposed to go up north one screen, where we will then be given further instructions."

They did as instructed, and found a captain standing by the dock. "What are you travellers doing here?" he asked them.

"We need to find a town to the west of here, as there's some sort of governor named Albert Youla who is terrorizing a province of this kingdom," Ronald said.

"You'll need a boat, as the only town I can think of is Relaxville, and that is on an island about 15 kilometres west of here," the captain replied.

"Do you have a boat?" Pixie asked.

"I used to," the captain replied. "But the sharks out there ate it up. Right around the time that business guy, what's his name...? Demarché came in. It seems like he unleashed some sort of potion or something on those sharks, as they had never attacked any ships until now."

"So, what do we do?" Ronald said.

"If you can find me a ship, then I can take you there," the captain replied. "My crew is over there in the lighthouse waiting for the chance to get back out to sea."

Ronald and Pixie then walked away, and Ronald asked, "Now what do we do?"

Pixie's phone rang, and she checked it, and found a message that said that they had to head one screen to the north. "I guess we have to go up north another screen," she replied.

They then headed up north to the next screen, and saw that there was a boat shop there. They went inside, and found a salesman waiting. "Welcome to my boat shop!" he said. "What do you need help with?"

"We need a shark-resistant boat so that we can defeat Albert Youla on the island to the west," Ronald replied.

"Well, you're just in luck! I happen to have a perfect one that should suit your needs in stock! And it's yours, if you can solve my puzzle!"

"I guess we have no choice," Ronald replied. "What is the puzzle?"

The salesman then showed them, and it involved having to build a model ship, which was a replica of the one that the salesman had, but without any instructions. Ronald and Pixie quickly went to work, and it took them about 10 minutes to finish it, much to the shock of the salesman. "You're the first two to *ever* solve that puzzle!" he said.

"I've had a bit of practice building models using only my imagination," Ronald said.

Pixie looked at him, stunned. "How is that possible?!" she asked. "Your only experience is in marketing!"

"I used building blocks growing up," Ronald said. "And, sometimes I still play with them. I have a few in my room. I also play a bit with my girlfriend's nieces and nephew."

"Well, a deal's a deal," the salesman replied. "The boat will be at the dock."

Pixie and Ronald then headed back to the dock, and just as the salesman had promised, the boat was there. The captain and his crew were already on board, and were getting ready to set sail for the tropical island. "Well, there you are!" the captain happily said to Ronald and Pixie. "We were looking for you when the boat arrived!"

"We didn't know that the boat would come so fast," Ronald replied. "We had to walk back, you know."

"Whatever the case, thank you so much for getting us a boat!" the captain said. "The guy who brought it said that it is shark-resistant! Music to my ears!"

"That's what we were told, too," Ronald said.

"Anyway, get on board! We've got an island to sail to!"

Ronald and Pixie promptly got on board, and the ship set sail for the tropical island. After a while, they arrived at the dock of the island, and everyone got off. As Ronald and Pixie started looking around the island, they encountered enemies right away. These enemies were more dangerous than the ones they had dealt with in the plains region. In addition to monsters, they had to face dangerous plants, which sprayed poison and sleeping gas, and caused status effects during battle. Ronald and Pixie were able to defeat their opponents, but had to use some of the items they had bought to recharge and protect themselves from the poison attacks. Also, the spiked shoes that they had received as one of their experience gains allowed them to stomp on the plants and defeat them. After travelling a few more screens, along which they had to engage in a few more battles, they arrived at Relaxville, which was the village on this island. After resting at the inn for the night, they then made their way through the village to gather any information they could about the governor's mansion, including how they would get there. Through their conversations, they found out that they would have to travel through the jungle in order to reach the mansion, and were warned that the jungle was very dangerous. They were also warned about the governor himself, as he was a dangerous man. The villagers also urged Ronald and Pixie to stock up on items from the shop in town, advice which they heeded to. Once they felt that they had everything they needed, Pixie and Ronald started for the jungle.

Inside the jungle, they immediately encountered some very difficult jungle creatures that they had to fight off. It required a lot of time and energy to fight off the creatures, but after they defeated them, they received some much needed level-ups. They then looked ahead, and noticed that the jungle was getting thicker. "I sure hope that we don't have to deal with a ton of monsters!" Ronald said.

"Same here," Pixie agreed, nodding her head. "I just hope that this jungle isn't too deep."

However, the jungle was exactly that, and it became even more dangerous as they went on. Instead of having to face enemies only from the front, they had to encounter that attacked them from all sides, including the plants that they had first encountered after docking, which were hidden in the trees and bushes. This kept Ronald and Pixie completely off guard, and affected their battle strategies. This also meant taking a few more turns in order defeat their opponents. However, defeating these difficult monsters allowed them to gain a few level ups, including better attacking and defence abilities, as well as giving them some new special abilities. To ensure that they didn't go too far off course, they stuck to the pathways. After travelling through what seemed like an endless number of screens, due to having to turn in various directions, they finally made it to the governor's mansion. The home, which looked like those found on Caribbean plantations, had a colonial era look to its exterior, with the facade having a combination of white sidings and stucco. It also had large balconies, and some outdoor furniture from the Southern plantation era on them. The property had its own sugar farm, papaya trees, as well as some vegetables gardens.

As they approached the gate, Ronald and Pixie were immediately attacked by guards. These guards were more difficult than the ones they had faced at Hylerd's mansion, and it took 10 turns to finally defeat them. After levelling up, they entered the gates, and went through the courtyard before entering the mansion. Once inside, they had to deal with another set of Youla's goons, who had been waiting for some time to battle Ronald and Pixie, and who attacked the unprepared duo when they entered. However, despite the difficulty of the battles, they were eventually able to defeat all of the enemies that they had faced, and for which they received another increase in their experience level. After this set of battles, they continued making their way through the mansion. Unlike Hylerd's mansion, they saw that Albert Youla had already done some redecorating, as the walls and flooring resembled what a plantation owner would typically decorate his house with. The walls had colonial, US independence-era, and Southern plantation-era paintings, wallpaper, and furniture, while Youla had put in hardwood flooring all over the house. This was opposite to the simple style that Martín preferred. Also, there were portraits on the walls of Youla and his family, Demarché and his family, and even some of Youla's friends. As they walked through the mansion, they had to defeat Youla's administrators, and these battles were also quite difficult for Ronald and Pixie. However, they were able to prevail over their enemies, and they were also able to earn a level-up after defeating the final administrator. Finally, they made it to Youla's personal vegetable garden, where they saw him watering the plants. Youla looked up, quite shocked that Pixie and Ronald had made it through the mansion. "Oh! You made it here!" he said in a Spanish accent, eyebrows still raised in shock. "I'm surprised my goons didn't defeat you!"

"Well, we're here, so clearly they weren't successful," Ronald said.

"Now, where's that briefcase?" Pixie asked.

"I have it with me," Youla replied. "But you won't get it from me! Now, we fight!"

This battle took much longer than the one they had with Hylerd, and was much more difficult. Youla had more special abilities than Hylerd as well, including the power to call on the plants and vegetables to attack Ronald and Pixie together, which not only caused damage, but could also cause negative status effects. They were able to defeat the plants in short order. However, the whole battle required 15 turns in all, as the difficulty of it forced them to take turns to heal and deal with status issues. Using the abilities that they had acquired from the level ups in this tropical paradise, they were eventually able to defeat Albert Youla. Finally, when Youla was defeated, he said, "I can't believe a weak girl and a puny boy beat me! How could this be?!"

Before Ronald could answer, Pixie said, "I'm not weak! I'm really strong! Maybe you shouldn't judge a book by its cover the next time you have to deal with a girl!"

"And, I can lift a good amount of weight," Ronald added.

"Oh, Tony Demarché, I have failed you!" Youla said, just as he was about to disappear.

A few seconds later, he disintegrated, and the briefcase then dropped to the ground, with Martín appearing out of nowhere. "Oh thank you, Pixie and Ronald! I owe you a debt of gratitude for getting me out of that cell! I didn't know how long I was going to be trapped in there!" he said.

"You're welcome," Ronald said. "We had a bit of trouble with Youla, but we did it."

Francisco Martín then picked up the briefcase and handed it to Pixie. "Take this, as it will be needed to help you to figure out where you must head to next on your journey," he said.

"Okay, thanks," Pixie said.

After taking the briefcase from Martín, Ronald and Pixie were then transported straight back to Relaxville, where they were thanked by the villagers for getting rid of Youla. The villagers also warned them that the remaining two governors were even more dangerous, and that Demarché himself would not be easy to bring down. After saying their goodbyes, Ronald and Pixie headed back to the dock to board the captain's ship, where they then sailed back to the mainland.

Upon arriving at the dock, they thanked the captain and his crew, and them immediately made their way back to the castle. When they entered the lobby, Pixie headed straight for the stand and placed the briefcase on it. When she did this, the same light and dust appeared as it did after the first briefcase had been placed on it. Once the magic light was finished, the front of the second briefcase showed "SW." "So, do we have to go to the southwest area of town for the next briefcase?" Ronald asked.

"No," the king replied. "Your next destination is to the southwest *of* Wallapville. There is a desert area that is located there."

"Oh," Ronald said. "Is it tough to go through?"

"Oh yes!" the queen said. "You will need *lots* of water just to get *through* the desert! And, Demarché has unleashed many desert monsters there as well."

"Yikes!" Pixie said. "Well, we'd better get going, Ronald!"

"Yeah," Ronald said. "Well, let's go!"

Meanwhile, at Demarché's mansion, Demarché was looking very worried. "Those two defeated Youla!" he said. "I can't believe it! I thought they wouldn't be able to deal with Youla's strength! I guess that cowgirl and that average guy are a lot stronger than I thought! I'd better inform Gregorious (the governor of the desert area) about the threat that he will be facing!"

Ronald and Pixie left the castle, and made their way to the shops to buy some items for their trip. On their way there, they were warned by the various townsfolk of the dangers lurking in the desert, including how some of the monsters unleashed by Demarché could pop out from the sand, which was similar to what Ronald and Pixie had encountered in the fantasy game's desert. At the shops, they loaded up on various healing and attacking items. Each one of the shopkeepers also gave them large amounts of water to ensure they didn't get thirsty. Any travellers that had previously attempted to travel through the desert not only had to deal with the monsters unleashed in it, but they also ran out of water. This forced them to dig into the sand, which yielded dirty groundwater, the result of a spell that Demarché had cast to ensure that no one could survive the desert. Therefore, the shop owners did this to prevent the alternative. Ronald and Pixie thanked them, and then travelled south to the southern area of town, then turned west to the southwestern area of town, and finally to the southwestern exit gate.

The desert area was just as difficult as they were told. Ronald and Pixie constantly had to deal with dust storm twisters, which also negatively affected their statuses. The enemies, for the most part, were situated away from the pathways, and were mostly desert-type enemies, including a spiked being, scorpions, evil cacti, and different types of mummies. The monsters were also extremely fast. As soon they saw Pixie and Ronald, they would attack them, which caught them by surprise. However, the monsters were no match for Pixie and Ronald, who used their enhanced strength and abilities to counter their enemies' strengths. They were able to make their way through the desert, and gained a level-up in the process. The heat was also very intense, and they found themselves drinking a lot of water to stay hydrated. At this point, they were very grateful to the shopkeepers for giving them all that extra water. They also noticed that this desert contained no oases, which was opposite to the desert area they had navigated through in the fantasy game. This reality meant that they did not have a place to rest, unlike the other game. They made sure that they did not stay off of the path because they knew that there were sand monsters lurking under the sand just waiting to attack them. After what seemed like an eternity, they finally made it to Dune Town, the village in this desert terrain.

Inside the town, they quickly looked for an in to rest in, as they were quite fatigued from their desert journey. This allowed them to fully recuperate, which brought their health and ability points back to 100%. After they were fully rested, they then walked around the town to ask the townsfolk about Gregorious, and where they would find his mansion. They were told that Gregorious was a very evil being, and was making things quite difficult for the townsfolk. He had cut off many of their revenue streams, and instead was taking kickbacks and diverting tax money to himself and to Demarché. They also mentioned that the mansion resembled a pharaoh's palace from Ancient Egypt, as the first governor wanted the residence to fit in with the desert surroundings. The villagers also mentioned that the mansion was located to the north of town, and that the real governor, Tillstrum, had been locked up in a prison somewhere to the east of town. They were explicitly told that they were not to try to rescue Tillstrum because he would be immediately freed once Gregorious was destroyed, and that it was more important to get to the mansion. Pixie and Ronald were also told that they needed to solve a puzzle in order to unlock the mansion's gates. After receiving this information, Pixie and Ronald first headed to the shops to stock up on the necessary items, especially water. They then headed to the village's north, and continued their journey to the mansion.

Once they were back in the desert, they had to go up three more screens in order to get to the mansion. They faced many more enemies along the way, who were difficult for Ronald and Pixie. The sand-dwelling monsters were coming up out of the ground, meaning that Pixie and Ronald had to be that much more alert so as not to be ambushed by these creatures. Every time they encountered these creatures, they had to go through 3-plus turn battles to defeat these monsters. And even though they faced many opponents, they were only able to level up once. However, they persevered and eventually were able to make their way to the governor's mansion. Once at the mansion's gates, they saw that the puzzle involved having to move blocks around to fit the holes in order to have a switch fall down, which would open up the gates. They struggled with this puzzle for an hour, but put their brains together and were finally able to finish it, after which a green switch fell down from the sky. Pixie immediately jumped on this switch, and the gate sparkled before opening up. The courtyard in this mansion looked like an oasis, as it had ponds, palm trees, lemon and lime trees, and even a pool. It also had statues, but it did not have any special plants or flowers growing because of the nature of the desert landscape. As they walked along the front pathway, Ronald noticed that no one was waiting to pounce on them. "What...no guards? What's going on here?" he asked.

"Maybe they're waiting for us inside, and want to catch us off-guard so that they can defeat us more easily," Pixie replied.

"Yeah, we'd better enter this mansion carefully. I mean, you never know how these games can turn things against you."

As they approached the front door, they took a deep breath, and opened the door slowly, being wary of any guards that may be waiting for them on the other side. As they entered the mansion, they looked in both directions, and then closed the door. Ronald saw some guards hiding behind some statues, and said to Pixie, "There they are! Let's get them!"

"Crap!" the guards said as Ronald and Pixie ran up to attack them.

Ronald got the first strike in, and thus started the battle. Ronald was in midair at this point, and used an acrobatic trick that he had learned from Dawna to put together a very powerful attack on the first guard, which allowed him to defeat the guard. He then got to go again on his regular turn, and used one of the abilities he had earned to defeat the second guard.

Pixie's turn was next, and she used a very powerful ability to defeat the third guard, leaving only one left. In his turn, the final guard used an ability that increased his defence capabilities, before the battle returned to Ronald. However, Ronald was able to use the same manoeuvre that he had used on the first guard, and was able to penetrate through this guard's defences. Pixie finished off the guard, which ended this battle. After collecting the coins, they then made their way through more rooms, where they encountered and defeated more of Gregorious' goons, before finally reaching his room. Once inside, Gregorious said to them, "So, cowgirl and normal guy! You finally made it! I've been waiting for you!"

"Your reign of terror over this province is over, Gregorious!" Ronald said.

"Yeah," Pixie added. "And we can either do this the easy way, where you hand over that briefcase in that locked cage, or we can do this the hard way, where we kick your butt!"

"I don't think you'll have *any* success today!" Gregorious said arrogantly. "I'll be the one who wins here!"

The fight then started, and Ronald and Pixie used their enhanced abilities and skills against Gregorious, and after only 6 turns they were able to defeat him. "Noooooooo! How could I lose? To *them*?!" he said as he blew up.

After Gregorious had disintegrated, Tillstrum magically arrived. "Oh thank you, Ronald and Pixie!" Tillstrum said. "I'm finally free of that prison cell! I can't believe that I had to live in there for so long!"

"You're welcome," Pixie said. "Now, about that briefcase...."

"Oh yes!" Tillstrum said. He then pulled out a key from his pocket, and unlocked the cage. He handed the briefcase to Ronald and said, "You're almost done collecting these briefcases! Just one more to go, and then you can go after Demarché!"

"Is the last place a difficult place to go?" Ronald asked as he took the briefcase.

"Oh yes! That Snow King is very difficult to beat! He has a lot of abilities that will cause problems for you!" Tillstrum replied. "Now go! There isn't any time to waste!"

Ronald and Pixie were then whisked back to the courtyard of the Wallapville castle. They entered the doors, where Ronald placed the briefcase on the stand. After the magical animation and the circle of light, the briefcase then had written on it "SE." "Well, looks like the final briefcase is located in the southeast," he said.

"Yes!" the queen replied. "Now, go! You've almost broken the force field! You cannot waste any time! Our daughter is waiting for you!"

"And, I'm sure Demarché is getting anxious," the king added. "He knows that he's in trouble, and that he has to protect himself!"

Meanwhile, back at Demarché's mansion, it was clear that he was not happy at all. "How can this be?!" he yelled to his staff. "*Gregorious* was defeated by those two?! And so *easily* at that?! He was supposed to be impossible to beat! Those two were supposed to be no match for him!"

"Well, sir, you can't underestimate people like that," his secretary said. "You have to be careful with heroes of *any* stripe."

"I sure hope the Snow King can defeat them! Otherwise, I'm in trouble here! I can't be left with nothing! Not after all the effort that I've put in to take over this kingdom! And especially not when I am so close to getting access to all of these resources that would make me the richest man on the planet, and allow me to control any country that I desire!"

While Demarché was busy worrying, Ronald and Pixie had left the castle to tackle the Snow King, but not before they had gone to the shops to stock up on some items. They also bought winter clothes, which they immediately put on because they were warned about how cold the southeastern area of the kingdom was. They then headed for the southeastern part of the town, and exited through the southeastern entrance gate, making their way to find the final briefcase.

The landscape that they now had to endure was an icy, wintery area, which also had a lot of snow falling, combined with a strong, chilly wind. As they made their way through the landscape, Ronald said, "Boy, this sure isn't like that other game! I remember how the heroes in that game could travel through a landscape similar to this without having to wear winter clothing, and they were just fine. In fact, in that other game they didn't have to worry about the issues of going through a desert, unlike this game where we had to deal with that desert landscape."

"What did I tell you when we first arrived?!" Pixie said.

"That this game isn't the other game."

"Exactly! Now, let's keep going."

As they continued on, they encountered winter-themed monsters in the next screen, including frozen plants and evil snowmen. They were able to fend off the creatures, and in the process, they levelled up, while also picking up the coins and items that they were awarded for defeating the monsters. They then travelled a few more screens, after which they faced more enemies along the way. They were easily able to defeat them, and travelled along. Finally, they made it to Snow Village, the village of this wintery area. They decided that they were tired from the day's travels, and thus stayed the night at the inn to refresh. When they woke up, they saw that there was a healing item waiting for them on their nightstands. They took the bottles which said "healing items," and they then walked around town to ask where they could find the final briefcase. The villagers mentioned that the old governor, Rufus Penguin, had been deposed by a loyal minion of Demarché, the Snow King. The new puppet governor erected the Snow Castle, which was located to the east of the village, and from where he directed the affairs of the province. This was in contrast to Penguin, who did not have his own mansion as he felt that having such a place was a display of arrogance. Instead, Rufus Penguin had a house within the village, and would meet with the citizens at the community hall to discuss provincial business. Penguin had been arrested by the Snow King, and was thrown into a dungeon located somewhere within the Snow Castle. Since then, the Snow King had been making life difficult for the villagers, including using his power to freeze things to keep those that he did not like at bay. He did things like covering their houses in snow, or freezing their pipes and doors. Such spells would only be undone if the villagers paid the Snow King a ton of money. They also mentioned to them that the Snow King, in addition to using his freezing power, had other powers that he would readily use during battle if given the chance.

After thanking the villagers for their time, Ronald and Pixie then went to the shops to buy more healing items, as well as powerful attacking items, before heading east for the Snow Castle. On their way to the castle, they encountered more wintery enemies. They were able to hold their own and defeat these monsters, and even received a level-up after defeating the enemies. They travelled another four screens before they made it to the outside of the Snow Castle. They were not given any chance to catch their breath, as they were immediately attacked by the Ice Guards of the castle. It took them 5 turns to defeat the Ice Guards, after which they entered the gates. The outside of the castle was nothing but snow and ice, though it resembled a fairy-tale castle, complete with pointed spires. The courtyard was also completely frozen, except for the path to the entrance, and was decorated with ice statues of the Snow King, ice fountains, and even ice sculptures. After entering the castle, they saw that the interior looked like an ice palace, completely decorated with more ice statues of the Snow King. Ronald and Pixie kept their guard high for any goons or monsters that may attack them. As they made their way through the castle, they were attacked by ice goons created by the Snow King. It took quite a bit of effort, but they were able to defeat them, while gaining a few level-ups along the way. After going through a number of rooms, they finally made it to the backyard of the castle, where the Snow King was standing, waiting for them. "I've been waiting for you two!" the Snow King said. "I knew you would come eventually! That is why I am prepared for battle!"

"Just hand over the briefcase," Ronald said. "We already know how this is going to end."

"No, you don't!" the Snow King replied. "This is going to end completely differently compared to the previous governors that you defeated!"

"So you want to do this the hard way?" Pixie said. "Okay, let's go!"

The battle then started. Ronald and Pixie found out that The Snow King was definitely much more powerful than the previous governors that they had faced. Moreover, the Snow King had the ability to heal himself. This made the battle even more that much more difficult. Ronald and Pixie quickly became frustrated as any of their work was being immediately erased when the Snow King used a turn to heal himself. Although, at the times when this happened, Ronald and Pixie would take advantage of this opportunity to use a healing item themselves. More importantly, Ronald and Pixie did not give up, and used any ability and item they possessed to battle the Snow King. Finally, after a 25-turn battle, they were able to gain the upper hand and defeated the Snow King. When this happened, he said, "Oh, Lord Demarché! I have failed you! Now there is no way to prevent these two from coming after you! I'm very sorry!"

He then exploded, and the briefcase dropped to the ground. Pixie quickly picked it up, after which they were magically whisked away to Snow Village, where they met with Rufus Penguin. "Oh thank you, Ronald and Pixie, for rescuing me!"

"You're very welcome," Pixie said humbly.

"That Snow Castle dungeon was so cold!" Penguin said. "I didn't know if I would *ever* get out of there! And he had locked me up in chains so that I could not knock down the icy prison bars!"

"Well, you're out now, so there's nothing to worry about anymore," Ronald said.

"Yes, and you know what that means!" Rufus Penguin said. "Now, it's time to get rid of that nuisance, Tony Demarché!"

"Yeah," Pixie said. "We'd better get back to the Wallapville castle and put this thing on the stand to break the force field."

However, unlike when they defeated Gregorious, Ronald and Pixie had to walk back to Wallapville. They headed west through the wintery landscape, and were greeted by a host of the winter enemies. Their confidence and great abilities showed, as they had no problems defeating their enemies, and gained a level-up also. After making it through the final screen, they entered the southeastern entrance gate to Wallapville. They took off their winter gear, and then made their way to the castle.

As they entered the castle, they heard the queen say, "Oh wonderful! You finally got the final briefcase!"

"Now, put that thing on the stand this instance!" the king commanded. "We need to break that force field!"

Pixie then placed the briefcase on the stand, after which the ground suddenly started to move. "What the...? Is this an earthquake?" she asked, fearful for her life.

"No, it's not!" the king said. "Just watch!"

Suddenly, a rainbow beam of light shone brightly on the stand, and the final briefcase had written on it "N." The stand then went under the floor, and reemerged after a minute. In their place instead was a large button. "Push that button!" the queen ordered.

Pixie obeyed the order, and pushed the button. Suddenly classical music started playing for about a minute, which confused both her and Ronald. When the music finally stopped, Pixie asked, "What was all that about?"

"The force field's broken!" the king replied. "We will soon be able to see our daughter again!"

"Yes, husband, we are!" the queen added joyfully. "You two! Head north this instance, and get our daughter back! We will get the palace ready for her return! Oh, it is going to be a wonderful celebration! I can't wait to see our beloved daughter again!"

"Yes, my dear wife, neither can I!" the king replied jubilantly.

At Demarché's mansion, he was infuriated over the fact that Ronald and Pixie had been able to collect all of the briefcases, and which led to the breaking of the force field. "That Snow King was *useless!*" he huffed angrily. "I can't believe that man and woman were able to beat him! He was supposed to be *invincible!*"

"So, what do we do now, sir?" his secretary asked.

"Well, we now have to prepare for their arrival! You just know they're going to be on their way!"

"What should we do to prepare?"

"Call a company meeting this instance, and tell everyone to meet inside the boardroom downstairs! We have to make sure that everyone is ready for battle so that they don't reach my office and rescue the princess!"

Meanwhile, Ronald and Pixie decided that they would leave for Demarché's mansion in the morning, and therefore made their way to the inn to rest for the night. In the morning, they first headed to the shops to purchase the final set of items that they would need. Wallapville's residents were ecstatic that the force fields had been broken, as it meant they were able to travel north without restriction, though they still had to wait for Demarché's mansion to be destroyed in order to visit the other country. They also knew that Demarché was now in deep trouble, and that the princess was going to be rescued very soon. They had already begun preparations for the celebration of her return, as the decorations for the party had already started going up. They wished Pixie and Ronald good luck, and told them that they believed in them. Ronald and Pixie thanked them, and then started for the northern end of the city. At the northern gate, they took a collective deep breath, and started for Demarché's mansion.

The northern landscape was a thick forest, although it was not as dark and creepy as the one that Ronald and Pixie had travelled through in the fantasy game. However, they had to be vigilant for the monsters that inhabited this area. These ghouls had been unleashed by Demarché when he first arrived, just in case someone had managed to break through the force field. These monsters came in various forms, including plants, spiders, insects, and even a ghost-like creature. But, because Ronald and Pixie had been able to gain so many new abilities and strengths in this game, they were able to defeat them without too much trouble. After travelling north for about five screens, they arrived at the gates of Demarché's mansion. The dwelling looked just like the large estates owned by many billionaires and dictators in the real world. It had a large front lawn, and a flower garden in the backyard. It also contained statues of Demarché and each of his loyal now-former governors, as well as various fountains. They even saw a few animals roaming the property. However these animals were not dangerous, as they didn't attack any visitors. "Whoa! I think the closest that I've been to one of these types of properties are the ones that I've seen on the documentaries," Ronald said, admiring the place. "This is *huge!*"

"Yeah, I know," Pixie said, nodding her head in agreement. "We don't have these in Video Game City. Wealth accumulation and hoarding is strictly forbidden there."

"Oh? What's the penalty?"

"Trust me. You don't want to know."

"That strict, eh?"

"Strict, harsh, prohibitive. Whatever word you want to use to describe it."

When they went to open the mansion's gates, they found that they were locked, while the top of the walls were covered in barb wire to prevent anyone from trying to scale them. "So, how do we get in?" Ronald asked as he looked around for a way to get in.

Pixie looked at her phone, and said, still staring at the screen, "It says here that we have to enter from the back."

"Let's do that, then."

As they started making their way around the perimeter of the mansion, they ran into some of Demarché's goons. Pixie and Ronald were able to easily defeat them, and quickly found the back gate, which was unlocked. As they went to open the gate, they were immediately met by a series of guards that had already been informed of their arrival. While the battles were lengthy, with each lasting about 6 turns, they were not overly difficult for Ronald and Pixie. After they had defeated the last guard and levelled up, Ronald and Pixie entered the mansion. Once inside, they saw that the interior looked just like any billionaire's or dictator's mansion, with the walls being covered with a variety of artwork and paintings. The furniture inside were all luxury items, though there was also some furniture that looked like it came from the Renaissance and Colonial eras. As Pixie and Ronald were going through the mansion, they were immediately met by several of Demarché's employees. These were the lowest-level employees of his organization who had not received much training in terms of how to do battle. As a result, they were very easy to defeat. In fact, none of the employees were able to get a turn in. Ronald and Pixie then made their way through the different rooms, and defeated more low-level employees of Demarché's company. They then went up a staircase to the second level, and were met by mid-level employees. These people were more difficult to beat, as they had been given much more training in how to do battle. Each of these employees were able to get in a turn while facing Ronald and Pixie. Each battle in the second-floor rooms took Ronald and Pixie a few turns to defeat their opponents. After clearing the second level of the mansion, they went up to the third level. Here, they had to deal with middle managers of the magnate's organization, and it took a great deal of effort, and subsequently more turns, to defeat. And, Ronald and Pixie were able to attain couple of level ups after their victories, after which they then proceeded to the fourth and final floor of the mansion. Each room contained an office of Demarché's senior management, starting with his vice-presidents, and these people were tough! In facing these people, Ronald and Pixie each required at least 12 turns to defeat them. After beating the vice-presidents, Ronald and Pixie levelled up, and then made their way to the rooms that contained the executive offices. Here, each successive opponent was more difficult than the previous one. However, they held their own and killed these minions. And, because of the difficulty involved in defeating a couple of the executives, Ronald and Pixie gained more level-ups, which further increased their strength. These extra rewards aided in defeating the remaining four executives, after which they received more level-ups. Finally, they headed to Demarché's office to face Demarché himself. As they approached the door to his office, they stopped and took a deep breath. Ronald then asked Pixie, "Well, are you ready?"

"Ready as I'll ever be," she replied. "Let's go inside and beat this guy."

They then opened the doors and entered the office. Demarché's office was large, almost like a penthouse suite. His desk, for which he had a leather chair, was located at the back of the office, in front of a window that gave him a view of his front lawn. At the front of the office, near the entrance, there was a leather sofa, some leather chairs, and even a bed in case he was working late into the night and he didn't want to go to his bedroom. The office also contained a golf station, an aquarium, a statue, a large figurine, and also a small table with some chairs around it. To the right of the back window was a jail cell, where the princess was locked inside. When she heard the doors open, she looked up, and saw Pixie and Ronald coming in. "Oh good! Finally, some heroes have arrived to rescue me!" the princess said excitedly. "I've been stuck in this cell for an *eternity*!"

Ronald was about to head to the desk when Demarché magically appeared. "So the cowgirl and the average guy have *finally* arrived!" Demarché said. "Well, I guess I will have to finish the job that my minions and my employees couldn't do!"

"Yeah, right!" Ronald said. *"You're* going down next!"

"No, *you two* are the ones that are going to go down," Demarché replied, with a scowl on his face. "If you want something done, you have to do it yourself. You can't find *any* good help these days!"

"No," Pixie said. "*You're* the one that is going down! We're not going to be defeated!"

"We'll see about that!" the magnate said. "I didn't build an empire without bringing down people like you along the way!"

"We're different than those other people," Ronald said. "We're *way* tougher than the other people that you brought down! And besides, you haven't earned anything! You've stolen so much from those other people!"

"Enough talking!" Demarché said, quite infuriated. "Let's settle this, *now*!"

The battle then started. Pixie and Ronald went first, and each of them used an attacking item that they had bought in Wallapville, which did quite a bit of damage to Demarché. Unfortunately, Demarché had the ability to heal himself, and used his first turn to bring himself back to 100%. Pixie and Ronald then each tried jumping attacks, which again inflicted some damage to Demarché. Demarché, who was very strong, showed his vigour on his next turn, and inflicted a large amount of damage on both of them. Pixie and Ronald were forced to use each of their next turns to heal up. Demarché charged again, but used an attack that caused less damage than he had on the last one. Pixie and Ronald then replied by each using an ability that they had acquired during the various battles in this game, which had some effect. The rest of the battle interchanged between healing, attacks, and use of items by Ronald and Pixie. In all, it took about 35 turns for Demarché to finally be defeated. When this happened, he wailed, "Noooooooooooooo! I've been defeated! How could this be?!"

"That's what you get for getting arrogant!" Ronald yelled back.

"But I'm supposed to be *invincible*!" Demarché said. "My empire! It's *ruined*! I've got *nothing* now!"

Ronald ran and got the key from Demarché's desk, and opened the jail cell. Suddenly, an earthquake started, startling everyone. "What's happening?" Ronald asked, scared and looking around in fear.

"The mansion's crumbling!" the princess yelled as she got out of the prison cell. "When you beat Demarché, and opened up this jail cell, it set in motion a self-destruct sequence!"

"What do we do now?" Pixie asked.

"Put this guy in the jail cell!" the princess responded.

Pixie, Ronald, and the princess then threw Demarché into the cell, and locked the door. "No!" Demarché said. "I'm going to be *killed* if I'm stuck in here when the mansion implodes!"

"Good!" Ronald said. "That means you won't wreak havoc on anyone else!"

"So, how do we get out of here?" Pixie asked. "If we try to make our way through the mansion, we'll be killed as well."

"Out the window!" Ronald said.

Ronald, Pixie, and the princess crashed their way through the window, and landed on the shrubs below. No one was hurt, and they ran out the back gate, circled the perimeter to the front, and then headed into the forest. In the distance, the mansion imploded, and nothing was left but rubble. "Well, we're safe now," Ronald said as he looked back. "Let's head back to town."

In Wallapville, the people of the kingdom welcomed back the princess, and gave Pixie and Ronald a hero's welcome. A parade was held, after which everyone headed back to the castle. The king thanked Ronald and Pixie for defeating Tony Demarché's minions, not to mention Tony Demarché himself, and, most importantly, for returning the princess to the castle safe and sound. The king also thanked the international community for sending Pixie and Ronald to deal with the magnate, as without their help, the magnate could have inflicted a lot more damage than what had already been done. The king then asked one of the servants to bring the heroes' rewards, and after a few moments, the servant returned with medals of honour. "Ronald, Pixie, these are for you," the king said.

"What? More medals of honour?" Ronald said, surprised. "I don't know if I really deserve it."

"Oh, will you listen to that!" the king said. "So humble! No, you deserve these for all of your heroism and bravery. Without you two, who knows what would have happened?"

"Thank you, your highness," Pixie said. "I really appreciate this honour."

"You're very welcome, Pixie," the king said.

After the ceremony, the portal opened up, signalling the end of the game. The king looked over, and was confused as to what that white flashing door was. "What's *that* thing?" the king asked.

"It's a portal," Pixie replied.

"A portal?" the king said. "I don't remember there being any portals in this game."

"Well, you see, I'm the traveller of the video game world, and I'm Ronald's guide through this world."

"Traveller? I've never heard of such a thing. Is that even allowed?"

"Well, it is for me. I came to an agreement with The VGG five years ago."

"Oh, okay. The VGG never mentioned this to me. And since we've never gone on 'vacation' to Video Game City or to any of the 'tourist games,' we haven't interacted with anyone who might have heard of you. Is this your first time in our game?"

"Yes, it is."

"Oh! Well, in that case, we are glad that you were able to come to this game! I hope you had fun playing it! And we hope that you make an effort to come back sometime!"

"It was okay. As for me coming back, we'll have to see what happens in the future."

"Fair enough. Now, you mentioned something about being a 'guide.' What do you mean by that?"

Pixie then explained how Ronald was from the real world, and how in order to get home, he had to play a particular number of games in a certain order unknown to him. She then explained how the portals were the way to get into the games, and they only opened up once Ronald had successfully beaten the game. "Oh, that's very interesting," the king said once Pixie was finished explaining. "I never knew that it was even possible for someone from the real world to come here."

"Well, it happened, so now I have to do this," Ronald said. "With that portal open, we've got to get going."

"Well, in that case, thank you very much Pixie and Ronald, for bringing our daughter back to us," the queen replied.

"You're welcome," Pixie said.

"And, good luck on the rest of your journey," the king said. "I certainly hope that you make it home safely."

"Thanks," Ronald said. "So do I."

Pixie and Ronald then hugged the king, queen, prince, and princess, and said their final goodbyes. After that, Pixie and Ronald walked over to the portal, and before entering it, they waved goodbye to all of the people at the castle. The people waved back, and some even yelled to them how grateful they were that Pixie and Ronald had come to the kingdom. Everyone wished them good luck on the rest of their journey. Once this was done, Pixie and Ronald entered the portal, and made their way to the next game.

CHAPTER ELEVEN

As soon as they exited the portal, Ronald and Pixie's clothing automatically changed. They were now both attired in winter gear, including thick winter jackets, thick pants, gloves, boots, tuques, and neck protection. Ronald then looked around and saw that they were on a ski hill, and that there were a good number of skiers and snowboarders going up and down the gondolas and ski runs. He also observed that the resort was located at the base of a mountain called Mount Wallace, and it had three peaks. Ronald also noticed that this resort was in the midst of a bitterly cold winter. "Where are we?" Ronald asked.

"I don't know," Pixie replied. "I've never been to this type of a place before."

"You mean you've never gone skiing or snowboarding?"

"No. In The Simulation of Real Life - People Version, the guy that created me *never* let me go to the ski resorts. And, I've never really had a chance to come to these types of games during my travels."

"Are you allowed to participate in this game? I'm asking because your clothes also changed."

"I'm not sure. I think that I'm wearing these clothes to ensure that I don't freeze to death. It could be another one of those games where we actually feel the effects of the weather."

Pixie then looked at her phone to find out what game they were in. She started to say, "It's something called XTreme Snowboard Racing and Freestyle-."

However, Ronald cut her off before she could finish the sentence, saying in excitement, "Did you say XTreme Snowboard Racing and Freestyle?"

"Yes."

"Awesome! I have that game at home! Not only that, but I also know how to snowboard, so this is going to be easy for me! And, with it still

176

being August back home, the ski hills are obviously closed. So this is a perfect way to get in some snowboarding practice before the ski season opens!"

"Okay. But how much do you play this game?"

"Oh, I play it *a lot*! So, I have no issues with the dynamics of this game!"

"That's good, then. It should help you out."

Pixie then checked to see if she was allowed to participate, and it turned out that she wasn't. "However," she added, "the only reason that my clothes changed was to make sure that I kept warm, as the weather in this game can cause people to freeze and get sick from the cold. It also looks like this is another tourist destination for people from the video game world, so I'm allowed to ski or snowboard or do whatever I want in here, as long as I'm not involved in any of the competitions."

"Oh, well, at least you can learn how to ski or snowboard here."

"I don't think I want to. I might get really hurt. So while you're competing, I'll just take in some of the activities around the resort. But first, let me check what you're required to do."

"Don't worry about that, Pixie. As I said earlier, I've played this game a lot, so I know what to do. You have fun."

Ronald then started to head to the gear shop to purchase the remaining snowboard gear that he needed, when Pixie yelled to him, "Wait! Where are you going?! You don't even know what your task is!"

Ronald stopped, and turned around to Pixie to tell her, "Yes I do! I just have to make it up to that third peak up there, and win either the trick or race events on the mountain."

"No, that's not it…!"

However, Ronald had already walked far enough away that he couldn't hear the rest of what Pixie had to say. If he had bothered to stay and listen to Pixie, he would have known that in order to open up the portal to the next game, he was required to win both the race *and* trick events, including the one-on-one challenges, and also was required to rank first overall on the entire mountain. Instead, he went straight into the gear shop and, before buying anything, he checked his wallet to make sure that he had something in there to make purchases with. After he saw that he had a debit card that read "XTreme Snowboard Debit Card," he then looked around the shop for snowboard boots and a snowboard. Once he picked out his gear, he paid for it, and then headed straight to the first race course. The game was set up such that each peak consisted of three race courses, two half-pipes, two big air runs, which was one or more jumps followed by a quarter-pipe, and two slopestyle courses, which contain rails, objects, and jumps scattered around the course for competitors to perform a variety of tricks. In order to enter the events, any competitor wishing to participate merely had to arrive at the starting gates, where they were then automatically assigned a slot. On the race courses, each competitor had to go through two qualifying heats, and then the final race. In order to advance to the next round, the competitor had to place in the top three of their run. In each race, there were six competitors that duelled against each other. They did not have to follow any gates, and could take alternate routes on the courses, which eventually connected back with the main course. On the trick courses, the competitors only had to compete in one qualifying run, and if they received a score in the top 10, they would advance to the final run. In all of the specialties, if the main player won a gold medal in each of the events on the peak for that respective discipline, the player would have to square off against one of the in-game characters in a one-on-one challenge for that particular discipline. The only exception was the final race challenge, which was a race against the mountain's top-ranked competitor down the entire mountain, and could only be unlocked once all of the other one-on-one challenges were successfully completed. There was also a "Momentum Meter," which filled up as the competitors completed tricks on either the race courses or on the trick-based courses, and this gave them the ability to move faster, or to do more difficult tricks. Moreover, a racer earned cash prize if they won a medal.

Ronald got off of the gondola, and headed to the starting gates for the first race. After he was assigned a slot in one of the middle starting gates, Ronald went to take his place. The starting gun went off, and all of the competitors were off. Ronald didn't worry too much about doing tricks on this course, as his main goal was to finish in the top three. Unfortunately, he forgot just how punishing this game was, and was knocked down on the very first turn, leaving him at the back of the pack. "Ow!" he said as he fell down. "What was that?!"

He quickly picked himself up, and worked hard to catch up to the rest of the pack. It took him a while, but he eventually caught up with some of the other racers, and found himself in fourth place for a while. About halfway down the course, he caught up to the third-place racer. Just as Ronald was about to pass him, the third-place racer knocked him down hard, and he suddenly found himself in last place again. He had trouble catching up again, as the jumps affected his speed, and he crossed the finish line in last place, meaning that he didn't advance to the next round of qualifying. When he got out of the stadium area at the bottom of the course, he said, "I completely forgot how these races can go. I forgot that sometimes, these racers try to knock you down to prevent you from passing them."

He then decided to focus solely on the trick events. Since these disciplines were individual events, and therefore didn't require him to be on the course at the same time as other people, he felt that he would be able to advance to the third peak with relative ease. He decided to start off with the half-pipe courses, as he remembered that when he last played this game, he had set a new high score record. He went to the half-pipe at the bottom of the hill, and was automatically entered after approaching the starting gate, and was told that he could start his qualifying run when he felt ready. Ronald was all ready to go, and started the run almost immediately. He used all of the allotted time he was given, pulling sets of tricks that were increasingly more advanced, including one where he did a grab with one of his boots off of the board. He placed first in this run, and advanced to the final. In the final run, his "Momentum Meter" was fully filled, which allowed him to do the most difficult and insane tricks, which had the crowd going wild. He finished first in this event, and was awarded the gold medal.

Ronald then went on to the next half-pipe course, which was a little higher up the mountain. Because his "Momentum Meter" was filled from the previous competition, he could do the difficult and crazy tricks right from the start of his qualifying run. He finished first in qualifying, and then finished first again in the final run by completing even more insane tricks than in the qualifying run, which earned him another gold medal. Once the medal ceremony was over, a snowboarder named Chantal came over to him and said, "Hello there, Ronald! It seems like you dominated the half-pipes here! How about we go at it again on this half-pipe, just the two of us in a one-on-one competition?"

"Is that a challenge?" Ronald replied.

"Yes, it is! And I'll beat you, as this is *my* peak!"

Ronald and Chantal then went back to the start of the run, and Elise went first. She obtained a score higher than the one he had scored to win the gold medal, which shocked him. "How the heck am I supposed to beat that score?" Ronald said to himself after she was done.

He then took a deep breath, and started his run. Using all of the allotted time, he took advantage of his full "Momentum Meter" and completed even crazier tricks than he had attempted in his gold-medal run, including some where he wasn't even on his board. After the run was over, he was relieved once he saw that he had scored higher than Chantal. "I can't believe that you *beat* me!" she said. "How did you do that?!"

"I can't believe it either," Ronald replied. "I'm just as shocked as you are. But, I did it, and that's all that matters."

"Well, congratulations. Good luck on the rest of the mountain."

Ronald then headed for the big air runs, both of which were located at the bottom of the first peak. There was no time limit on to complete these events. Instead, Ronald only had to do one trick on the jump, and one trick on the quarter-pipe, and that was it. On the first course, he took advantage of his full "Momentum Meter" to land very tough tricks, which allowed him to place first not only in the qualifying run, but also in the final run to win the gold medal. In order to get to the second big air run, he required a ride from one of the resort's employees on their snowmobile, as there was no way for him to ride up the mountain on his snowboard, and no gondola was nearby. On this course, he used the same strategy as on the first course, which earned him first place in both the qualifier and in the final, and which earned him the gold medal. After the medal ceremony on the second big air course, he was challenged by a guy named Robert to a one-on-one challenge. "You're on, Robert!" Ronald replied.

They then went back to the start of the course, and Robert went first. Unfortunately, he didn't land his jump trick nor his quarter-pipe trick, which resulted in a lower score. Ronald then took his turn, and did some very simple tricks, as he knew that he didn't have to take too many risks because he had to beat a very low score, and easily beat Robert. After the run was over, Robert congratulated Ronald, and Ronald went on to the slopestyle courses.

He made his way to the first slopestyle course by boarding down the peak, and entered the event once he approached the starting gate. In the qualifying run, he attempted some difficult tricks, but fell hard when trying to stick the landing. Despite this, he managed to finish in the top 10 in this round. In the final run, while he was a little more cautious, Ronald successfully completed several really crazy tricks, and won the gold medal as a result. He then used the gondola to head up to the second slopestyle course, and again had some trouble in the qualifying run, and was barely able to finish in tenth. However, in the final run, he was able to regain his form, and was able to do well enough to squeak out a gold-medal victory. After the medal ceremony on the second slopestyle course, a woman named Emily came up to him, and said, "Yo Ronald! That was pretty impressive! But let's try this course again, one-on-one, and see who's the best!"

Ronald accepted, and then the challenge began. Emily went first, a but missed a few tricks, which led to her scoring quite low. Ronald then took his turn, and attempted some difficult tricks, but nothing too risky, as he felt that they weren't necessary because Emily had scored quite low. He easily won the challenge, scoring 10,000 points higher than Emily, and when he arrived at the finish line, she congratulated him on his run. Then, the operator of the ski hill came up to Ronald and said, "Congratulations, Ronald! You've successfully completed the requirements of Resort Peak, and you now get to advance to Middle Peak!"

"Thanks," Ronald replied.

"You must immediately head to the gondola that will take you up to the lodge of Middle Peak. It is waiting for you!"

The operator gave Ronald directions to the gondola that he needed to take. Ronald headed there, and once he arrived at the gondola station, he got on. After a 10 minute ride, he arrived at the Middle Peak lodge, and headed straight for the equipment shop to buy more advanced gear. After purchasing what he was looking for, he continued on to the trick events on Middle Peak.

Ronald decided to start off with the big air events as he was able to get a really high score the last time he played the game. He remembered that on this peak, there were two huge jumps followed by the quarter-pipe on both of the courses. However, as he was starting on a new peak, his "Momentum Meter" was reset to zero, meaning that he couldn't start with the crazy and insane tricks. As soon as he arrived at the starting gate of the first big air course, he was allowed to start his qualifying run right away. On the first jump, he got some wicked air, and pulled off a really tough trick. He landed it cleanly, and immediately prepared for the second jump. At the second jump, he was able to get even more air than the first one, and he completed a number of highly advanced tricks before landing cleanly. On the quarter-pipe section of the course, he was able to get even more air than the previous section, and was able to do one more difficult trick. After his run was over, he looked at the scoreboard, and saw that he had placed first overall. In the final run, he used the same strategy as the qualifying run, and ended up winning the gold medal in this event.

He then headed straight for the gondola to head to the second big air course. After he got off, he saw that this course was set up similarly to the first one, and therefore used the same strategy as the first big air course, which allowed him to finish first in both the qualifying and final heats, which earned him the gold medal. It also helped that Ronald's "Momentum Meter" was full after the first big air course. He took full advantage of this and attempted the most crazy tricks he could with the airtime he got on the second course. After completing the second big air event, a boarder named Willie came up to Ronald and said, "Hey Ronald! You did well on the big air courses! But you haven't beaten me one-on-one! Let's ride this course again, just you against me!"

Ronald accepted the challenge, and they started the course again. Willie started first, and achieved a really high score, much higher than the one that Ronald was able to get on his gold-medal winning run on this course. Ronald was up next. After taking a deep breath, he started his run, and put together a series of high-difficulty and very crazy tricks on both jumps, followed by a series of difficult tricks on the quarter-pipe. When the run was over, Ronald looked at the scoreboard, and saw that he had barely outscored Willie. However, he was happy to have defeated him because it meant that he had finished the big air portion of the peak.

He decided that he would do the half-pipes next. These half-pipes gave all competitors 30 seconds more than was given on the first peak, mainly because the courses were longer than the ones on the first peak, and there was no way anyone could finish the run within one minute. Ronald approached the course, which was on the lower part of the second peak, and was entered as soon as he arrived at the starting gate. With his "Momentum Meter" full, he was able to put together a run that combined a variety of amazing and crazy tricks, which earned him first place in the qualifying round. He used the same approach in the final run, and won the gold medal. He then made his way up the peak to the second half-pipe via a gondola.

Inside the second half-pipe, using the full "Momentum Meter" to his advantage, he pulled off a series of very advanced tricks in both the qualifying and final runs, and finished with the gold medal. After the medal ceremony, a woman named Yvette approached Ronald, and said, "Hi Ronald! You really did amazing out there on the half-pipes! Those were some crazy tricks you put together!"

"Thanks," Ronald replied.

"But, I'm the queen of the half-pipes on this peak! You haven't done anything until you beat me!"

"Is that a challenge?"

"Yes, it is! You, me, this half-pipe, one-on-one. What do you say?"

"I accept your challenge."

Ronald and Yvette then went up to the starting gate, and Yvette went first. She put together a really solid run, crashing only once, and put up a really high score. Ronald went next, and he used the exact same strategy that he had used during the events, and put up a score that was more than 100,000 points higher than Yvette's. After he finished, Yvette congratulated him, and Ronald moved on to the slopestyle courses.

The next course was located in the middle of the peak, and therefore could be reached only if one rode down on a gondola. After arriving at the course, he was entered into the competition once reaching the starting gate. He made sure that he did not get arrogant, even with his full "Momentum Meter," and therefore was cautious not to try too many risky tricks that could hurt his chances to qualify for the final. It worked, as he qualified with a fifth place showing. In the final, he took more chances, and landed all of the tricks, and finished with the top score, and won the gold medal. He then rode down to the second slopestyle course on the peak, and used the same strategy as the first course. It worked again, as in qualifying heat he placed fourth, and then he won the gold medal with a fantastic ride in the final run. After the medal ceremony, a man named Quincy came up to him and said, "Hey Ronald! Good work on winning the slopestyle events on the peak! But you haven't proven anything yet until you've beaten me! So let's redo this course, just the two of us, one-on-one!"

Ronald accepted the challenge, and they went back to the top of the course. Quincy went first, and he put up a pretty good score by landing some fantastic tricks. Ronald was next, and he pulled off an even greater number of difficult tricks, including some jaw-dropping ones. When he finished the run, he became excited after seeing that his score had easily topped Quincy's. They shook hands, and Ronald prepared to move on. The ski hill's operator then appeared, and said, "Congratulations, Ronald! You have successfully completed the requirements for Middle Peak, and you now advance to TOM Peak! A gondola is waiting for you to take you there right now!"

"Thanks," said Ronald. "Where is the gondola?"

The operator gave him directions to the gondola that he would need. After arriving at the gondola, Ronald got into it, and took the ten-minute ride. The gondola dropped him off right in front of the TOM Peak lodge, where he immediately headed for the gear shop to upgrade his snowboarding gear. After purchasing the items, he rode down to the slopestyle course at the base of the peak to continue on with the trick events on TOM Peak.

He arrived at the starting gate, and was automatically entered into the event. His "Momentum Meter" was reset back to zero since he was starting on a new peak, which meant that he could only do some simpler tricks and rail grinds to start with. However, this was fine with Ronald, as he decided to use the same strategy as he had used on the slopestyle courses on the second peak. It worked, as he placed seventh in the qualifying run, and in the process filled up his "Momentum Meter." In his final run, he went all out with the difficult tricks, and successfully landed them all, winning the event in the process. He then took the gondola to the second slopestyle course, and used the same strategy, this time finishing eighth in qualifying before going all out to win the gold medal in the final run. When the medal ceremony was over, a guy named Paul rode up to him and said, "Congratulations on winning the gold in slopestyle on this peak, Ronald! But you haven't proven yourself yet until you beat me, the master of slopestyle on this peak! I'm going to wait for you at the top of this course so that we can settle who the *real* trickster is!"

Paul then walked up to the top of the course, and Ronald guessed that in order to accept the challenge, he had to follow Paul. Ronald made his way to the top, and the challenge started as soon as he reached the starting gate. Paul was really good, and put together a string of really difficult tricks. As a result, he put up a really high score, definitely one that would be difficult to beat. Ronald, with his full "Momentum Meter," went all out on the crazy and insane tricks, and was successfully landed each and every one of them. After he had reached the bottom of the course, he saw that his score just barely beat Paul's, but Ronald didn't care as it was enough for the win. After receiving his congratulations from Paul, Ronald headed for the big air courses, starting with the one at the bottom of the peak.

The big air courses on the third peak were much longer than the ones on the first two peaks, as there were three jumps, followed by the quarter-pipe at the bottom of the runs. After entering the competition, Ronald used his full "Momentum Meter" to his fullest advantage. On each one of the jumps, he was able to get a lot of air, and put together a string of some mind-boggling tricks, and more importantly was able to land them all. On the quarter-pipe section of the course, he was able to get a good amount of air, and put together a combination of easier tricks, which earned him first place in qualifying. In the final run, he followed the same strategy, en route to the gold medal. Ronald then took the gondola up to the second big air course, where he duplicated the same routine as on the previous course, finishing first in both the qualifying and final runs, the latter resulting in a gold medal. After the ceremony, a woman named Tiffany approached Ronald and said, "Hey Ronald! You may have won the big air events on this peak, but you aren't anything until you beat me!"

"So, does that mean you want to challenge me?" Ronald replied.

"Of course that's what it means! I'll see you at the top of the run!"

Ronald followed her to the top of the course, and they started their one-on-one challenge. Tiffany went first, and put together a very good run with a score that topped what Ronald had scored in the final run of the event. Ronald was up next, and before beginning his run, he took a deep breath, and gave it all he had. He put together a series of crazy tricks after each jump, and landed them, though barely. Then, on the quarter-pipe, he put together a series of even more extreme tricks, and again was barely able to nail the landing. They both looked up at the scoreboard, and saw that Ronald had just squeaked past beat Tiffany, winning by only 10 points. Tiffany then congratulated Ronald, and he then rode down to the half-pipe at the bottom of the peak.

The half-pipes on TOM Peak were even longer than the previous two peaks, and the runs were 2 minutes long, thus allowing competitors to do some crazy things during their runs. As Ronald approached the starting gate, he took a deep breath, then entered the event. In the qualifying run, he put together a great series of insane tricks, and placed first. Then, in the final run, he completed even more difficult tricks, and landed each and every one of them, which garnered him the gold medal. He then took the gondola to the half-pipe at the top of the mountain, and used the same strategy that he used on the first half-pipe. He placed first both in the qualifying and the final runs, and won the gold medal for his efforts. Once the medal ceremony was over, he was approached by a guy named Barney, who said, "That was impressive, Ronald! But you have yet to beat me one-on-one! So, let's see who's the better man at half-pipes!"

They both then headed to the start, where Barney went first. He attempted some very insane tricks, but missed on some of his landings. However, he was still able to put up a respectable score. Once he was done, Ronald took some time to compose himself, as he thought that once he was finished with this challenge, he was on his way to the next game. After a few minutes, he felt he was ready, and then started his run, where he put together a very impressive showing, hitting a lot of crazy tricks, though he was lucky to land some of the tricks. Once the run was over, he saw that his score was much higher than Barney's. In fact, it was 500,000 points higher than his opponent's. Barney congratulated him, and then Ronald waited patiently for the portal to open.

He waited in the empty stadium area for about half an hour, and started wondering why the portal wasn't appearing. "What the...? What's going on here? The portal should have opened up by now!" he said to himself.

After waiting for about five more minutes, he decided to call on Pixie to find out what was happening. "Pixie?! Come here right now! I need to ask you something!" he yelled.

He waited a few more minutes, and saw that Pixie hadn't shown up. Ronald suddenly realized that he probably had to pause the game in order to get help from her, just like he had to in all of the other single-player games he had played up to this point. Once he recognized this fact, he yelled, "Pause!"

Pixie then arrived, and said to Ronald, with a clear look of smugness on her face, "Yes, Ronald? What seems to be the problem?"

"The portal. It hasn't appeared yet, and I've been waiting for...."

Ronald then checked his watch, and said, "38 minutes! What's going on here?"

"You didn't complete the tasks of this game," Pixie replied condescendingly.

"How is that possible?! I completed all of the trick events successfully in the game!"

"But, that wasn't the only requirement of the game. It's only *half* of it! You became so arrogant thinking that you knew everything you needed to do in this game that you didn't give me a chance to tell you that you are required to finish *all* of the one-on-one challenges in this game, and that you also have to rank first overall in the rankings."

"What? How could that be? That's *way* different than when I play this game at home!"

"Gee, maybe if you hadn't run off when we first arrived here I would have been able to tell you *exactly* what you needed to do in this game! Remember that here, the parameters are much different than when you play the games at home."

"Well, what's my ranking right now?"

Pixie then checked her phone, and after waiting for a few minutes for the information, she told Ronald, "You're ranked 40th."

"That's it?! After all of the stuff I've been through already?!" Ronald said, surprised.

"Yes, that's it."

"So what do I do, then?"

"I would suggest that you go back to the first peak and start the races over again. Remember, you can't move on until *all* of the one-on-one challenges are completed."

"You mean I even have to do the one-on-one race challenges in the backcountry?"

"Yes!"

"But in that first race, I was knocked down...*twice*! It's almost impossible to win those things."

"Well, you'll just have to keep trying. Don't you want to get home?"

"Yeah, I do."

"Well then, you'll have to keep at it. You'll win, eventually."

"Okay, fine. I'll keep trying."

Before he left, Ronald said, "Pixie, just one more thing."

"And that is...?" Pixie asked.

"How do I check my ranking so that I don't have to call on you every two minutes?"

"You should have a ranking card in your wallet. That's something else I couldn't tell you because you left so quickly."

Ronald, still not too happy with the difference in the rules between how he played at home and what was required here, checked his wallet, and found the ranking card. It showed 40th, exactly as Pixie had told him. He then rode his way to a gondola, and got onto it and headed back to Resort Peak to restart the racing portion of the game.

After getting off of the gondola, he went straight to the first race course, and was entered into the race after approaching the starting gate, and was assigned to the gate at the very left. After the race started, he tried to avoid getting hit by the other racers, but was unsuccessful, as he was knocked down four times, and ended up finishing last, thus preventing him from moving on. Ronald immediately headed back to the top of the course, and started again. In the qualifier of what was now his third attempt at this course, he was able to finish fourth, but still was not able to move on. After this race had ended, he decided to check his current ranking, and pulled out the card. He noticed that he had dropped from 40th to 48th. He sighed in frustration, and wondered to himself, "What do I have to do to move on in these races?"

He then made his way back to the top of the course, and tried it again. This time he was able to finish third in the qualifying run, which meant that he could now move on to the next heat. In the next heat, he finished third again, which qualified him for the finals. In the final run, he finished fourth, and therefore didn't win anything. Luckily, however, when he checked the ranking card again, he saw that he had risen up to 43rd, which relieved him somewhat. However, he said to himself, in frustration, "I'm going to be stuck here *forever*! I'll *never* get home!"

Begrudgingly, he then went back up to the top, and attempted the race again. In the first heat, he finished third, and did so again in the second heat. Finally, in the final run, he finished first. After seeing his placement on the scoreboard, he jumped off of his snowboard and ran around the stadium area in excitement. "Woo-hoo! *Finally*! I won a race!" he yelled.

Ronald then walked in front of the stands, raised his board in excitement, and then high-fived everyone in the front row. After he had finished celebrating, the medal ceremony started, and he proudly accepted his flowers and his gold medal. After the medal ceremony had ended, he looked at his ranking card, and saw that he had risen all the way up to 32nd. Ronald, now having regained his confidence, rode to the nearest gondola, and made his way up to the second course on the peak.

In the first qualifying run, he barely finished third, as during the race he and a female racer were engaged in a heated battle, with there being numerous position changes. Ronald made his final move just before the finish line, and was able to sneak his board just ahead of hers. He did even better in the semi-final heat, as he finished in second, a good second because there was no one around him when he crossed the finish line. Finally, in the final race of the course, he finished first after a really tough one-on-one battle with a male boarder, who had done his best to knock Ronald down so that he could finish in first. After the medal ceremony, Ronald checked his ranking card, and saw that he was now ranked 27th. He then took a gondola up to the final race course on the peak.

On this course, he finished first in all of the heats, though he had to work harder in order to avoid getting hit by the other competitors. On a couple of occasions, he even used the alternate routs to ensure that he was alone, and that he wouldn't get knocked down by the other racers. After the completion of the medal ceremony, a woman named Riley came up to him and said, "Hey Ronald! What you did on the tracks was pretty impressive! But, now it's time to beat me, one-on-one, in the backcountry! I'll be waiting for you there!"

Ronald then made his way to the gondola, and asked the operator to take him to the backcountry area for the peak. As he arrived at the starting line, he saw that Riley was already waiting for him. "So," she said, "you decided to show up! Let's get this thing started!"

They then started racing, and she was very aggressive in the race. Ronald had to avoid her punches a few times, as Riley was clearly trying to create a large amount of separation between them. However, Ronald was able to maintain his focus, and steadily got ahead of her. By the end of the race, he had built up a sizeable lead, winning the race in a time of 3:12.58, which was 45 seconds ahead of Riley. After the challenge was over, Riley congratulated Ronald, after which he made his way to the nearest gondola, and headed to the second peak.

The first course of this peak was located at the base. After entering the race, Ronald was placed in one of the middle gates. He finished third in the first qualifying heat, and then finished first in the semi-final, and finally finished first in the final, and thus won the gold medal. The focus on Ronald's face was now really showing. After he had made his way to the next course, he again was assigned to one of the middle starting gates. On this course, he finished first in all of the heats, en route to the gold medal on this course. After receiving his medal, he then took the gondola to the race course located at the top of the peak, and finished first in all of the races there as well. After the medal ceremony had ended, a man named Claude came up and said to Ronald, "Congratulations, Ronald! You beat the courses! But, let's see how you do in the backcountry against me!"

Ronald accepted the challenge, and rode his way down to the starting area of the backcountry course, where Claude was waiting for him. "Great! You're aren't chicken after all!" Claude said. "Now, let's get going! I've got some stuff to take care of at the resort, and I don't want to waste anymore time!"

Claude turned out to be a much tougher opponent than Riley, as he was faster and even more aggressive, as he did his best to knock down Ronald many times. To counter this, Ronald used some of the alternate paths down the peak, while also blocking Claude's attempts to punch him when they were close together. Ronald also did some tricks on the jumps and fallen trees, which allowed him to keep his "Momentum Meter" full in case he needed an extra burst of speed. After he had crossed the finish line, Ronald saw that he had defeated his opponent by a few tenths of the second. Nonetheless, he let out of a sigh of relief. Claude congratulated him, and Ronald then rode to the nearest gondola and made his way to the first race course of TOM Peak.

Here, Ronald was assigned to the last gate on the right. Before getting into position to start the race, he checked his ranking card, and saw that he had shot up all the way to 15th, which made him happy because he realized that he was now quite close to finishing this game. He then went into position, and waited for the race to begin. He had some difficulty in the first qualifying run, as the racers were even more aggressive than those on the first two peaks. He barely fended off his opponents, but did well enough to in finish third place. He managed to do a little better in the second heat in terms of fending off the others, and finished in third place. In the final run, he was finally able to get things together, and used his trick ability to fill up his "Momentum Meter." As a result, he was able to put a large amount of distance between himself and the rest of the pack, which allowed him to concentrate on the course rather than who was racing beside him. He was able to cross first and win the gold medal, after which he pumped his fist in the air in celebration. After the ceremony he took a gondola to make his way to the second race course.

Ronald then used the same strategy on this course as he had used in the finals of the first course get some distance between him and the other racers. Ronald was now solely focused on mastering the course, and did not want to worry about other racers trying to knock him down. His strategy worked to a degree, as he was able to finish the first heat in a clear third. In the second run, he was able to finish in second, and once again had enough breathing room to be able to just worry about the course, and figure out the lines that he needed to take on the course. Ronald gave it everything he had in the final race, using all of his speed boost while refilling his "Momentum Meter" by completing some tricks, which allowed him to further activate the speed boosts. This strategy enabled him to build a comfortable lead. He was able to stay ahead, and finished in first, thus winning the final gold medal in the game. After the ceremony, he checked his ranking card, and saw that he was now ranked second, meaning that he still had to win the one-on-one challenge in order to get the top ranking. Just then, a woman named Piper came up to him and said, "Hey Ronald! That was impressive, how you dominated out there! But, you haven't completed your task yet! You're ranked second, right?"

"Yeah," Ronald replied. "Why do you ask? And how do you even know that?"

"I check the rankings all the time. And, I'm ranked number 1! If you want to get out of this game, you'll have to beat *me*! So, here's what we're going to do: The two of us are going to have a little race in the backcountry! And it's not just going to be the backcountry of this peak. No, no, no! That would be too easy. It's going to be the backcountry of the entire *mountain*! After all, you have to have a challenge in order to win, right? *If* you win, you'll be ranked first overall, and will have completed all of your tasks to get out of here. But if you lose, then you'll have to start the game all over again! So, do you feel like gambling?"

"Well, if that is what it takes for me to move on, then I accept your challenge."

"Oh, you're going to be in for a rough ride," she said with a smug smile.

"I don't think so. I feel like luck is on my side this time around. Let's just get to the top of this mountain and get this thing going."

They then hopped onto the snowmobile of one of the mountain's employees and headed for the top of the mountain. It was very cold, snowy, and even icy, so they both had to watch their footing when they walked to the starting line. As the race started, they had to watch that their boards did not get off line, as the ice was making the ride very difficult. After getting past the icy areas, they gave it all they had as they went down TOM Peak. The race was indeed very close. After they had entered Middle Peak, Piper had managed to build up a slight lead. Ronald countered this by attempting some tricks to boost up his "Momentum Meter." After it was filled up, he started alternating between using speed boosts and attempting tricks in order to keep the meter full. This strategy allowed him to slowly catch up to Piper, and eventually pass her. Piper had focused on using up her entire speed boost, which came to haunt her as she started losing momentum. She was eventually forced to attempt some tricks, but crashed, as she had tried to do more tricks than she could realistically handle based on the amount of airtime that she actually had. After they made it to the end of Middle Peak, Ronald had built up a comfortable lead on Piper, who was now really struggling to keep up. Ronald then sped up as he went down Resort Peak, which left Piper well behind. As he was approaching the finish line, Ronald noticed that he was all alone. He also saw that a stadium area had been erected at the bottom of the hill, where everyone in the resort was sitting to watch the race. The crowd, including Pixie, cheered Ronald on as he came into view. A large roar was audible as he crossed the finish line. The resort's owner, who was also calling the action, came up to Ronald after he had finished and said, "Congratulations, Ronald! You have successfully completed all of the tasks of this game!"

The owner then reached for a plaque that read "#1 Overall Racer in XTreme Snowboard Racing and Freestyle," and handed it to Ronald. "This is for you! Again, congratulations on your accomplishment!"

"Thank you, sir," Ronald said as he took the plaque.

Piper then finally crossed the finish line, and was clearly disappointed with how things had ended. She then got off of her board, and walked over to Ronald. "Good job, Ronald," she said to him. "I guess you wanted this more than me."

"Yeah," Ronald said, "but my legs are *killing* me! Now I see why you people put on a tough face after doing these all-peak races, because these things are *hard*!"

"We definitely do! Now I hope you show more appreciation for what we do when you play this game."

"I definitely will!"

Pixie then came out from the stands, and said, "And, I hope you learned that you should not be so arrogant and think that you know everything about any game you play!"

Ronald nodded in agreement. The portal then opened up, and Pixie said to Ronald, "We'd better go."

"Hold on a minute," Ronald said. "I have to do something first."

Ronald then walked over to the stands, and lifted up his board to the crowd to celebrate. He then shook and high-fived the hands of every person in the front row, who were still congratulating him on his accomplishments. This just made Pixie laugh, and she thought, "If this is what happens in the real world when they win an event, then these people are just *weird*!"

After Ronald was done, he walked over to Pixie and told her, "Okay, I'm finished celebrating. Let's go!"

They then headed for the portal and entered it, making their way to the ninth game of their journey.

CHAPTER TWELVE

When they got out of the portal, Ronald and Pixie found themselves in Downtown Calgary at the City Hall LRT train station, which was right in front of Old City Hall. Their clothes also changed back to normal, and they noticed that it was a nice summer's evening. However, not realizing that he was still in the video game world, and that this was only the video game version of Calgary, mainly due to the realism of the modern video game systems, Ronald was smiling from ear to ear and said, "Finally! I'm home!"

"Uh, Ronald, are you sure?" Pixie asked as she looked around.

"Oh, I'm sure!" Ronald replied happily. "I recognize this area. We're right in front of City Hall! And over there, it's IAC Plaza! And there's the Performing Arts Centre, where the Downtown Calgary Concert Hall is located!"

Ronald then turned around, and said, "And look! The Downtown Library!"

"But Ronald-," Pixie started.

"Don't worry about me anymore!" Ronald interrupted. "It was great getting to know you Pixie. I really enjoyed your company. But, I've got to get home now."

"But-."

"Don't be concerned! I can take the LRT from here. As I said at the start of the dancing game, there's a bus stop near my house, so once I get to Dalhousie Station in the northwest, I can take the buses home."

Ronald then crossed 7th Avenue and was standing on the platform on the other side of the street, waiting to board his train home. Pixie was still trying to get his attention that they were still not in the real Calgary, but rather were in a video game rendition of it. After waiting for about an hour, Ronald looked at his watch and said to himself, "What's going on here? I know that Calgary Public Transit Service has issues, but since the new mayor came in, it has really improved a lot. A train should have *been here* by now!"

In the meantime, Pixie had crossed the street and joined Ronald on the platform. Then she asked him, "Is there a problem, Ronald?"

"Yeah," Ronald replied. "The train hasn't arrived yet. And it's been an *hour*! I mean, this just isn't like Calgary Public Transit Service! If something went wrong, they would already have informed their customers about it."

"That's what I've been trying to tell you! You're not home yet!"

"What? How is that possible?"

"Look around here! Does the real Calgary look like some 3D-pixellated world, like a video game would?"

Ronald then looked around, and saw that this indeed was *a* Calgary, but not *the* Calgary. All of the buildings had a pixellated tone to them, then he took a look at himself and saw that he still was a 3D-pixellated person. Once he realized this, his heart sank, and he looked to Pixie and said sadly, "The train's never coming, is it?"

"No, it's not," she replied compassionately.

"So you mean I'm *never* going to get home?"

"Oh, you will, eventually. But right now, you're still in the video game world, though I'm not sure what game it is."

She then pulled out her phone to look for some details. She found out that they were now in a game called ISR Simulator - International Street Racing. In this game, Ronald had to race souped-up cars around various racetracks in the world. The cities he would race in were grouped into regions: the Canadian region was comprised of Calgary, Vancouver, Toronto, and Montreal; the US region was made up of Las Vegas, San Francisco, Chicago, New York, and Miami; Europe had London, Paris, Berlin, and Prague; and the Rest of the World was made up of Tokyo, Sydney, Australia, and Auckland, New Zealand. In order to win the game, Ronald not only had to win the most money, but he also had to earn the highest reputation, which could only be achieved by beating the top racer in each location and region, as well as having to defeat the Ultimate Racer of the game. After hearing this, Ronald said, "Well, that explains why we're in Calgary. I remember playing this game before at a friend's house, and I know that it starts in Calgary."

"Yeah, that's what it says here," Pixie agreed, nodding her head as she looked at her phone. "I guess this is the first location that you have to race in."

"But it's been so long since I last played, so I don't remember where the first track is. Would you have any idea?"

Pixie looked at her phone, and after a few minutes, she said, "Aha! I've found it! But, this is the first time I've ever been in any game that is played in your hometown, or even your home *country*, for that matter."

"Oh, so, I guess you don't know where the first track is physically located, do you?"

"No, I don't."

Pixie then held up the phone to Ronald's face to show him the address, and asked him, "So, do *you* know where this place is?"

"I sure do!" Ronald said. "Remember, I used to work Downtown!"

Ronald then led the way to the location shown on Pixie's phone. As they walked there, she said, "You know, this is the first time that I've ever been to any racing game."

"You're not a big sports fan, are you?" Ronald asked her in a subtle tone.

"I think that was made obvious when we were in that hockey game. So, to answer your question, no, I'm *not*!" she replied.

"From what I remember, I think I this game has a monetary system. How exactly would I be able to make purchases?"

Pixie looked down at her phone, and then said, "You have a debit card in your wallet."

"Good, that makes me feel much better," he said in a relieved tone.

When they arrived the track, they saw all of the racers there. Ronald checked his pockets to make sure that he was indeed provided with a wallet. After finding it, he then searched for the debit card which said "ISR Simulator - International Street Racing" on it, and pulled it out after finding it. Before he went to talk to one of the racers about how he could purchase a car, he asked Pixie, "Are you allowed to compete with me?"

"Let me check," Pixie replied.

She then looked at her phone and said, "No, I can't. But I *can* travel with you, and I *can* stay with the spectators here and watch the races."

"Okay. Well, I'll see you after the first race, then."

Ronald then went up to one of the racers, and asked him about where he would be able to buy a car. As it turned out, this person actually had a car that he wasn't using anymore, and offered it to Ronald for $2000. Ronald accepted the offer, and pulled out the debit card to pay for it, after which the racer pulled out a purchase machine to complete the transaction. Ronald then noticed that he had another card in his pocket that showed him his bank balance, and the balance had now decreased from $10,000 to $8000. Ronald then asked about the courses in the game, and the racers mentioned to him that he had to race on five different courses in each respective city, with each race being five laps in length. He would be racing against nine other people, and after each race he would win money, with the winnings being dependent on his placing. The amount of money earned would decrease according to placing, with the 1st place finisher winning the most amount of money, and the last place finisher would win the least amount of money. Also, cars would get damaged in the game, and it would cost money to repair them. Therefore, Ronald was advised to keep his racing as clean as possible. Furthermore, the money he earned could also be used to buy better cars, which he was strongly advised to do, as the races would get more difficult through the regions. It was also mentioned that there was an entrance fee for each race. The only exception was this first Calgary race to allow for people who were just starting, or were broke, to be able to start building up their bank accounts. The city challenge races were unlocked after Ronald won all of the races in the region, while the regional challenge races were unlocked only when he won all of the races in the region. The final showdown against the Ultimate Racer would commence once all races in the regions were conquered. After receiving this information, Ronald then entered the race, and he was given a slot as to where he would start.

In this first race, Ronald started in sixth place, and anxiously was waiting to get going. A few minutes later, the lights turned green, signalling the start of the race. He immediately started passing cars on the first lap, and eventually found himself in second by the end of the first lap. After two more laps, he was able to pass the first-place car, and stayed in that position all the way to the checkered flag. Ronald won $10,000 for finishing first, which gave him more than enough money to buy the best car available in Calgary which went for $8000. With the leftover money, he was able to buy some upgraded car parts. After completing all of his purchases, Ronald saw that he only had $3000 left in his bank account. He then headed to the next track, and was mindful to keep his purchases in check, as the second race's entrance fee was $1000.

Ronald arrived at the next course, and then registered himself for the race. He was slotted in third place because he had won the previous race He was able to get into first place early on, and kept the lead en route to another victory. He won $12,000 in this race, which allowed him to buy the remaining car upgrades he needed. However, these purchases now left him with only $5000 in his account. He then drove with Pixie to the third course, and paid the $2000 entrance fee. In this race, he was slotted in first place, a position that he never relinquished during the race, and won $15,000. Ronald went to the fourth course, and paid the $3000 entrance fee, and won that race as well, and was $18,000 richer as a result. In the fifth and final race, Ronald had to pay a $5000 entrance fee, and won this race as well, as well as the top prize of $20,000. After the race ended, he got out of the car, where he was met by the top racer in Calgary. The racer said, "Okay, Ronald. You may have won the races here in Calgary, but now it's time to beat *me*! Let's go!"

Ronald hopped right back into his car, and the race immediately started. These city challenge races were just one lap, and if he won, not only would he win the race and move on to the next location, but he would also win his opponent's car. However, if he lost, while he wouldn't lose his car, he would have to start at the beginning and re-race all of the city's courses all over again. And only after winning all of those races again would he be able to return to the one-on-one challenge against the city's top racer.

Ronald did everything he could to win the race. However, he was no match for the top racer, who handily defeated him. As a result, Ronald had to start the Calgary races all over again. Ronald did not lose hope over the fact he had to re-race all of the Calgary courses. In fact, it only increased his determination. And his resolve showed, as he handily won all of these races again, and was ready to face the top Calgary racer again. This time, Ronald learned from his mistakes from the previous race, and was able to win this duel. The other racer came over and congratulated Ronald, and told him that if he wanted to come back and race in Calgary, he could do so without having to go through the circuit again. Ronald was also informed that there would be a garage in each city where the racer's car would be readily available to them. The reason for this was because the developers and programmers of the game designed the game in such a way as to ensure that players could access all of their cars from that garage, including any ones that they bought. All Ronald had to do was look for a sign that said "ISR Simulator - International Street Racing Car Shop," use his debit card in the card reader, and he would be able to access all of his cars in the garage. Ronald was also informed that all future purchases were to be done from the garage. After this, Ronald and Pixie were whisked away to Vancouver for the next set of races.

When they arrived, Pixie was given directions as to where they had to go for the first of the Vancouver races. After receiving this information, Ronald and Pixie wasted no time and headed straight there. Before entering himself, Ronald bought a new car, and a few upgrades, which cost him $80,000. However, he made sure that he didn't fully upgrade the car as any further upgrades would mean that he wouldn't have enough money to pay the $10,000 entrance fee. After registering for the race, he was slotted in fifth. Once the race began, Ronald immediately started passing the racers in front of him, though it took him three laps to overtake the lead. He managed to keep the lead and crossed the finish line in first place, winning himself $30,000. He used some of this money on upgrades, but made sure that to save enough for the $12,000 entrance fee for the next race. While he started in third in the second race, Ronald was quickly able to overtake the others and won this quite easily, winning $33,000. After fully upgrading his car, he proceeded to the next race, which had a $14,000 entrance fee, and was slotted in first to start. Ronald never lost the lead, and won that race as well, and getting the $35,000 top prize. He didn't buy any new cars or upgrades for the fourth race, and instead only paid the $16,000 entrance fee. He won that one as well, and won $38,000. Finally, he entered the fifth race, which had an $18,000 entrance fee. Ronald's confidence was in high gear, which showed in his decisive win. His victory in the fifth race netted him $40,000, after which he was challenged by the top racer of Vancouver. Unlike the one-on-one challenge in Calgary, he won this race easily, mainly because the Vancouver racer kept crashing, which greatly damaged his car and affected its performance. After receiving his congratulations, he was told that he could return to Vancouver to race on any one of the courses that he wished to. Ronald and Pixie's next stop was Toronto.

The first thing Ronald did in Toronto was buy a new car, completely upgraded, which came at a cost of $100,000. He then entered the first race, which had an entrance fee of $25,000, and he was slotted to start in fourth place. In this race, he had some difficulty passing the cars in front of him, as his opponents were really experienced and skilled. He was only able overtake the lead on the final lap, and had to really fight to keep the lead. His win in this race earned him $50,000, and afterwards, he took the attitude that a win was a win. He then entered the next race, which had an entrance fee of $27,000, and was slotted in first. He did not relinquish this position once during the race, and in fact built up a commanding lead and won $55,000 for his efforts. He immediately entered the following race, which had an entrance fee of $30,000, and was again slotted in first to start the race. He struggled on this winding course, and in fact feel into fifth during the first two laps after crashing a couple of times. However, he was able to recover, and managed to overtake the lead with half a lap to go, and came out in first place, and won the $60,000 prize. After the race, he spent $10,000 to repair his car, which had incurred a great deal of damage in those crashes. After the car was repaired, he entered the fourth race, and paid the entrance fee of $33,000, and was again slotted into first. This time, he didn't relinquish the lead, and won the race, along with the top prize money of $65,000. He then entered the final race, and parted with the entrance fee of $35,000. His skill really showed in this race, as he started and finished in first place, winning $70,000. He was then challenged by Toronto's top racer, and he flat out dominated this race, winning by over 2 minutes against this opponent. After being congratulated and told that he was more than welcome to return to any of the Toronto courses anytime, Ronald and Pixie were whisked away to Montreal.

After they arrived there, Ronald took a look at his bank balance, which now stood at $178,000, and asked Pixie, "Say, Pixie, where do I place on the money lists?"

"What do you mean?" Pixie responded.

"Well, my bank balance card shows that I have $178,000 in cash. Where does that rank?"

"Let me check."

Pixie then took a look at her phone, and saw that Ronald was ranked first overall. After she told him, Ronald said, "Really?! That seems odd because I've already spent a lot of money on cars and car upgrades. I also had to spend $10,000 to repair the damage that I sustained in the fourth race in Toronto. Do the cars and upgrades somehow count in those rankings?"

Pixie again looked at her phone, then said, "It would appear it does. I guess it takes the resale value of your cars into account when calculating your overall money ranking."

"Cool!" Ronald said. "Well, I guess I should buy another car so that I can continue on with this game, and beat the Montreal courses."

"Okay. Just make sure you are left with $40,000, as that is the entrance fee for the first race here."

"Okay, I will."

Ronald then bought a new car and fully upgraded it, spending a total of $120,000. He then went to the first course in Montreal, and paid the hefty entrance fee. He was then slotted into first, which was a surprise to him. "Why am I slotted there?" he asked the race organizer.

"Because you've done really well in the other cities," the organizer responded. "That, and your car is worthy of starting there."

Ronald then hopped into his car and headed for the starting line. When the race began, he was quickly passed by a couple of cars, and ran in third for the first couple of laps. However, he managed to regroup, and he passed those two cars in the next lap, and didn't lose his lead, on his way to the win and $80,000. He then went on to the next race, and paid the entrance $43,000 fee, and was again slotted in first. He won this race again, never relinquishing his lead, and earned $85,000 in the process. He then entered the next race, which had an entrance fee of $45,000, and he easily won that race as well, winning $90,000 in the process. He then went on to the next race, and paid the $47,000 entrance fee, and won that race as well, getting $95,000 for his efforts. He then entered the final race, and paid the $50,000 entrance fee, and won the race and $100,000. After he had finished the final Montreal race, he was challenged by the top Montreal racer, and easily won the challenge. After being congratulated and told he could return to the Montreal courses at any time, Ronald was then met by the top street racer in Canada, who came up to him and said, "So, Ronald, looks like you've won a lot in this country. But, you can't call yourself the King of Canada until you beat me! So, let's get the race going!"

The regional racing challenges were two laps each, and took place in the final city within the region where the races were held, but on a different course. Unlike the city races, if Ronald lost, he would be able to redo the regional race until he won, and would not be sent all the way back to the beginning of the region. But if Ronald won, he not only would get to move on to the next region, but he would also win the car of the region's top racer, which would be readily available to him in his garage. Therefore, this race was held in Montreal. Ronald and the top Canadian racer got into their cars and started the race. Ronald's opponent was tough. The two racers ran neck-and-neck in this race, and constantly kept passing each other. However, on the final lap, Ronald finally was able to make his move and overtook his opponent. When they both crossed the finish line, Ronald won by just half a second, but it was still a win. This allowed Ronald to move on to the US portion of the game. He was congratulated by the Canadian racer, after which Ronald and Pixie were sent off to San Francisco.

When they arrived in San Francisco, they landed right at Fisherman's Wharf. Pixie quickly took out her phone to find out where they had to go, and found out that they had to head to a course located somewhere near the Golden Gate Bridge. They then got into Ronald's car from Montreal, and drove to the location using the directions given. When they arrived, Ronald bought a new, fully upgraded, top of the line vehicle for $200,000. After purchasing the car, Ronald then entered the first race paying the exorbitant $60,000 entrance fee, and was slotted in second. Ronald easily passed the first-place car on the first lap, and continued building up his lead as the race went on, and won the race $125,000 for his efforts. He entered the next race, which had a $70,000 entrance fee, and started and finished in first place, winning $135,000. In the third race, which had an $80,000 entrance fee, Ronald started in first place, but lost three positions early on to some very skilled drivers. He had to work hard to squeak out a win at the finish line, and won $144,000. The fourth race, which had a $90,000 entrance fee, was a very tight race wire-to-wire. However, Ronald was able to build a lead after some skillful driving, and won the race, winning $150,000 in the process. The fifth race, which had an enormous entrance fee of $100,000, saw Ronald dominate the field, en route to a victory and the $155,000 prize. He was then challenged by the top San Francisco racer, a race which Ronald dominated, due to having a more powerful car than the other racer. After receiving his congratulations, Ronald and Pixie moved on to the Las Vegas races.

After arriving in Las Vegas, Ronald was amazed to see his that bank balance was a whopping $392,000. "Wow! This balance is building up, isn't it?" he said.

"Yes, it is," Pixie said. "I think you'll be able to attain the top money ranking easily, as you're buying the best cars, and getting them fully upgraded. Plus, you're racing very cleanly, so you haven't had to spend too much money on repairs. The hard part is going to be those top-racer challenges, not to mention that race against the Ultimate Racer."

Ronald nodded as they headed straight for the street racing area. After arriving there, Ronald bought the best car available, fully upgraded, for $250,000 before entering in the first race, which carried an entrance fee of $125,000. He was slotted in first place for this race, and Ronald didn't have too much trouble. Ronald easily won the race and the $175,000 prize. He went on to the next race, and paid the $130,000 entrance fee, and won this race decisively as well, and was awarded $180,000. The third race had an entrance fee of $135,000, and Ronald dominated this one too, winning the top prize of $185,000. In the fourth race, which had a $140,000 entrance fee, Ronald won by driving defensively, which prevented anyone from passing him, and nabbed the $190,000 prize. The fifth and final race course had an entrance fee of $150,000, and was one which proved to be more difficult for Ronald. While he didn't crash, he did lose position several times, as the competition was that good. However, on the final lap, he made a strong charge, and came all the way bay from fifth to first, barely overtaking the lead right to the finish line. In fact, the race went to a photo finish, and it was determined during the review that Ronald was victorious by a margin of .001 seconds, which was enough to give him a $200,000 payday. He then raced against the top racer in Las Vegas, and won this challenge easily, as the other racer crashed so badly that he completely blew up his car. After Ronald was congratulated, he and Pixie then made their way to Chicago.

When they arrived in Chicago, Ronald immediately checked his bank balance, and saw that it had the same balance as when he first arrived in Las Vegas. As a result Ronald went to the garage to get the car that he won in the one-on-one challenge in Las Vegas, but didn't upgrade it, as he was going to buy the best car available in Chicago once he had the money. After getting the car from the garage, he headed to the first track, which carried an entrance fee of $175,000. However, he was slotted in ninth due to not having the best Chicago car. Despite this, Ronald was skillfully able to move up during the first three laps, and eventually won the race by passing the racer that had held the lead from the beginning on the final lap. For his efforts, Ronald received $225,000, plus a $35,000 bonus for his near worst-to-first showing. With this money, he bought a new, fully upgraded car for $300,000, and then reentered the last race in Las Vegas because he was just short of the $183,000 fee needed to enter the second race in Chicago. In that Las Vegas race, he easily won with his brand new car, and the $200,000 first place prize. He returned to Chicago, and was able to afford the entrance fee for the second race, where he was slotted in first. He never looked back and won the race, along with the first place prize of $237,000. He then entered the third race, paying the $189,000 entrance fee. He was slotted in first to start, and he made sure to keep his focus on the track rather than the other racers, and this strategy allowed him build a comfortable lead. He won the race and the prize of $244,000. Ronald then went on to the fourth race, which had an entrance fee of $193,000, and was able to win this as well, netting the prize of $250,000. In the fifth race, Ronald paid the $200,000 entrance fee, and he struggled in this race. The drivers were much more aggressive, and the track itself was a really tough one, especially with its tricky turns that seemed to come out of nowhere, especially after long straightaways. However, Ronald was able to tough it out and win by two seconds, which netted him the $260,000 prize money. Ronald was then challenged by the top Chicago racer, and they went on to the race. Ronald won the race easily, and received the customary congratulations from his opponent. After shaking hands, Ronald and Pixie went on to New York.

When they arrived at New York, Ronald saw the that he would not be able to immediately afford the prices for both a fully upgraded car, even a lower-end one, and the entrance fee for the first race, which had a hefty $215,000 price tag. As a result, he decided that he would return to Chicago to run in a couple of races to build up his bank account so that he could afford both the first race's entrance fee and the top car over there. He then asked Pixie to use the menu system on her phone so they could return to Chicago, which she did in a matter of minutes, and they returned to Chicago. He re-entered the fifth race twice, and won it both times, receiving $520,000 total. He saw that his bank account balance now sat at $573,000, and he decided that he would run the fifth Chicago race one more one more to be safe. He re-entered the fifth race again, and won it again. He reviewed his balance after the race, and after being satisfied with it, he asked Pixie to return them to New York.

In New York, he didn't buy the best available car, but rather bough the second-best available car instead, and fully upgraded it, which came at a total cost of $320,000. Ronald then entered the first race, and paid the $215,000 entrance fee, which still made him cringe. In this race, he was slotted to start in second, as he didn't have the best car in the city. However, Ronald found the car okay, and was able to pass the person running in first place on the first lap. He didn't give up the lead, and raced his way to the win and the $275,000 prize. He then entered the second race, paying the $225,000 entrance fee, and won this race as well, and won $283,000 for his efforts. Ronald moved on to the third race, paying the $230,000 entrance fee. In this race, he had to work really hard to fend off the competition. His confidence and skill really showed, and he was able to squeak out a win by beating the second-place person by 1.5 seconds, and received $292,000 for winning. He moved on to the fourth race, which had a $236,000 entrance fee, and found this race easier than the previous one. He won the race, and received $300,000 as the prize money. The fifth course had an entrance fee of $240,000, which made Ronald blink because of the high fee. Ronald was able to win this race as well quite easily, and netted $310,000 in prize money. He was then challenged by the top racer of New York. Ronald got into his car, and started the race. This was a difficult one to race in because he didn't have the best car available in New York, something his opponent tried to use to his advantage. He was able to keep his opponent in his view, and made a move in the final few turns to pass him, and just held on for the win. They both got out of their cars, and Ronald was congratulated for his skills, and then Ronald and Pixie were sent to Miami.

As soon as they arrived in Miami, Ronald saw that the prices of the cars here, fully upgraded, were exorbitant. He then decided to go to the garage to get the car that he had just won in New York, and fully upgraded it at a lower cost. Once the car was upgraded to the Miami standards, which came at a cost of only $123,000, he went to the first race course, and paid a

$250,000 entrance fee, and was slotted in tenth because he had what these people considered an inferior car. However, Ronald showed them that he had a great car and great skill, and quickly rose from last to first in the first couple of laps, and held onto his lead through the final three laps. In addition to winning this race, and the top prize of $325,000, he also won a $100,000 bonus for going from worst to first. After the race, everyone looked at him shocked, and wondered how he could have done so well with such a "lousy" car. All Ronald could do was shrug, and he and Pixie moved on to the next track.

Here, Ronald paid the $258,000 entrance fee, and was slotted in ninth, as the people here still were doubting his abilities because he was racing, in what was still deemed an inferior car. However, Ronald proved them wrong again, quickly passing all of the other cars in front of him in just the first lap. He continued building up his lead to win the race, and received the top prize reward of $335,000 plus a $75,000 bonus, which again shocked everyone. Ronald then entered the next race, paying the $265,000 entrance fee, and this time was slotted in first, as the race organizer did not want to pay Ronald a bonus if he was able to win this race after starting in one of the bottom four spots. Ronald won this race as well, easily building up a large lead, and received $343,000. He then entered the final race of Miami, which had a mind-blowing $275,000 entrance fee. Ronald started this race in first place, and never looked back, en route to a victory and the $350,000 reward. Ronald was then challenged by the top Miami racer. After being looked down by the other racers in Miami, Ronald took this challenge personally. He won this duel easily, as his opponent crashed multiple times in this race. After the race, he was congratulated, and when Ronald got out of his car, the top US racer came up to him and said, "So, Ronald, you were able to win all of these races here in the USA. But, if you want to prove you're the King of the US, you have to beat me!"

Ronald accepted the challenge, and he got back into his car. This race was much more difficult, as the other racer's skill, not to mention his vehicle, were showing. Ronald persevered through it all, and was able to defeat the other racer by .23 seconds, which allowed Ronald to win both the race and his opponent's car, not to mention allowing him to move on to the European races. After being congratulated, Ronald and Pixie headed to the European region to for the races there.

Upon arriving in London, England, Ronald took a look at the prices for cars here, as well as the entrance fee for the first race. The steep prices made Ronald's decision quite easy. He decided it would be better to just upgrade the car that he had won from the US' top racer, as this car far was more advanced than any of the other ones he possessed. He and Pixie then headed to the garage, and paid $165,000 to upgrade the car, which was a real bargain compared to the $500,000 he would have had to spend on a new car. He then went to the first course in London, and paid the $300,000 entrance fee, and was slotted into first because everyone here had heard about how well he had raced in the US, and the organizers weren't interested in paying him any bonus money. Ronald showed them how much skill he had, winning this race decisively, and by more than 15 seconds. He was even more surprised at how powerful his car was, which gave him even more confidence. For his victory, he was paid $375,000. He then moved on to the next race, and paid the entrance fee of $310,000, and easily won this race as well, netting $387,000. He went on to the third race, paying the $317,000 entrance fee, and kept shocking everyone. He won this race too, and received $393,000. The fourth race, which had an entrance fee of $325,000, gave Ronald more problems than the previous London races. He was able to hang on and win it by 3 seconds, and received $400,000 for his efforts. The fifth race had Ronald paying a $330,000 fee to enter, and then he went on to dominate this race, winning by 23 seconds, and got $410,000 as his prize. He was then challenged by the top racer in London. However, Ronald showed his extreme prowess in this race, as he easily won it and his opponent's car. When the race ended, Ronald was congratulated by his opponent, who told him that he could return to any one of the London tracks if he wanted to, before he and Pixie moved on to Paris.

When they arrived in Paris, Ronald looked around the area, and saw that they were in front of the Eiffel Tower. "You know, before I got laid off, I was planning a trip to France," he said to Pixie. "I know this isn't the same thing as the real Paris, but it's still pretty cool to get to see the Eiffel Tower in person. And, I was also looking at going to Germany, too, in the same trip."

"Wow, that's amazing," Pixie said. "Do you have the money to do it?"

"I do. But not the motivation. I mean, it hurt pretty badly when I was laid off."

"Yeah, you told me that in the dancing game. Are you going to do it once you get home?"

"Maybe next year, meaning 2014. I mean, after being in these games for so long, and seeing that they can be a lot more dangerous than I thought, I will definitely need a break from them."

"I can imagine. You really did seem to have a life before you lost that job. And, I'm glad that you've learned that you can't escape to our world to deal with your problems."

"By the way, how many games are there left to play after this one?"

"I have no idea. Remember, The VGG said that they would inform me only *after* you complete the last game that you are required to play."

Ronald could only shrug, and it was quite evident that he was homesick. They then went to the garage to upgrade the car that he had won from London's top racer, spending $200,000 in the process. Before they went to the first track, Ronald asked, "Oh, Pixie, what's my reputation ranking in this game? I know I rank first in overall money, but I don't know where I rank in that other thing."

Pixie looked at her phone, and said, "Oh, it looks like you're getting a good reputation. No one here is taking you lightly, so that's a good thing."

While Ronald was satisfied with the answer, he was still determined to show everyone that he was indeed the best. They then arrived at the first track, and Ronald paid the $350,000 entrance fee to enter. He was slotted in first, because everyone had heard that they couldn't take him lightly, even if he wasn't driving the best available car in the city. In this race, he finished in first, though he had to fight some hard battles with the second- and third-place cars throughout the race. He won by only .4 seconds, and for his efforts, he won $425,000. He then entered the next race, which had an entrance fee of $360,000, and found himself in another tough battle. He was able to win the see-saw battle, and won $432,000. Ronald moved on to the third race, and paid the $370,000 entrance fee. He had quite a bit of trouble with the winding track, but won in a photo finish, winning by .01 seconds, and received $440,000. The fourth race, with an entrance fee of $375,000, was even more difficult than the previous three. Ronald fought all race, and won by a slim margin on the final lap, which earned him $450,000. The fifth course had an entrance fee of $382,000, making Ronald cringe. Here, he was able to build up a good lead, and didn't relinquish it despite the best efforts of the other racers, and won by 3 seconds, getting $460,000. He was then challenged by the top racer in Paris, and Ronald was able to win that race as well. His opponent congratulated him, and told him that he could return at any time that he wanted, after which he and Pixie moved on to Prague.

When they arrived in Prague, Ronald took a look what it would cost to buy the best car in Prague, and what the entrance fees were like. He could only shake his head, as the prices were very stiff. He then decided that he would continue upgrading the cars that he had won, and as a result decided that he would upgrade the car that he had won from the Paris racer. The total cost of upgrades for that car was $225,000, and after they were completed, he and Pixie made their way to the first track, where the entrance fee was $400,000. Ronald was slotted in first, and never gave up the lead, and won $475,000 for his efforts. He then went to the second race, and paid the $404,000 fee, and won this race decisively as well, winning $482,000. The third race had an entrance fee of $410,000, and Ronald handedly won this race, getting $490,000. The other racers were quite impressed with Ronald's skill and determination. They knew that he was a force that could not be reckoned with. He went on to the fourth course, which cost $415,000 to enter, and continued his domination, netting $495,000 for his efforts. The fifth race had an entrance fee of $425,000, which made Ronald roll his eyes. However, this track proved to be more difficult for Ronald. The track had more turns, and was more windy. The other racers did their best to take advantage of this. However, Ronald was able to hang on, and won the race and $500,000. The challenge against the top Prague racer also proved to be quite difficult. There were numerous lead changes, but in the end, Ronald came out in top, though a photo review of the finish was called to make sure that that was indeed the result. After examining the photos, the race organizers determined that Ronald did indeed win, but the margin of the victory was just .001 seconds. But, it was still a win, which allowed Ronald to move on to Berlin, not to mention receiving the racer's car. After being congratulated by his opponent, Ronald and Pixie then headed on to Berlin.

After arriving in Berlin, Ronald decided that he would spend $623,000 to buy the second-best car available there, and fully upgrade it. He felt his that his bank balance was high enough to allow him to do this and retain the top ranking in the money standings. He also saw that there was still more than enough available to pay the $435,000 fee required to enter the first race. After receiving his car, he went to the track, and entered the race. He was slotted in first, and didn't lose the lead, winning by over 25 seconds, and earning $510,000. The second race had a fee of $446,000, and Ronald continued his dominance, winning the race and netting $525,000. He moved on to the third race, and paid $450,000 to enter it, winning it by over a minute over the second-place racer, and getting $532,000. Next was the fourth race, which had a fee of $455,000 to enter. He was able to win this race too, though it this a little closer than the first three, as the margin of victory was 10 seconds. For his win, he received the prize of $539,000. The fifth track had an entrance fee of $463,000, and proved to be quite difficult. It had a lot of turns, and very short straightaways. Ronald had to really concentrate here, and was even passed a few times. However, he was able to recover and regain the lead, and was able to win by 29 seconds. However, the margin was so high only because there was a major crash behind him on the last lap that slowed down all the other racers. For his efforts, he received $548,000. He was then challenged by the top racer in Berlin, and easily won that race. After being congratulated, Ronald was then challenged by the top European racer, who said, "Okay. So you won all of the European races. But let's see how you fare against the best of the best in *all* of Europe!"

Ronald accepted the challenge and got back into his car, and headed to the starting line. This course would prove to be tough, as it was narrow and windy. After the lights turned green, the race started. This race was quite the duel, as Ronald and his opponent were engaged in a battle where neither one was able to build a good up lead. There were even a couple of close calls near the walls for both drivers. As they approached the finish line, Ronald managed to just pull away, and won by only a second over his opponent. When he got out of his car, Ronald was congratulated by the racer, and was told that he was always welcome to come back to Berlin, or any of the other European tracks. Ronald and Pixie were then sent to Sydney for the final region's races.

After arriving in Sydney, Ronald saw the infamous Opera House and said, "You know, when I return home, I should also look at making a trip here. I would *love* to see a show at the Sydney Opera House."

"I'm sure that would be fun," Pixie replied. "But, stay focused! You still have some races to win! There is no time for daydreaming or sightseeing right now."

Ronald nodded his head, and they then headed to the garage. Ronald decided that he would pay $225,000 to fully upgrade the car that he had just won from the top European racer, thus reducing the expense of a new car. Once the upgrades were completed, he and Pixie went to the first track, where Ronald paid the $475,000 entrance fee, and was slotted to start in first. In the race, he didn't surrender the lead, and dominated the entire way, en route to the win and $575,000. He then went on to enter in the second race, paying the $480,000 entrance fee. He easily won that one as well, getting $583,000 as his reward. He moved on to the third race, paying $485,000 to enter, and dominated here as well, winning $590,000 for his efforts. The fourth race, which had an entrance fee of $493,000, gave Ronald some difficulty. He and the second place finisher duelled the whole race. However, Ronald pulled ahead and won, which earned him $598,000. He went to the fifth race, and paid $500,000 to enter. This race was close, but Ronald was able to get a 3 second advantage over the racer in second place, and won the race and $602,000. After the fifth race was over, he was challenged by Sydney's top racer. Although this racer was tough, Ronald maintained his focus and was able to win the challenge. Ronald's opponent was quite gracious in defeat, and said he was welcome in Sydney at any time. Ronald and Pixie then headed on to Auckland.

In Auckland, Ronald first decided to first upgrade the car he had just won from the racer in Sydney, which came at a cost of $250,000. After the upgrades were completed, he then moved on to the first race, where he paid $515,000 to enter, where he was slotted in first place. The other races kept Ronald on his toes. They tried to pass him few times during the race but Ronald was able to fend them off, and finished in first, earning $625,000 for the victory. He headed on to the second race, and paid the $520,000 fee. He found this race much easier than the previous one, and quite handedly won the race, getting $634,000 for his efforts. In the third race, which had a $527,000 entrance fee, Ronald had to deal with some very aggressive opponents. At one point, he barely avoided a crash. On the third lap, when he was battling for position, one of the cars behind him suddenly knocked into second-place car, which fishtailed in Ronald's direction. His skills showed here, as he avoided getting caught up in the wreckage, and found himself all alone in first after crossing the finish line. For the victory, he earned $640,000. The fourth race, which had a $535,000 entrance fee, was even more challenging. The track was winding with short straightaways and lots of chicane turn combinations. Ronald managed to win the race, though he won by .0001 seconds. Even after the race was over, the officials had to examine photos of the finish, and some video was also consulted. In the end, it was determined that Ronald had indeed won, and was given $646,000 for the victory. The final race carried an entrance fee of $550,000, and was easier than the others. Ronald was able to win this one with less effort, as he managed to get a 10-second lead that he did not lose, and got $658,000 for the win. He was then challenged by the top Auckland racer, and won that race handily. He had built up a 1 minute lead halfway through, and that lead increased to well over 3 minutes ahead by the time he crossed the finish line. After receiving the customary congratulations and well wishes for his win, including being told he could return at any time he wanted, Ronald and Pixie went on to Tokyo for the final series of races, including the one against the Ultimate Racer.

In Tokyo, Ronald decided that he would buy the best car available in the game. The cost was a hefty $750,000, fully upgraded, but Ronald didn't want to worry about the difficult Tokyo tracks. He then went and entered the first race, which carried a mind-boggling fee of $575,000. In this race, Ronald saw just how tough the Tokyo racers were. A number of times, he found himself running as low as sixth. Ronald used pure determination to come back, overtaking the lead on the final lap, en route to the win. The prize he won was of $675,000. He then entered the next race, at a cost of $585,000. He found this race to be just as close as the first one. But he persevered, and won the race and the $700,000 prize. The third race, which had a fee of $600,000, was also tough. Once again, Ronald won it on the final lap, and was awarded $725,000 for his efforts. The fourth race, which had an entrance fee of $615,000, was no less difficult. Ronald had battled hard, and on the final straightaway, Ronald came out of the final turn faster than the second place racer, and was able to fully pass him halfway down the straight to win by .5 seconds to earn $750,000. In the final 5-lap race of the game, Ronald paid $630,000 to enter, and once again found himself in a very competitive race. This was another see-saw battle, however, on the final lap, Ronald was able to make his charge, and eventually won by 4 seconds due to being able to come out of the turns faster and cleaner than his competitors. For his efforts, he won $775,000. Ronald was then challenged by the top racer in Tokyo. Ronald was able to win the race easily as the other racer crashed out and completely damaged his car beyond repair. After winning this race, Ronald was congratulated by the Tokyo racer, and then was challenged by the top Rest of the World racer. Ronald showed his skill here, decisively winning this race as well. Ronald was congratulated by his opponent, and was invited to return to Tokyo anytime he wanted to. Finally came the Ultimate Racer, a man adorned in tattoos and all-black leather. As Ronald was getting out of his car, he was approached by the

Ultimate Racer, who said, "Good job, Ronald! You have proved how good you are so far! Now, is your final test! To prove that you are the best in the world, you have to beat me!"

The challenge against the Ultimate Racer required Ronald to win a 3-lap race against him in a neutral location, meaning that the race would not be held in any of the cities that Ronald had already raced in. As it turned out, the city that they would race in was Los Angeles, as the developers of the game determined that this city had the best street racing culture and the most challenging street racing courses. Also, Ronald found out that he could attempt this race as many times as he needed to in order to win and move on, as there was no punishment if he lost. Furthermore, Ronald was only allowed to use the car that he had won from the Rest of the World racer, which already came fully upgraded. After receiving these details, Ronald, Pixie, and the Ultimate Racer were immediately whisked away to Los Angeles. When they reached the starting line, there was no crowd there, and only Pixie was allowed to watch the race. Ronald got into his car first, after which the Ultimate Racer got into his. After the lights turned green, the race started. Ronald quickly found out why this guy was called the Ultimate Racer, as he pulled ahead almost immediately. For the next two laps, Ronald trailed, but slowly chipped away at the lead. By the time the white flag appeared, signalling the final lap, Ronald was just half a second behind. He used his turning skills to further cut into the lead, and was able to pull even with the Ultimate Racer with half a lap to go. Ronald then started to hedge his way forward through the turns, and pulled away in the final straightaway, winning over the Ultimate Racer. When the race was over, Ronald found out that he had won the final race in the game, but only by .73 seconds. However, he was just thrilled to have won because it meant that he was moving on to the next game. After they got out of their cars, the Ultimate Racer said, "Congratulations, Ronald! You beat me, and you proved just *who* the King of the Streets is! You have completed your tasks for this game, as your final balance of $1,676,000, along with the cars that you own, ranks you first overall in the money rankings. You have also earned the highest reputation amongst the street racers."

"Thank you," Ronald said. "I really appreciate hearing that."

The portal then opened, and before Ronald and Pixie were allowed to go into it, the Ultimate Racer stopped them. "Ronald, first I have to give you something before you go."

The Ultimate Racer then opened the trunk of his car and pulled out a plaque saying, "The Top Racer in ISR Simulator - International Street Racing." He handed it to Ronald, and Ronald said, "Thank you! I wasn't expecting anything in return for this!"

"You're very welcome," the Ultimate Racer said. "You truly deserve it."

"Before I go, I have a question to ask you."

"And that is?"

"Do I get to keep the money and the cars that I earned in this game?"

The Ultimate Racer laughed and then shook his head and said, "No. Are any of those things real when you're playing these games in the real world?"

"No."

"So, what makes you think that it's different as a result of you playing here in person?"

"Because I already have all of the medals and plaques that I received from the other games, and I know I'm allowed to take them home with me."

"Well, those are the only things that you get to keep. The money and cars stay with us. Otherwise, it could cause a large number of problems both for you and for us if you took those other things home with you."

Ronald contemplated what the Ultimate Racer had just said. After pondering it for a minute, he then said, "Okay. It does make sense when I think about it. I mean, it would be tough to explain to everyone where I got that much money, and where those types of cars came from, when I haven't been working for the past number of months. And I'm sure The VGG would not be too happy about it, either."

"Exactly."

"Well, thanks again."

Ronald then motioned to Pixie that it was time to go, and they headed for the portal. They entered it and made their way to the tenth game, not knowing that it led to the final game that Ronald was required to play before he would finally be allowed to go back home.

CHAPTER THIRTEEN

After exiting the portal, Ronald and Pixie found themselves in the middle of a war-torn region of the US Midwest. This area contained buildings that had been blown down or damaged by fire, scorched earth, and fire-damaged cars. However, there were no dead bodies littering the area. Ronald then looked around and remembered seeing this place on a documentary. He then turned to Pixie and asked, "Say, are we somewhere in Missouri?"

Pixie then looked at her phone, and said, "That's what it says here. Central Missouri, to be exact. But, I don't think you're in the real world yet."

"That, I guessed. But, what are we doing here?"

Just then, Ronald's clothes then changed, and he was wearing military combat gear. He took particular notice at the flag patches on his shoulders. On his left shoulder was a Canadian flag, and on his right shoulder was a flag that was unrecognizable to him. "Which country does this flag belong to?" he asked as he pointed to his right shoulder. "I mean, the one on my left is the Canadian flag, but I have never seen this other one before, and I've seen a lot of flags, and I've read a lot of books about them, too."

Pixie then looked at her phone again, and said that they were in a game called Operation Midwest: The Fight for Freedom. The flag on his right shoulder was that of a new country located in North America. It was set in 2026, a few years after another financial crisis had led to the collapse of the US economy and the US dollar, which resulted in such financial turmoil that the US couldn't pay its debts. During 2023, it had tried to ask its major creditors for debt forgiveness, but those countries and entities refused. Their justification was that the US had for so long demanded debts owed to it to be repaid, and therefore they should be held to account. The US then desperately went to Canada and Mexico to ask for debt forgiveness. However due to the lack of faith in US banks, and also a lack of trust that the US would reciprocate the gesture if they ever needed help in the future, Canada and Mexico made huge demands, including forgiveness of debts they owed to the US and its banks, as well as territorial demands. The US government initially balked, but both countries reminded the US that no one else in the world was willing to forgive US debt, and as a result they were in no position to negotiate. The US eventually conceded and agreed to the demands in early 2024. They gave Canada not only some of their pre-Confederation territory, namely Washington state, Oregon, northern Minnesota, northern Maine, northeastern Vermont, part of North Dakota, and part of the Alaska Panhandle, but also ceded to Canada Idaho, Montana, the rest of Minnesota, North Dakota, Alaska, Maine, and Vermont, and New Hampshire. The latter was a compromise for Canada's initial demand that the US return *all* of Canada's pre-Confederation territory, which had also included Ohio, Illinois, Indiana, Wisconsin, Michigan, and parts of New York and Pennsylvania. Mexico received most of the land it had held prior to both the Gadsden Purchase and the Mexican-American War, with the exception being Texas because it had declared independence in 2021 after its citizens voted in a referendum to secede from the US. Hawaii had also separated from the US, declaring independence in 2022 via a referendum, and had cut off relations with the US after the declaration. Instead, Hawaii decided to forge closer ties with Australia, Japan, and China due to their closer proximity. "What?!" Ronald said in disbelief. "Yeah right! As if *that* will ever happen!"

Pixie emphatically replied, "Well, when you're caught in a bind, and no one else is willing to help you out, you will do *anything* to receive help. And, from what I read here, the US hasn't exactly been the nicest of neighbours."

"I guess. But, this is just a video game, and based on what I know, *that* will *never* happen! Anyway, what else is in the backstory to this game?"

Pixie then looked again at her phone. She mentioned that the residents of the ceded territories enjoyed being a part of their new countries as they offered many social programs, especially universal healthcare, which meant that they would save a fortune, including possible bankruptcy from any health-related costs. Their new countries also offered them more freedoms compared to their previous situations. Feeling that they also could do better on their own, in mid-2024, the remaining territories of Wyoming, Colorado, Kansas, and Oklahoma, as well as Kansas, Iowa, Missouri, Arkansas, Illinois, Wisconsin, Indiana, Ohio, and Michigan all came together and unilaterally declared independence without any referendums. They named their new country Fertana because of the fertile lands it contained, and this new entity was quickly recognized by many countries around the world. The US was now only left with Louisiana, Pennsylvania, New York, southern New England, the District of Columbia, all land south of the Ohio River to the Gulf of Mexico, which included Mississippi, and all of the states bordering the Atlantic Ocean. The US was determined to regain Fertana because the unilateral secession had led to a further loss of prestige. It already had to deal with the humiliation of having to give up so much land to both Canada and Mexico in exchange for a small amount of debt forgiveness, and the US was not willing to be further humiliated. As a result, the US invaded Fertana in late 2024 to avenge all of its losses. In invading the country, they couldn't use drones because they had been declared illegal by the international community in 2020. Some senior US officials had even been arrested and tried at the Court of International Crimes a few days after the new law had passed for using these weapons. These officials were eventually convicted of their crimes, and were currently serving their sentences. However, the US found great resistance from Fertana's residents, who enjoyed living in their new country because they enjoyed the new freedoms they had, and enjoyed having more say in how their country was run compared to before. So, they were really incensed when US troops started invading. Almost immediately, they started raising militias, while also asking the international community to help them defend their new country. Canada and Mexico stepped up to help their new neighbours, whom they felt were being bullied by the US into submission. It should also be noted that Canada, Mexico, and Fertana were working on a new "Fair Trade" deal, as the International Forum for the World's Communities and the Trade Committees United had both declared the Continental Free Trade Agreement for North America null and void in 2022 due to Texas and Hawaii declaring independence. Canada and Mexico also felt that the US, if successful in regaining Fertanan land back, would come after *them*, looking to recapture the land they had acquired in exchange for forgiveness of US debt. Moreover, they had a suspicion that the Americans wouldn't just be satisfied in regaining the land they had lost. Instead, Canada and Mexico feared that the US would then look to look to dominate *all* of North America, and turn the whole continent into one country called United States of America. Latin America had also answered Fertana's call, as they felt that helping a new country in former US land was the perfect way to get its revenge on the US for how they had been treated by the US government and its corporations. Furthermore, all of those countries that had previously allowed the US military to keep military bases had now kicked out all of the US soldiers, and confiscated the land on which the bases formerly stood. The bases were subsequently torn down, and new developments were arising on those lands.

The US had also called on its allies to help it recapture its former territories. However, only one stepped up, and that being Texas, which still had strong ties to the US, including using the US Dollar as its currency. Israel did not step up because, with the collapse of the US, this meant the end of US financial support for the country. Instead, they had come to a quick agreement during 2024 to unify with the Palestinians in Gaza and the

West Bank, including breaking down the wall that they had finished building in 2018. They called their new country IsPal, with its capital being Jerusalem. This new country was built on the premise of multiculturalism, which had equal rights for everyone. The Palestinians were even allowed to move into the settlements as neighbours with the Israelis, and in some cases shared apartments with their new countrymen. The new country told the US that it was too fragile to get involved in any major wars, and needed to concentrate on making IsPal work. Other Middle Eastern countries also refused to help, as they didn't see any benefit in helping out a crumbling empire. Furthermore, they were of the opinion that the US would never help them out in similar circumstances in the future unless the outcome only benefitted US interests. The UK and Australia also decided to abstain, citing a conflict of interest due to the Commonwealth and other historic ties that they had with Canada. China and Russia stayed out of the battle for two reasons: One was that their rival and enemy was finally on the verge of complete collapse, and the other was because they saw this conflict as a North American war, and therefore it was not in their strategic interests to get involved. However, some of Fertana's citizens were still loyal to the US, and when they were called upon by the US to take up arms against Fertana, they immediately heeded to the call to reunite their country. "Whoa!" Ronald said in shock after Pixie had finished discussing the game's description. "Do you really think all that could happen?"

"Well, if the US is as alienating and horrible as it says here, then anything's possible," Pixie replied. "I'm not a fortune teller, and I won't speculate on future events. And like you said, this is just a video game, and is intended for gamers that enjoy the military-combat genre of games."

"But this is the *first time* I've ever heard of a game like this, with those types of things happening. Why would a video game studio build something like that?"

"Maybe it's based on what could happen if real-world events continue as they do. Or, maybe the developers wanted to create a game that was different compared to all of the other ones out there in this genre. I know I've heard that most of the military games that have been created are based in countries located in either Europe or Asia. And when some country is trying to break away, or there is internal strife, the US is always involved in trying to the rescue the new country, or whatever allies it has. So it seems this game is considering things from a different perspective, and making people think about how the US would react if a territory was trying to separate from *them*, or if there was any internal trouble within its own borders."

"Oh, okay. But what happened to the outside territories that the US controlled? Like Puerto Rico?"

"It says here that they all became independent nations, as they had no interest in helping out the US, but rather wanted to put their energies towards building their countries, including getting an economy running, and rebuilding their cities and infrastructure."

"Okay. Well, since I'm the only one wearing military gear, I guess that means that I'm the only one allowed to participate in this game, right?"

"Yes, it does. But, if you need my help, just yell 'pause,' just like you did in the other games where I was only allowed to be an observer."

"Okay. But, if I *do* need your help, please don't react like you did in that crime-fighting game."

Pixie laughed, then said, "Don't worry, I won't. The leaders of this game already assured me that there's more to do here than there was in that stupid police station lobby."

"Okay, that's good. So, where exactly am I supposed to go?"

Pixie checked her phone, and then said, "There's a military base located 10 miles north of here where your unit of the pro-Fertana soldiers are stationed. Wait a second. *Miles*?! What the heck is a 'mile?!' I know about metres and kilometres and other metric units of measurement, because that's what we use in the video game world. I even know about feet, inches, pounds, and Fahrenheit, because we use all those things for measuring height, weight, and cooking temperature. But what is *this* thing?"

Ronald started laughing as he replied, "It's a unit of measurement based on the British Imperial system. Not many countries use it anymore, as most countries have switched to the metric system. I think the US is the only country in the world to still solely use the old system. In Canada, we mostly use the metric system, although in practical and convenient cases we use the old system."

"Like when?"

"Like when describing our height and weight, and when we're cooking food."

"Okay, so just like us here. But what is the conversion from a mile to a kilometre?"

"One mile is 1.6 kilometres, and one kilometre is .6 miles."

Pixie then did the calculation on her phone, and said, "Whoa! This base is 16 kilometres from here! That's pretty far!"

"It is," Ronald replied, "but I can handle it. Will I have to worry about getting shot?"

"No, you won't, as this territory was secured for Fertana early on in the war. They're having trouble with areas further north of the base, and especially to the east and south."

"Okay. Well, I guess I'll see you later. If I don't need your help, I guess we won't see each other again until the end of the game."

Ronald then started to walk in the direction of the base, when he heard Pixie yell at him from behind, "Ronald! Wait!"

Ronald stopped, turned around, and asked, "What now?! I have to get to that base so that I can get this game over with!"

"Well, there's one more thing I have to tell you."

"And that is…?"

"In this game, just like in the dancing game, there are real-world players playing on either side of the battle. But there is a difference. They will appear as avatars of their real-world selves, meaning that you can actually interact with them. And another warning: you may end up having to face your friends from the real world. And, they may recognize you."

"I don't think that will be a problem because no one that I know plays these types of games."

"Oh, okay. I had to warn you though! Well, off you go, then."

Ronald then turned around and just shook his head. Suddenly he stopped, and realized that there was one more issue that Pixie hadn't mentioned. He turned back and said to her, "Say, Pixie, there's just one thing that you didn't talk about."

"And that is?" Pixie asked.

"Exactly where in the war are we?"

Pixie blushed in embarrassment, and said, "Sorry! I should have mentioned that!"

She then looked at her phone, and relayed the details to Ronald. They were now in the middle of the war, and the pro-US side had already captured the area between the Great Lakes and the Ohio River, and were now making advances into Iowa, Missouri, and Arkansas. They now had stationed some troops in Illinois, as they were using the captured territories as a base to move further north and west. Ronald's unit, along with some of the Canadian and Latin American units, would be working not only with the Fertana units stationed in Iowa and Northern Missouri, but also with the northwestern and western Fertanan regiments, both of whom were fighting to drive the Americans and Texans out of Iowa and Missouri. Also, the southwestern Fertanan troops were rushing to aid those located in Southern Missouri and Arkansas. There were also other Canadian units, as well as part of the Latin American contingent, helping the Fertanan units deal with the US troops in Wisconsin, Michigan, and Ohio, while the Mexican and the rest of the Latin American soldiers were fighting against the Americans and Texans in Illinois, the south, and the southwest. "Okay, thanks," Ronald said after Pixie had finished explaining. "That really helps me out a lot."

He then turned around again, and began walking to the military base, noticing how everything along the way had been destroyed. After he had walked for about two hours, he finally saw a military base in the distance. He stopped before approaching to examine the flags to make sure that he wasn't heading to one of the US bases. He saw the base had both a Canadian flag and the Fertanan flag flying in the wind, and breathed a sigh of relief. Confident that he was approaching the right base, Ronald continued on, and entered the base.

Upon entering the base, Ronald asked around as to where he had to go to check in. He was told that the check-in for all the soldiers that had volunteered or had been drafted was located at the front of the base, in the reception area. He then headed there, and when he arrived, he saw that the office was really small, as there was not much more than a desk, some bulletin boards, and a room at the back. Ronald approached the receptionist and told her, "Hi, I'm Ronald Charlton. I was told to come here to check-in immediately."

The receptionist looked at her computer and said, "Yes. Please head this way to take your physical. After you pass it, you will then receive your equipment."

"*Physical*?! I wasn't told about any physical! I thought that this was a video game!"

"Well, with the realism of video games these days, including the development of devices that require you to be physically active in the games, we need to make sure that all of our soldiers are in tip-top condition. You have to realize that this won't be easy!"

Ronald just rolled his eyes and followed the receptionist to the area where the physicals were being conducted. He went through his physical, and after it was over, the doctor told him, "Wow, Ronald! You're in really good shape! You passed easily! What's your secret?"

"I work out a lot," Ronald replied.

"Well, it really shows," the doctor said, still quite impressed.

The doctor then pointed to another area of the base and said, "You will have to go to that building to get your equipment."

Ronald nodded and proceeded to the other building, where he was given the necessary guns and ammunition required for this game. He was then sent to the training grounds to learn how to fight. The training was really vigorous, but Ronald pushed as hard as he could. Once his training was over, he was directed to join his squadron, which was going to be put through some exercises before its first battle. During the exercises, Ronald noticed that there were some avatars of people from all around the world, and he even recognized a few that he went to high school with. These people also recognized Ronald, and after the exercises were completed, they came up to him to talk to him. However, he walked away because he had no interest in talking to anyone, as he was completely focused on doing what was required to get out of the video game world once and for all. He headed straight to the mess hall for dinner, and then after that he went to the bunkers to rest, as he knew that this game would be tough and would require every ounce of strength in him.

The next day, he and the rest of the squadron were woken up at 6:00 am, as the officers of their unit wanted to get to the battlefield, which was located to the north in Northern Missouri, as early as possible in order to sneak up on their enemies. They all quickly got ready, had breakfast, picked up their equipment, and headed out to the battlefield using a large number of military transport trucks.

Just before they arrived, the officers stopped the unit to give the soldiers their instructions on how to handle the battle, including what to look out for, and what was the best time to advance on the enemy. The unit then parked their vehicles about 2 kilometres away from the battlefield, and the soldiers got off and continued on foot. When they arrived at the battle site, they saw that their opponents had not arrived yet. The unit used the extra time to get into position, and then waited patiently for the enemy. About an hour later, the pro-US side arrived, and Ronald's unit immediately opened fire on the enemy before the enemy was able to get into position, much to the shock of their opponents. The opponents scrambled in trying to counter the attack, but before they were able to fully compose themselves, Ronald's unit made a charge, further catching the pro-US side further off-guard. However, they were quite resilient, and were quickly able to turn things around, which made the battle much more difficult than Ronald's unit had anticipated. The battle was quite bloody, with both sides amassing a number of casualties in a short period of time. However, they persevered, and by the end of it the pro-Fertana side won the battle and were able to reclaim this part of Missouri for Fertana. They then secured the area, with some troops carrying the wounded and dead to the nearest medical unit. The unit also left a sizeable number of troops in the area to guard the territory, while the rest headed back to the base. The dead avatars of players in the real world also disappeared, with a "Game Over" message showing up on their television screens in the real world.

At the base, the officers debriefed them, and told the soldiers how proud they were of them for fighting so well, while also reminding them that the task was not done yet, as there would still be a number of battles to fight in Iowa before they could move on to the eastern areas. The next day the troops were again woken up early in order to try to catch the US side again by surprise. They travelled further to the north into Iowa. They once again parked their vehicles about two kilometres away from the battlefield, and them marched the rest of the way on foot. However, they arrived at the battle site at the exact same time as the pro-US side. This battle was long, and unfortunately for Ronald's unit, it went heavily in favour of the US side. "Retreat!" the pro-Fertana soldiers heard the squad captain yell half an hour into the battle.

The soldiers ran, doing their best to dodge the gunfire from the charging pro-US soldiers. While some soldiers were hit, most made it back safely to the vehicles, which raced back to the base. This battle was a major setback for the Fertana side, as they had strongly believed that they would win this battle, and would be able to make some headway into Iowa. The soldiers were demoralized, wondering what they would do next. The officers told their troops to take the rest of the day off to recuperate. However, the senior officials huddled in the office to come up with a new strategy. Many of the soldiers walked around the base to get some fresh air. However, Ronald headed straight for the bunkers to avoid letting anyone in the real world know what he was doing actually *inside* the game, especially because he was concerned about what The VGG might do to him if he accidentally let anything slip out. He took off his uniform and dressed in his civvies, and then just lied down on his bed to read some books that were nearby. The only time he left the bunkhouse was for meals, and when it came time to sleep, he fell into a deep slumber, strangely relaxed despite what had happened earlier in the day at the battle.

The next day, all of the soldiers were called into the meeting room to discuss the new strategy that the officers had come up with. In the meeting, the lieutenant said that the mistake that the unit had made was that they had attacked the pro-US side from the front, as that was something that could easily be anticipated. Instead, what the unit was now going to do was sneak up on them. They would now send only a few soldiers to the front of the battlefield to act as a decoy, while the rest would attack form behind to surprise the enemy. Ronald was among the few who volunteered to act as a decoy, as he felt that he could provide a great distraction. Interestingly enough, his old high school classmates didn't offer their services as decoys, which surprised Ronald as many of these people had acted like the "tough guys" during their high school days. Once the plan was conceived, the unit then headed back to the battlefield to retry the second battle.

After they had made it into Iowa, the unit then split into groups, with the decoys hustling to the front, while the rest of the squadron went around the battlefield, ensuring that they were not spotted by the enemy side. As the decoys were making their way to the battlefield, one of them asked, "Do you think we'll be successful this time around?"

"I hope so," Ronald said. "I recognized some of those on the enemy side yesterday, and trust me, they are easily distracted, and can be quite arrogant. So, when we show up, we will have to do our best to find a hiding spot quickly, because as soon as they notice us, they will start wondering why there are so few of us attacking from the front."

When Ronald and his group arrived at the battlefield, they saw that the pro-US side was already waiting for them, anticipating another advance. Ronald and the rest of the decoys then scrambled to find a place to hide behind some bushes, where they then overheard a conversation between some of the enemy soldiers. "What's going on?! The Fertana side should have *been here* by now!"

"I don't know. It seems odd."

"You know, maybe they got scared after what happened yesterday, and don't want to take any chances! Maybe they only sent a few soldiers to spy on us. After all, we did put a good beating on them!"

Ronald peaked over the shrubs, and in the distance, saw the rest of his unit advancing. He then told his partners hold their position, and then he came running out of the bushes. He yelled to the enemy soldiers, "Hey! You want to know where we are?! Well, we're right here!"

"Ha!" said the pro-US soldier in an arrogant tone. "That's *it*?! Where's the rest of your crew?!"

"They sent me, so here I am!"

"Oh, this is going to be *easy*! Don't worry, guys. *I'll* take care of him! You just wait here!"

Suddenly, in the distance, the captain of Ronald's unit yelled, "CHARGE!"

"What was that?!" asked one of the enemy soldiers.

The pro-US soldiers turned around, and saw the charging pro-Fertana unit coming from behind. The other decoys joined Ronald, and the three of them charged from the front. "Oh crap!" an enemy soldier said in shock.

The enemies scrambled to get into position, but it was too late, as the Fertana unit successfully won the battle without any casualties, and forced the pro-US side to retreat. In the next few battles, the unit continued to use the same strategy and were able to take Iowa relatively unscathed, which was a boon for morale. The unit then made their way eastward into Illinois, where they won some very tough battles, which allowed them to advance on towards Chicago. Meanwhile, news of the unit's success in Northern Missouri and Iowa had spread to some of the other units. This increased morale amongst those groups as well, which they used to their full benefit. The southwestern pro-Fertana squadrons were able to successfully drive out the joint American-Texan forces from Arkansas, Southern Missouri, and the rest of Illinois. Also, the Fertanan units in Wisconsin and Michigan were also able to drive out the pro-US side from those areas, as well as areas around southern Lake Michigan. After their respective victories, these two units then joined Ronald's unit in Chicago, where then formed a larger battalion. After the unification of the squadrons, the officers used the next couple of days to come up with strategies on how best to attack the pro-US side and drive them out from Chicago. Ronald decided to stay in the bunkers outside of mealtime so that he could mentally prepare for the upcoming battle, and to ensure that he didn't accidentally let out the secret about his journey. After the conclusion of the officers' strategy session, the unified squadron was briefed on the strategy. Ronald's unit would attack the city from the south, the second unit would attack from the north, a third would attack from the west, and a fourth would come in from the east. They were told to rest up, as the battle would be very tough and demanding. The next day, all the solders were woken up at 4:00 am. Despite the early wakeup call, he focus and determination showed on all of their faces. The units quickly headed to their assigned positions, with Ronald's unit heading south. Ronald's unit was to face a very tough opponent, which was comprised of the largest contingent of US-Texan soldiers in the area, who were well prepared and in top physical condition. When the battle started, Ronald's unit saw just how difficult their enemy was. The first several hours was a see-saw battle, with both sides enduring heavy casualties. Ronald's unit did their best to hold their own, and continued to battle. The biggest obstacle that the unit faced was that the US-Texan forces were hiding out in many of the apartment buildings and business offices, which helped them greatly to maintain their cover. These forces would come out briefly to fire on their opponent, and then quickly returned to their hiding spots. Meanwhile, the other pro-Fertana units, due to having to deal with smaller enemy squadrons, had an easier time in their battles, and were easily able to take the north, west, and eastern parts of Chicago. After conquering these parts of the city, the other three pro-Fertana units then reunited and made their way south to assist Ronald's unit. This gave Ronald's unit a major boost as they were still in a stalemate in South Chicago. When the larger unit caught up with Ronald's unit, one of the leaders of the unit said, "Good! We've finally got backup!"

The officers quickly came up with new strategy on how best to overtake their enemy. They decided that Ronald's unit would attack from the south, and the rest would attack from the other three directions. Then, the order came, "Attack the enemy...NOW!"

Ronald's unit then charged up from the south, while the other forces attacked the north, east, and west. This battle continued to be difficult. The American and Texan units proved to be tough, and refused to go down easily. It took several hours for the unified pro-Fertana force to penetrate into enemy lines. However, when they did, the battle started going in favour of the pro-Fertana squad. It took approximately six hours for the pro-Fertana side to finally overtake their enemy, and this was due to two major factors: the larger numbers, and an attitude of never giving up until the fight was won.

Motivated, they continued on. The unified squadron from the Chicago assault was now split into two. One unit went through Northern Indiana, where they were able to drive the pro-US side out, thus reclaiming the territory for Fertana, including Fort Wayne. The other unit, who were just as inspired as the other contingent, went to Southern Indiana, and were able to drive out pro-US forces and reclaim the area, including Indianapolis. In Ohio, those pro-Fertana units, upon hearing of the success in the other areas, became more motivated, and started making gains on the pro-US forces, driving the enemy further and further out. Eventually, the successes added up, where all pro-Fertana units were now quite close to one another. Ronald's unit was eventually able to defeat the US troops in Toledo and other places in Northwest Ohio. The Southern Indiana unit took back both Cincinnati and Dayton, while the other Ohio units were able to take control of the eastern part of the region, including Cleveland, Akron, and Canton.

After another successful set of battles, the only pro-US stronghold was Columbus, and the pro-Fertana sides now surrounded the city. Here, all of the pro-Fertana units now combined into one mega-unit. All of the officers worked together on a strategy to reclaim Columbus, and thereby guaranteeing once and for all Fertana's independence. The soldiers of the now-united army were told to take the rest of the day off while the officers devised the strategies for the assault. Once again, Ronald decided to head to one of the bunkers to ensure that he didn't reveal to anyone in the real world about what he was doing in the video game world. The only time he came out was for meals. He spent the rest of his time reading and thinking about how many more games he had left before the final portal opened. When night fell, he went into a deep, relaxing sleep, hoping for the best the next day.

The next day, all of the soldiers were woken up at 4:00 am, and were ordered to report for a morning briefing. At the meeting, they were divided into four units, and were asked to join their new units immediately before the strategy would be discussed. Once all of the soldiers had joined their new units, the officers then went over the plans for the final assault to drive out the joint American-Texan forces from Fertana once and for all. Each unit was assigned a particular quadrant of Columbus, where they would attack the pro-US units stationed in that quadrant. Ronald's unit was assigned to attack the northwest quadrant. The strategy was to push the enemy side to the grounds of the former Ohio State House, where a final battle would be held. The view was that sheer numbers would be the driving force in helping Fertana win. After the officers had finished debriefing the army, his unit went immediately to their post to await further orders. After arriving there, their squad leader received instructions that they were to start attacking, and they went into Columbus. This series of battles was very tough, as the US-Texas side was formidable. However, as the casualties mounted, the Fertana force was able to penetrate into the area, causing the enemies to feel overwhelmed. The pro-US forces started retreating for the Ohio State House. Ronald's side continued marching forward, defeating the pockets of pro-US resistance that were still present. They were able to push other US Loyalists inwards, eventually making their way across two bridges into Downtown Columbus before stopping just before the final turnoff to the State House. They held their position there, and awaited further instructions for the final assault. The other units, after suffering initial setbacks, were also able to penetrate into enemy lines, and began getting the upper hand. They, too, made their way into Downtown Columbus, and before long the pro-US army was surrounded, with their only remaining stronghold being the State House. Finally, the officers of the pro-Fertana army gave the go-ahead for the final charge, and all four units converged on the Ohio State House. After a short battle, the pro-US army surrendered, realizing that their numbers were no match for the pro-

Fertana side. Upon hearing this, the Fertana side celebrated, raising their hands in victory, and letting out triumphant cheers, knowing that the war was over and that the pro-Fertana side had won, meaning that Fertana's independence was secured.

A treaty signing was held soon after, officially ending the war. Canada and Mexico had their claims to the territories they had gained a few years earlier formally enshrined, while Fertana was officially recognized as a country by the US, with its territorial rights also being enshrined in the treaty. The treaty also contained a provision that any US, Texas, or Loyalist soldier who was not willing to stay in Fertana and pledge allegiance to the new country had to leave within a year, or face jail time for treason. The treaty also required all signatory countries, including the Latin American countries, to stay out of the internal affairs of each other unless formally requested, thus preserving each country's sovereignty rights. And if anyone *did* try to interfere in matters relating to another signatory country without prior permission, their leaders, including the heads of state/government and high-level security and intelligence officials, would immediately be sent to the Court of International Crimes to face trial for treaty and sovereignty violations. After the treaty was signed, the pro-Fertana soldiers headed to Chicago, while the US and Texas soldiers began heading home. Loyalist soldiers and residents started making plans to move to either the US or to Texas.

During the next week, festivities were held all across Fertana to celebrate the official independence of the new country. In Chicago, a formal independence ceremony was held, and Ronald and Pixie took in the festivities. The new President, who was elected by the military and other senior officials on an interim basis until formal general elections could be held, declared November 25, 2026 as the official date of independence, which from that day onwards would now be known as Fertana Independence Day. He further declared that each year onwards, the week beginning Independence Day would be a national holiday celebration, meaning that people didn't have to go to work that week. He formally thanked all the Fertanans who had come forward to fight for the new country against the Americans, and also thanked all of Fertana's allies for all of their help. He added that he hoped that Fertana and the other countries could now forge new friendships. He also mentioned that he wished that Fair Trade, and not Free Trade, would be the basis for any future deals with his new friends, as he felt that being fair in deals was essential to having sustained partnerships. Finally, he said that he and Fertana's leaders had decided that Chicago would be the new capital, and that construction of a federal legislative house would begin soon. It would be up to the individual states if they wanted to keep their capitals and their respective legislatures in their current cities, or if they wanted to move them to new locations. When the President had finished speaking, the crowd let out a boisterous cheer, happy and relieved that, finally, the new country could get on with the business of working on building up the democratic, economic, and political structures that would hopefully sustain it for many years to come.

No soldiers or officers were given individual awards, as the President felt that it was unfair to recognize only certain people, especially since securing independence would not have been possible without the efforts of everyone involved. Instead, he called the victory a "team effort," emphasizing that in a team, everyone's contributions are just as important, win or lose. After the initial shock, the officers and soldiers realized that it was better this way, since there would be no controversy over who was more deserving of recognition, and thus would reduce jealousy amongst the soldiers. After this, the crowd cheered, and the ceremonies then ended. The crowd then dispersed and went on to enjoy the other events of the festivities. Just then, Ronald's clothing changed back to normal, and the portal opened. Upon seeing it, Ronald said to Pixie, "Well, I guess it's time to leave. So, where are we headed to next?"

Pixie looked at her phone, and a look of shock came across her face. "What's wrong?" Ronald asked, concerned about what was happening.

"It looks like that's the final portal to your home," she replied, "and The VGG is letting me go with you, if I want to."

"Cool!"

Ronald then walked over to the portal. Just before he was about to enter, he noticed that Pixie wasn't there beside him. He looked back, and saw her standing there. "Aren't you coming?" he asked Pixie.

"No, I'm not," Pixie replied.

Ronald then walked away from the portal towards Pixie. He stood in front of her, and asked, "Why not? I thought you always wanted to travel the world. Well, this is your chance to do so!"

"Yeah, I wanted to travel the 'world.' But, not *your* world. I just wanted to travel this world."

"Oh. But aren't you the *least bit* curious about the real world?"

"Not really."

"Why not?"

"What will I do there? I mean, over in the real world, money is the only thing that seems to matter, and I have nothing to offer it."

"But you have a degree."

"Yeah, from a university that doesn't even exist in the real world! That's not going to get me anywhere!"

"With your beauty, you have plenty to offer! Like being a model!"

"Yeah, right! As if I want to go into that brain-and-soul-sucking profession!"

"What?! Some models aren't dumb, you know! I know a couple who went to university with me, and they could have done anything they wanted, but they went into modelling because they just liked that more. But, whenever we met before I got laid off, we would have the most intelligent discussions."

"Trust me, those types of people are in the minority. And, from what I understand, in the real world, anyone who becomes a model immediately starts acting less intelligent, and they become corrupt because they always forget the people that supported them."

"Well, you could do other things. I mean, modelling isn't the only thing a smart girl like you could do."

"Well, I would also have to deal with mortality, instead of immortality. And, I happen to like immortality, as I *never* have to worry about something killing me. Besides, the last thing I want to do is complicate your life in the real world."

"How would you do that? You've become such a great friend to me."

"You've got a nice girlfriend, and someone who really loves you. But, even though she's okay with you having all of these female friends, she may get jealous of me, and may even feel threatened by me. I mean, you've never dated a girl like me, nor one who looks like me. I doubt you even have had *friends* who look like me. So, that may threaten her, and you'll then have a *whole other* set of problems to deal with beyond unemployment."

"Well, I guess you've got a point. But, it sure would have been fun to introduce you to my brother, just so that he could see that not *all* women are as corrupted as he thinks."

"Well, I think he would have had other problems to deal with by having me in the picture."

"So, I guess there's no convincing you, then, to come home with me?"

"No. No chance at all."

"So, what are you going to do, then?"

"Well, after you enter the portal, I'll be heading back to Video Game City, and I might take a vacation and go travel to the games where we saw those tourists, and the other 'tourist games' that exist. I need one after this journey. After the time off, I'll just continue on with my travels around the video games."

"Well, I guess this is goodbye, then."

"Yeah, I guess it is."

"Will we ever meet again?"

"I doubt it. The chances of another person from the real world coming here, or a person from this world ending up there, are *very* slim."

"Okay. Well, it was great getting to know you. It was a pleasure to have you around during this trip."

"And so were you. I'm really going to miss having you around."

"Same here. Bye, Pixie."

"Bye, Ronald. I hope you get home safely."

"Thanks."

They then hugged, and Ronald then walked back to the portal. He looked back one more time at Pixie, smiled, and waved to her. Pixie, who was now very emotional, waved back, and smiled. Ronald then went into the portal, knowing that he was finally going home, and that he never would have to live in the video game world ever again.

CHAPTER FOURTEEN

As Ronald travelled back through the long 3D tunnel, all he could think about was everything that he had gone through in order to reach this point, and how Pixie would now be living without him in the video game world. Then, his thoughts turned to what he was going to do when he did get home, especially with Dawna. He started thinking about what plans he would make this week with Dawna, and even what they could do next weekend. That is, if it still wasn't raining outside. After about ten minutes, he could see his family room coming into view in the distance, and guessed that he was about five minutes away from getting back to his house. He also saw Mitch standing there, and Ronald was wondering just how much time had passed in the real world since he had been transported into the video game world. It was still Sunday, August 11, 2013 in Calgary, however it was about twenty minutes after Ronald had been sent through the portal into Video Game City. As it turned out, Mitch saw the lightning come into the house, and was checking the entire house to make sure everything was okay. He had just come down to the basement after examining the upper two levels, and saw that Ronald was nowhere to be found. He had checked all of the other rooms in the basement, but still couldn't locate Ronald. Mitch returned to the family room, looked around in confusion, and said, "Ronald? Where are you? I just saw the lightning come inside the house. I was just checking to see if everything was okay. *Are* you okay?"

Ronald could hear his brother, but was still quite deep within the portal to answer Mitch. After a few more minutes of silence, Mitch said again, "Ronald? If you're playing some sort of a game, this isn't funny!"

As the family room came closer into view, Ronald yelled from the tunnel, "Mitch! Look out!"

Mitch looked around confused, wondering where the noise was coming from. He then asked, "Ronald? Is that you?"

Ronald yelled again, "Mitch! Get out of the way!"

Mitch just stood there, and then turned around just in time to see Ronald come flying out of the TV and land on top of him. "Ooph!" they both said as they hit the ground.

"What was that?!" Monica yelled from the living room upstairs.

"Don't worry, Mom! I found Ronald!" Mitch yelled from the floor.

Ronald and Mitch then got up, and Ronald then scolded his brother. "I *told* you to get out of the way, didn't I?" he said.

Ronald then calmed down and asked, "Are you okay?"

"Yeah, I am," Mitch replied, checking his body for injuries. "What the heck were you doing *inside* the TV?! Is that even *physically possible*?!"

Ronald then explained that when the lightning came inside the house, it had hit the game console, and sent him into the video game world. He then told Mitch about everything that he had gone through to get back home, including the games that he had to play. When Ronald finished explaining, Mitch said, "What?! How can that even *happen*?! That's not even *possible*!"

Ronald then reached into his pockets and pulled out all of the awards and medals that he had won during his adventures in the video game world, and said, "Then, how do you explain *these*?!"

Mitch just stared at them, wondering if the items were even real. "Where did you get them?" he asked, pointing at them.

"Like I just said, I've been actually *inside* the video game world, and at the end of most of them, the video game people gave these to me."

Mitch just stared blankly, and then touched them. When he saw that they were indeed real, he was taken aback, and gave a look of shock. "When Mom warned you last week that your addiction to the video games was so bad that one day you would end up *inside* them, I didn't think she was actually *serious*!" Mitch said in disbelief.

"I don't think she thought it was possible, either," Ronald said. "Neither did I. And neither did those people in the video game world. But, it happened, and the only way I could get out was to physically play those games."

"So, how come no one came home with you?"

"I asked the guide, but she refused."

"You had a guide with you as well?"

"Yeah."

"Was she hot?"

"Oh yeah! Like right out of a magazine!"

"Is it just any plain old magazine, or a particular one?"

"A fitness magazine. Though, she also looked like she could have been inside a magazine targeted towards men."

"Oh, I guess she was in really good shape, then. And, at the same time, very easy on the eyes!"

"Yeah, I guess. But she is a much nicer person than a lot of models are, especially the ones from those men's magazines."

"That's good that she's actually a really good girl. But, wow! You had someone like that as your guide. But, why did she refuse to come here? Was there a rule against it?"

"No, she was allowed to come home with me. She just didn't want to come because she felt more comfortable living in the video game world. And she didn't think there was anything for her in our world."

"Oh, okay. That would make sense. But I don't think anyone's going to believe you when you tell them this story!"

"I'm not going to! And neither are you! This is our secret, okay? The last thing I need is for Mom telling someone, and then I have the media coming after me to talk about my experiences."

"Fine. Though, it still is amazing that something like that could even happen."

"I know."

"So, what do you want to do with this game that you were playing all day?"

"Save it, then turn the system off. We can do something else for the rest of the day."

"Okay!" Mitch said excitedly.

Mitch then proceeded to save the game and turn off the Invisio 4. After he was done, he asked Ronald, "So, when's the next time that you're going to play these games?"

"It's going to be a *long* time before I play another video game," Ronald replied. "Especially after what I've just been through!"

"Finally! It's about *time* you stopped playing those things!"

After Mitch turned off the system, they then went upstairs. When they got to the living room, the first thing Ronald did was apologize to his parents for his behaviour since his layoff, and said that he was sorry for being mad at them. They accepted his apology, and then he called Dawna. During the conversation, he apologized to her for his behaviour and how he had treated her, and how much he really appreciated and cared for her. Dawna accepted it, and then apologized herself for not being more understanding, and said she was deeply sorry for constantly yelling at him for playing the video games, especially since she knew that he was really depressed. They then made plans for the following weekend to go to a Calgary Stampeders game, as the forecast called for rain for the rest of the week. When Ronald hung up, he spent the rest of the day with his family to help with setting up the new stereo system. Unfortunately for all of them, that was all they could do because, while the thunder and lightning had stopped, the rain didn't. As a result, they were stuck indoors.

On August 21, Ronald celebrated his birthday with his friends, family, and girlfriend. Everyone was quite amazed at how much Ronald had changed in the last week and a half. They all wondered what had come over him, and what helped him to get out of his depression and stop playing the video games. However, whenever anyone questioned him about it, he just kept silent about it. Even when his parents prodded him for an answer, Ronald just said that he finally realized video games weren't the answer to his problems, and that the video game world was a lot crueller than he had thought. Not only that, but Ronald's sudden change in attitude meant that his family was going on vacation after all. They decided that they would head to the Okanagan, after which they would spend a few days in the Canadian Rockies. On top of that, Ronald had signed up for rec league basketball and floor hockey, as he now wanted to do more than just work out at the nearby gym. Even his friends from the rec leagues were surprised, as they thought that Ronald was never going to go back and play.

After the birthday dinner, Monica brought out the cake and everyone sang "Happy Birthday" to Ronald. After he had blown out the candles, Monica then sliced the cake and served it to everyone there. After everyone had finished eating the birthday cake, Ronald then opened up his presents. After he had opened the last one, he thanked everyone for their thoughtful gifts, and then went on to say, "Everyone, I've got a very important announcement to make."

Dawna, thinking that Ronald was going to propose to her, couldn't contain her excitement. However, that was not the announcement that Ronald was giving. Instead, he said, "I know I've been very difficult to deal with these past six months, and I want to thank you all for being so patient with me, even when I wasn't the most pleasant person to be around. To all of you, I am truly sorry for my behaviour."

It was quite an emotional moment for everyone. After everyone forgave him, he continued, "Now, in the past week and a half, I've been thinking about everything that went wrong just before I was laid off from Pacific, and I have come to one conclusion. And that conclusion is that the employees didn't have any say in hiring their new boss, and management was not willing to listen to their input, even when it was obvious that the new boss was clearly bad for business."

Dawna initially looked disappointed, but then calmed down, realizing that maybe it was best to not rush into marriage. She was in the midst of getting on with life after competitive volleyball, as the Canadian National Women's Volleyball Team had recently informed her that she was not going to be on the team anymore. And, more importantly, Ronald had to get his life back on track after his layoff and everything that he had gone through since then. Everyone else was really confused about what Ronald was trying to say. Finally, and one of his friends asked, "So, where are you going with this?"

"Well, I'm thinking that it's time to look at business differently," Ronald replied.

"And that is…?" Dawna asked in rebuttal.

"A worker co-op," Ronald said. "One where the workers not only decide what direction the organization is going to go in, but where they also have a say in who will be their managers, and who will be on the executive team. That's the only way to prevent the Betty Morgans of the world from ever coming in and causing havoc on both their organizations and their employees."

"So, how does this affect you?" Mitch asked.

"I am going to start my own business, and I have decided that it will be a worker co-op," Ronald said. "Each employee will own the same number of shares as I do, even though I'm going to head this new company. They will also have an equal say in how the business is run, and we will all share in the profits."

"You do realize that some of them could gang up on you and throw *you* out, don't you, dear?" Monica asked in a concerned tone.

"But, that's why we involve all of the employees, management and executive," Ronald said. "If it becomes quite obvious that a clique is forming, and they look intent on causing problems, they can be thrown out before they do any damage. And, besides, some of you have worked with me, and you know I'd do my best to be a really good boss."

"True," said another friend of Ronald's, who had worked with him at Pacific IT and Consulting with him. "But, that still isn't foolproof. I mean, you still could end up hiring someone like Betty Morgan because she's really good at playing the office games, and really good at making herself look good during interviews."

"What did I just say, though?!" Ronald responded. "If there are a ton of complaints about someone like Betty Morgan, they can be dealt with much more easily in a worker co-op setting than in a traditional business setting. That person then has to answer to the entire organization, and *especially* to their staff. Moreover, there may be other people in the organization that have observed the bad behaviour too."

After a lengthy discussion, some of Ronald's friends then came forward and offered to work in Ronald's company, as they were already looking at quitting their current jobs. Some of these people included those still employed by Pacific IT and Consulting, as they knew that the company was on a downward spiral and was headed towards bankruptcy because of Betty's team. When they asked Ronald when he was going to get started on this idea, he said, "A week after we get back from BC. That way, I can get my mind back into work mode."

They then enjoyed the rest of the evening, and played some games, including video games. However, Ronald surprised everyone by not wanting to participate in the video games.

The following spring, on April 5, 2014, Ronald and Dawna were taking a stroll through Fish Creek Park, and were enjoying the scenery and each other's company. It was a bright and sunny day, and the temperature was a comfortable 15 degrees Celsius, making it the perfect day to take a walk in the park and see the budding flowers, trees, and bushes, as well as deer, owls, coyotes, beavers, and other animals inhabiting the park. However, they made sure that they kept their distance from the animals so they wouldn't be attacked. They took many pictures that day, whether it was a beautiful flower budding, or anything else of interest. As they were walking, they talked about how her job was going, and how he was doing emotionally. Then, Dawna just stopped and said, "So, Ronald, I've noticed that you don't play video games much anymore. What exactly happened to you last August?"

Ronald kept silent, and now had a nervous look on his face. He was doing best to maintain silence on the matter. "Well? What went on?" she asked again.

"Well, um…," Ronald said, looking down, still nervous about whether or not he should say anything.

"Ronald Charlton, I'm your girlfriend! What did we agree to when we became exclusive?!" Dawna said, now getting angry with him.

"That we wouldn't keep secrets from each other," he replied begrudgingly.

"That's right! Now tell me what happened in August before I really get mad!"

Ronald then finally agreed to tell her, and said, "Well, you remember that Sunday when we had that major thunderstorm?"

"Yeah."

"Well, lightning struck my game console, and I was sent into the video game world."

Dawna's face was one of disbelief, as she did not believe that Ronald was telling her the truth. "Ronald, if you're not going to tell me the truth, then just say so! Don't come up with some cockamamy story about how you were sent into the video game world!" she said angrily.

"But I *am* telling you the truth!" Ronald said.

"What proof do you have?"

"You remember how you went into my room to get something before we left for Banff the weekend before my birthday, and you saw all of those plaques, medals, and other awards on my desk?"

"Yeah."

"How do you think I got them?"

"I don't know. I thought that maybe you did something during the week and had gotten were really lucky."

"*Seriously*?! You honestly believe that I could have received *that many* accolades in just one week, especially when all I did was play video games for months on end? And especially since I was not involved in *any* other activities during that week? Don't forget that those leagues that I'm playing in didn't even start until late October."

Dawna then thought about it for a minute, and then looked shocked. "You mean that can actually *happen*?!"

"It *did* happen!" Ronald replied. "And, I had a guide, too. A female guide who looked like a fitness model, but who could also be in one of those other magazines, especially the men's magazines!"

"It can't be! I mean, I remember a scientist friend of mine saying back in university that there was a theory about alternate universes and alternate worlds, and that it was impossible to know if these things really existed, or if there was even a way to travel to them."

"Well, I don't know if a mode of transportation is available to travel to another world, but *I* certainly got sent to *that one*. But, you can't tell *anyone*, okay?! I don't need anyone, whether it be the media or scientists, coming after me to discuss my adventures in that world. Next thing you know, I'll start having people, including photographers, bugging me everywhere I go about what I had to go through."

"Okay, I won't. I don't want my baby to be hounded by the public. I know how much you value your privacy. But, I have one question for you."

"And that is…?"

"If you were transported into that world by lightning striking the game console, how exactly did you get out?"

"I had to play a certain number games, which turned out to be 10, in a certain order set by The Video Game Government, the government of that world. I wasn't even told when I actually *entered* the final game. The VGG only informed Pixie, my guide, *after* I had finished the final game that I could go home. If she didn't get a message saying so, I had to keep going."

"Whoa! That must have been tedious!" Dawna said, shocked at how much Ronald actually had to go through. "I know I wouldn't be able to handle constantly playing game after game after game without knowing if I would ever get home."

"Oh, it became annoying, all right," Ronald said, nodding his head. "I mean, in the fifth or sixth game, I was already getting frustrated. I was even in a game that had a 3D version of Calgary in it, and I thought I was home, when I actually wasn't."

"I know that game! One of my friends has it, and he made me play with him once. But, how did you travel between games?"

"Via a bunch of portals. When I finished one game, the portal to the next game would open up. And when I had finished the last game, the portal that appeared was the one that took me home. And I fell right onto Mitch when I got out of the 3D tunnel that led to my family room via the TV."

"Ouch! Did either of you get hurt?"

"No, but it did catch Mitch by surprise. Though it was strange that the portal *into* the video game world was through the console, and the portal out of it was through the TV."

"And I guess he's the only other one who knows about what you went through, right?"

"Yes, he is."

"Another question. How come this guide didn't come home with you? Was there some sort of rule against it?"

"She was allowed to come with me. She just didn't want to."

"Why not?"

"Let's just say that she was more comfortable living in the video game world than in our world, and leave it at that."

"Okay, fair enough. But I am curious about another thing. What did she look like? And did you have feelings for her?"

"Well, she was in shape, and was good looking. But, I only have feelings for you, Dawna. I only saw Pixie as a friend."

Dawna smiled at the answer, and they continued walking. After they walked further along the trail, Dawna asked, "So, how's your company doing?"

She had never really asked before because she didn't want Ronald to feel like she was putting a lot of pressure on him, as she knew that startups and new companies took a while to really get going. She also knew that Ronald was probably under a lot of stress already, and didn't want him to become mad like he had become a year earlier. But Ronald didn't mind, and said, "It's actually doing surprisingly well."

"Oh? How so?" she asked curiously.

Ronald's new company, which was called Custom IT Design Cooperative, was involved in the same industry as Pacific IT and Consulting. The company had officially started on September 16, 2013, a week after his family had come back from their vacation. Ronald was the head of the company, and was also heavily involved in the marketing department. The initial employee-owners included not only those of Ronald's friends that had agreed to join his company on his birthday, but also some of Ronald's former coworkers from Pacific IT. They all joined because not only did they like the industry, but also liked the idea of being involved in the decision-making in the company, including who would be in the executive ranks. Some of the workers went into the consulting area, while the others went into the IT area, but everyone helped each other out when needed. When the company started making announcements in October 2013 to potential clients about their company, including the services it provided, they were overwhelmed with responses, especially from Pacific IT's former clients, who had been looking for new suppliers for some time after dropping Pacific due to the poor service given after Betty's friends started there. Also, those clients that had previously worked with

Ronald and some of the others at the new company remembered the excellent service and high-quality results they had received from them. Therefore, they had called up Custom IT Design about what services could be provided, and Ronald and the company were only too happy to resume the working relationship they had with these people. Not only that, but these clients recommended Ronald's organization to other companies, who eventually also became clients of Custom IT. Pretty soon, word had spread around Southern and Central Alberta about the high quality of work that Custom IT produced, which led to many more clients approaching the company. The result was that Ronald and the rest of the marketing team didn't even have to make proposals and cold calls in order to get new clients.

When their first job posting came out in January 2014, the response was overwhelming, as many people working in other organizations also liked the idea of working for a company that they owned, and liked the idea that they would have a say in how the company was being run. It helped that some applicants came from backgrounds where they had worked for nightmare bosses and indifferent executives, and were trying really hard not to have to go through those experiences again. The company moved quickly in hiring new people, as they were dealing with an avalanche of calls from potential clients. In fact, they hired more than initially anticipated, as the business was growing faster than expected.

As for Pacific IT and Consulting, they were driven into bankruptcy in November 2013, mostly due to the incompetence of Betty's team, and the unwillingness of the executives to do anything about it. Moreover, Betty's team had also convinced the executives to have the company go deep into debt, although the exact reasons for taking on the debt were never made clear, and this debt also became too much for the company to handle. While many of the employees were able to get other jobs, Betty and her friends had trouble finding other jobs, as word had spread around the business world that her team had single-handedly caused the spirited downfall of a once booming company. Furthermore, no one was willing to give a reference to Betty and her friends, afraid that their reputations would be ruined as well. The executives also had trouble finding work, as other companies were hesitant to take a chance on them because of how incompetent they appeared in dealing with the problems that suddenly plagued the company after Betty's arrival. While they were aware that *something* was going on, made evident by the fact that they were losing clients like crazy, the executives didn't link the problems to the Marketing Department. Instead, they continued blaming the problems on the Consulting and IT departments, and in fact unfairly fired some people from those departments for supposedly driving away business.

When Ronald had finished explaining everything, Dawna stopped suddenly, which almost made Ronald fall flat on his face. "Whoa!" she said in a shocked tone. "You just started that company in *September*! And you and all of those other people were just laid off *last year, in February*!"

"Well, that's what happens when you treat people poorly, and don't take your work seriously," Ronald replied. "And, don't you think that we were all surprised when, on the first day we announced that we were looking for clients, we were bombarded with so many emails and phone calls?"

"No wonder you looked so flustered by the time Christmas came!"

"Yeah, we all were! But, with all of the new hires, including the 20 people that started last week, it's made things a little bit easier."

"Are you going to hire any more people? Because it sounds like your company's growing a little too fast."

"No, I think we'll be good for now. This week, I saw that all the employees were more relaxed, and even I'm finding myself more relaxed. So, I think that staffing is good for now."

"Oh, okay. That's good to hear, because I don't want you to have another issue like last year. You know how much I worry about you."

"Thanks. I also don't want to have to go through what I had to last year."

They then continued walking on the trail, wondering what their futures would hold. But there was one thing that Ronald was certain about. And that was he would never have to go back to the video game world again, where he could only interact with video game characters. Instead, he was now going to do his best to enjoy the sights, smells, sounds, tastes, and the feel of the real world. Moreover, he would do his best to also enjoy the company of the people of the real world, especially Dawna. If there was one thing his journey had taught him, it was to appreciate what he had in the real world, and to not escape into a virtual world. And he was never going to forget that.

ABOUT THE AUTHOR

Ashad Mukadam was born and raised in Calgary, Alberta, Canada, and he still makes this city his home with his parents, Nizar and Nasim, and his brother, Ayuz. After finishing high school in June of 2001, he went on to the University of Calgary in September of that year, where he finished his Bachelor of Commerce degree in 2005 with a major in Management Information Systems. He worked in the IT field for a while, but realized that he enjoyed writing. His passion for writing led him to return to school in September of 2008, where he attended the University of Calgary. He finished his Bachelor of Arts degree in Communications Studies, With Distinction, in April of 2010, and graduated in June of that year. After he finished, he took some time to volunteer with CJSW and The Gauntlet to help him prepare for the world of journalism, while he also helped out as a blogger for the Ismaili Soccer League to help him improve his blogging and writing skills. From September 2012 to May 2013, he worked in different positions, being a marketer for a fitness company from September to November 2012, and a freelance journalist for various publications around Southern Alberta from October 2012 to May 2013. Now, he is a professional writer, as he writes books, and he is also looking at becoming a professional photographer.

www.ingramcontent.com/pod-product-compliance
Lightning Source LLC
Chambersburg PA
CBHW030538030726
47495CB00004B/1043